FIND ME

J.S. MONROE read English at Cambridge University, worked as a freelance journalist in London and was a contributor to BBC Radio 4. Monroe was also a foreign correspondent in Delhi for the *Daily Telegraph* and was on its staff in London as Weekend editor.

Follow J.S. Monroe @JSThrillers or visit Facebook.com/FindMeBook

J. S. MONROE

FIND
ME

HEAD OF ZEUS

Typeset by Adrian McLaughlin

Printed and bound in Great Britain by
CPI Group (UK) Ltd, Croydon CR0 4YY

Head of Zeus Ltd
First Floor East
5–8 Hardwick Street
London, EC1R 4RG

WWW.HEADOFZEUS.COM

For Hilary

FIND
ME

Though I am old with wandering
Through hollow lands and hilly lands,
I will find out where she has gone,
And kiss her lips and take her hands

—W. B. YEATS, FROM
'THE SONG OF WANDERING AENGUS'

I *found her a few minutes ago, in the corner, her upright wings pressed together like hands in prayer. Did she take one look at my life and choose to conceal her beauty? I can't blame her.*

Dad taught me to love butterflies. If one was trapped in the house, he would abandon whatever he was doing to set it free. Yesterday, when we were out on his boat, he found one – a pearl-bordered fritillary, he said – resting on a sail bag in the sunshine. He called me over, but it flew off as I approached. We watched in silence as it flitted away, carefree, brave, too far from land to survive.

I'm not sure what this one is. I want to prise open her wings, bring some colour into my rinsed-out life, but that would be a violation. And there's been too much of that already.

'It's just resting,' Dad says. I didn't see him appear, but his voice never startles me. He's been here a lot in recent weeks, leaving as quietly as he arrives. 'The underwing markings help to keep it unnoticed.'

I will try to go unnoticed, keep what beauty I may still possess for Jar. And one day, with Dad's help, I will spread my wings in the sun again.

PART ONE

I

It is five years since her funeral, but Jar recognises her face at once. She is standing on the up escalator, he is descending, late again for work after another night out on the wrong side of town. Both escalators are crowded, but he feels that they have the Underground to themselves, passing each other as if they are the last two people on earth.

Jar's first impulse is to call out to Rosa, hear her name above the din of rush hour. But he freezes, unable to say or do anything, staring at her drift up to the surface of London. Where is she going? Where has she been?

His heart rate picks up, palm moistening on the black rubber handrail. Again he tries to call out, but her name sticks in his throat. She looks distracted, anxious, out of sorts. The stowaway hair has gone, replaced by a shaved head, at odds with his memory of her. And her posture is less upright than he remembers, weighed down by an old rucksack, with a floral-patterned tent bag hanging below. Her clothes, too – baggy Ali Baba trousers, fleece – are dishevelled, unchosen, but he'd know her shadow on a furze bush. Teal-blue eyes dancing beneath a serious brow. And those pursed, mischievous lips.

She glances down the escalator, searching for someone perhaps, and steps into the flow of passing commuters. Jar scans the people below as a sheet of newspaper slides past him in a warm blast of wind, twisting and folding in on itself. Two men are pushing through the crowds, moving people aside with the quiet confidence of authority. Behind them, a row of digital adverts flip like playing cards.

Frustrated, Jar looks to either side of a knot of tourists blocking his way, as if this might somehow disperse them. Don't their London guidebooks explain about standing on the right? He checks himself, remembering his own first hesitant days in town, fresh off the plane from Dublin. And then he is free, skidding around the bottom of the escalators like a child before making his way back up again, opting for the central flight of steps, two at a time.

'Rosa,' he calls out, approaching the barriers. 'Rosa!' But there is no conviction in his voice, not enough belief for anyone to turn around. Five years is a long time to keep the faith. He scours the crowded ticket hall and guesses that she has turned left for the main concourse at Paddington.

A few minutes earlier, more broke than he should be a week before payday, he had slipped through the barriers behind an unsuspecting commuter. Now he must do the same again, tailgating an elderly man. He takes no satisfaction from this, no pleasure from the ease with which he avoids detection as he shows the man where to put his ticket and steps through the barrier with him. Deceit masked as the kindness of youth.

He runs until he is at the centre of the concourse, where he stops for breath, hands on knees, beneath the high arcing span of Brunel's austere station. Where is she?

And then he spots her again, heading towards Platform 1, where the Penzance train is preparing to leave. He zigzags through the crowds, cursing, apologising, trying to keep her rucksack in sight.

As he spins around the corner of a booth selling greetings cards, he sees her up ahead, beside the first-class carriages of the train, glancing over her shoulder. (They used to slip cards bought from shops like this under each other's college-room doors, trying to impress with student irony.) Instinctively, he turns around too. The two men are walking towards them, one with a finger to his ear.

Jar looks back at the platform. A guard blows her whistle, ordering Rosa to stand aside. Rosa ignores the shrill warning, swings open the heavy door and shuts it behind her with a finality that reverberates around the station.

Now it's his turn to approach the train. 'Stand away,' the guard shouts again, as the carriages start to move.

He runs to the door, but she is already walking down the aisle, looking for a space, apologising as she knocks against someone's seat. Keeping parallel with the accelerating train, he watches her place the rucksack in a rack above her and sit down by the window. For the first time, she seems to be aware of someone beyond the glass, but she ignores him as she settles down, picking up a discarded newspaper, glancing at the luggage rack.

The train is moving too fast for him now, but as he runs, Jar smacks his hand against the window. She looks up, wide eyed with alarm. Is it Rosa? He can't be sure any more. There's no flicker of recognition, no acknowledgement that she knows him, that they were once the loves of each other's lives. He falters, slows to a walk and stops, watching the train pull away as she stares back at him: one stranger to another.

2

Cambridge, Summer Term, 2012

I know I'm not meant to be writing this – there should be no record, no contrails left in the Fenland sky, as my counsellor would say – but I have kept a diary all my life and I need to talk to someone.

I went out again tonight with the drama crowd. Looks like I've got the part of Gina Ekdal if I want it. I keep telling myself I'm doing all this for Dad.

Well, not quite everything. I dropped an E when we first arrived in the pub. The candles on the tables burned like crucifixes – beautiful, prophetic perhaps – but it was not what I had hoped for. I think I kissed Sam, the director, and possibly Beth, who's playing Mrs Sørby. I would have snogged the entire cast if Ellie hadn't intervened.

I won't try that again, but I'm determined to wring every ounce out of what time I have left here. I know this crowd, this life, isn't me, but it's an improvement on my first two terms ('Michaelmas' and 'Lent', as Dad insisted on calling them – I'm sticking with the seasons). It's so easy to fall in with the wrong set, harder to extricate yourself without causing offence or coming across all superior.

After the pub we went for a meal, even though I wasn't hungry. I don't know where it was, some place down by the river. I was still pretty drunk – until it was time to pay.

And that's when I met him. Why now, with so little time left? Why not in my first term?

He was making his way around the table, taking payment from each of us. One bill, split fourteen ways, can you believe it? But this guy never complained, not even when he came round to me and my card didn't work.

'The machine's acting up,' he said, so quietly I could hardly hear him. 'We're out of range. Best you come up to the till now.'

'Sorry?' I said, looking up at him. I'm not short, but this guy was tall, a big bear of a man with a clean-shaven chin and a soft Irish brogue.

He leant down, checking that no one else could hear. His breath was warm and he smelt clean. Sandalwood, maybe.

'So we need to try your card again, nearer the till.'

There was something about the look he gave me, an avuncular, reassuring smile, that made me get up from the table and follow him over to the till. And I liked his big tidy hands, a discreet ring on his thumb. But he wasn't my type at all. The wide sweep of his jawline came together too sharply at the chin and his mouth was pinched.

It was only when we were out of earshot that he turned to me and said in a louder voice that my card had been rejected.

'I've been advised to take the card from you and cut it up.' He grinned. His big face brightened and gained better proportions when he did that: the chin softened and his cheekbones rose up.

'What do we do?' I asked, pleased that we seemed to be in this together. I've been broke since the day I arrived.

He looked down at me, realising for the first time, I think, quite how drunk I was. And then he glanced across at the table.

'The cast?' he said.

'How did you guess?'

'No tips.'

'Maybe they'll leave one in cash,' I said, suddenly defensive of my new friends.

'That would be a first.'

'You're not an actor yourself then,' I said.

'No. I'm not an act-or.'

He made me feel embarrassed by the word, rhyming the second syllable with 'roar'. 'So what do you do when you're not being rude about my friends?' I asked.

'I'm a student.'

'Here? At Cambridge?'

It was a stupid, patronising question and he spared me an answer.

'I write a bit, too.'

'Great.' But I wasn't listening. My mind was already wandering back to my contribution to the bill and the fact that I had no means of paying. I don't want any of the cast to know I'm penniless, even if it goes with the profession. And I can't tell them that my financial worries – all my worries – will soon be over. I can't tell anyone.

'There's enough money in the tip box, from other diners, for me to cover it,' he said.

For a moment I was lost for words. 'And why would you want to do that?'

'Because I think it's the first time you've hung out with these people and you're trying to impress them. Not being able to pay might cost you the part. And I'm already looking forward to coming to watch. Ibsen's all right, you know.'

We looked at each other in silence. He caught me by the elbow as I swayed too much. I was starting to feel very sick.

'Are you OK?' he asked.

'Can you take me home?' The tone of my voice – slurred, pleading – sounded all wrong, as if I was listening to someone else talking.

'I'm not finished for another hour.' He was looking at Ellie, who'd come over. 'I think your friend needs some fresh air,' he said to her.

'Has Rosa paid?' Ellie asked.

'All done now.' He handed back my card.

And that's as much as I can remember. I didn't even get his name. All I'm left with is first impressions: a man unhurried by the world, living life at his own measured pace – time on the ball, as Dad used to say. And beneath that calm exterior, is there a wildness in check, passion restrained? Or is that just wishful thinking on my part?

I feel ashamed now. Neither of us had any money, but there he was, an Irish writer working in a restaurant, without complaint, serving tight-fisted students to pay his bills, and I am defaulting on a maxed-out credit card.

Part of me – a big part – hopes to see him again, but I don't want him to be involved in what lies ahead. I'm still scared that I've made the wrong decision, but I can't see another way out.

3

Jar sits at his desk reading through the excuses from colleagues who have failed, like him, to make the daily 9.30 a.m. conference. Every day he is amazed by the chutzpah of other people's explanations. Yesterday, Tamsin group-emailed to say that she would be late after the fire brigade had had to rescue her from her bathroom. Cue lots of gags about firemen's lifts when she finally arrived, flushed-faced, blouse wrongly buttoned.

Today's offerings are more prosaic. Ben's washing machine has flooded the kitchen floor; Clive blames a cow on the line for his late train in from Hertfordshire; and this from Jasmine: 'Left house without wallet, now retrieved, running late.' Maria, the *grande dame* of the desk, is on better form: 'Husband's eaten children's packed lunch, will have to make them another.' Not bad, Jar thinks, but nothing to rival Carl's peerless excuse from last summer: 'Just getting my act together after Glastonbury. Might be a few days late.'

Carl is Jar's only real ally in the office, on for a pint after work, relentlessly cheerful, always wearing headphones around his neck. (If he's doing the tea run, he goes around the office signalling a large T with his hands.) He's a jungle MC when he isn't running the music channel on the arts website they both work for, telling everyone who will listen that jungle isn't retro, never went out of fashion and is more popular than ever. He also has an unhealthy knowledge of computers, often forgetting that Jar has no interest in app development or programming paradigms.

Jar had considered group-emailing the office from Paddington, to explain his own lateness, but he wasn't sure how it would have gone down: 'Just seen my girlfriend from uni who took her own life five years ago. Everyone tells me I'm imagining things, that I must move on, but I know she's alive, somehow, somewhere, and I'm never going to stop looking until I find her. She wasn't ready to die.'

He has told Carl everything, but not the others. He knows what they think. What's a prize-winning young Irish writer, debut collection of short stories a critical if not commercial success, doing in the seventh circle of office hell in Angel, chasing web-traffic figures by writing click-bait on Miley Cyrus? It was unfortunate that the first piece he was asked to file was on writer's block: ten authors who had lost their mojo. Sometimes he wonders if he ever had it.

In recent months, he has seen Rosa increasingly often: at the wheel of passing cars, in the pub, on top of the Number 24 bus (front seats, where they always sat when they were in London, riding up to Camden). The appearances have their own name, according to the family GP back in Galway: 'post-bereavement hallucinations'.

His father has other ideas, talking excitedly of the *spéir-bhean*, the heavenly woman who used to appear in Irish visionary poems. 'How can you be so insensitive now,' his mother chided, but Jar doesn't mind. He is close to his da.

He spent a lot of time at his home in Galway City in the immediate aftermath of Rosa's death, trying to make sense of what had happened. His father owns a bar in the Latin Quarter. They would sit up late, talk through the sightings, particularly one, on the Connemara coast. (He did all the talking, Da listened.) Some he knows are false alarms, but others, the ones he can't challenge...

'You look like death, bro,' Carl says, slumping down in his chair, which lets out a hiss of air. 'Just seen a ghost?'

Jar doesn't say anything as he logs into his computer.

'Christ, sorry, bud,' Carl says, shuffling through some promo CDs on his desk. 'I thought—'

'I bought you a coffee,' Jar cuts in, passing him a latte. He doesn't want to prolong his friend's embarrassment. Carl's a little overweight, baby faced with a mop of fair, dread-locked hair and a cherubic smile, and has an annoying habit of abbreviating words in his emails ('unforch' for unfortu-nately) and saying things like 'fave', 'bless' and 'fairs', but he possesses less malice than anyone Jar knows.

'Cheers.' There is an awkward pause. 'Where did it happen?' Carl asks.

'I'll do today's doodle,' Jar says, ignoring him.

'Are you sure?'

'It's Ibsen. Old pal of mine.'

They take it in turns to write stories about that day's Google doodle. They are meant to log on to Australia's Google page the night before, steal an eleven-hour march on the sleep-ing world, but they often forget. The stories are buried on the website, where no one can see them, but they're a shot in the arm for traffic figures, as people click idly on the search engine's embellished logo of the day.

Half an hour later, having filed far more than was neces-sary on Ibsen, mostly about Gina Ekdal's character in *The Wild Duck* and an extraordinary student performance in

Cambridge five years ago, he is down on the street, sheltering from the rain with Carl in an alleyway by the office entrance that smells of last night's beer and worse.

'Soft old day,' Jar says, filling the silence. He can tell Carl is preparing himself to raise an awkward subject and looks around for a distraction. 'Pizza eater, four o'clock.'

'Where?' Carl asks.

Jar nods across the road at a man walking along the pavement, talking into one end of his mobile phone, which he is holding horizontally in front of his mouth – like a slice of pizza. Carl and Jar watch, smiling. They both have a thing about people who talk into their mobile phones in funny ways: the furtive caller who whispers behind a cupped hand; the person who moves the phone back and forth between ear and mouth. The pizza eater, though, is one of their favourites.

'I know it's not my business,' Carl says, drawing on a cigarette as the man disappears into a crowd. He holds the cigarette between his chubby thumb and first finger like a child writing with chalk. 'But perhaps you should think about seeing someone, you know, about Rosa.'

Jar stares at the middle distance, hands sunk deep in his suede jacket, watching the traffic push through the rain and spray in the street beside them. He wishes he had a cigarette too, but he's trying to give up. Again. Rosa never smoked. He's come down to keep Carl company, let him know there are no bad feelings from earlier. And to dodge the 11 a.m. conference.

'I think I might have found someone who could help,' Carl continues. 'She's a bereavement counsellor.'

'Been hanging out with undertakers again?' Jar asks, recalling Carl's recent ill-fated experiment in 'funeral dating'. Working on the principle that pheromones tend to fly at funerals – 'there's a lot of grief in lust, and a lot of lust in grief' – Carl had crashed a few wakes in the hope of finding love, not necessarily the widow, but someone foxy and confused in black.

'She swiped right.'

Jar looks at his friend in surprise.

'OK, she didn't. She's helping me with a story.'

'About Tinder?'

'Thought I might be interested in some new research they're doing on the beneficial effects of music in shrinks' waiting rooms. Play a bit of old-school jungle and people open up more.'

'Jump out the window, more like.' Jar pauses. 'Thing is, this morning makes me more convinced than ever that Rosa's alive,' he says, taking the cigarette from Carl and inhaling deeply.

'But it wasn't her, was it?'

'It could have been, that's the point.'

They stand in silence, watching the rain. Hope's a private, fragile thing, Jar thinks, easily extinguished by others. He inhales on Carl's cigarette again, and hands it back. He can't blame him for being sceptical. They are about to head back up to the office when Jar's eye is caught by a movement, a tall man taking a seat in the window of Starbucks, across the street. Black North Face jacket, collar up, unremarkable brown hair, indistinctive features. Faceless and forgettable, except that it's the third time Jar's seen him in two days.

'Do you recognise that man?' Jar says, nodding at Starbucks.

'Can't say I do.'

'Swear he was in the pub last night. And on my bus yesterday.'

'Are they following you again?'

Jar nods in mock agreement, expecting his friend's ridicule. He's mentioned it to Carl before, the feeling that he's being watched.

'D'you know, one in three people suffer from paranoia?' Carl says.

'That few?'

'The other two are watching him.'

Jar wants to offer a token laugh, something to show that he's fine, just imagining it all, but he can't.

'The feeling I got when I saw her on the escalator...' He pauses, allowing himself one more glance at the man. 'Rosa's out there, Carl, for sure she is. Searching for a way back.'

4

Cambridge, Autumn Term, 2011

It's two weeks since I arrived here, and I am missing Dad more than ever. I thought the change of scene, a new start, would break the cycle, but it hasn't. Not even the fog of Freshers' Week can mask the great hulk of my grief. We were a double act, salt and pepper, Morecambe and Wise (his favourite show), closer than any of my friends seem to be with their fathers. Thrown together by fate, no say in the matter, that's just how it was.

I got so angry in The Pickerel last night when people started badmouthing their parents. Then the girl in the next-door room, who is also studying English, dozy Josie from Jersey, asked about me. Of course the mood changed when I explained, a missed beat in the drunken hum of the pub, no one quite sure what to say, where to look. For a moment, I saw myself from above, wondered if that's how Dad sees things these days.

Five minutes ago, when I woke to sunlight pouring in through these cheap college curtains, he was still alive and we were going out to lunch together in Grantchester. I was planning to tell him about my first weeks at Cambridge, the clubs I've joined, the people I've met. And then I remembered.

Dad used to talk all the time about this place. We only came here once together, in the summer, a week before he died (it still feels so strange writing that). He was his usual restless self that day. Dad just had incredible enthusiasm for life, an energetic intelligence. Given the chance, he would have shown me around Cambridge on his fold-up bike (the one he cycled to work on), or we would have jogged (he had the lean physique of a fell runner). Instead, we walked, at pace, me struggling to keep up.

He began by showing me around what he kept calling his college, which was men-only in his day. Can you imagine? It's comforting to know that he was here before me, walking the same paths, crossing the same hallowed courts. And then he took me punting, said that's what you did. At least he wasn't wearing a straw boater.

Uncharacteristically, there were moments of quietness that day, and he explained that things were difficult at work. He never spoke much about his job and I usually didn't ask. All I knew was that it had taken us to various embassies around the world, mostly in south Asia, and that he worked in the Foreign Office's Political Unit, sending reports back to London that he joked no one ever read.

For the last two years he'd been based in London. I'm not sure if it was a promotion, but he still travelled occasionally. I was old enough to look after myself when he was away. And old enough to accompany him to work functions when he was back, including a garden party at Buckingham Palace last year. He wore the same blazer he was wearing that day on the River Cam.

'I've got to go to India,' he said, ducking unnecessarily as we passed under Clare Bridge.

'Lucky you.'

I regretted my tone. I knew he didn't like being absent for long stretches.

'Ladakh,' he added, smiling.

He hoped that this would somehow soften the blow. We had a happy trip together there once, to Leh, where we hung out in hippy cafés on the Changspa Road, watching young Israelis drive into town on Enfield Bullets as they tried to seek some solace in the mountains after national service. It's possibly my favourite place in the whole world. I want to have a job one day that allows me to travel like Dad.

I watched him nod at a punt passing us in the other direction. Two proud parents sitting in the front, prodigal son steering them down the Backs. I'm sure that my father's career was hampered by his insistence on being there for his only child. He pretty much brought me up himself, with the help of an ayah or two along the way.

'Promise me you'll try everything when you get here,' he said.

I remember not liking his tone, the suggestion that he might still be away when I went 'up' to Cambridge, as he insisted on saying, but maybe hindsight is skewing my memory. That sunny afternoon, however, he was not himself; more reserved, fewer jokes.

'Sign up for all the clubs and societies,' he continued, a false levity in his voice. 'Give everything a go, the whole damn life here. I remember joining Labour, the SDP and the Conservatives all in the same night.'

'Is that why you're so good at this? Because you joined a punting club?'

'I learnt how to punt to impress your mother. First time I took her out, the pole stuck in the mud – easy thing to do. I just shouldn't have clung on to it when the boat drifted away.'

'Dad!' I said, with mock exasperation. I could see the memory made him happy rather than sad, a smile creasing the corner of his mouth, the side he always used to whisper silly things out of when we were meant to be being serious. 'It's pronounced "Ma'am" as in "spam", and remember to curtsy,' he'd said moments before I bobbed in front of the Queen in heels that sank into the Buckingham Palace turf.

I find it hard to imagine being able to do that: smile at the thought of him. Right now it just makes me want to curl up in this narrow college bed and die.

5

Jar knows that there's something wrong the moment he steps out of the lift. The door to his flat is open, a sharp triangle of light slicing the darkness of the landing. His breath shortens.

'Wait here,' he says to Yolande, whom he was kissing in the lift seconds earlier. They had met in a pub at the top of Brick Lane, where he often stops off after work. A pattern has emerged in recent months. After a 'post-bereavement hallucination', as he now knows he must call this morning's sighting of Rosa, he seeks the comfort of a stranger. A misguided attempt to move on with his life: strangers somehow making him feel less unfaithful to her memory.

He pushes the door further open, but it catches against something. Forcing it, he steps inside, blood pulsing at his temples. The flat – one big room, a kitchenette at the far end, bed at the other – has been ransacked, the floor littered with books pulled from the bookshelves that line every inch of the walls. Some of the shelves have been wrenched and are leaning limply into the room like storm-torn trees. He closes his eyes, trying to rationalise what's happened.

Burglary is not uncommon in his towerblock, the most recent series of break-ins blamed on crackheads north of the

Hackney Road. Nic Farah, a photographer one floor down, had his computer lifted last week. And a TV and sound system were stolen from a flat on the sixteenth, four floors below him, a few days earlier. As a half-hearted precaution, Jar has taken to hiding his twelve-string guitar under the bed.

He steps through the snowfall of books on the floor, snatching at his father's copy of *More Than a Game* by Con Houlihan. Instinctively, he knows that none are missing. It's not what they – whoever 'they' are – came here for. He bends down beside the bed. His guitar case is still there. He is about to stand up but decides to pull the battered case out. Anything to distract himself, stop the thoughts chasing each other around his head. Reassured by the case's heaviness, he opens it beside him on the bed. The guitar is safe, undamaged, further confirmation that this isn't a regulation burglary. Good guitars like his are easy enough to sell for cash.

'I'm guessing it's not normally like this,' Yolande says, standing in the doorway. Her voice is polished. Jar is shocked by how easily he has forgotten her. 'Shall I call the police?'

He should have made his excuses at the bar and left, not brought her back here. She isn't even technically a stranger. She had caught his eye the last time he went in to see his publisher, walking past him with a box of books to be signed by an author more in favour than he would ever be. And then there she was in the bar tonight. It would have been rude not to go over and talk to her.

'No,' Jar says. He strums an impatient chord on the guitar before putting it away. 'Nothing's been taken.'

'How do you know?'

'Because there's nothing *to* take now.' Jar snaps the guitar case shut and paces around the room.

'So many books,' she says, watching him. And two more coming tomorrow, Jar thinks: *Young Skins*, by Colin Barrett, to compensate for this week's Jennifer Lawrence story, and Anne Enright's *The Green Road* for a One Direction quiz. Futile attempts to maintain some sort of cultural equilibrium in his life. He's running out of room.

'Let me help you clear up,' Yolande says, at his side now, a hand on his shoulder.

Jar flinches at the contact. She is too good to be involved in his life. As he watches her retrieve a book, something catches his eye in all the mess. It's a photo of Rosa. And it shouldn't be here. He doesn't keep any reminders of her in the flat, no trace at all. It's a rule of his. Did someone leave it, like a calling card? And then he remembers that he'd used the photo as a bookmark when he was at Cambridge. It must have fallen out of a book.

He bends down to retrieve it, staring at her face. Rosa always did know how to get his attention. He loves her studiousness in this one: at her desk, not looking at the camera, chewing on a pen. He's seen so many images over the past five years that he worries he can no longer remember what she was really like, his memory of her shaped by photos.

'I ought to be heading home,' Yolande says, looking over his shoulder. Her voice startles him. How long has he been staring at the photo?

He knows she is owed an apology, an explanation at least, but he doesn't know where to begin.

'OK,' he says, turning away from Rosa's accusatory gaze: another one-night stand you've treated shabbily.

Jar looks at Yolande for a moment. A different night, another life, they would be making drunken, languid love by now, falling into bed after he had wooed her with an Irish ballad on the guitar, one of the songs that he used to hear so often in his old bedroom, his father's voice floating up through the floorboards of the family-owned bar in Galway.

'I'm sorry. Will I come down with you, hail a cab?'

'It's fine,' she says. 'Really.'

But he insists and they descend in the lift together in silence.

'You loved her very much, didn't you,' she says as the lift shakes itself to a halt on the ground floor. 'She was lucky to have known that.'

Outside on the street, she hails her own cab, but he waits until she is inside and heading into the night – to Mile End, he thinks she said – before walking back to his block of flats with new purpose, or is it fear? What happened in his flat tonight means that someone – who, he is still not sure – is starting to take him seriously. Someone who wants to know how much he's found out about Rosa. And possibly try to stop him, too. A van door closes in the distance. He presses the button for the twentieth floor and steps back outside the lift as the doors slide shut. Not waiting for the empty lift to rattle up into the night, he heads out the back entrance of the block of flats and cuts across another estate to a row of lock-up garages.

He's learnt over the years that paranoia is a corrosive disease, eating away like acid at the edges of his rational mind, but he allows himself one certainty this evening: his flat wasn't visited by burglars. The chaos was too choreo-graphed, too methodical for crackheads. In recent days he has had the feeling of being watched, followed home from work, observed from coffee shops, a sensation that he has so far managed to dismiss. Tonight changes everything.

He unbolts the locked side door of the garage and steps

inside, turning on the fluorescent strip light. His actions feel more valid now. He isn't expecting this place to have been burgled too, but it's still a relief to find it exactly as he left it yesterday. He sits down at the computer, switching it on as he looks around the small, cold space. Rosa always feels closer here.

Three nautical charts of the north Norfolk coastline, taped together, dominate one breeze-block wall. Red-marker-pen arrows have been drawn on to the charts, indicating the direction of currents; beaches as far west as Burnham Deepdale and Hunstanton have been circled. Next to the charts is an Ordnance Survey map of Cromer. Green-coloured pen lines lead out to photographs and CCTV stills neatly stuck to an adjacent pinboard.

The wall behind the computer table is a patchwork of photographs. On the left-hand side are images of Rosa from university. On the right are unconfirmed sightings since her death, some of them crossed out. He didn't take a photo at Paddington of the woman he thought was Rosa. Instead, he sticks a photo of the station on the wall, draws a question mark next to it with a red marker pen and adds the date.

He keeps everything to do with her here, in an effort to preserve some sort of normality in the rest of his life. The endless Freedom of Information requests to St Matthew's (her college), the police, the hospital, as well as his correspondence with the coroner (exempt from FoI). There's the more personal, too: a Margaret Howell nightshirt (bought by her aunt when she got into Cambridge), her favourite perfume (scent she'd found in the spice market in Istanbul), one of the funny cards she'd slipped under his college door.

When people visit the flat, they think he's moved on with his life. He likes that, wants people to believe he's over her.

No one need know that it's here in this draughty lock-up that he feels most alive, surrounded by images of the woman he loved more than he thought it was possible to love another human being. If someone walked in on him now, they would mistake him for a stalker. In some ways that's what he is, except the woman he is hunting is meant to have died five years ago, jumping to her death on a wild night in Cromer, 130 miles away on the north Norfolk coast.

He checks through his personal emails. His father has sent him a few lines about hurling over the weekend and a link to a match report in the *Connacht Tribune*. Jar's cousin was playing. 'Conor didn't come within an ass's roar of scoring. Visit us soon, Da.' Jar smiles as he moves to flip accounts to his work email, but his eye is caught by another message in among the junk.

It's from Amy, Rosa's aunt, a picture restorer who lives in Cromer. Amy and Rosa had always been close, but the bond between them grew even stronger after Rosa's father died. Rosa often went up to the seaside town for weekends, welcoming the chance to get away from the cauldron of Cambridge life.

Jar was invited along too but it wasn't always easy. Amy bears a painful physical resemblance to her niece. She has also spent much of her life on medication, rollercoastering in and out of depression. Amy's spirits seemed to lift, though, whenever Amy was with her. They would sit quietly in the filtered sunlight of the sitting room, where Amy would paint intricate patterns in henna on Rosa's arms and hands as they chatted about her dad.

Jar doesn't blame her for what subsequently happened and he has stayed in touch since, their relationship, like Amy and Rosa's, blossoming in mutual bereavement. Amy is an ally, equally paranoid, the only person Jar knows who doesn't believe Rosa is dead. She has no explanation or theory, just a 'sixth sense', as she puts it, which makes the upbeat tone of her email tonight all the more intriguing:

> Jar, I've been trying to ring but couldn't get through. We've found something on the computer that you might be interested in. It's to do with Rosa. I'm around all week if you want to come and visit. Call me.

Jar glances at his watch and considers ringing Amy now – it's late but he knows she never sleeps well. Then he remembers his phone is on the charger back at the flat. He'll ring her first thing in the morning – from the train to Norfolk. After tonight's burglary, he might be running out of time.

6

I t's been a week since I saw Him in the restaurant. If you had asked me then how I imagined we'd meet up again, I'm not sure I would have said as naked as the day I was born on the banks of the River Cam. But that's what happened last night and I'm still not quite sure how.

At least I now know his name. He's called Jarlath Costello, 'Jar' to his friends, and he's from Galway. His father runs a bar in the city, his mother's a psychiatric nurse in Ballinasloe. Jar's doing an MPhil in Modern and Contemporary English, having read Irish Literature at Trinity College, Dublin. As I thought, he's a couple of years older than me. And ten times more sensible.

After we finished our rehearsal, the whole cast went out for a drink at The Eagle, where Watson and Crick did their DNA thing. Later, when the evening started to wind down, three of us – Beth, Sam the director, and me – took a walk along the Backs. It was a warm June night and the moon was almost full, bright enough to cast shadows.

'Anyone fancy a dip?' Sam asked, looking at me. He'd been flirting a lot over the past few days and I can't say I minded the attention, although I worry about my motives. An aura has

29

already built up around him as a director, that unsaid consensus that in a few years he will be something big in the real world.

Beth hesitated, watching my response. I knew she fancied Sam too, but I'd been trying to put that to one side, determined that it wouldn't get in the way of what I hoped was our growing relationship. I'm still attempting to prove to myself that I can do what students are supposed to do: get drunk, skinny-dip, forge lifelong friendships, have lots of energetic sex, maybe even learn something.

I must have paused too long, for the next moment Beth was stripping off and running across the grass, her body shockingly white – and far too nubile – in the glassy moonlight.

'Come on then,' she whooped, as much to herself as to us. She'd seized the initiative, laid down a challenge, and I was going to match her all the way.

Without pausing, I took off my clothes too, running towards the riverbank in the hope that it might seem like a less flagrant act when combined with doing something else. I didn't look back to see whether Sam was following us. I just wanted to join Beth in the water as quickly as possible.

I felt no embarrassment until my knickers caught on my toe and I hopped the final few yards before jumping in. I couldn't help noticing that I made more of a splash than Beth, which annoyed me. And then I was annoyed that I'd even noticed.

The river was much colder than I expected, but I swam over to Beth, who was treading water beneath Clare Bridge, looking back at Sam.

'Is he coming in?' I asked, as indifferently as I could manage. I wanted to turn around, but that would have suggested that I was as interested in seeing Sam naked as she was.

'How is it?' Sam called out. He was still very much in his clothes.

'Aren't you joining us?' Beth asked.

'These will get wet on the grass,' he said, gathering up both our piles of clothes. Oddly, I felt more self-conscious about Sam handling my knickers than seeing me naked, but he bundled them up briskly, like a mother picking up washing from a teenager's floor, and walked over to a bench that was set back from the bank.

Beth turned to me. I could tell she was thinking what I was thinking: Sam never had any intention of swimming.

'You're a chicken, Sam,' Beth called out. 'A big fat lazy cock hen.'

'He could have left them where they were,' I said.

'He's auditioning us,' Beth said, swimming back to the shore.

I trod water, watching as Beth lifted her dripping white arse out of the river and sashayed across the grass towards Sam, who was now sitting on the bench, our clothes piled up next to him. She made no effort to walk quickly or cover herself.

Suddenly it wasn't funny any more. I didn't want to be auditioned, to submit myself to Sam's scrutiny.

'Are you staying in there all night?' he asked.

If I have to, I thought. A better friend than Beth would have brought my clothes to the bank. The game had been won and she could at least have been magnanimous in victory, but she'd already pulled on her clothes and was sitting next to Sam, his arm slung around her shoulders, keeping her warm.

And then I watched as they got up and walked away, arm in arm.

'See you back at college,' Beth said, calling over her shoulder. 'Catch us up.'

Yeah right. Trying to ignore the creeping cold, I looked around me, at the fabled Backs bathed in moonlight, King's

College Chapel rising up in stately silhouette. I should be enjoying Cambridge, I thought, my time here, but I'm not. That reminder made me feel at peace with the decision I've made. I miss Dad so much it hurts.

There was a May Ball further down the Cam, at Queen's College. The distant hum of music and student exuberance carried up the river. I'd like to go to our own college ball, at least I think I would, to prove that I can enjoy things like that, but the ticket is too expensive. Three people have asked me, offering to pay, but it feels like a contract for sex.

I thought back to the day Dad punted me down there, the last time I saw him alive. He would have approved of the skinny-dipping but not Sam's behaviour, even less Beth's. I only had myself to blame.

I suddenly felt vulnerable, my clothes too far away from the bank for comfort. In the distance, a group of students was heading my way. And that's when I spotted Him, walking over Clare Bridge above me.

There was no question it was Jar, the heft of his big frame silhouetted in the moonlight. And there was something about his long-strided walk: purposeful, going somewhere with his life, not treading water like me (waiting for an end that can't come quickly enough). At least he was on his own, hands thrust deep in his jacket pockets.

Should I sink lower into the water, I wondered, hope he doesn't see me, or front up and call out, ask him to bring my clothes over?

'Hi there,' I said, realising for the first time how cold I was. I needed to get out.

For a moment he didn't respond, but then he stopped, as if he was processing the voice, recalling it from some deep vault in his writer's brain.

'Down here. The girl who couldn't pay for her dinner.' It was a lousy calling card, but I couldn't think of anything better to say.

Jar was peering over the edge of the wall now, his arms cradling one of the big stone balls that line each side of the bridge.

'Let me guess now,' he said, seemingly unsurprised to see me skinny-dipping in the river at midnight. 'Method acting? Some weird audition?'

'Kind of. Only I don't think I want the part.'

'You look frozen.'

'Can you get my clothes?' His comment had made me feel much colder, dangerously so. 'Over there, on the bench.'

'You're lucky no one ran off with them.'

I started to swim for the bank, watching as Jar walked across the bridge and over to the bench, where he picked up my clothes. We reached the bank at the same time.

'I'll leave them here,' he said, making a conscious effort not to look in my direction as he held them out and turned his back.

For a moment I wondered if I was too cold to pull myself out of the water. My arms were aching and I sank back in after the first attempt.

'Are you OK there?' Jar asked, turning his head sideways, as if addressing someone he couldn't quite see in the dark.

I wanted to ask him to help, but it would have been too awkward. Instead, I summoned the strength and hauled myself out.

'I'm fine.'

We'd both clocked the approaching group of drunken students, now walking towards us on the path that runs parallel with the river. Chivalrously, Jar had positioned himself in between them and me. I pulled my clothes on as swiftly as I could, not bothering with my bra and trying to ignore the catcalls.

'The nick of time. Are you OK?'

'Fucking freezing.'

'Here, take this,' he said, giving me his jacket. 'Go on now,' he added as I hesitated.

I wrapped myself in his large suede jacket, aware of sandalwood again, just like in the restaurant, and we walked down towards King's College, away from the students, who'd lost interest.

We hadn't discussed where we were going. I just wanted to walk to keep warm and he seemed fine with that. Soon we'd turned up through King's College and into town, chatting about his home in Galway, his time at Trinity College and the move to Britain. As we talked, I subconsciously weighed up being cold against having to make a decision about what we were doing, where we were going, his place, mine or our separate ways, and I wasn't ready to decide yet. It turned out he's just begun working on a novel, on top of his MPhil, and was out walking in an attempt to think through the ending.

'Someone once told me that writing a novel is like telling a joke,' he said as we headed up Hobson Street. 'You know the punchline, but there are lots of ways of getting there.'

'But you don't know the punchline...'

'My father used to love *The Two Ronnies*, always had it on in the pub – when he wasn't watching *Dave Allen*. His favourite part was when the little fella sat in the big chair and told those long shaggy dog stories. The actual joke was not important, it was the way he told it. I thought the ending wouldn't matter.'

'Have you come up with one tonight?'

'Early days,' he said. 'My two main characters have only just met.'

7

Jar replied to Amy's email, telling her that he wanted to come in person instead of talking over the phone, and he is now on the Coasthopper bus from King's Lynn to Cromer. He took an early train out of King's Cross, using all the cash he had left in his emergency fund (kept in a battered old Persian teapot at the flat – another item that the 'burglars' had left untouched).

He feels a surge of adrenaline when Cromer pier comes into view. He always does. Five years ago, Rosa was seen on the town's CCTV, approaching the Victorian structure at 1 a.m., a rough sea pummelling its iron pillars. A man who has never been traced rang the police shortly afterwards to say that he had just seen a figure jumping off the pier's end. The emergency services were called and the town's inshore lifeboat launched. A vicious riptide flows beneath the pier and that night the current was running east to west, which would have carried anyone in the water out into the North Sea and around to the Wash. CCTV cameras on and around the pier, some of which were found to be faulty, had no record of a person leaving.

Jar has visited Cromer a number of times in the intervening years, to see Amy and to stand here, high above the roiling

35

water, trying to imagine what might have happened – whether the woman he loved, and who he thought loved him, had chosen to end her life there. The memorial service was postponed until after the coroner's inquest. Everyone expected her body to wash up on one of the beaches along the north Norfolk coast, but she was never found.

At the delayed inquest, the suicide note addressed to Amy, with whom she had been staying the night she died, the call to the emergency services, the police report and the character assessment from her college dean, which dwelt on her grief for her father, were enough for the coroner to declare her presumed dead. It was little consolation that her death was recorded as misadventure rather than suicide.

She had written a letter to Jar, too, which was also presented to the coroner. It was an email in her drafts folder (Amy's one had been left there too) and wasn't long. He knows the words by heart:

Jar, I'm so sorry. Thank you for the late happiness you brought into my life and the love we shared. I hope you go on to find the peace that eluded me in this world. In the end, the loss of Dad has proved more than I can bear, but already I feel closer to him, knowing what lies ahead of me. I just wish I didn't have to leave you behind, babe, the first true love of my life and my last.

Jar has often wondered if she deliberately chose a stormy night to head down to the pier. In her last weeks at college, he had helped her to write an essay on pathetic fallacy. Her mind was more disturbed than he realised at the time – he accepts that now – but it still doesn't make sense.

After stepping off the bus, he heads straight for the hotel

where Amy has arranged for them to meet: the Hotel de Paris, an Edwardian timewarp popular with coach parties. He is early and had planned to walk down the pier first, but the choice of venue – why not meet at her house? – has made him nervous. Or perhaps it's being in a seaside town unfairly out of fashion that troubles him: the dawn-like stillness of empty streets and closed-up shops, the sense that last night's party has moved on.

Inside the hotel, which overlooks the pier, wood-panelled signs indicate the 'Ladies Powder Room' and 'Games Room'. There's a minstrel's gallery of sorts above the main reception, a dizzying patterned carpet, chandeliers, and heavy gilt-edged portraits on the walls. Jar heads down to the cocktail bar, past a poster advertising house doubles and Bacardi and colas, and a glass cabinet displaying bottles of Prosecco and Pinot Grigio.

Amy is early too, sitting in the far corner of the deserted main bar, nursing a cup of coffee. Jar swallows hard, the deafening echoes of Rosa threatening to fell him before they've even spoken: the same high brow and long, dark hair, an unseasonal purple velvet coat and bohemian knee-length boots. But there is none of Rosa's playfulness. Instead, a heaviness hangs over her, something that Jar once saw in his mamó shortly before she died: eyes wearied by years of pain. She's having one of her down days, he thinks.

'Am I late?' he asks, closing his eyes as he kisses her on the cheek.

'I'm in no rush,' she says. Jar remembers how time seems to slow down around Amy when she's like this. 'Coffee?'

A bored waitress wearing a pinny emerges through a swing door that slams with disapproval behind her. Jar jumps, but Amy doesn't seem to hear it. He orders a double espresso, taking in the empty, high-ceilinged room: the dark varnish of the bar, ornate cornicing, a sketch of the lifeboat. He feels a sudden pang of homesickness, for the family bar in Galway, his father.

'Our revels now are ended,' his da likes to bark at closing time, standing on a chair among the throng of locals and tourists. 'Or, in the immortal words of William Shakespeare, haven't any of you feckin' eejits got homes to go to?' (He can curse the bladder out of a goat, can Da.) Sometimes it feels like Jar's whole childhood was misspent sitting on a bar stool, dipping his finger into the beer-spill tray as he listened to Da chatting to customers, telling American tourists about the fourteen tribes of Galway, weaving his spell of Gaelic bonhomie. If his mother hadn't made a point of sending him to bed every night, he would have stayed up till dawn. 'Well how's the wee fella ever going to learn about the world?' his father would complain, ruffling his hair.

'You look well,' Amy lies. Jar knows he's not in good shape. A darkness around his eyes, too much over the belt.

'You too now,' he lies back. Today she looks older than her forty-something years, her hair more obviously flecked with grey. And she seems suddenly anxious, glancing around the empty room. Jar turns too, expecting to see someone, but they are alone.

'You were lucky to get a table,' he says.

Amy humours him with a fey half smile. She is wearing more make-up than usual, but it fails to conceal the darkness beneath her own eyes. Rosa never wore make-up, he tells himself.

'I brought you a present,' Jar continues, removing a copy of *Where Heaven and Mountains Meet: Zanskar and the Himalayas* from a cotton bag he's been carrying.

She takes the book and flicks through it, stopping at a

photo of a barefooted pilgrim walking precariously along the frozen edge of the Zanskar River. 'There was no need,' she says. Another half smile, more heartfelt this time.

'It was one of Rosa's favourites,' he adds.

'Thank you, Jar,' she says. 'How's the writing?'

'Katy Perry's keeping me busy.'

Jar sounds more defensive than he means to be. He's used to people asking him about his writing, but he has got no better at explaining that he hasn't written a word of fiction since Rosa died.

'How's Martin?' he asks. Amy's husband used to work as a pharmacologist at a contract research organisation, overseeing pre-clinical trials for various drug companies, but he left his job some time ago.

'Doing more freelance work, still applying for jobs. Cycling more than ever. And he's determined to finish his novel. You know how it is.'

Jar nods. He hasn't seen Martin for a while, but not out of choice. He bonded with him at their first meeting, after Martin announced that he had enjoyed Jar's collection of short stories and was an aspiring writer himself. On the surface, it was an unlikely alliance, given that Jar knew nothing about Martin's other all-consuming passion, cycling, or the pharmaceutical industry, but Martin turned out to be something of a polymath. He'd been offered a place to read English at Cambridge, impressing the interview panel with his theories on 'the medicalisation of identity' in the Beat Generation, but had settled on the more practical world of pharmacology and later specialised in psychopharmacology.

Martin also shares Jar's reservations about counselling. Amy wants Jar to get help for his post-bereavement hallucinations – she knows some good therapists – but he is less keen.

He is about to ask about Amy's own job – she is back working two days a week as a picture restorer at the Fitzwilliam in Cambridge – when she interrupts him.

'I know I am a bit paranoid, but...' She hesitates.

'Join the club.'

'Has anyone been keeping an eye on you recently?'

He smiles, holding her gaze. Sometimes he thinks they should actually set up a club together, just the two of them. (Motto: 'Even paranoids have enemies'.)

'I feel watched every day,' he says. 'Sometimes by Rosa, usually by others, most recently by a man sitting in the window of a Starbucks café. And last night my flat was burgled.'

'Jar, you should have said. I'm so sorry.'

'Nothing was taken.'

Amy looks at him for an explanation, but none is forthcoming. Jar is wary of revealing his latest conspiracy theory, that whoever burgled him was trying to establish how much he has found out about Rosa's death. Amy is fragile at the best of times and he doesn't want to alarm her.

He watches her fiddle with the single wrapped biscuit that came with her coffee. Her nails are bitten, unloved. Once, when he had accompanied Rosa to Cromer, Amy had sat with them both and painted his nails silver.

'And you?' Jar says, resting his hand on Amy's arm. It pains him to see her like this. 'Are you're feeling watched too?'

'We were always careful when Martin was still working,' she says, staring out of the window, recalling a faraway past. 'Kept a lookout, noticed things.'

Jar was aware that Martin's work had come to the attention of animal rights activists. His career in pharmaceuticals was the main reason why Rosa's father had fallen out with him shortly after they got married, and why Rosa wasn't so keen on him, either. That and the speed with which Martin had put Amy on medication for her depression and anxiety.

'The police used to tell us what to watch out for in the street, around the home,' Amy continues.

'Is Martin still a target?'

'It's been a while. We keep an eye out.'

'And?'

Amy sits up, as if she's suddenly remembered why she is there, and speaks with more animation. 'I've just had this feeling in recent days that our house is being observed, that's all.'

'What does Martin think?'

'He's says it's to be expected: paranoia is a common side effect of withdrawal. I'm trying to cut down again.'

'That's good,' Jar says.

'I'm seeing a therapist. Martin's not over the moon, as you can imagine. I tried when he first left his job, when I thought we were starting out on life again, but then...' Her voice falters. 'Rosa's disappearance knocked me back a bit.'

'Of course.' Jar pauses. Sometimes, because of her medication, Amy talks to him as if he's a stranger, forgetting the hours they have spent discussing Rosa. 'It knocked us all. Why do you think you're being watched?'

'We have a lot of CCTV and alarms around the place, but they're more for my benefit. I'm the worrier. Martin thinks life's too short.'

Her words hang awkwardly in the air. They both know it.

'You mentioned Rosa in your email,' Jar says, steering the conversation back.

Amy casts her eyes around the room and then turns to him, focused again.

'Two days ago, I took my laptop in to a local man in town who fixes computers. I'm trying to be more independent these days. The laptop had died and I wanted to see if anything could be saved. I rang Martin on his bike ride to explain what I was doing. He's very particular about our computers and I knew he would want to know. Turns out the hard drive was corrupted. He managed to retrieve most of the files, but there was one folder that couldn't be accessed.'

Amy picks up a plastic bag at her feet and passes it to him under the table with the furtiveness of a drugs dealer.

'It's the hard drive. What's left of it. The man transferred all he could on to my new computer.'

Jar holds the bag in his hands, resisting the temptation to peer inside.

'Take it,' she says.

'I don't understand.'

'Martin came straight home from his bike ride when I rang him. He took the drive down to his shed and couldn't open the folder either, but he managed to decipher its name.'

'And?'

'It's called "Rosa's Diary".'

For a moment it feels like Jar is gripping Rosa's hand under the table rather than a plastic bag. She is with them in the hotel, talking about Ladakh, her desire one day to visit the region in winter, walk the icy Zanskar.

'She must have downloaded it on to my laptop when she stayed that last night,' Amy says. 'She often used it for her emails when she was here. It's probably nothing, but...' Her voice trails off mid-sentence.

Jar feels sorry for her, the warped world they inhabit, where there are no coincidences, only connections. They can both see the oddness of Rosa downloading her diary on to their computer.

'We thought you might know someone who could open

it,' she continues, with more confidence now. 'Maybe one of your techie work colleagues. That guy Carl you're always talking about. I know Martin didn't always see eye to eye with Rosa...' She forces a smile. 'But the next day, after a particularly long ride – he says he does all his thinking when he's out on his bike – he returned quite animated, started talking about her in, well, affectionate terms. He also said that you were the only one who had really understood Rosa.'

Jar looks away.

'Perhaps it was guilt. Later that night, he announced that we ought to hand the diary over to you. It was the right and proper thing to do, he said, seeing as you two were together. He asked me to give it to you.' She pauses, turning her wedding ring. 'I think Rosa meant it to be found one day, Jar. It might have some answers.'

8

It was late by the time we reached Jar's rooms. We'd walked the streets of Cambridge for more than an hour, stopping off in All Saints Passage for a kebab, which we shared and both regretted, and then, finally, he asked what I'd like to do.

I was still feeling cold inside from my dip in the Cam, but I didn't want our evening to end. He's a good listener, or perhaps he just couldn't get a word in edgeways. There's something about his manner that made me unburden myself, tell him more than I've told anyone since I've arrived at Cambridge. If only I could talk about the one thing that's looming ever larger in my life, darkening or brightening the horizon, I'm not sure any more.

'Can you show me your etchings?' I asked, linking my arm in his for the first time. He looked at me and then smiled as a group of drunken students pushed past on King's Parade.

'Aren't I meant to ask that?'

'OK then.'

'Would you like to come up for a—' Another student knocked into his shoulder, rocking his broad frame sideways, but he didn't react.

'For a what?' I grinned.

'For a coffee,' Jar said. 'Better make that a whiskey.'

His rooms were spacious compared to mine, a lot tidier,
too. Big windows overlooking King's Parade, a bedroom off
a decent-sized sitting room – the sort of *Brideshead* accom-
modation that people might imagine when they think of
Cambridge. I wandered around, trailing my hand over the
worn burgundy leather sofa and armchair. He even had a
fireplace. The walls were lined with books – Yeats, Synge,
Heaney – and his laptop was resting closed on a desk in the
corner, an anglepoise light hanging its head in shame above
it. A row of Irish whiskey bottles stood on the windowsill, a
Villagers CD propped up next to one of them.

I still had no idea where the evening was heading, but I felt
comfortable in Jar's company, enough to ask him if I could
change out of my damp clothes while they dried.

'I would run you a bath, but it's a couple of miles down the
corridor,' he said, passing me his paisley dressing gown from the
back of the door. 'We don't want the neighbours talking now.
You can change in there,' he added, nodding at the bedroom.

'Here's fine,' I said. We were standing in the sitting room,
beside the sofa. 'You saw it all down by the Cam anyway.'

'I wasn't looking. Would you like a whiskey?'

'Not even a peep?'

He didn't answer as he fetched a bottle and glass from the
windowsill and poured a generous measure.

'Here, it'll warm you up,' he said, passing me the glass.
'Twelve-year-old Redbreast – single pot still Irish whiskey.
Sherry cask, first-use bourbon barrels. Plenty of fruit and
spice with oak variations.'

'How can I resist?' I whispered. We were standing close
now, facing each other.

'That's what my da says, anyway. He gives me a bottle of the stuff every New Year, along with extensive tasting notes.'

'Where's your glass?' I asked.

'Oh, I've already drunk my life's allocation.'

'That's not fair.'

'I can't complain.'

'On me, I mean.'

'Besides, I write better when I'm sober.'

'I didn't know you were planning to write tonight.'

We were so close now our faces were almost touching.

'It never seems to stop. Let me help you,' he said, unbuttoning my shirt. His big fingers – clean, manicured nails – were steady, untrembling. I wondered if he was surprised that I wasn't wearing anything underneath, already had me down as a bra-free feminist.

I took a sip of whiskey, felt it sear my mouth and held it there. As he slipped off my shirt, watching me, my lips, I leant in to kiss him, closing my eyes – properly-deliriously-student-happy for the first time since I arrived in Cambridge – and shared the whiskey. He let it into his mouth and swallowed.

'Not much resistance there,' I whispered.

He drew me gently to him, kissed my neck, and then my mouth again. We stopped as I took off his jacket and shirt. I was in no rush, savouring the measured pace, but the rhythm quickened when we kissed again and I felt his bare skin against mine. I slipped my hand into his jeans, holding him tightly as he slid his fingers down the front of my knickers. We stumbled towards the bed, giggling at our awkward, increasingly urgent dance. For a moment he paused above me, and I wanted to tell him everything, but I knew that would be unfair: the burden of my chosen path must rest with me and me alone.

Afterwards, as we drank more whiskey in bed, I apologised if I'd knocked him off the wagon. He hadn't struck me as an alcoholic, reformed or otherwise. I wanted to talk to him more about his past in Dublin, the life of excess so at odds with his calm manner.

'It's nothing complicated,' he said, as if reading my thoughts. 'My father runs a bar in Galway, ergo I've drunk all my life. I then went to university in Dublin, where I drank some more, usually in The Pav, the campus sports bar, but sometimes off campus at John Kehoe's, which serves the best pint of Guinness in Dublin.'

'And now?'

He looked at the whiskey in his glass. 'The first drop I've had since I arrived.'

I nudged him in the ribs, nodding at the row of bottles on the windowsill.

'Purely medicinal. My life's better now, more ordered.'

'Until tonight.'

'It's different. I'm not alone.'

He put an arm around me and we lay there in contented silence, my leg hitched over his, under the sheets, until he turned and fixed me with his eyes.

'You're not telling me something,' he said, without any accusation. I could feel my stomach tighten.

'I've told you more than I've told anyone for a long time.'

'Are you happy?'

'I am tonight.' Happier than he will ever know, but his words had pulled the magic carpet from under us.

'And do you usually sleep with someone so soon after meeting them?' he asked, smiling. I wasn't listening. What had I done?

'Rosa?'

47

'Never,' I replied, but he knew something had changed. The intimacy of the night had evaporated.

'Me neither.'

We lay in silence.

'Can I write something down?' he said, as if he was asking to turn off the light. 'I always think I'll remember later, but I never do.'

'What time is it?'

'Late. Stay here tonight. Please.'

I watched him as he got up from the bed, pulled on the dressing gown I'd worn earlier and walked over to his desk, where he opened up his laptop and began to type at once. It wasn't much of a spectator sport, but I lay back, wondering what he was writing.

'Almost done,' he said over his shoulder.

Maybe I'm flattering myself, but I couldn't help thinking that it was about us, the frisson of our first encounter. My eyes started to well up and I pressed my lips together until they hurt. I knew it wasn't fair on him. I've promised not to get close to anyone, least of all someone like Jar.

I got out of bed and walked across the room, putting my arms around his shoulders as I kissed the top of his head.

'I have to go,' I managed to say, my eyes pricking with tears.

9

J ar walks out of the hotel ten minutes after Amy, who insisted that they leave separately. Her anxiety is unsettling rather than reassuring, a mirror to his own paranoia.

He heads for the beach, telling himself that he wants to fill his lungs with air, listen to *the murmuring surge*. But the pier soon pulls him with a force he's unable to resist.

It should hold no significance – Rosa didn't die here, he tells himself – but as he walks past the Pavilion Theatre and stands at the far end, beside the lifeboat house, the sobs start to come, buckling his knees. It's been a while since he cried and he allows the tears to flow. The events of the last couple of days have brought things to a head, made him accept what he's always known. It will be impossible to get on with the rest of his life until he finds out what happened to Rosa.

His hands tighten on the railing as he stares down at the pillars below him, where lengths of snagged old fishing lines blow in the wind like cobwebs. It's a big drop down to the water – at least forty feet. Jar tries not to think about how long it would take for a body to hit the surface. Next to him is a life-ring and a sign saying 'No Diving'; beyond that an emergency phone. Did Rosa consider using it?

He looks out to sea, where the distant shapes of wind

turbines interrupt the horizon, then turns and walks towards a group of local fishermen and some tourists who have gathered. A few are crabbing, using clear buckets and bright orange reels; others spin with rods. A man is taking a break on a bench that looks more like a bus shelter. There's a beheaded mackerel and a short black-handled knife at his feet, a half-empty glass of Guinness in his hand. Beside him is an iPad, no doubt to record any catches, and an empty bottle of Lucozade.

Jar hears a phone ringing and, after a moment, realises that it's his own.

'Jar, it's Amy. Where are you?'

'On the pier,' he says, shielding his phone from the wind.

'Get yourself away from there, away from Cromer.'

Jar looks around him, glancing at the huddle of hooded fishermen. One of them catches his eye.

'Is everything OK?' he asks, his stomach tightening.

'The police are here.'

'Where?' Jar scans the shoreline for flashing blue lights. 'What's going on?'

'They've taken away my new computer. And they're asking about the old hard drive. They're looking for Rosa's diary, Jar. I know they are.'

'Have you told them anything?' His mind is racing; calculations, consequences.

'Martin thinks the computer man must have tipped them off.'

'About Rosa? Why?'

'Maybe he thought her diary might be evidence, I don't know. He was asking about Rosa, knew all about her death.'

The line drops before he can reply. Jar suddenly feels very exposed on the pier. *They're looking for Rosa's diary, Jar.*

I know they are. They – the people who burgled his flat, the man in the café opposite work – don't want him to know what happened to Rosa that night, don't want him to read her version of events. Did they follow him up from London on the train, clock his meeting with Amy at the hotel? He sets off down the other side of the pier, away from the fishermen, his thoughts churning like the sea beneath him.

'Jar! Where are you going?'

Jar stops in his tracks and turns. A woman, ten yards behind him, near where he was standing, has stepped up on to the lower railings, face obscured, arms held high above her head.

'Don't you love it when the wind's whipping up the waves like this?' she calls out.

'Rosa,' Jar says, walking towards her. 'Will you please get down from there.'

'It reminds me of Cornwall, when the sea comes crashing over the harbour wall.'

'You're scaring me now,' Jar says, breaking into a run as Rosa climbs another rung of the railing, leaning out to sea to balance herself.

'I'm not going to do the song, if that's what you're worried about.' Rosa turns to him, smiling, her arms stretched out either side of her now, as if she's about to sing. 'Just kidding.'

Jar grabs her around the waist and holds her there, his head pressed against her back. Then she turns to face him, slides down off the rails and hugs him, burying her face in his neck.

'You all right?' a voice says. Jar turns to a man standing next to him, the fisherman who had caught his eye.

'Fine,' Jar says. 'I'm fine.' Jar releases his grip on the railings. There is no one else around.

*

At the post office, on his way to catch the bus, Jar buys a padded envelope and gives Carl a call, propping his mobile under his chin as he picks up a pen.

'It's Jar. I need your home address.'

The hard drive is a tight fit, its sharp corners pushing against the envelope, but it will have to do.

'Everything OK? Your group-email said you'd gone to A&E after injuring your tongue with a clothes peg.'

'I'm fine,' Jar says, hoping his latest excuse had spread a little happiness in the office. 'Just need the address. Gibson Street, isn't it?'

'Number nine,' Carl says, giving the Greenwich postcode too. 'Are you sending me flowers? Bless.'

10

Cambridge, Spring Term, 2012

J ust when you think you know what someone's like here, you realise you don't. I thought Phoebe and I were friends, the first proper friendship I've made at uni, but things shifted between us at Formal Hall tonight, in a way that I hadn't expected.

Phoebe and I got on from the moment we met in Freshers' Week – she shares my misgivings about the drinking-club crowd, the banter boys and their initiation rites. She likes a drink or three, just without the need to join an eighteenth-century student dining club, and is not bothered by her weight or her unkempt hair, which has been shaved at the back but is like a stack of brambles on top, held in place with a bright headband.

She's also into radical student politics, which I think will be good for me, and claims that the intelligence services have already got a file on her anti-establishment activities. ('Badge of honour,' she said, when I asked if she was worried. 'And at least you'll know why I ended up at the bottom of the Cam.')

She's one of the kindest people I know, too, a good listener (you have to be, with me). One night when I was feeling particularly low about Dad she knocked on my door, asking if I had a phone charger she could borrow, and obviously saw that I had been crying. She gave me a hug and then went off to make me a hot water bottle (it's what her mother does for her whenever she's upset).

We ended up chatting all night, talking about Dad, death, how you want the world to show some respect and stop spinning, at least for a few minutes, when someone dies, but life moves on. I told her about how the house was cold-called by a broadband provider the night Dad died. 'Is Mr Sandhoe there?' the voice asked. It wasn't the seller's fault. Everyone has to earn a living. I wanted to scream and shout, tell him that Dad had just died, but instead I put the phone down without saying a word and sobbed.

'That was very big of you,' Phoebe said, as dawn was breaking. 'I would have told them to fuck off and die.' She was up on my desk, hugging her knees, drinking Drambuie from a miniature bottle I'd found (we were that desperate).

Anyway, tonight, at dinner in Formal Hall, I found myself opposite Nick, a second year who had sat down with the sole purpose of chatting me up. I was meant to be going to dinner with some other people, but they'd stood me up and he spotted me on my own.

Nick's reputation for getting freshers into bed is well known. (His favourite routine involves asking girls to have a bath with him, playing it down, as if he is suggesting an innocent game of Scrabble.) I was determined not to show any interest, but then he began to reel me in. Maybe it was the setting. Eating in hall is a strange, medieval experience but one that I think Dad had in mind when he urged me to try everything. There's no electric lighting, just candles set in silver candelabras – on the tables, not floating, *Harry*

Potter-style – and we have to wear our college gowns. Waiters with white gloves appear out of the shadows with food, we order wine that is brought up from the cellars, and the plates have the college coat of arms printed on them. As for grace, it can take a good minute for one of the fellows to recite – in Latin, of course.

So there I was, finding myself – against my better judgement – increasingly taken by this boy, listening to him sounding knowledgeable on Ladakh and its pre-Buddhist pantheon of gods, even though he's never been there in his life. He seemed to know all about Neemu, too, the village where Dad and I acclimatised to the altitude after we flew into Leh from Delhi. And he talked with confidence of the Nubra Valley, the Kargil conflict of 1999 and how he would like to visit a tiny border village he's read about called Turtuk – only the same tiny village that Dad and I once visited.

'They say Turtuk's apricots are the sweetest,' he said.

All I could do was nod. Pathetic, in retrospect. I realise now that he'd just been on my Facebook page and read up on Wikipedia. But I was hooked, which was why I didn't see Phoebe approaching our table.

I could sense she was momentarily puzzled, as Nick made space for her to sit down next to him. Only last week, I was pouring scorn on Nick's rumoured ambition to shag every fresher in St Matthew's. But then something happened. As she took her seat, they kissed each other on the lips.

I turned away and looked back at Phoebe, who was smiling at me. Her plump cheeks were flushed like ripe Braeburns and I could smell alcohol on her breath. I looked at her for an explanation, but none was forthcoming. The wine was reddening her eyelids and she looked more vulnerable than triumphant.

'Last week,' she said. 'We got together last week.'

'That's great,' I said, dabbing my lips with a napkin. A more unlikely couple it would be hard to imagine, but maybe I'm missing the point of Nick. In Freshers' Week, apparently, he persuaded Genevieve, a first-year Classics student, to lie naked with him on the floor of his rooms, surrounded by more than a hundred candles. They didn't have sex: he just liked the tableau.

And now, tonight, my head is full of ungenerous, irrational thoughts. Why didn't Phoebe tell me they're going out? I should be pleased for them. Nick isn't my type – I was just making polite conversation at Formal Hall. But I know that, for a few minutes at least, while we sat together in the candlelight chatting about India, I forgot that Dad had died.

II

'I met her last night,' Carl says, holding out a business card. 'That bereavement counsellor I was talking about.'

'The one who plays jungle in her waiting room?' Jar says, taking the card. He reads the name: 'Kirsten Thomas'. They are sitting under the Westway, watching a group of children being given a skateboarding lesson. Beyond the wire fence, on the far side of the skate park, Hammersmith and City trains are running up into Paddington, met by walls covered in graffiti.

'Kirsten's an older woman who happens to be very hot,' Carl continues.

'Not really what counselling's about,' Jar says.

'Makes it more interesting when she asks you to lie on the couch.'

'That was Freud.'

'He wouldn't have said no.'

'To what?'

'Fancying his therapist. "Can I call you mother?"'

Jar knows he should laugh with his friend, particularly when he's going out of his way to help him, but he's not in the mood.

'Anyway, this Kirsten,' Carl continues, relishing her name,

'she specialises in grief. Post-bereavement hallucinations. And she's American. Did I mention that? Hot American, like the pizza. Are you hungry?'

Jar takes a sip of his latte. Carl's always hungry.

'And for the record, she didn't discount my theory about funeral dating. Said it's tasteless and disrespectful and inappropriate, but the science is sound.'

Jar hopes Carl finds love one day, for the sake of female mourners everywhere.

They've been sitting here for thirty minutes now, trying to shelter from the icy wind that slips through the subterranean skate park like a pickpocket. Carl promised it would be worth the wait.

Jar returned from Cromer on Thursday, satisfied that no one followed him on the bus to King's Lynn, or the train back to London. He didn't go to work on Friday, preferring to lie low in his flat. It's now Saturday morning and this is the first time he's been out.

Despite his own formidable computer skills, Carl hasn't been able to open Rosa's diary, but he is intrigued by the challenge and knows a man who can. Which is why they are waiting incongruously with all the west London fathers, trying not to look like a couple of child molesters.

Anton, his bulging Rasta hat ballooning out behind him, lifts a hand, five fingers spread out, as he sweeps past on his skateboard, a pair of bulky headphones perched on his head. Jar glances at his watch. Behind Anton, a group of young children – they can't be older than six, Jar thinks – follows him like a string of ducklings, pushing along on tiny boards, oversized helmets wobbling.

The dads are sitting in the stands with him and Carl: Notting Hill bankers, Jar guesses, wearing baseball caps in reverse and weekend jackets padded at the elbows and shoulders. Some of the mums are sitting in their 4x4s, jacked up on the pavement outside, preferring to sample the gritty end of their neighbourhood from the comfort of their cars.

As the lesson ends, an older child slips off his board, which shoots into the stands, coming to rest at Carl's feet. Carl bends down but then seems to think twice about returning the board. Looking up, he sees the boy, unhurt, getting up off the ground and walking towards him.

'May I?' Carl asks the boy.

The boy smirks but doesn't protest.

'Is that a good idea now?' Jar says.

'I used to pop shove-it with the best of them,' Carl says, getting on the board and pushing off with surprising smoothness.

'Ten years ago. When you were *fifteen*,' Jar calls out after him. But it's too late. Flushed with confidence, Carl tries to flick his board in the air and falls heavily. The boy who lent him the board goes over to help.

'I'm fine,' Carl says. 'Bruised pride, nothing more.'

Five minutes later, they are standing in a rusting forty-foot shipping container at the back of the skate park, where repairs are carried out. Anton, lesson over, leads the way, past a workbench covered in decks, trucks and wheels, to a desk at the end, where there is a bank of three computers, tools everywhere and the hard drive that Amy gave Jar.

Anton sits down on the stool, one leg bouncing as he spins back and forth between the screens like an agitated City dealer.

'The file's na' corrupted,' he says in a heavy Jamaican accent. Jar takes a moment to tune in. 'It's encrypted.'

'What do you mean?' Jar says, glancing at Carl, who seems less surprised. 'I mean, I know what encryption is, but—'

'Someone's made it look like a corrupted file,' Carl says.

For the next five minutes, he acts as a translator, not of Anton's Rasta patois, but of the technical jargon. For some reason best known to Rosa, each of her diary entries has been separately encrypted. After working through the night, Anton has managed to extract a couple of them in no particular order.

'It's not going to be cheap,' Carl whispers. Anton has his headphones on again, music playing, head nodding. (Carl's own headphones are slung round his neck.)

Jar detects a certain excitement in his friend's voice. Anton hands him a memory stick with the two diary entries on it. He then writes down a Hotmail address and password on a scrap of paper. After Anton has extracted each diary entry, he explains, he will put it into the drafts folder of the Hotmail account, where Jar can retrieve it. This way, the diary entries will never be transmitted across the internet.

Jar wonders if he is being ridiculed here – Carl says the drafts-folder system is regularly used by terrorist cells keen to avoid detection by the intelligence services – but both men seem to be taking him seriously.

After agreeing on a fee – subbed by Carl – they leave the skate park and walk back down towards Ladbroke Grove, stopping off to look at some vinyl at a stall where the Westway passes over Portobello Road.

'I thought it would be more,' Jar says.

'He likes the challenge. It's not every day you come across encryption like that. Not unless you work for GCHQ. They tried to recruit him once, you know.'

'Who? Anton?'

'He turned them down. Didn't want to grass people up.'

Jar doesn't wish to appear ungrateful, but the memory stick is burning a hole in his pocket. Every time he encircles it with his fingers, he is holding Rosa's hand – just like he was in Cromer when Amy passed him the hard drive under the table.

'I ought to make a move,' he says, as nonchalantly as he can. 'I can get you the money next week. Payday.'

Carl keeps flipping through old jungle records: DJ Dextrous, Remarc, Ragga Twins.

'I've got to ask, Jar. Was Rosa into key-generation algorithms at uni?'

'Not that I know of.' It's a question that's troubling Jar, too. How did Rosa know how to encrypt the files? He can't remember her ever showing the slightest interest in computers.

'And why download the diary on to someone else's computer?'

'She didn't intend anyone to find it. Not straight away.'

'Or read it. I know it's Rosa, and you two were an item and all, but it's still nosing about in someone else's private diary, right?'

'Don't think I haven't asked myself that.'

'Hey, Rebel MC,' Carl says, holding up an old album. 'Ras Tafari.' Jar smiles at him and turns away. In another life, Carl will return as a Rastafarian, no question. Carl puts the record back and leans against the stall. 'This is going to stir up a lot of things,' he says. 'Reading her diary.'

'Maybe an explanation.'

'Is that what you're hoping for?'

'A why would be nice, if not a how.'

'Call Kirsten. Please.'

Jar can't bring himself to say yes, but he gives Carl a look as he leaves to suggest that he might.

As he turns on to Ladbroke Grove, his phone rings. It's Amy. Jar has tried to ring her several times since they met in

Cromer, but her phone has been switched off. For a moment he thinks the line has dropped, but then she speaks.

'They're trying to frame him, Jar. He's not like that.'

'Like what? I can barely hear you.'

Jar stops opposite the Tube station, glancing up and down Ladbroke Grove as he checks the reception on his phone. Amy sounds like she is drunk.

'Is it about the old hard drive?' he asks.

Over the next few minutes, Jar manages to establish what's happened. Martin has been arrested on suspicion of possessing indecent images. It's a ridiculous allegation, Amy says, a set-up, but enough for her to start popping her pills again. There's a further complication, too.

'Martin hasn't told them about the old drive,' she says.

'Where do the police think it is?'

'In the bin.'

That's good, Jar thinks. Very good. 'And where's Martin now?'

'In Norwich. They're still questioning him. What should we do, Jar? This isn't about any photos. They're after the diary and they think he's hiding it. He'll have to tell them, sooner or later, explain that we gave the hard drive to you.'

'I need more time, Amy. Another few days.'

'Have you managed to open the diary?'

'Some of it. It's taking a while to access the files. They can't charge Martin if he's done nothing wrong.'

There is a silence before Amy speaks, Jar's 'if' lingering in the ether.

'I'll call you,' she says.

As Jar walks up on to the Tube platform, the thought crosses his mind that Martin just might have indecent images on his computer. No children of his own, those two strange rescue dogs he used to keep – 'smoking beagles', Rosa called them. But it doesn't wash. Martin's not like that. The authorities' focus is Rosa, not her uncle – and Jar's own efforts to prove that she is alive. And they are watching him now, desperate to get their hands on her diary, knowing that there is something Rosa's been waiting to tell him.

12

I haven't come to Cambridge to study drinking games. And I have no interest in rugby (even though Dad loved it). So why did I spend last night with a group of college players and public-school groupies whose idea of a good night out is getting lashed at The Pickerel and then setting fire to their pubes with sambuca?

I don't want to upset anyone, that's my problem. And when everyone in my block is heading out for the evening, it seems rude to say no, be the killjoy, say I've got work to do. No one likes to be left on their own, not in their first year. And I thought it would be good for me. Getting out of my room. I've spent too much time in here recently, light off, curtains drawn, writing this diary, hoping it might help to lift the darkness that wraps itself ever more tightly around my life.

At least I managed to leave early last night. I slipped out when everyone was using their empty beer glasses as binoculars, and meandered down King's Parade, trying to imagine how Mum and Dad had met here. I wish I'd asked Dad more about their time as students.

That day when he took me punting, we also went for tea at the Kettle Pot, opposite King's, his arm around my shoulders as he ushered me to a table in the big bay window overlooking the famous chapel. He was very insistent we sit there, said it was where he had first dated Mum.

'Your dean's a good man,' he said, smearing too much jam on his hot buttered crumpet.

'You know him?' Dr Lance: bearded, serious, a world authority on Goethe.

'We were undergraduates together,' Dad said. 'When everyone left, he stayed on, took to the academic life.'

'He seemed OK at the interview.'

In truth he'd left little impression on me and I was struggling to recall his face. I had expected him to do something weird when he interviewed me – set fire to the newspaper he was reading, somersault out of the window mid-conversation – but it was a very straightforward exchange, quite different from the myth of the Oxbridge interview.

'Some of the best people in the FO have been recruited on his recommendation.'

'I'll bear that in mind, when I need a job.'

'I've asked him to keep an eye on you.'

'Dad,' I sighed, but he had a point. I had been asked to leave a few places in my time, including my last school, but it was after A levels and the place was a dump.

'In a good way. Most students only get to see their dean when they've done something wrong. He'll be looking out for you. There if you ever need any help.'

'Can I ask you a question, about us?' I said, sated after our crumpet fest.

'Sure.'

I paused, feeling guilty about bringing up Mum's death.

She took her own life a year after I was born. The family doctor said it was nobody's fault – postpartum psychosis – but Dad never forgave himself. 'If Mum hadn't died, would you have been more successful, in your career?'

He laughed, throwing back his head like in the photo I have of his wedding, when his best man was making a speech. His laughter was always infectious, unselfconscious. 'Do you know something that I don't?'

'What I mean is, a lot of people in your situation would have got in more help.'

'Your mother and I had vowed to bring you up ourselves. If you're asking me if my job might have gone in a different direction...' He paused. 'I can't answer that.'

'Well I'm sorry if I have held you back.'

'Don't be ridiculous. You can only play the cards in front of you. If Mum hadn't died, we might have had more children, less money. Who knows? I might have taken a different job altogether, outside the FO.'

'It must have been very hard. In the early months.'

'This is a merry conversation.'

'I just need to know.'

'Of course. New chapter, no longer my little—'

I cut him short with a don't-you-dare face of disapproval. Another pause. We were always easy in each other's company, no need to talk if we didn't want to.

'Did you ever think about ending it all as well?' I said at last.

He looked at me before answering, his face suddenly serious, sad. I'd never asked him that before and I don't know why I decided to ask him then. It was a cruel question, selfish. I knew he'd suffered over the years, had had days when he'd come home and hadn't spoken a word, had stayed up late in his study, risen red-eyed the next morning, an empty bottle of whisky in the recycling bin.

'Sometimes it seemed the easiest thing to do. But she would have been furious!' He laughed again, less effusively this time. 'And I couldn't bear the thought of you losing both of us.'

I rested my hand on his. His eyes were moistening.

'Thank you.'

'All I ask in return is that you care for me when I'm old and dribbly.'

Dr Lance wants to see me tomorrow. We meet up a few times a term – he clearly feels even more responsible for me since Dad died – but this time I sense it will be different. He has written me a sweet note, said it's been brought to his attention that I'm not happy (underlined). Understatement of the year.

I've been thinking a lot about Dad's words in recent days, what stopped him from following Mum and taking his own life. *Sometimes it seemed the easiest thing to do.* Would Dad be 'furious' with me? And was he ever furious with Mum? I didn't know it was possible to be this down, to miss someone so much, for life to feel such a disappointment. Perhaps it's because I'm conscious of how much I'm meant to be enjoying myself here.

The new college counsellor will be there tomorrow, too, along with Dr Lance. I wasn't even aware we had one until I heard that all the boys are pretending to be suicidal just so they can spend time with her. She's mint, apparently. A hottie, as Dad would have said.

13

Jar has always questioned Carl's taste in women, but he's right about Kirsten Thomas. It's Monday morning and he's sitting in a high-ceilinged room in a Georgian town-house on Harley Street, allowing his eyes to linger on hers longer than he should as she outlines her terms.

'My first session is always off the clock,' she says breezily. New England, Jar guesses. Maybe Boston. 'But in your case, I'd like to make you an offer.'

Me too, he thinks, returning her smile, then checks himself: Jaysus, you're behaving like Carl. He takes in his surroundings, wondering if all Harley Street consulting rooms are like this. She is sitting on one side of a large oak desk, he is perched on a chair in the centre of the light and airy room. A chandelier hangs from the high ceiling, the floor is reclaimed pine boards.

There's no couch – he makes a note to tell Carl – but a sofa and one armchair are arranged beneath the tall window. A wooden Venetian blind shields them from London life beyond. In the corner there's a washbasin, and he spots a box of tissues on the floor, beside the armchair. He thinks of all the people who must have sat in these rooms, unpacking their problems for an hour only to put them all away again and step back out on to the street.

'I'm writing a paper that I'm hoping you might be able to help me with. It's called "Bereavement among the imaginative: grief reactions, post-bereavement hallucinations and quality of life".'

'Catchy title.'

'I've written about the condition before, but I'm now kind of interested in how it affects artists. Novelists.'

'You think we imagine it? Make it all up?' Jar doesn't mean to sound aggressive, but he resents the suggestion of creativity.

'Not at all. Quite the opposite, in fact. Maybe the condition manifests itself better in the artistic.'

'So what are you offering?'

'Six free one-hour sessions, starting tomorrow. Before I see my first client of the day. Are you a morning person?'

Jar doesn't answer. Instead, he looks again at her cropped blonde hair and blue eyes, trying to guess her age: mid-forties? Her face is magazine-model attractive rather than unusual: high, sculpted cheekbones, wide mouth, snub nose. There's nothing mysterious or exotic about her, but on the plus side she's not interested in playing up her unquestionable assets. Light make-up – maybe a clear sheen on her full lips – and her clothes are anything but revealing: buttoned-up cream blouse beneath a brown jacket, skirt to her knees. No heel.

'I'm not sure why I'm here, if I'm honest,' Jar begins.

'That's OK.'

'My friend—'

'Carl, he told you to come. I'm glad. He said he would.'

'I was expecting to hear music,' Jar says, nodding towards the door. '"Therapy" by All Time Low, that kind of thing.'

'British humour, huh?' she says, managing a smile.

'Irish, actually. We tend to find comedy in most things, even death.'

The mention of death stills their conversation like oil on water, which is Jar's intention. He looks towards the window, a cue to move on, get to the business end of their meeting. It's then that he becomes aware of a quirk in her breathing: an occasional sharp intake of breath, as if she's been frightened by something.

'If you are OK with my offer,' she says, 'I'd just like you to turn up here and talk.'

'Talking's a way of life where I come from.'

What's he saying? Playing up his Irish roots to impress the blonde American?

'I'm guessing Dublin,' she says.

'Galway City.' He knows he should stop there, but he can't help himself. 'Ireland's "cultural heart",' he adds. 'Birthplace of the late, great Peter O'Toole.'

She holds his gaze, looks away, and takes another breath just before she speaks, making that curious sound again.

'I'm a psychoanalyst by training, Jar. I rely on a method called free association, developed by Sigmund Freud. You say whatever comes into your head and I look for unconscious factors that might explain your behaviour.'

Carl wasn't so wrong after all, he thinks.

'I'll need you to tell me everything about your bereavement and the subsequent sightings,' she continues. 'It will help me and I'm confident it will help you.'

'How much did Carl explain?'

'Can we assume nothing?'

'If it's easier. But I'm guessing he said that my girlfriend – Rosa Sandhoe – died five years ago, that we had a brief relationship at university, and I subsequently drank myself into oblivion in a misguided attempt to get over her. The truth is less simple. We loved each other with a passion for the few months that we were together, an intensity that I have never experienced before or since. I drink slightly less now, but I still miss her every day. What's more, I think that she's very much alive. Rosa was a happy person when I knew her, despite the loss of her father – her suicide was out of character, a belief reinforced by sightings of her that have become more real in recent months.'

Has he said too much, been too candid? Jar decided before he arrived here that there would be limits. He won't mention Rosa's diary, not specifically, even though its discovery – and the effect it might have on him – is what's brought him here. He feels guilty enough that he's reading it – Anton has passed on six decrypted entries now: how they met at the restaurant, skinny-dipping in the Cam, their first night together – and he doesn't intend to breach Rosa's confidence further by sharing the contents with anyone else. He's also troubled by her version of events.

'Do we have a deal?' Kirsten asks, smiling at him.

An hour later, Jar is sitting at his computer in the lock-up garage, about to read for the third time the latest diary entry that's arrived, when his phone rings. It's Amy, sounding more coherent than the last time they spoke. They talk about Martin – the police have released him without charge – and then the hard drive. It's four days since she handed it over in Cromer.

'He had to tell them we'd given it to you,' she says. 'I'm sorry. It's Rosa's diary they're after, Jar.'

'How much did he tell them?'

'Your name and address. He had no choice. Have you managed to read any of it yet?'

Jar can feel time running out as they speak. He tells her about Anton, how he's decrypting the entries one by one and placing them in a drafts folder.

'Ask this Anton to copy all the files,' Amy suggests, as Jar logs into the drafts email address. 'That's what they are coming for. And Jar?' There is a pause. 'Her diary's bound to stir things up. I know you weren't keen before, but you should really think about getting some help. Talk to a therapist. I can recommend a few.'

'I already am. Had my first session today.'

'That's great. Who with?'

'An American in Harley Street.' Even Jar's impressed by how that sounds.

'Was it helpful?'

'Early days. I'll let you know.'

After a few minutes of chat, Amy says she's coming to London later in the week and it would be good to meet up. Jar agrees and they hang up.

The diary entries never arrive in the drafts folder in any particular order. The one on the screen now is from Rosa's second term at Cambridge. Jar hates himself for it, but he can't help always scanning the text first to see if she has mentioned his name, left him a message, a crumb of comfort.

When he had first read this entry, it was with a twinge of disappointment that he realised she'd written it in the spring term, before they met. And before an important meeting with the college dean, Dr Lance, a man Jar has written to many times over the past five years. An Oxbridge recruiting sergeant for the intelligence services, if the rumours are to be believed: the old tap-on-the-shoulder-over-a-sherry routine.

All Jar knows is that Dr Lance has never replied to his letters, emails or phone calls, refuses to see him whenever he turns up in person.

He flicks back to the beginning of the document and starts to read, shocked again by how much sadness Rosa managed to conceal from him, how little he really knew her.

Was she pretending that hot summer's day when they cycled out to Grantchester Meadows with a bottle of cheap cava? He'd disappointed her by asking if they needed to bring glasses – his da has a thing about glasses in the pub, used to get Jar to polish them every morning before school ('You never know when the Pope might pay us a visit.').

'You're so old-fashioned,' she'd teased, swigging from the bottle as she lay back in the sunshine by the river. He had never felt happier than he did that day, lying with her in the long grass and planning their future together. Had it meant the same to her? Did she write about it? He's sure she was happy too, which makes the disconnect between his memory and hers all the more unsettling.

14

Cambridge, Summer Term, 2012

Strange things, May Balls. They're held in June not May and they cost more than most students can afford. I'd never seen a champagne fountain before, not even at any of the diplomatic parties Dad took me to, but I saw one last night, watched people having their heads held under it until they gagged (posh waterboarding).

Everyone else in my year seemed to be going to our college ball, and, well, what the hell, I thought: Dad would have been appalled if I'd not gone. Besides, I had three bids on the table, all offering me a free ticket.

I went with handsome Tim in the end, having told him up front that I had a boyfriend back home. He seemed fine with that in a way that made me feel bad. But I told myself I was lying in order to be more truthful: to dampen any sexual expectations (mine as well as his).

If I'm honest, I also decided to go because I thought it would be good for me. I hadn't seen Jar since our skinny-dipping encounter, but I couldn't get him out of my head. I had to keep reminding myself that this was not the time to fall in love. That if Jar was thinking about me for even a fraction of the time he was filling my thoughts, it would be unforgivably cruel to him. (I also had to keep reminding myself that he might not care a fig, of course.)

Tim insisted on having cocktails in his room with a few close friends before we went across the road to join the ball. I'd been to his room a few times before. It's a nice enough place, but nothing to compare with Jar's. A party was already overflowing down the corridor when I arrived in a cream taffeta ball gown that I found in a charity shop on Bene't Street. For a moment I wondered if I wasn't the only one he'd bought a ticket for. Tim's one of the most social students in college, thanks in part to Tim's Bar, a late-night shebeen he runs in his room every Friday, when he serves cocktails to all and sundry. His dad's a wine merchant in the City, so sourcing industrial quantities of alcohol isn't a problem. Money isn't either. He's also very sporty, more into cricket than rugby, and good-looking in a Greek god sort of way, but I wouldn't have given him a second thought when I first met him if it weren't for the fact that he's also profoundly deaf.

'I thought a quiet tête à tête might scare you off,' he said, kissing me on both cheeks when I found him in the corner, shaking cocktails. Like all the men present, he was wearing a black tailcoat with white bow tie.

His own speech is generally good – a few telltale words are a bit nasal – but he relies on lip-reading and minimal hearing in his left ear to understand what other people are saying. When I first met him, I was flattered by the attention, the close face-to-face engagement, until I realised he does that with everyone. He needs to have a clear view of your lips.

'Moscow mules,' he said, gesturing at an array of full glasses laid out on the table. 'Grab yourself one while you can.' Then, to the room, and my embarrassment, he slung an arm around my shoulders and called out, 'Everybody, this is Rosa, my date for the night.'

A loud cheer went up and glasses were raised as I felt my skin prickle. There was only one thing for it. I knocked back mine in one and grabbed another.

'So you're Rosa Sandhoe,' someone in a far more expensive gown than mine said. She'd come up to the table for a refill and looked like a rower: broad across the shoulders, strong chin, ruddy complexion. 'Lucky girl.' I sensed that Tim was more of a catch than I'd realised. Then her smile hardened. 'Don't forget to move your lips when you squeal.'

Ten minutes later we were queuing at the porter's lodge to be signed in. Ahead of us we could hear the hum of drunken revelry and music: sitar and tabla and, in the background, the throb of electronic dance music.

First Court took my breath away. It had been transformed into a luxurious Rajasthani palace, mirror-work drapes glinting in the spotlights, incense burning, vast images of elephants with bejewelled howdahs projected on to the ivy-clad buildings.

The sitar and tabla musicians played, sitting cross-legged on velvet cushions in the corner, as waiters opened bottles of champagne: rows and rows of them lined up on a table like an army of marionettes. Centre stage, though, was a magnificent champagne fountain, bubbling over three tiers. Waiters dipped glasses into it and handed them out to guests as they arrived, while others replenished the fountain by emptying bottles theatrically into the top.

'I hope you don't mind there's no headline act,' Tim said as we took our glasses and walked on into Second Court. 'Trinity spent twenty grand on Pixie Lott. Personally, I'd rather drink decent champagne all night.'

'I thought the Villagers were playing,' I said.

'Not exactly U2, are they?'

It was a timely reminder of our differences. Jar introduced me to the new band from Dublin in his room that night and I've been listening to nothing else since. I was expecting their set to be the highlight of my evening.

We decided to take a tour of what was on offer before meeting his friends back in the Scholars' Orchard for a hog roast. The exotic theme continued into Second Court, which felt more Moroccan. In the dimly lit corners students were lying back on cushions, smoking hookahs as they watched belly dancers shake their stuff.

Phoebe was there with Nick, who was sitting on a rug next to her. She wasn't wearing a ball gown – too bourgeois for her. We'd seen each other a few times since that dinner in Formal Hall, but it hadn't been the same. No confidences shared any more. That she was still going out with Nick made me think better of him. He could have gone with anyone in St Matthew's but he'd chosen Phoebe, not for her looks but for who she was: a feisty politico. I gave her a friendly smile as we passed. She looked wasted, her eyes glazed as she puffed on a hookah, and didn't seem to notice me. Nick raised a hand, like a tired Indian chief, his face shrouded in smoke.

We met fire-breathers and magicians as we wandered on through the Fellows' Garden, one side of which runs along the Cam. Hammocks, Moroccan lanterns and pea-lights, glowing softly like fireflies, had been strung in the trees, and coal braziers were burning in the shadows. There was a funfair down by the river, and a floating casino, which Tim said he was keen to visit later. He also wanted to go to the comedy tent. And the fortune teller. I liked the idea of the silent disco. Maybe the spa area, too.

'The sign of a good May Ball is the shortness of the queues,' Tim said as we passed a crêpe stand. (He went to three balls last year and is going to two this year.) We saw stalls offering hot dogs, waffles, burgers, oysters and candyfloss. Later, at dawn, there would be smoked salmon and scrambled eggs, full English breakfasts, kippers and kedgeree. No queues, no money required. It was all free (sort of).

'Thanks,' I said, putting my arm through Tim's as we made our way back to the Scholars' Orchard. I've made the right decision to come here, I thought. This is what Cambridge life's all about, isn't it? At least I've known it, if only briefly.

The first person we met was the girl with the rowing shoulders who'd come up to me in Tim's room. She was drunk and managed to peel me away from Tim while he talked to her partner.

'How are you finding him?' she asked, her arm linked firmly in mine.

'Tim?' I said, trying to stay near him, but she was strong and walked me off down the orchard. I didn't want to make a fuss.

'Just to warn you,' she said. 'He keeps his eyes open when he's fucking you, likes to watch your mouth so he can hear you moan. It can be disconcerting the first time.'

'I should be heading back,' I said, glancing over my shoulder at Tim, who was still talking to her partner.

'This is your first ball, isn't it?' she asked, her arm pressing harder against mine.

'You're hurting me.'

'I'm sorry,' she said, loosening her grip a little. 'There's always a lull at these things. After dinner and before the headline band starts playing. That's when he expects a return on his investment.'

'It's not like that,' I said. I just need to get away from her, I thought, but she was much stronger than me.

'And he likes it rough, lots of noise. There's a quiet place at the far end of the Fellows' Garden where he always goes. Beyond the casino boat. Make sure you're ready. It might hurt less. And remember to move your lips when you squeal.'

She exaggerated the movements of her mouth as she said those last words, her tongue licking against her top teeth as she spelt them out.

'Everything all right?' Tim said when we rejoined him. He put one arm lightly across my shoulders. 'Hannah's not been leading you astray?'

I smiled weakly as he exchanged glances with the rower who'd just had me in an arm lock.

After sharing wild sea bass in the candlelit dining pavilion, my head spinning with the earlier cocktails, Tim's choice of wines and Hannah's words, he suggested we walk over to the casino boat. My stomach lurched. Hannah, sitting diagonally opposite, raised her eyebrows as she sipped on her wine.

In my mind I'd envisaged an innocent smooch on the dance-floor at dawn if I was drunk enough, nothing more. Tim had been a perfect gentleman up to this point and I'd have had no reason to suspect him of wanting anything else from me if it hadn't been for Hannah.

As we walked towards the Fellows' Garden, Tim's arm slipped from my shoulders to the small of my back. I told myself it was because I was less steady on my feet than I had been and he didn't want me to slip.

All around us, as we entered the garden, couples were lying on rugs beneath the trees, some awake, a few passed out. Hannah and her man had hung back, saying they were going for a moonlit punt.

'Rosa, I need to clear my head a little before I gamble away my family inheritance at the roulette table,' he said. 'Shall we go for a walk? Down by the river?'

I thought I was going to be sick. I'm just being a prig, I told myself. And Hannah's a fantasist, has her own jealous agenda. I glanced at handsome Tim, his white tie still immaculate beneath his wing collar, the lights in the trees, the moon's reflection on the river, Cambridge's *jeunesse dorée* in all our privileged splendour.

Dad would have loved the whole thing, for its ephemerality: a moment in time, full of youthful promise and naïve ambition, before we step out into the world and discover that none of it is real.

Why can't I just enjoy Cambridge like everyone else? Instead, I've chosen to turn my back on it all. I hope to God Dad would understand why.

'Stay here,' I said. 'I'll be back in a minute.'

15

Jar googles 'Kirsten Thomas' again after he's finished reading, to check that he didn't miss anything when he looked her up earlier, before his introductory meeting with her this morning.

She's a fully qualified Freudian shrink, certified by the American Board of Psychiatry and Neurology after completing a four-year residency at the University of South Carolina School of Medicine. To judge from the testimonials on its website, the Harley Street consulting rooms where she practises cater mainly to Americans in London. She arrived in the UK a year ago.

Jar stands up to stretch, arms almost touching the walls of the lock-up, and wonders idly if Rosa's counsellor still works at her old college. Rosa never mentioned that she was seeking help from anyone (that was the problem). Or that Dr Lance was in any way concerned about her happiness. It makes him feel less hostile towards St Matthew's, which he has always accused of heartlessness, negligence.

No counsellor is listed on the college website. Instead, students are encouraged to talk to their tutor, or the college chaplain, nurse or welfare officer. The university offers a counselling service, but Rosa specifically mentioned a college counsellor. A minor distinction, but Jar can't help feeling it's an important one.

After shutting down his computer and bolting the door behind him, Jar walks back to his flat, glancing up and down the street before taking the lift. The sense of being watched has grown in the days since his return from Cromer, but he's confident that no one has discovered the lock-up. It makes the burglary of his flat easier to deal with: they came looking for evidence of Rosa, his search for her, and found nothing, but he knows they will be back, keen to get their hands on the hard drive.

He also knows that he should make an appearance in the office, not least because he's run out of decent excuses and will soon be sacked. Normally, he likes to hang around his flat on a Monday morning, unpack book deliveries, do the cryptic crossword, check his Amazon rating, but since the burglary, the flat no longer feels safe, a place to linger.

Carl's pleased to see him when he finally pitches up just before lunch. (He's so late that the up escalator is in sleep mode.) Even more pleased when he tells him about his early-morning visit to Kirsten.

'No couch,' Jar says, picking up a story about a shortlist for yet another literary prize. (Longlist stories are the worst to write, he thinks: all those hyperlinked titles.)

'Bet you still charmed the pants off her,' Carl says. 'Turned on the blarney.'

'It was a meeting of minds.'

'Of course it was. I hope she's helpful.'

'Thanks, honestly now,' Jar says, struggling with his computer. 'Did you have a problem logging in today?'

'No slower than usual.'

Jar is used to the office computers acting up, but he's never seen this message before: 'This account is already in use.' He reads it out to himself, but loud enough so Carl will hear. Carl knows about these things. He leans across from his desk to have a look.

'Did you log in remotely from home and forget to log out?' he asks.

'I never log in outside office hours, Carl. On principle. I'm not even sure I know how.'

Carl gets up and stands in front of Jar's keyboard, his fingers moving fast. He logs out of the web-based system and logs in using the standard office work-experience username.

'It's definitely your ID,' he says. 'The computer's working fine.' Carl logs out again. 'Try now,' he says.

Jar enters his username and password, but the same message flags up on his screen.

'Are you sure—'

'I'm sure.'

'Then I suggest you ring technical support. Because someone's currently in your account.'

'You serious now?'

'It's probably nothing. Then again, it might be senior management reading your emails. It has been known to happen.'

Keith over on the technical support desk is more interested in crushing candy than sorting Jar's problem, but after hearing him out (while still playing on his computer), he tells him to try logging in with the office work-experience account.

'I've done that,' Jar says, peering down at Keith. 'I sit next to Carl.'

Mention of Carl changes things. Carl knows more about IT than the IT department. 'What's your username?' Keith asks, minimising Candy Crush and calling up the company log-in window.

'JarlathC.'

'Password?'

'Is that normal? To just give it out like that?'

'Do you want me to fix this or not?'

'Rosa081192,' he says quietly.

Keith sits up in his seat, expressing interest in Jar's case for the first time. Still looking at the screen, he reaches across to his phone and dials an extension.

'I think the Syrians are back in town,' he says.

Jar is asked to follow Keith to a part of the office that he didn't even know existed: down in the labyrinthine, dimly lit bowels of the building beside the post room, with no windows and stale air. So this is where everyone's requests for technical help are ignored, Jar thinks, looking at the row of terminals and the sallow faces behind them.

Jar watches as Keith and two others gather around a terminal.

'JarlathC,' Keith says to the man with the keyboard. Then, to Jar, 'Password again?'

Jar feels even more uneasy about sharing it. 'I'll type it,' he says.

The IT staff part reluctantly as he leans forward and enters 'Rosa081192'. He knows everyone is watching which keys he presses, but it feels defiant in a small way.

'Who's "Rosa" when she's at home?' Keith asks.

'Don't forget her birthday,' someone else says.

Jar ignores them, looking at the screen. The same message flashes up: 'This account is already in use.'

'And you're definitely not logged in anywhere else?' Keith asks.

Jar is about to answer when someone else at another screen to his left interjects. 'He's not. IP address is showing as US.'

'The Syrians are good at spoofing,' Keith says to Jar. And then, turning to one of his colleagues, he adds, 'So much for your new packet filtering, Raj.'

Jar wishes Carl was there to translate. Only last week his friend was telling him about a group of hackers called the Syrian Electronic Army, sympathetic to Bashar al-Assad, who'd been targeting the computer systems of various UK media organisations. This, though, seems to be personal. What happens next makes his mouth dry.

'That's my inbox,' Jar says, looking at the screen, which is now showing his work email account. 'How did you manage to log in?'

'We didn't,' Keith says. 'We can watch what they're doing, but we can't log them out. Not unless we shut down the entire company email account.'

'And what are they doing?' Jar asks.

'Remotely accessing your email account to search through your messages, by the look of it.'

'Is that legal?'

Snorts all around. Maybe this is how they spend their days, Jar thinks: watching staff send emails to each other slagging off senior management. He must remember to be ruder to the IT department.

'Should we send out a group-wide alert?' Keith says.

'This isn't the Syrians,' Raj says.

Jar watches the screen as it switches to his sent mail: work messages to Carl, his editor, other colleagues and freelance contributors mixed in with hundreds of emails to Dr Lance, Amy, the Information Commissioner's Office, the RNLI, the Cromer coastguard, the UK Missing Persons Bureau, the Foreign Office. He wonders if anyone in the room notices these messages, whether they care. Most people use their email for non-work business, don't they? The cursor begins to scroll down the list before it moves rapidly to the top right-hand corner, logs out of the email, and exits Jar's account.

'The good ones figure out that we're watching them,' Keith says, as if he's just singlehandedly seen off the enemy.

'Do we know who it was?' Jar asks.

'National Security Agency?' Keith suggests, playing to the crowd. 'I suggest you get a new girlfriend.'

16

My plan was to head straight for the porter's lodge, sign out of the ball and walk over to Jar's rooms. I knew it wasn't the right thing to do – by Tim, whose intentions were entirely honourable for all I knew, or by Jar, who didn't need me arriving back in his life at two in the morning – but I've been trying to live truthfully while I can, no matter how little time I have left.

The civility of earlier had disappeared from First Court, where a student was drinking from the champagne fountain, her body supported on either side by two boys as she arced her head backwards under the top tier, her breasts popping out of the top of her gown as she gagged on the fizz.

As I reached the porter's lodge, I bumped into Nick, who I'd last seen with Phoebe, smoking a hookah. He was distraught, his eyes wide with fear.

'Rosa, it's Phoebe. I can't find her anywhere.'

I'd never seen him so agitated, hadn't realised just how much he cared for her. 'Where did you last see her?' I asked, glancing towards the porter's lodge.

'In Second Court. She wanted to go for a walk in the

Fellows' Garden. I told her to wait while I charged our glasses. When I got back she'd gone. That was half an hour ago.'

'She did look a bit—'

'She hasn't been herself tonight, Rosa. Lost her mojo. Quite scary actually. Lots of odd remarks. Will you help me look for her?'

I didn't want to go back to the Fellows' Garden, bump into Tim, but I couldn't just walk away.

'OK,' I said, and found myself walking back through First and Second Courts.

As soon as we entered the Fellows' Garden, we both knew something was wrong. There was a commotion in the far corner, on the opposite side from the Cam, and two security staff with walkie-talkies ran past us.

We followed them, along with a group of other curious students. It's strange how you know something awful has happened before there's any empirical proof. It's something in the air, perhaps, a metallic taste in the mouth. The pea-lights in the branches above us no longer seemed so soft and inviting, the braziers suddenly burned more fiercely.

A crowd had gathered near the wall at the very back of the garden, where there were no lights. The grass was worn there and it had been marked out of bounds all evening by wooden fencing and rope. As we drew near, people were peeling away, hands over their mouths. There was no panic, just a numbing stillness spreading through the garden like heavy fog. Instinctively, I reached out for Nick and linked my arm through his.

'Oh God, oh God,' he was whispering. I couldn't see anything from where we were standing, but he unlinked my arm and made his way through the crowd. Already, a security guard was ushering people away. 'Everyone back. Can you all move *back*.'

And then I saw her, in a tree to our left, head limp, her body hanging from a low branch. She was moving, but only because one of the security guards had grabbed her legs, around the knees, and was trying to support her weight, take the strain off the ligature around her neck.

I couldn't bear to watch any more. Nick had stepped forward and was helping the security guard hold her body. 'Somebody call an ambulance – please,' I heard him say, but it was already too late. Everyone apart from Nick seemed to know that.

I offered a prayer and fell to my knees, looking around: silence, disbelief, tears. So this is how it feels for those left behind, I thought.

I don't want my own death to be like that, ripping up the lives of others, but I have run out of options.

17

'Do you find it comforting, when you see Rosa?' Kirsten asks, sitting at her desk.

'Frustrating.'

Jar is on the sofa in the window of Kirsten's consulting room in Harley Street, not finding their first formal early-morning session easy. After the troubling incident with his office email account yesterday, he went out on the tear with Carl, drank too much for a Monday evening. The daylight is torturing his eyes.

'Do you talk to her?' she asks.

'When I see her?'

'It's not uncommon for people to reach out to a loved one when they are experiencing a hallucination, try to engage them in conversation.'

'Occasionally, yes.'

'Can you tell me about it?'

Jar stays silent, listens to the street outside: a moped driving past, a fading police siren. He hasn't had time to process what happened on the pier, when Rosa was standing on the railings. He closes his sore eyes, thinks back to another time when he saw her by the sea.

'I was staying with a family friend in Cleggan, on the

Connemara coast. It was just after daybreak and I went for a walk, up to Cleggan Head, to get a view of the bay and the islands, spread out like giant lilies in the sea. I remember at one point it was boggy underfoot. That's when I saw her. She was in my peripheral vision, to the left, walking along beside me. I didn't want to turn and look at her in case she vanished. It was comforting, to be sure – having her with me. The memorial service had been a few weeks earlier and I was still feeling raw.'

'What did you say to her?'

'She spoke first, picked up on something I'd said shortly after we first met in Cambridge, when I told her that I was a "bogger" – someone who doesn't live in Dublin, who's beyond the pale. A culchie. She laughed at that, said she'd never heard the expression before.'

'What exactly did she say?'

'It was after my foot slipped in the mud. "Clumsy bogger," she joked. "You should have stayed in Dublin." "I'd never have met you," I replied. She didn't say anything else after that. I kept talking though, asked her what she thought of the music we'd chosen at her memorial service. We left the church to "What a Wonderful World".'

There is a pause. He can hear the sound of Kirsten's pen writing on paper and then that odd intake of breath again. He wonders if she emits a similar sound, louder perhaps, more of a gasp, when she's making love. He tries to shut out the image, uncouple his train of thought and concentrate on her questions.

'Why do you find it frustrating, when you see her?' Another silence. He senses that he's being boxed into a corner, like a defence witness.

'Because you know you're hallucinating?'

Jar nods, despite himself. The mood in the room shifts imperceptibly, the ensuing silence no longer awkward, more an invitation to reflect. That's her job, he thinks: getting people to the point where they want to open up. Clever, manipulative. Hence the box of tissues at his feet. He hears her breath again, just before she speaks.

'Why did you come here today, Jar?'

He feels his eyelids throbbing. Does he tell her that his life is being destroyed by the belief that Rosa is alive? That the love they had for each other was stronger than the lure of the Norfolk sea and her apparent suicide was out of character? That he is still drinking too much and suspects he's being followed everywhere? That he has become a cynical and jaded human being, worn down by a job he dislikes and the extinction of a once-promising talent to string sentences together?

Or does he confess that he welcomes the prospect of spending an hour each week talking about Rosa? (Even if it is to an older woman he knows she would have disliked – Rosa had a thing about bottle blondes.) Carl listened in the early days, but Jar can tell he's bored by it all now. He doesn't blame him. Amy still listens. So does Da, but Jar feels guilty whenever he brings Rosa up in conversation; his parents are too old to worry about their grown-up son. It's Kirsten's job to listen.

'Talking about her keeps the memories alive,' he offers finally.

'And the hope that she's alive too?'

He doesn't answer.

'I've got to be straight with you, Jar,' she says. 'No one I've spoken to about post-bereavement hallucinations believes their loved ones are still alive. They see their hallucinations more in terms of an ethereal trace, a contrail left in the sky.'

Where has he heard that expression before?

'You mean an apparition? This isn't a ghost story.'

He listens to the sweep of her fountain pen, guessing her handwriting is rounded, well formed, as he wracks his brain.

'I'm going to ask you a very blunt question. I don't mean to be insensitive, I just need a single-word answer, the first that comes to mind.'

'Go ahead.' Here comes Sigmund, he thinks.

'What would you have felt if Rosa's body had turned up?'

Jar pauses. Despite the warning, he is unsettled by her question.

'Suspicious,' he says, his voice quiet but firm. They look at each other in silence. Kirsten pushes back her chair and comes over to sit next to him on the sofa.

'I'm sorry,' she says, placing one hand briefly on his forearm. It's not a flirtatious gesture, but he isn't prepared for the inevitable intimacy that follows, her face now close to his, the scent of citrus. She rests her notepad on her lap and pulls the hem of her skirt – shorter than yesterday? – over her knees.

'For these sessions to work for both of us, I need to understand your current state of mind, ask occasionally awkward questions, analyse your answers. It's part of the free-association method I mentioned yesterday. Then we can talk more meaningfully about the hallucinations. Is that OK with you?'

Jar nods, turns away and then looks back at her. She is still staring at him.

'Why "suspicious"?' she asks.

He notices that the second button on her blouse is undone. It must have fallen open when she moved from the desk to the sofa. She can't have done it deliberately – everything about her manner today is professional, neutral, denuded of all sexuality – but the flash of flesh is distracting, enough for him to drop his guard, confide more in her than he intends.

'Because I think her death was faked.'

'Faked by whom?'

'If I knew that, I wouldn't be here now.'

He glances at his watch, suddenly resentful of the meeting, her, Carl's insistence that he come here, the ease with which he has been distracted.

'It's not my area, but isn't faking a death quite a hard thing to do?' she persists.

'I've never tried.' But he's looked into it, in more depth than she will ever know, studying every permutation and practitioner, from a man in Milan called Umberto Gallini who can make people disappear (for an eye-watering fee) to 'canoe man' John Darwin. Lost at sea is as good a method as any.

'Are you a naturally suspicious person?' she asks.

'I never used to be.'

'What else makes you wary?'

The traffic warden across the street who watched him ring the intercom on her front door today, he thinks. The removal men lingering on the stairs outside his flat this morning.

'All these questions,' he says, swallowing hard.

He's remembered now. The first diary entry Anton sent him: *There should be no record, no contrails left in the Fenland sky.*

'It's not what you expected?' she asks, getting up from the sofa and moving back to her desk. Her hips have a subtle sway.

'I don't know what I was expecting,' he says, managing a smile, his thoughts tripping over each other. *No contrails left in the Fenland sky.* 'I'm sorry. I don't mean to sound ungrateful now. It feels good, for sure, talking it all through like this. I've always found talking helpful.'

But it feels anything but good and she knows it. 'Does it truly?' she asks.

'I can see it helps,' he lies. He needs to get away from her.

'That's great. I appreciate your honesty. May I ask you one last question: did Rosa write you a farewell letter, an explanation at all?'

'A suicide note, you mean?'

'I didn't want to call it that.'

'She did.'

Where's she going with this? *I just wish I didn't have to leave you behind, babe, the first true love of my life and my last.* He has vowed never to share Rosa's final letter with anyone.

'Was it useful?'

'Ambiguous.'

'But she was someone who liked to write?'

'How d'you mean? She was always putting off essays.'

Jar doesn't see the next question coming.

'What about a journal? Did she ever keep a diary?'

The words resonate in the cool, still air. *Did she ever keep a diary?*

'Reading it can sometimes help those left behind,' she adds.

He looks up, returns her intense gaze. How much does this woman know? How much has Carl told her?

'A diary?' he says, thinking of the latest entries he read last night about Phoebe and the college ball, hoping there are more waiting for him in the drafts folder. 'No, she never kept a diary.'

18

Cambridge, Summer Term, 2012 (continued)

I wasn't the only one to leave early. The May Ball committee, on the advice of the police, decided to cancel the rest
of the evening.

I didn't see Nick again, or Tim. I could have found him,
used the excuse of Phoebe to explain why I hadn't returned
to the casino boat, where I'd left him, but I just wanted to get
away from the college as fast as I could.

I walked over the bridge and down towards King's Parade,
hoping that Jar wouldn't mind being woken at such an hour.
There were other people from the ball wandering the streets
in their finest – Cambridge's privileged diaspora. A girl in
tears, being comforted by her partner. A couple on the wall
beside King's College porter's lodge, talking quietly, a bottle
of champagne at their feet.

It took a few rings of his doorbell before Jar came to the
door in his dressing gown. I was crying and wearing a ball
gown and it was two in the morning, but he let me in without
saying a word. The moment the door was closed, I fell into
his arms, sobbing. He held me tight until the tears stopped,
and then moved me gently upstairs and on to the leather

sofa in his sitting room, pushing aside some cushions and a blanket.

Over a whiskey, I told him about the night, first about Phoebe, then we talked about Tim. My worries about him suddenly seemed so petty compared to the tragedy that followed in the Fellows' Garden.

'If they found Phoebe quickly, she might have a chance,' Jar said.

'They didn't. She was gone, Jar, I'm sure of it. The ambulance left without a siren.'

'There's no traffic at this time of night.'

'Her head was hanging so heavy.' I couldn't get the image of her in the tree out of my head. Jar poured another whiskey.

'You can't go blaming yourself, Rosa.'

'I could have been a better friend to her. And Nick. He'll never recover from that. His face when he saw her...'

Jar hugged me closely as I cried again, feeling safe in his warm embrace. I should never have gone to the ball, I thought, or walked out on Jar that night.

As I sat there holding him tightly, thinking that there was nowhere else in this world I'd rather be, I heard a noise in Jar's bedroom behind us. I swallowed hard, pulling away from him.

'Is there someone else here?' I managed to whisper, wondering if it was possible for my evening to get any worse. I couldn't blame him if he'd got a girl staying over.

'Niamh, my cousin,' he said, wiping a tear away from my eye. I wasn't sure if there was a knowing smile playing faintly on his lips. 'She's over from Dublin for a few days.'

I started crying again. 'Hold me tight, Jar,' I said. And never let me go.

'I shouldn't have left Tim tonight, walked out like that,'

I said, regaining my composure. 'For all I know, he just wanted to place a few bets in the casino.'

'And this Hannah, presumably she's Tim's ex?'

'Probably.'

'In that case, I wouldn't believe a word the floozie said.'

The doorbell downstairs was ringing.

'Busy night,' Jar said, getting up from the sofa as his cousin appeared at the bedroom door. 'Niamh, this is Rosa. Rosa, Niamh.'

Niamh came over and sat down next to me. 'Everything OK now?' she asked, a hand on my arm. God, was it that obvious? I must have looked wrecked.

'I'm making a tea, do you fancy one? Seeing as we're all up.'

'Go on then,' I said. Niamh had kind eyes, like Jar's, and her Irish accent was stronger, but she was short and gamine, with none of Jar's heft. I remembered him saying something about her being an artist.

As she fetched a boiling kettle from the bedroom, I wondered if she'd heard our conversation. I didn't have the emotional energy to tell her about Phoebe.

I hope to God Phoebe survives. There's a chance, as Jar said. She can't have been there long.

'Who's at the door?' Niamh asked.

We both listened. I could hear Jar's voice but not the other person's. Then the door closed and Jar came back up the stairs. I looked up and saw him in the doorway, with Tim beside him, his white tie undone, eyes red, hair a mess.

'I just wanted to check that you're OK,' he said, sheepishly.

I glanced at Tim and then Jar, wondering how Tim had found me, why Jar let him in.

'Do you fancy an Irish whiskey?' Jar said to him and then smiled at me, as if to tell me that everything was in hand.

'Or a tea?' Niamh said.

Tim looked at me and then Jar. 'A large whiskey.'

For a moment I wondered if Jar and Tim knew each other, whether the whole evening had been another set-up, but it turned out Jar just wanted to give Tim a chance to explain himself. A bit of male solidarity, which irked me, but Jar also knew how bad I felt about walking out on him. More than anything, I think he just felt sorry for Tim, for me, for everyone who'd been at the ball, and over a new bottle of twelve-year-old Yellow Spot ('toasted barley, newly cut hay, hint of grapes') he encouraged us to talk about Phoebe.

As dawn broke, Jar made us all scrambled eggs and bacon, our alternative May Ball breakfast, which the four of us devoured as if we'd not eaten for days. He put on the Villagers, too, who I never did get to see at the ball.

In a quiet moment on the sofa, Tim apologised for Hannah, hoped she hadn't upset me. Jar was right, of course. They used to go out and she's never forgiven him for splitting up. He didn't know that I'd been about to walk out on our evening, had just assumed that I was swept up in the awful events of the Fellows' Garden, and I left it at that.

'How did you know where I was?' I asked.

'I asked a few people in the street if they'd seen a beautiful girl in a ball gown wandering around on her own.' He paused, glancing across at Jar and Niamh, who were washing up. 'Is Jar the chosen one then?'

I nodded, feeling guilty that I'd misjudged Tim and grateful to Jar for allowing some closure on the evening, as my counsellor would say.

I wonder if Dr Lance ever called Phoebe in, whether she met the foxy college shrink. Phoebe always had a complicated relationship with authority. I realise more than ever now how lucky I am. It could have been me swinging from a tree.

19

Jar's mind clears the moment he steps out on to Harley Street and into an ordinary day. The sky is an electric blue and people are on their way to work, clutching takeaway coffees, talking on phones, messenger bags strapped across shoulders. A few people are running, light rucksacks on their backs. On the corner, an orange-tanned woman – all fur coat and no knickers, Jar thinks – hails a taxi.

He could do with an espresso himself, as he glances at the brass plates beside the doors of the Georgian houses he passes, a snapshot of affluent hypochondria and vanity: dental implants, colon hydrotherapy, aesthetic surgery, mindfulness hypnotherapy, thread-vein removal, leech therapy, laser teeth-whitening. He got off lightly.

The session with Kirsten was unnerving, though. Her line of questioning was odd, even allowing for Freud: asking if Rosa kept a diary. And that reference to *contrails left in the sky*. He's more troubled that he confided in her, fell briefly under her fleshy spell.

It's as he reaches the corner of Harley Street and New Cavendish Street that he sees the car pull up beside him. The next moment its doors are open and two men are standing on the pavement, blocking his way.

'Jarlath Costello?' one of them says.

Jar nods.

'Police,' the man says, flashing a badge at him. Jar thinks he sees the words 'Metropolitan Police', but he can't be sure. 'Please step inside the car.'

'What's this all about?' Jar asks, his heart pounding. But before anyone answers, another man, approaching from behind, grabs his arms and handcuffs his wrists behind his back.

'Jaysus, this is absurd,' he says as he is bundled through the car's rear side door, his head pushed down.

'Jarlath Costello, I'm arresting you on suspicion of committing offences under the Sexual Offences Act and the Obscene Publications Act,' the man beside him in the back seat says. 'You do not have to say anything, but it may harm your defence if you do not mention when questioned something which you later rely on in court. Anything you do say may be given in evidence. Do you understand?'

'I don't understand, no,' Jar says, but he knows exactly what's going on. The police are following up on the hard drive, the one that Amy gave him. It's the only explanation. He leans back against the headrest, trying to remain calm as his mind processes the implications. Finally, after five years, the authorities are taking his investigations into Rosa seriously.

He feels weirdly elated as they speed through the West End traffic. At Oxford Circus the driver turns on the siren. It sounds as if it's coming from a different car, another world.

Jar's never had much time for the police, even less so since they failed to investigate Rosa's disappearance properly. It's another reason why he was reluctant to report the burglary of his flat.

The siren falls silent. He should request a lawyer, he thinks. That's what people do in this sort of situation. But he doesn't need one. He just needs to hear them spell it out – *we're after Rosa's diary because in it she might explain what happened, how she's still alive* – and he'll be happy.

When the car reaches the police station on Savile Row, Jar is manhandled into the foyer, where his wallet and phone are taken from him and signed for. He's then led to an empty cell, where he sits on the concrete floor, back against the wall.

At least time on his own allows him to work through every scenario and there's one that won't go away. He's been arrested under the Sexual Offences Act and the Obscene Publications Act, which suggests they have a strong case against Martin, Amy's husband. If the computer man really did find indecent images on his hard drive, as well as Rosa's diary, it doesn't look good for him. Or Anton. Or Carl. Jar has no wish to involve anyone else in this.

Two hours after his arrest, he is released from his cell and led to a small interview room with a table, a recording device and two wooden chairs. A tall, angular man sitting in the far chair rises to his feet as Jar enters.

'Miles Cato,' he says in a Scottish accent. Borders, Jar thinks, trying not to be thrown by the polite reception: the extended hand, this man calling himself Miles, with his urbane manner and chalk-striped suit. He's not like any policeman Jar's met before, and suspiciously friendly for the British.

They sit down at the table. Miles leans in towards the tape recorder, arms folded, giving his name and the time and date of their interview. Jar glances at the inert machine. There are no lights, nothing to suggest that it's been turned on.

'I don't think it's working,' Jar says.

'They never do, in my experience.'

Jar flinches at his thin-lipped smile. This is why people insist on a lawyer, he thinks.

'I'm sorry about earlier,' Miles continues, sweeping a hand through his thinning sandy hair as he pushes back his chair, scraping its wooden legs on the concrete floor with a sound that returns Jar to a cold classroom in Galway. 'The sooner we can get you out of this place, the better. May I call you Jar?'

He's been called Jarlath since his arrest. How does he know to call him Jar?

'Why am I here?' Jar asks.

'We need your help.'

'Who's we?'

Jar has Miles down as Oxbridge-educated, early forties, his expensive tan more merchant banker than policeman. The cochineal-red socks and brown brogues don't look like they've been on the beat either. He doesn't answer Jar's question. Not directly anyway.

'I think you know Martin, possibly you know Amy better. He was recently arrested on suspicion of possessing indecent images. Are you familiar with such things?'

The question is put to him matter-of-factly, as if he's been asked whether he takes sugar with his tea.

'Of course I'm bloody not.'

'We think they're level four, one short of the worst. Not pleasant.'

'I'll take your word for it. Amy told me he's been released.'

'Amy's been very helpful. Explained how she met you in Cromer last Thursday and handed over her old computer's hard drive. As far as I'm concerned, there was no need for you to be arrested today. Her late niece's college diary was found on the hard drive – corrupted, I gather – and she thought you might like to read it, given you were once an item at university. Touching.'

Miles offers a small, camp smile. Jar doesn't like him, his

aquiline nose, where their conversation is going. Rosa is not centre stage here, she's barely in the wings.

'What you both couldn't possibly know is that Martin's been on our radar for a while now and we think the hard drive might have once contained a folder of images that contravene the Obscene Publications Act. The man who was trying to fix Amy's computer came across some...' He hesitates. 'Some unusual file traces on an external hard drive and then discovered a catalogue reference to some encrypted image files on another hard drive – possibly the one you were given. He rang us to raise the alarm.'

Or did he ring someone about the diary, Jar wonders, his phone call running up a red flag somewhere in Whitehall that caught the attention of Miles Cato, whoever you are.

'Not the first time he's tipped us off. Amazing what you find, fixing people's home computers.' Miles pauses. 'I just need you to return the hard drive, Jar. We have no interest in Rosa's diary.'

He's bluffing, calculated that it's too late to stop him reading it. *We have no interest in Rosa's diary.* Jar tries to shut out the words, extinguish them from his mind. Miles needs to establish how much he knows, whether Rosa's spilt the beans about her disappearance.

'Haven't you got enough to charge Martin with already?' Jar asks.

'Not yet. He's good with computers, covers his tracks. But we think he slipped up when he copied some encrypted images on to his wife's computer. I'm assuming you've taken the drive to someone who knows how to recover corrupt files. We want it back, Jar. Intact. It's potentially important police evidence.'

Evidence that she's alive, Jar thinks. 'Including the diary?'

Jar fixes Miles with a stare, searching for a clue that he is right, that this is all about Rosa. But Cato's face remains blank, inscrutable.

'Exactly as it was when Amy handed it over,' he says coldly. 'You've got until nine o'clock tonight.'

'And if I can't manage that?'

'We go public about today. An Obscene Publications arrest never looks good, I'm afraid, particularly when combined with the Sexual Offences Act.'

20

Cambridge, Spring Term, 2012

I finally got to see Dr Lance today after our meeting was rearranged several times. The college counsellor, an American woman called Karen, popped her head around the door at the end for a quick chat, but more of her in a minute.

I'm still trying to work out why Dr Lance really wanted to see me. It was different from our normal awkward chats, where we have sat eating his wife's homemade shortbread and drinking green tea while he asks if I am OK, whether I need to talk to anyone about Dad's death.

To his increasing concern, I've turned down all offers of bereavement counselling, from the university when I first arrived and from our GP last summer, immediately after Dad's death. The timing wasn't great, I suppose. Dad died a month before the start of my first term and I had to make a decision: either I postponed going up to Cambridge for a year while I got my head around what had happened (too much introspection) or I threw myself into it, hoping that the excitement of starting university would take my mind off everything (problems further down the line).

I opted for the latter and somehow it seemed

counter-productive to sign up to counselling while I was trying to dull the pain with Freshers' Week. It hasn't worked, of course. My first two terms at Cambridge have been an unmitigated disaster: too much pressure to enjoy myself, the reality falling far short of my high expectations. A constant sense of people achieving things elsewhere.

I should have delayed university until I'd come to terms with Dad's death. I realise that now. A year, two years, whatever it took. Instead, I've been in denial, letting his death fester in the background, from where it's cast ever lengthening shadows across my life here.

Dr Lance didn't hold back this time. No awkward silences while we waited for his interminably slow kettle to boil. He'd heard that I was unhappy and seemed to think that talking about Dad – their time together at college, the unique nature of his work at the Foreign Office and so on – would cheer me up.

I started crying immediately, which was perhaps his real plan. He wanted to flush out my grief, and it worked: months of suppressed pain, no one to talk to. (I always talked to Dad about anything that troubled me, even during the 'terror years', as he called them, when puberty turned me into a teenage monster.)

Dr Lance doesn't look like a man used to emotion in his life, but he couldn't have been sweeter, or less embarrassed, offering me a (clean) chequered hanky and resting a hand on my shoulder while I gathered myself. Maybe it's his beloved Goethe that makes him so at ease in the presence of grief.

'I'm sorry,' I said, blowing my nose.

'It's quite all right. I'm sorry I didn't realise something was amiss sooner. You seemed so together. And independent – until recently. Everyone was very concerned after your last supervision.'

Probably because I hadn't finished my Marlowe essay on *Hero and Leander*, but I didn't say that. Dr Lance steepled his fingers beneath his cropped beard, ginger with streaks of silver.

'I do think it's time you talked to someone, Rosa. We now have a very good in-house counsellor at St Matthew's, which might be easier than going through the university's welfare services.'

'I miss him every day,' I said. My face was red, my mascara smudged.

'Of course. We all do.'

'And I feel so guilty when I'm not enjoying myself here, doing the things that I know he would have wanted me to do.'

'There's a lot of pressure for these three years to be the best of your life. They invariably aren't. Mine weren't. Which is partly why I stayed on.'

'Sometimes it feels like an eclipse, a darkness racing across the fields, the sun going out in the middle of the day, when I'm supposed to be at my happiest.'

'Have you had any suicidal thoughts?'

I paused, surprised by his change of tack.

'Tragically, we lose too many young people at this fragile stage of their lives,' he added. I wondered if he was about to bring up Mum's death, even though she died a few years after uni. The three of them were quite a gang at Cambridge, apparently.

'Dad did, at his lowest moments. We talked about it once. I'd be lying if I said I haven't thought about it too.'

'Karen is a trained bereavement counsellor. I've asked her to drop in today. Is it all right if I call her now?'

I nodded, watching as he picked up his phone and rang her.

Two minutes later I was shaking Karen's hand and we were being ushered by Dr Lance to the sofa in front of his fireplace.

'I'm going to leave you in Karen's capable hands,' he said, his fingers touching my shoulder again before he left the room.

I was a little wrong-footed, conscious of how I looked after so much crying, but Karen must have been used to tear-stained student faces.

It was immediately obvious why all the boys in college are feigning depression to be on her books. Karen has blonde, shoulder-length hair, enviably high cheekbones and powder-blue eyes. Beautiful in an obvious sort of way. Nothing wrong with that, I suppose. Nor that she's American. I couldn't really place her accent – East Coast? – but she had a manner about her that was at once reassuring without being patronising.

'Dr Lance has told me all about you,' she said. 'And your mother and your wonderful father. I think I can help if you're willing to let me.'

'I'd like that,' I said.

'There are a lot of options open to us,' she added. 'Different ways to improve your life.'

There was only one thing that was unnerving about Karen: she did this short intake of breath just before she spoke. It was as if she'd suddenly remembered to breathe. The more she talked – about the sessions she wants me to attend, her background working with young people, her interest in post-bereavement hallucinations – the more I couldn't help noticing it, until in my mind it became a deafening gasp.

Dad would have found it funny.

21

J ar looks for a public phone as soon as he is released from the police station. After searching for ten minutes, he finds a phone box on New Bond Street and calls Carl at the office. He doesn't want to risk making a call on his mobile.

'Wassup?' Carl asks, in his faux gangsta voice. 'The boss is pissed at you. I've been trying your mobile all morning.'

'I was arrested.'

'Arrested? By the police?' Who else, Jar thinks. The Salvation Army? 'What for?'

Jar fills him in on Amy's husband, the case against him, hears the excitement fade from his friend's voice, the fear creeping in.

'But it's a bunch of malarkey, Carl. They're after the diary.'

'Of course they are. I get that.' Carl pauses. 'But, you know, just supposing there are dodgy images on the hard drive… Could we be done for handling them?'

'There aren't any, trust me.'

'I still need to ring Anton, warn him.'

'They want the hard drive by 9 p.m. Can you get it back from him by then? I would go myself, but…' Jar looks out of the phone box, checks the street.

Carl agrees, reluctantly, to collect the hard drive, says he will go over to Ladbroke Grove after work, meet Jar back at the Savile Row police station at 8.30 p.m. 'I don't like this, Jar. Anton won't either. I'm just going to ask for the drive back, spare him the details.'

'I also need him to copy the diary before we hand it over. Can he do that?'

'I can ask. Are you coming into the office now?'

'Tell the boss I've got splinters embedded in both corneas and was last seen wandering into heavy traffic, looking for an eye clinic.'

'Ouch. How many days off are you after?'

Jar loves his friend, but he hasn't got time to discuss sickie strategies. And his job feels more of an irrelevance than ever now. He needs to get back to his flat, check for more diary entries. They might be the last ones he reads if Anton can't copy the files. He's also got a plan to prevent Miles Cato from reading the diary himself. Or at least to slow him down.

22

Cambridge, Autumn Term, 2011

A man came to see me today, an old work colleague of Dad's. Dr Lance introduced me to him in his rooms. He's called Simon somebody – he didn't give me a card.

Over a sweet sherry – yup, some old people still drink the stuff – in front of Dr Lance's fireplace, glowing with coals, he asked if I knew the exact nature of Dad's work at the Foreign Office, what he'd done for his country. I told him what Dad always told me: that he worked for the Political Unit, writing boring reports on far-flung countries that no one bothered to read.

'Not quite,' Simon said, glancing across at Dr Lance. He had a kind, almost cheeky face, at odds with his middle age. If it wasn't for the dark suit, he could have been mistaken for a children's entertainer. Or maybe a vet, someone who's patient with puppies.

I was being flippant, my usual defence when I'm feeling emotional (it's known as 'week five blues', apparently). Any talk of Dad is likely to set me off, particularly when someone is singing his praises. I was also a little resentful at having been summoned back to college from the Sidgwick Site, via a text message from Dr Lance, just when I was finally getting into my Coleridge essay.

'It's been decided to honour your father posthumously by appointing him to the Order of St Michael and St George,' Simon said, running the sherry around his glass.

'Sounds impressive.' Order of St Michael and St George – he would have liked that.

'He's been appointed a Knight Commander, a KCMG.'

'I'm sure he'd have been very proud. Tickled.'

It wasn't the right word – the sherry talking – but I wasn't ready for all this talk of knights and commanders. Simon humoured me with a fleeting smile.

'We were wondering if you would accept the honour on your father's behalf,' he continued. 'Next week.'

'Where?'

'St Paul's Cathedral. Private chapel, small service.'

'Sounds like he did more than he was letting on,' I said.

I always knew Dad was not being entirely honest with me whenever we talked about his work, but we seemed to have arrived at an unspoken understanding that I wouldn't ask too many questions and he wouldn't offer any more details.

I don't think he was a spy – he used to make disparaging remarks about the 'spooks' at the High Commission in Islamabad – but I guess I just thought his work was important and if he didn't want to tell me more about it, there was probably a good reason. All I know is that his job took us to some incredible places over the years: India, Pakistan, China, Hong Kong.

'He did a lot of good work with young people,' Dr Lance said, looking at Simon for agreement. Or was it for his approval? 'Saved a lot of lives.'

'Really?' I said, surprised. Dad had never mentioned

working with young people, though he once said he wished he'd been a teacher.

'Extraordinary work. His death has left a big hole in a lot of lives,' Simon said.

I looked away at the fireplace, my eyes brimming. It's just over two months since Dad died and I'd be in denial if I said I was even beginning to come to terms with him not being around, not being available at the end of a phone. He would always take calls from me, even in important meetings. I think it was a promise he'd made to himself.

'I'd be honoured to accept the award on Dad's behalf,' I eventually managed to say. 'Thank you.'

'Excellent. There's one other thing, though,' Simon continued. 'It's been brought to our attention that some journalists have been asking about your father, the exact circumstances of his death. I'd be grateful if you could let me know if anyone tries contacting you directly.'

'What are they asking?'

'The usual Fleet Street stuff, whether he was a spy. We're not commenting and nor should you.'

I've still got the card of a journalist who approached me at Dad's funeral. I should have thrown it out. I'm not sure why I've kept it, or why I didn't mention it then. Perhaps it's because there's a grain of doubt in my mind too about Dad's death, not that it was suspicious or anything like that, but that I don't know the full story of his life.

I don't have the mental strength right now to ask questions. All I know is that the Foreign Office launched its own internal inquiry, which concluded that Dad died in an accident: a car crash in the Himalayas, outside Leh, in Ladakh – one of my favourite places in the world, despite its treacherous roads. He was trying to establish the nature of the Chinese

114

threat along India's border with Tibet. At least, that's what he told me in so many words when he rang from Heathrow. 'Send my love to the Dalai Lama,' I'd joked. I think they were the last words I ever said to him.

'He wasn't a spy, was he?' I asked, as Simon turned to Dr Lance, signalling that our meeting was over. I didn't expect him to answer.

'No,' he said. 'He was much more important than that.'

23

'It's just a coincidence, Jar,' Carl says, sipping on a fresh pint.

'You say that,' Jar replies, more drunk than he should be on a Tuesday night. 'But how many female bereavement counsellors do you know who are a) American b) drop-dead-gorgeous blondes and c) take small but weirdly audible breaths just before they speak? Answer me that.'

'So Kirsten's a spice now, is she? You've changed your tune.'

'I wouldn't kick her out of bed for eating crisps. You know that. I know that. It's just a statement of fact. "Beauty is truth, truth beauty – that is all ye know on earth, and all ye need to know."'

Jar only allows himself to quote poets, particularly British ones, when he's drunk. 'You don't believe me, do you?' he continues. 'Don't you think it's weird now?'

'No. I don't, Jar. I don't think it's weird at all. It's pure chance. Serendipity.'

Jar's too drunk to make his case again, or mock Carl for attempting a word like 'serendipity', but he tries.

'I know you mean well, Carl, but there's a great deal of sense outside your head,' he says. 'I was arrested by the police this morning the moment I walked out of Kirsten's door on Harley Street. Literally, it was a few yards down the road from her gaff. She picked up the phone and called them as soon as I left.'

'Why would she do that?'

'Because I lied about the diary. She asked me if Rosa kept a journal and I said she didn't. It was the last question of the session, what the whole hour had been leading up to.'

Carl gives him a look. Jar knows how he must sound – paranoid, deluded – but he no longer cares.

'Why did you say she didn't?' Carl asks.

Jar glances at his friend as he takes another sip from his pint of Gat. For a second, the thought crosses his mind that Carl's in on this too. It's happened before – fleeting, irrational suspicions, threatening to poison the well of their friendship – but he has learnt to dismiss them as quickly as they arrive.

This time, it's harder. Carl was the one who introduced him to Kirsten, told him to let her help him. He and Carl go back a long way, he reassures himself: five years. They met soon after he moved to London. Not long after Rosa died...

'Will you answer me this,' Jar says, trying to move on. 'She used a certain turn of phrase. Said that most people think a post-bereavement hallucination is like a "contrail left in the sky". Rosa wrote something almost identical in her diary: "No contrails left in the Fenland sky." Said it was the sort of thing her counsellor would say.'

'And?' Carl raises his eyebrows.

'Don't you think that's strange? A curious expression for both of them to use?'

'No, I don't.'

'I googled it: there are only seven hundred occurrences of that phrase across the entire internet.'

'I've got to be honest, bro. This is not just some weird little OCD coincidence fantasy you've got going on here, it's a serious problem. You were lifted by the Feds.'

'Tell me about it. And then there was the hacking of my email account...'

'I could have been arrested too,' he says, ignoring Jar's earlier computer problems. 'And Anton.'

'There aren't any dodgy images on that hard drive.'

'You say that. But how do we know?'

'Because this whole thing about indecent images is just a cover. They're after Rosa's diary, Carl.'

There is a pause while both men nurse their pints, watching the barman mix Bacardi and Red Bulls for two young Asian students. Neither of them would normally frequent a pub on Piccadilly – tourist territory – but they both needed a drink after Carl, panting like a dog, had handed over the hard drive to Jar at 8.55 p.m. outside Savile Row police station. He had waited on the street, getting his breath back, while Jar went inside and gave the drive to the duty officer, who seemed to be expecting it. Miles Cato was nowhere to be seen.

They had met his deadline, but only just. Anton had kicked off about copying the disk, asking why Carl suddenly wanted it back. He protested even more when Carl asked him to add another layer of encryption on to the original folder. Jar hoped that would delay Miles Cato – buy him a few days, even a few hours – but he doubted it.

'Thanks for picking up the hard drive,' Jar says, by way of a peace offering.

'Anton wasn't happy.'

'He did encode it, though?'

'He disappeared for an hour.'

'How much do I owe you?'

'A lifetime's supply of bubble hash.'

'Is that what you promised him?'

'If it don't bubble, it ain't worth the trouble,' Carl says, glancing at his watch as he puts a drunken arm around Jar. 'She should be here any minute.'

'Who should?' Jar looks around the crowded pub, but he doesn't recognise anyone.

'Drop-dead-gorgeous Kirsten, of course.'

'Carl?' He can't believe what his friend has just said.

'Relax. She's off duty. Promised not to talk about this morning.'

'But—'

'I won't say a word about her Cambridge doppelgänger. Or contrails. Or weird breathing. I promise. Chill.'

Again Jar declines to bump his friend's outstretched fist. Instead, he searches his familiar eyes for evidence of betrayal. What the hell's Carl doing asking Kirsten to join them? And why has he just confided so much in him?

'I'm not comfortable with this. I'm her client. At least I was. I'm not sure I ever want to go back there.'

'Even more reason to enjoy her company this evening.'

'You could have warned me.'

'I thought I just did.'

'As she's about to arrive.'

'You'd have run off any earlier. She likes you. And she's hot.'

'She's all yours.'

'I'm a kept man.'

'Since when?'

'Since last night. If you'd bothered to come into the office this morning instead of getting yourself arrested, I would have told you all about Tatiana from Odessa.'

'I'm going to head on.' Jar is overwhelmed by a sudden need to leave the pub, be on his own, clear his head.

'Jar...' Carl's hand is on his arm now, restraining him. 'Stay for a bit. It'll be good for you. Have some fun. Enjoy the *craic*.'

'You don't understand,' Jar says, ignoring Carl's crude appeal to his Irishness. He's not falling for that. 'I lied to her today, couldn't get out of there quick enough.'

'Well lie again. She won't ask you anything about this morning.'

'Did you ring her?'

'She rang me. About the article I'm writing on music and shrinks. Then she asked if you were OK.'

'When?' Carl's his best friend, Jar thinks. Relax.

'Tonight. When I was at Anton's. I told her a drink would cheer you up, but we agreed it didn't sound too professional. She promised to avoid all office talk. Besides, you're not paying her, so it's not really a proper client–therapist relationship, is it?'

'Is that what she said?'

'It's my impartial reading of the situation.'

'M'lud. Jaysus, Carl.'

'Come on, Jar. You've got to get over all this. Move on with your life.'

'Are you two sure I'm not intruding?'

Jar spins round to see Kirsten standing next to him and smiling in a way that makes his stomach lurch. She's wearing a low-cut cherry-red dress and heels and is radiating warmth and charm – like a siren, Jar thinks.

'We were just talking about you,' Carl says, winking at Jar. 'What can Jar get you to drink?'

24

I'm not sure I can write much tonight. I feel numb, weird, fractured, as if I'm living in a parallel world to the life I lived before Dad died. A world identical to my own in every respect except for one.

Dad was buried this morning, alongside my mother, in the graveyard at Paul, high above Mousehole: the only constant place in our itinerant family's life. My mum grew up in this Cornish village, where I am writing now. Her mother lived here for sixty years, but the locals still considered her a foreigner (or blow-in, as they say).

Mum inherited a fisherman's net loft and came down with Dad whenever they were back in the UK. They used to walk along the coast path to Lamorna, drive over the moor to St Ives to buy a painting to take back to their drab Foreign Office quarters in Beijing, Islamabad or Delhi. Dad told me once how he'd had to return a picture to a gallery the day after they'd bought it. It was a painting of a beach, three bands of colour, yellow, green and blue, and late that night, when they were admiring its abstract simplicity over a bottle of wine, Dad suddenly thought he could trace the profile of a giant nude with huge breasts reclining in the dunes. It wasn't intentional, just an ambiguous shape, but once they'd seen it, the picture was ruined. 'Mum was quite cross, said I had a filthy mind,' Dad said.

He brought me down here a lot in the months and years after Mum's death. I remember tending her grave, cutting back the grass with a pair of children's red plastic scissors, looking at the neat writing on the slate headstone, asking Dad why there was a big gap below Mum's name. It was only when I was older that he explained that the space was reserved for him. 'Two-for-one offer at the undertaker's,' he joked.

There weren't any jokes today. Maybe even Dad would have struggled to see the funny side of his death, aged forty-six, in the prime of his life and career, killed in the Himalayas, a place he loved, by a truck driver who had fallen asleep at the wheel. I'm forcing myself to write these words, in the hope that it will make what's happened more real. *Killed in the Himalayas, a place he loved, by a truck driver who had fallen asleep at the wheel.* Right now, my brain refuses to process the fact of his death. Dad's died. Gone. I will never see him again. Never hear his voice. Link my arm in his.

Tomorrow I will visit the place where Dad told me to go in an emergency, if the world ever slipped off its axis. I have never been before, but he once gave me instructions. It worked for him at certain times in his life – he spent several days there after he lost Mum, he said, walking, camping – and I hope it might offer some solace now. I need something.

Amy – so sad today, heavily sedated – said that there'll be a memorial service in London in a few months, once everyone has got over the shock. There'll be more jokes then, I hope, stories shared, laughter remembered. Amy also said that I can visit her every weekend at her house in Cromer, if I need to get away from college. She misses Dad terribly but she's trying to be strong for me. I know the two of them didn't see as much of each other as they would have liked, because of Martin. She's promised that won't happen with me in the future.

I managed to get through my reading in the service: 'What is Success', one of Dad's favourite poems ('To laugh often and much... to find the best in others... this is to have succeeded'), which he liked to point out was wrongly attributed to Ralph Waldo Emerson. I'm not sure what everyone made of the poem. Amy tried to talk me out of reading anything in public, but I felt I owed it to Dad.

I wept before I stood up, when the coffin was first brought in, and I cried afterwards when we sang 'Dear Lord and Father of Mankind', but not during my reading. I felt strong then. I imagined Dad at the back of the church, arms folded, nodding encouragingly, like I'd seen him once at the doors of the school theatre, when he turned up from London just in time to watch me sing 'Oh, Look at Me!' in *Salad Days*.

It was a strange collection of people in the stout, weather-beaten church. There were a lot of his Foreign Office work colleagues, many of whom had travelled down on the train from Paddington to Penzance, although I noticed one or two important-looking people leaving afterwards in discreet government cars.

Dr Lance, who had interviewed me at Cambridge, came up for a chat in the King's Arms, the pub across the road, where Amy had arranged a wake (crab sandwiches, white wine, wild flowers we'd collected together from the hedgerows that morning). He was very sweet, said how much he looked forward to welcoming me to St Matthew's in October, although he quite understood if I wanted to postpone my university career. A place would be kept for me.

Fishing boats are returning now, passing across Mount's Bay on their way home to Newlyn, their navigation lights barely visible in the rain-streaked gloaming. I'm sitting at the same window where Dad used to perch with his binoculars, pointing out ships on the horizon. I wish I had paid more attention. The coal fire is smoking badly – Dad always used to curse its poor 'draw' (I never knew how that worked) – and it's cold in this old, wooden-walled house, but I'm glad I have a few days to myself. It was exhausting today, having to put a brave face on things while I really just wanted to run away across the moor and rail at the gods who have taken Dad away from me.

Some things I'll never forget about Dad:

- His silly voice as the Once-ler whenever he read me *The Lorax*.
- Finding him downstairs in his study one night, crying over family photos of Mum, him, and me as a baby, on holiday in Seville. She had been dead fifteen years.
- The sound of his laughter rising up from the sitting room when he was watching yet another repeat of *Dad's Army*.
- Singeing his bushy eyebrows when he set fire to a wet bonfire with petrol.
- Coming to a parents' evening at school with a bicycle clip still around one trouser leg.
- Standing on the sidelines at a netball match in the rain, cheering me on like it was an international rugby match (I'm sure he wished it was, but he never complained).

A man approached me in the King's Arms just as we were leaving the wake, said he would like a chat when I'm feeling stronger.

'I was trying to interview your father for a story I'm working on,' he said, standing at the bar with a pint in his hand – not his first of the day, I suspected. He was in his early fifties, two stone overweight, and might have been good-looking once, before the beer started to ruddy his face and swell his belly.

'I'm not sure this is the time or place,' I said. The only journalists I've met are the foreign correspondents who used to turn up at the High Commission in Pakistan for free drinks. They were a fun crowd and I felt similarly unthreatened by the man in front of me. He glanced around the room, which made me look too. 'Were you at the service?' I asked.

'That wouldn't have been appropriate. I shouldn't even be here now, talking to you. Will you call me in a month, two months? A year? Whenever you feel you can. I'd appreciate a chat.'

He handed me a card – 'Max Eadie, freelance journalist' – and moved off just as one of Dad's colleagues came over.

'Everything all right?' the woman said.

'Fine,' I replied, holding the card tightly behind my back.

25

J ar pushes back his chair, running a hand through his hair. He is at his computer in the lock-up, sober after a cold bath, unable to sleep. His evening at the pub in Piccadilly remains a blur. He hopes he behaved, didn't let on what he now knows to be true: 'Kirsten' is the same woman as 'Karen', the college counsellor who was introduced to Rosa by Dr Lance five years ago. He's sure of it. It was Kirsten who approached him through Carl; Kirsten who asked him about Rosa's diary. And Kirsten who rang the police when he lied. Jar just wishes he knew why she approached him, who she's working for.

He glances at his computer. It's 3 a.m. and he might not have much time. If the police can arrest him once, they can do it again. Miles Cato will want another chat when his people run up against Anton's encryption skills.

Max Eadie, Jar thinks, turning the name over in his head. Could it be the same journalist? In the first few months after Rosa died, a reporter had asked questions around Cambridge about her, but Jar has never been able to trace him.

It was Rosa's college who let it slip. One uncharacteristically indiscreet porter. Jar had travelled up to Cambridge in August, a month after Rosa died, determined to speak to

Dr Lance. The dean hadn't been replying to emails, or taking his calls, so Jar thought he'd try to doorstep him. He wasn't successful.

'Who shall I say wants to see him?' the black-suited man in the porter's lodge asked. He was what his mother would call a right-looking queer-hawk, Jar thought.

'Jarlath Costello.'

The porter watched him as he picked up a phone and dialled an extension. 'Not another journalist, are you?'

'I'm not a journalist. I'm a student. King's.' It was technically a lie. Jar wouldn't be returning to Cambridge in October for his PhD as planned, couldn't face it after what had happened. And he had just landed his first job on an arts website. 'Why do you ask?'

'Some reporter from London was poking around earlier. Asking questions.'

'About what?'

'Dr Lance's not answering his phone.' The porter redialled.

'What was he asking about?' Jar continued, surprised by his own persistence. 'The journalist.'

'The death that dare not speak its name. Student suicides. No answer from Dr Lance.'

'Can you remember what he was called?'

'Best if you make an appointment, sir.'

That was all. One London journalist 'poking around'. His interest might have been in Phoebe, of course, whose ghastly May Ball suicide had made all the papers in the summer. Rosa's own death had followed a few weeks later. It was covered by the local press as just another sad student suicide. Nothing was made of her father, who was simply reported as working for the Foreign Office.

Jar knows Rosa and her father were close. He wishes he

could have met Jim Sandhoe, having heard so many happy stories about him from Rosa. In the early days, using the basic journalism skills he picked up while working on the arts website, Jar tried to discover more, but he drew a complete blank. There was almost nothing about Rosa's father online, except for some open-source reports he'd co-written on the economy of south-east Asia. There was no evidence to suggest he'd worked for anyone other than the Foreign Office's Political Unit, although Jar soon realised that this was a department regularly used for official cover by the intelligence agencies. But now, it seems, his job was 'more important' than a spy's. He's never come across anything about a posthumous KCMG.

Jar searches for Max Eadie, grateful that his name is a relatively good one to google. There are no journalists, just a Max Eadie who runs his own corporate public relations company in London. He opens the website, clicks 'About Us' and looks at a photo of a jowly man in his fifties. His biography refers to an earlier career as an investigative journalist, a job that led him to 'understand the complexities of crisis PR management from both sides of the fence'. Clients include a number of unpopular banks. There's a 'crisis' contact number beneath each member of staff's biography, including a mobile number for Max Eadie.

Jar checks the street before he leaves the lock-up and walks back to his flat, keeping out of the pools of orange streetlight. There's a van parked at the end of the road that wasn't there earlier. And one of the cars opposite his block has gone. Relax, he tells himself. He will call Max Eadie first thing in the morning.

26

Silent Retreat, Herefordshire, Spring Term, 2012

The view from my room is beautiful: there's sunshine on the high ridge above us, a spring stillness in the valley below. I'm here to 'settle my mind', get in touch with an 'inner calm'. At least that's what Maggs, the nice man downstairs, said when we all gathered for our welcome chat. He was wearing jeans and a collarless white cotton shirt (no flowing robes). There was an enviable serenity about him and his talk was all about concentration and focus, living in the moment and letting go of the things that worry us: thoughts, emotions. Apparently he was a ski bum before he 'found himself' in Bali.

There's been no mystical mumbo-jumbo, although it wouldn't bother me if there was. I'm pretty open to this sort of thing, having hung out in the Himalayas. Dad used to meditate every morning when we were in Pakistan and we were just beginning to discuss the bigger issues in life when he died. I feel oddly close to him here.

The one catch is that it's a silent retreat, which might prove a challenge for me. We could ask questions during the welcome talk, but from now on we have to stay zipped.

We handed in our phones when we arrived, and no reading or talking is allowed.

I'm hoping this diary will get me through. It's strange how much we rely on talking in life. When I met people downstairs, I wanted to say hi, ask where everyone was from. One girl had a streaming cold, looked terrible, but I couldn't check that she was OK.

I'm sharing a room with another girl. After we came upstairs to dump our bags, we greeted each other with a nod and a smile. I had to bite my lip. I wanted to know all about her, compare notes about Maggs (OK, cards on the table, he's fit, which could prove distracting when we're trying to meditate – must keep eyes closed), ask her where she bought her gorgeous bangles, which look Indian.

It was Karen's idea to come here. After my meeting with her in Dr Lance's rooms, she arranged my first 'session' in her study, off Second Court. She let me do most of the talking: about Dad, how I've tried – and failed – to immerse myself in university life rather than wallow in grief, the very real prospect that I will drop out in the summer, maybe travel to India, visit the place where Dad died. I told her about the darker times, too, the nights I've been unable to sleep, my thoughts about ending it all.

'I don't think you should underestimate the effect of losing a parent,' she said. 'Both parents, in your case. If you need to take a break from university life, travel for a year, I'm sure Dr Lance would understand.'

'Do you think so?'

'We've talked about it already. And we all think it would be a good idea if you did take some time out. The first year at university is stressful enough without the added complication of grieving for a parent.'

'What about my studies?'

'They can wait.'

'The college would take me back?'

'Of course. I think visiting India could be very healing.'

She paused at this point and it was the first time I sensed that there was another agenda to our meeting. There was something about her manner that made me feel she was biding her time, waiting to take the conversation in another direction. I was not entirely surprised by what she said next.

'Or...' She got up from behind her desk and came to sit next to me on the sofa. Her eyes were an extraordinary blue and she was wearing a faint scent: lemons. Summery. 'You could decide that university is not for you, leave at the end of next term and do something completely different with the rest of your life.'

'I don't understand.'

'There are certain people who are just not suited to university, particularly in a place like Cambridge, where expectations can be so high. In my experience, working here and at Oxford, the unhappiest students are often the most gifted – in languages, the sciences, philosophy. From what Dr Lance has told me, you are an extraordinary student: double-first material.'

'I'm not sure about that,' I said, feeling myself blushing. It was strange, but the mere hint that I might not be spending another two years in that place had raised my spirits already.

'However, the prospect of dropping out of university can itself be very stressful. There may be a sense of personal failure and it doesn't look so good on a CV. Dr Lance is all too aware of this. He wants everyone who leaves here to go on and achieve their very best in life. We've talked a lot about you, how brave you've been, coming up here so soon after your father's death.'

'I'm not sure if it wasn't too soon,' I said. Tears were coming.

'We'll never know. Personally, I think you were right to give it a shot. And you're right to acknowledge now that it might not have worked out for the best. Dr Lance wants to help you. That's why he's brought me in. He was very fond of your father and it upsets him to see you so unhappy. I want you to go away from here for a few days, take time out to think about your life, where you want it to go. Calm things down a bit in that busy, brilliant brain of yours. When you come back, we can talk more about the options available, consider what's best for you, your long-term wellbeing.'

That's how she left it. And here I am now, sitting in a remote country house in Herefordshire, about to go downstairs for our first proper meditation session. Tomorrow we'll be woken at six for a six-thirty start, followed by more meditation after lunch (all the food is vegetarian). T'ai chi or yoga at the end of every session, two hours off in the middle of the day for walking. Bed by nine.

The college paid for my transport – a train down to London, then another one, a three-hour journey out to Hereford – and there is only one condition of my visit: I am not to mention it to anyone. I'm not sure why. Perhaps Dr Lance doesn't want a stampede of students rushing off for a few days' chilling in Herefordshire.

My roommate has come upstairs while I've been writing this and she's been sitting on her bed, writing too. A letter, I think. I couldn't help myself and scribbled my name on a slip of paper and handed it to her, along with a piece of dark chocolate. We're not supposed to have brought any food with us, but I smuggled in some 85 per cent cacao, figuring it was a health product, nourishment for the soul.

She wrote her name on the paper – she's called Sejal – and handed it back, adding a thank you for the chocolate. It was as she passed me the paper that I saw what the bangles are hiding: deep laceration scars on her wrist, healing now but quite recent. I'm amazed she survived.

She saw me notice them and we paused for a moment, acknowledging each other properly for the first time. Then I grabbed my pen and wrote on the paper: 'Which university are you at?' She hesitated before writing back: 'Oxford'. I took the paper and wrote again: 'Did Karen send you here?'

She looked at me with surprise and nodded.

27

'Thanks for making time to see me,' Jar says. 'I was intrigued by your message.'

Jar takes in Max Eadie's airy office, the views across Docklands towards Greenwich. He's spent many hours on the balcony of his own flat staring out at this building, watching the light on its apex wink through the night, brightening low clouds like lazy lightning.

It's the first time he's actually been inside One Canada Square and for a few tense moments downstairs he thought he would never make it.

'ID?' the guard on the turnstiles had asked. Jar took out his driver's licence, wondering if his details would flag up an alert of some kind. Was he about to be arrested again? Bundled away in a police van to be interrogated by Miles Cato? But he was waved through, observed by the guards as he walked over to the bank of lifts and waited for a lift to the twentieth floor.

Half an hour earlier, he'd felt watched when he left his block of flats, that same sense of unease he'd had in Cromer. The feeling had persisted on the Docklands Light Railway, when a man had stepped into his carriage at the last moment. He knows he is being paranoid, but the journey here has left him tense.

'Coffee? Tea?' Max offers.

'I'm fine,' Jar says. He likes to give himself thirty seconds when he meets someone new, enough to soak up first impressions, assess his own visceral response to another human being. Max is overweight – Jar adjusts his own shirt – and his cheeks are redder than they should be, suggesting joie de vivre or stress-induced drinking. A bit of both, perhaps.

A pair of reading glasses hangs around his neck and there is a set of golf clubs propped up in the corner. Old set, nothing flashy. Above them, on a bookshelf, a row of business directories and a battered copy of *An Indian Summer* by James Cameron. The linen suit is crumpled and baggy, and there is a food stain in the middle of his floral tie.

'I'm not here to hire your services, you do know that now?' Jar begins.

'I figured,' Max replies, cleaning his glasses on his tie. 'Crap,' he says, noticing the stain. He spits on his tie and rubs it with his fingers. 'Got any kids yourself?'

'None that I know of.'

'Don't let them hug you in a suit when ketchup's on the menu. Which it always is in our house.'

'I'll try to remember that.'

'I know what you're thinking. Old fart like me, young kids.'

'Not at all.'

'It's not a second wife. Nothing like that.'

Jar holds his hands up in mock protest, in a far-be-it-from-me-to-judge way.

'It's actually my third.' Max smiles. 'Did I offer you a drink?'

'No thanks.'

Jar wonders how Max ever got to be a crisis PR manager,

given his own seemingly shambolic life. 'I think you might have once written an article about Jim Sandhoe,' he says, keen to focus on what he's come here for.

'Never published, sadly. Not in print, anyway.'

'Is it still available to read?'

'It was a long time ago. Another life.' He glances around the expensive office, as if to remind Jar of his changed circumstances.

'I went out with Rosa Sandhoe, Jim's daughter, at university. The summer term, before she died.'

Max's face changes at the mention of Rosa's name, his lower lip pursing like the spout of a milk jug.

'I think you met her once,' Jar continues. 'At her father's funeral.'

Max winces. 'I remember her face: pretty girl.'

'What was the article about?'

Max sits back, picking at a molar. It's several seconds before he speaks. 'I've got a vivid imagination, Jar. These days I use it to dream up worst-case scenarios, try to predict where things might spiral, how bad a story could get. My clients buy into me because they think I'm authentic: I look how they imagine Fleet Street hacks should look.'

He waves one leg in the air, pulling up his trousers. 'Soles worn down from all those knock jobs, that kind of thing. *Déshabillé*. I don't tell them journalism's all iPads and twenty-something digital natives these days. When I was a journalist, my news editor dealt in facts. I once stumbled on a story about Rosa's father, but I couldn't stand it up. No proof.'

'Of what?'

Max pauses. 'I'm sorry about Rosa. Truly. I never wanted to doorstep her father's funeral, but... How well did you know him?'

'We never met. He died a month before Rosa started at Cambridge. But I think he worked in the Foreign Office, the Political Unit.'

Jar manages a knowing smile, journalist to journalist now. Max doesn't reciprocate, but his eyes have narrowed, as if he's taking Jar seriously for the first time.

'Was her father a spy?' Jar asks. 'Or more important than that?'

He watches Max absorb his words, looks for a flicker of recognition. Was the same thing ever said to him? If it was, he's not letting on.

'I'll give you the short answer. The long version might still be on the dark web, but I doubt it. The site that published my story has probably been closed down.'

'By whom?'

Max raises his eyebrows, as if it's too obvious a question to answer.

'I went to a redbrick, Warwick. Oxbridge wasn't for me. It wasn't for a lot of people who went there, as far as I can tell. Have you ever looked at suicide statistics at Oxbridge?'

'Can't say I have.'

Max wiggles a finger in his ear, vigorously. 'My point is that a lot of the country's brightest students are also the unhappiest.' Rosa used exactly those words in her diary, Jar thinks, when she was quoting Karen. 'Several individual cases caught my eye – the ones whose bodies were never found.'

Jar wishes he had tracked down Max earlier, but he never had a name. And he never came across his article. The dark web was always a no-go zone during his research, a place of moral turpitude and depravity. He should have been braver.

'There were certain coincidences – connections between the suicides and Rosa's father. Not big ones, but enough to work on. Evidence that those unhappy students might have met him in the months before they "died". I was convinced they were being given another chance in life. I just couldn't prove it. Rosa's body's never been found, has it?'

'It hasn't.'

'I can't offer you closure here, Jar, if that's what you've come for. My conspiracy theories are only going to make matters worse. Stir things up that perhaps should be left to rest.'

'That's a risk I'm prepared to take. Will you help me find Rosa?' Jar pauses, looking up at Max. 'I may have the proof you were looking for.'

28

Silent Retreat, Herefordshire, Spring Term, 2012

Day two of our silent retreat and I've listened to Maggs talk about mindfulness for most of the morning, practised an hour of t'ai chi, meditated (woken by a Tibetan gong at the end), taken a two-hour walk along Hatterall Ridge on my own and, er, signed the Official Secrets Act...

I'm still not sure I've done the right thing. I shouldn't even be writing about it here, but as no one's ever going to read this, I guess it's OK. (And I'm soon going to be taught encryption skills, making this diary even more private.)

Karen said everything would become clear shortly. And I suppose it has. In short, next term will be my last at Cambridge. (It feels *so* good to be writing that.) Instead, I've got an opportunity to work abroad for a while – with plenty of time to grieve. Then I'll see how I feel – about the job I've been offered, university, Dad.

It was after the meditation session that Karen found me, said she wanted to have a chat. She took me to a small room near the kitchens, overlooking what was once a walled garden, closed the heavy oak door and we both sat down. She pulled out a sheaf of paper – the Official Secrets Act – and put it on the round table between us.

Outside, a wood pigeon was calling. Dad loved birds, was a bit of a twitcher. 'You know what a wood pigeon is saying?' he asked me once, as we lay on the newly mown back lawn.

'Tell me,' I said.

'"My toe bleeds, Betty. My toe bleeds, Betty."'

'Don't be alarmed,' Karen began, observing me look from the window to the formal paper, the crown symbol. She touched my forearm and left it there for a moment. 'A very special opportunity has arisen,' she said.

'What sort of opportunity?'

'I must ask you to sign this before we can continue.'

'Are you serious?' I turned the paper around so I could read it.

'It's an indication of how highly they rate you.'

'Who's they?'

Karen didn't say anything.

'You mean you can't tell me?' I laughed, hoping that a smile would break over Karen's face, that she would explain all this was a joke, some new kind of treatment – espionage therapy – but she remained silent, her features set. I returned her gaze, stilled by its seriousness, glanced back down at the paper and read the first paragraph:

```
A person who is or has been a member of
the security and intelligence services, or
a person notified that he is subject to the
provisions of this subsection, is guilty of
an offence if without lawful authority he
discloses any information, document or other
```

article relating to security or intelligence
which is or has been in his possession by
virtue of his position as a member of any of
those services or in the course of his work
while the notification is or was in force.

'It's just a precaution,' she said.

So I signed it and listened to the wood pigeon again, wondering what I'd done, what this retreat in Herefordshire was
really about. I told myself that Dad must have signed it a
hundred times. *My toe bleeds, Betty. My toe bleeds, Betty.*
Had Sejal, my roommate, signed it, too? Was that why we
weren't allowed to talk to each other?

Over the next ten minutes, Karen gave me a few basic
details about the opportunity, explaining that I would be
based abroad, on American territory, and would spend the
first six months after the end of the summer term undergoing
tests and training. The salary, in her words, was 'competitive'
– something of an understatement. I won't be maxing out on
my credit card again.

'Once your core competencies have been established and
analysed, you will be given a more specific brief,' Karen
added, sounding more like a management consultant than a
counsellor.

'Would I be working for the intelligence services?' I asked,
looking at the Official Secrets Act again. The opaqueness of
the information she'd given me was frustrating, as was the
wording of the Act.

Karen ignored my question. 'If you're happy with what
I've told you, you will shortly be taken to another place, not
far from here, where you will be given more information. If
not, you'll be returned to college, where you will explain that

you've been on bereavement leave. At this stage, it's my job to establish your basic compliance with the offer that's been made to you.'

'And remind me exactly what that offer is?'

Karen could have been annoyed by my tone, but she was happy to run over the details again, like a waiter repeating the daily specials. 'You will leave Cambridge at the end of next term and spend a year abroad, first being trained, and then, as you embark on your new life, working in a role that cannot be discussed with anyone – friends or family, boyfriends.'

I'm sure she knew the effect her words would have on me, my delight at never having to return to university again.

'If you accept, you will have to break off contact with everyone,' she said, as if reading my thoughts. Did I blush? 'Are you close to anyone at the moment?'

I paused. 'No,' I said. *My toe bleeds, Betty.*

29

'Jar, it's two o'clock in the morning.'

'I know. I'm sorry. Can I come round?'

'What, now?'

Jar knows he's asking a lot of Carl, but he needs to talk about the latest entries from Rosa's diary. And, despite himself, he can't shake off the nagging thought that Carl is more involved with Kirsten than he's letting on. Why did he invite her to join them for a drink?

Half an hour later, he's sitting on the floor of Carl's flat. It's a small space, made more cramped by the records that take up every inch of the place: stacked on Ikea shelves, rising up from the floor like vinyl stalagmites. There's a faint smell of weed.

'Do you remember her ever mentioning a retreat in Herefordshire?' Carl asks, handing Jar a mug of tea. He's wearing a Congo Natty T-shirt and boxer shorts.

'Possibly. I remember her telling me she once went away from college for a few days, to clear her head. I think it was a mindfulness retreat of some kind. And Herefordshire rings a vague bell. It was before we met, her second term.'

'Are you surprised by how depressed she says she was?'

Jar glances across at Carl. It's a question that's troubled

him for the past five years, how he might have missed her depression, mistaken it for grief.

'There were times when she was not herself. Her moods were up and down, for sure.'

'But you never thought she was suicidal?'

'It wasn't in her nature.'

'But it was in her mother's.'

'She was more like her dad.'

Jar turns away, thinking again about the latest diary entry. Rosa had been protecting them both from something else, a new beginning. It fits with the email she left him – *I just wish I didn't have to leave you behind, babe, the first true love of my life and my last* – and is a less painful reason than suicide. She'd been swept up in something that she couldn't get out of.

'Her counsellor made her sign the Official Secrets Act, Carl. Tell me that's not weird.'

'Patient confidentiality.'

Jar looks up at him, his childish smile, and then casts his eyes down, ashamed that he ever doubted his friend.

'I don't know what to think here, bro,' Carl says, sitting at the table. He starts to read Rosa's diary on his laptop. Jar emailed him the last few entries, about the Herefordshire retreat, before coming over. 'Does it really change anything? Rosa was offered a job. Usually that happens when you graduate, but in this case they went two years early. She was a talented student, one of the best. And it wouldn't be the first time that the intelligence services recruited from Oxbridge. But Rosa didn't take up the job, because she died, Jar; because she chose, tragically, to take her own life. Nothing changes.'

For a moment, Jar knows that Carl could be right, but he pushes the thought away. 'I met someone today who was

investigating Rosa's dad before he died. He used to be a journalist, now works in crisis PR.'

'And?'

'He wrote a story that none of the newspapers would publish. It was about the number of student suicides at Oxbridge
and other top universities. Rosa's body wasn't the only one
that was never found. There were others.'

'And why didn't anyone publish the story?'

'He couldn't stand it up.'

'Maybe because it was bollocks.'

Again, Jar knows that Carl could be right. He under-
stands where his friend is coming from, can't blame him for
his scepticism.

'He thought the student suicides were connected in some
way with Rosa's father, that they had all met him in the
months before their deaths.'

'Why would they do that?'

'Because they were being given an opportunity to begin
again, make fresh starts, new lives. Just like Rosa says in
her diary.'

'The story wasn't published, Jar, because it sounds far-
fetched. The intelligence services do a lot of dodgy things, but
they don't go around faking student suicides and giving them
new identities.'

'Rosa's father worked for the Foreign Office, the Political
Unit. It's a common cover for spies.'

'So?'

'The article *was* published.'

'I thought you just said it wasn't.'

'On the dark web. And I need you to help me find it.'

'That's not how it works. You can't google things on the
dark web, Jar. That's the whole point.'

'There must be a way. Please?'

'The dark web gets such a crap press,' Carl continues. 'Sure, it's full of assassins and arms dealers, drug smugglers and grotesque human dolls, child abusers and Silk Road black marketeers – they're all down there. But there are plenty of things that aren't so bad about it. The Arab Spring began on the dark web. Bloggers in Beijing use it to get round the Great Firewall of China. The *New Yorker* has a site – Strong-Box – for whistleblowers. And if you're into Stravinsky, there are fifty thousand pages dedicated to "emancipated disso-nance" – I wrote about it last week.'

'The journalist mentioned something about a hidden site with an onion-suffix address.'

'That's a start.'

Jar watches as Carl minimises his email window, sighs and fires up his Tor software.

'Welcome to onionland,' he says, rubbing his hands on the sides of his boxer shorts in anticipation.

'Onionland?' Jar asks.

Carl gives him a withering look. 'Where every domain name ends in "dot onion".'

Jar was hoping that his friend might rise to the challenge. He's heard a bit about Tor ('The Onion Router'), how it con-ceals IP addresses, allows people to communicate anonymously over the internet, but he's never tried it. Edward Snowden used it to spill the beans – ironic, given Tor was originally developed in the 1990s with funding from the US Navy.

Two minutes later, Carl is diving the dark web, looking through various index pages of Tor hidden services – the Hidden Wiki, TorDir and TorLinks – that list an array of websites. As far as Jar can tell, it looks like the 'surface web' he's familiar with.

'The spooks hate the anonymity of Tor, of course,' Carl says, to himself as much as Jar. 'One of the NSA documents Snowden revealed – using Tor, natch – was a slideshow entitled "Tor Stinks". But it's not infallible. Sure, it can protect your site from traffic analysis – analysing patterns in communication – but it can't do shit about correlation attacks, if someone can see both ends of the communications channel, you and the destination website.'

Not for the first time, Jar hasn't a clue what his friend is going on about, but he is happy to let him talk. 'If there's a whistleblower element to this spy site, then it might also be accessible with a standard web browser using Tor2Web.'

It's just after 4 a.m. when Carl finally finds the article. Jar is asleep on the sofa.

'Yes, boy!' Carl shouts, slapping his leg. 'Got you.'

Jar sits up and stares across at the screen, bleary eyed.

'It's on a Tor hidden site for spy junkies,' Carl continues. 'Membership required, restricted access. Took a while, but I got us in. Do you want me to print the article out?'

'I do. Thanks.' Jar is standing beside Carl, staring at a passport photo of Rosa on the screen. She's one of six people in a grid entitled 'Student Suicides'. Next to her is an Asian girl called Sejal Shah – the same name as Rosa's roommate in Herefordshire.

Jar hasn't seen this photo of Rosa before and wonders where it was taken. He looks at it for a moment longer before turning to read the text below:

A high-ranking British Foreign Office official has links to a covert US intelligence programme that is suspected of recruiting some of Britain's brightest – and unhappiest – Oxbridge students with the promise of giving them new identities, Max Eadie reports. Suitable students are identified by college counsellors and then sent on a 'retreat' to Herefordshire, home to the headquarters of the SAS, before their suicides are faked and they are set up with new lives.

Taken on its own, it sounds far-fetched – 'bollocks', according to Carl – playing to its online audience of conspiratorial spy junkies. But there are too many similarities with Rosa's diary for Jar to dismiss the story outright: the mention of a possible recruitment centre at a military base in Herefordshire, the use of counsellors and student welfare services at top universities to identify suicidal students who might be ripe for recruitment. And the naming of six students, including Rosa and Sejal, as possible recruits.

None of the students' bodies has ever been found.

30

Silent Retreat, Herefordshire, Spring Term, 2012

Things moved quickly after I agreed to sign the Official Secrets Act. Karen told me to pack my bag and left the room with the document.

Ten minutes later, a black car picked me up at the back of the country house, in a courtyard that was once, presumably, reserved for servants and tradesmen. There was just a driver, and Karen and me in the back.

No one saw the car arrive, and no one, as far as I could tell, noticed us leaving. The rest of the students were deeply relaxed – sleeping, perhaps – in one of Maggs' meditation sessions in the main library at the front of the house.

'Have you taken everything from your room?' Karen asked. She was distracted, looking out the window as if checking to see if anyone had seen us leave.

'It's all in my bag,' I said. Except the chocolate, which I'd finished off with Sejal last night. I wondered again if she had also signed the Official Secrets Act. She'd left first thing in the morning. I hadn't thought to ask where she was going and she hadn't offered an explanation.

'Are we going far?' I asked.

J. S. MONROE

'No.' Karen was no longer herself: distant, on edge.

Soon the car was waiting for a barrier to be raised at the entrance to what looked like army barracks.

'Where are we?' I wasn't expecting an answer.

'Don't worry. You're not joining the army.'

The barrier closed and a man in uniform with a moustache and a weapon at his waist watched us drive past. He wasn't smiling.

It certainly beat turning up to a lecture, but there was still a strong air of the sort of institutional orderliness that I was hoping to have left behind. I'm not suited to orders, uniforms, acronyms. There were Ministry of Defence signs everywhere I looked, displaying unintelligible letters and numbers.

'This is the only time you'll be in a military environment,' Karen said, sensing my anxiety. I need to work on my acting skills.

Ten minutes later I was sitting in what felt like a classroom with five other students: the only one I recognised was Sejal. I'm not sure any of the others were at the retreat.

Karen was standing in front of us, with a man I was sure I'd seen before, but I couldn't think where. He glanced around the room, his eyes resting on mine for what seemed like a long time. There was something about him that was vaguely familiar. Had he been at the garden party that Dad took me to at Buckingham Palace?

'I want you all to meet Todd,' Karen said. 'I know the last few days have been kind of strange, but I think you'll realise what safe hands you're in once Todd has explained a little more.'

Todd smiled, pausing before he spoke. Late forties, chinos, open-necked shirt; looked like nothing could faze him. Time on the ball, as Dad would have said.

'It's very good to see you all,' he began. 'Truly.' For some reason, I was expecting him to be British, but he spoke with an East Coast accent, much like Karen's. 'I'm going to keep this short as there will be a lot for you to take in today. First off, welcome. Welcome to the Eutychus programme. Seriously, it's a privilege to be among such gifted students.'

A slight shuffle of feet, hands through hair. What's Eutychus? I caught Sejal's eye. She smiled.

'A unique opportunity lies ahead of you all, a second chance, something that very few of us are given in life. You will shortly have a choice: whether to embrace that chance wholeheartedly, or return to your old lives. It's a big decision, the biggest you'll ever make. In the meantime, put it out of your minds. You've all come recommended by your colleges, by Karen, but we've also been watching you over the past few months, analysing your mental strengths and weaknesses, your spiritual wellbeing, demeanour, character. Believe me, no one's gotten here by chance.'

We didn't look at each other that time. I think we were all taken aback at the thought of having been watched.

Dr Lance has had more of a hand in all this than I realised. I'm not worried, though. Todd's a reassuring presence. And I can't help but feel flattered that I've been chosen.

'We'll be running some more tests over the coming days. We're confident we've got the right people, but there's a chance that one or two of you will have to leave us. It would be a tragedy if anyone took that personally: you've done exceptionally well to get this far, trust me.'

Sejal had raised her hand. 'Can I ask a question?'

'Be my guest. There'll be a lot of questions in the coming days.'

'Are we going to be working for the American or UK government?'

'Do you have a preference?' Todd's manner was light and breezy, but I could see that underneath he was irked by Sejal's question. 'Last time I checked, we were allies.'

'Just curious,' Sejal said. I admired her sassiness.

'For the record, you'll be working for both. I hope that answers it for you.'

Sejal glanced over at me. We both knew very well that it didn't, that there will be more questions than answers in what lies ahead.

31

'You look tired,' Amy says, sipping on a coffee. Jar had gone back to check on his flat and the lock-up after seeing Carl, worried that he might have been burgled again (he hadn't), and then headed out to meet Amy at a café in Greenwich Park – her choice of venue. It's exactly a week since they met in Cromer. Once again, Jar has felt followed – a man at the far end of his carriage on the Docklands Light Railway looked over in his direction once too often – so he got off at Mudchute, walked through the tunnel under the Thames, to the *Cutty Sark*, and continued up to the park on foot.

'I've never thanked you for giving me Rosa's diary,' Jar says, sitting down at the table. He glances around the café as Amy pours him a coffee from a cafetière. Her hand is trembling.

For a moment, he thinks a man being served a pot of tea at the counter is the same person who boarded his train at Canary Wharf.

'Are you still seeing your American therapist?' Amy asks, not picking up on Jar's mention of the diary.

'I've had a couple of sessions on her couch,' he says, taking one more look at the man at the counter before focusing on Amy. He doesn't know whether to tell her about Kirsten, his theory that she's the same woman who counselled Rosa at Cambridge.

'How about you?'

'I'm hopeful the therapy's working. I'm slowly weaning myself off all the medication.'

'That's good. What's the story with Martin?'

'The police released him as soon as they got back what they wanted,' she says. 'It was a joke and they know it.'

'Is he OK now?'

Amy looks down. Jar notices the red-raw cuticle on her index finger. Rosa only spoke once about her aunt's marriage, hinting at an unhealthy imbalance.

'He's still furious with me for getting someone to look at my computer,' she says. 'For getting him arrested. Keeps saying I should have asked him to fix it. But he's always too busy.'

'In his shed?'

Amy nods at him and then turns away. Jar remembers their domestic set-up from his visits to Cromer: the large Victorian house on the edge of the town, Martin's 'shed' at the bottom of the garden, a no-expense-spared office where he seemed to live day and night, working on his big novel, when he wasn't out cycling.

'The police arrested me, too – after a session with my counsellor on Harley Street. Risky business, therapy. A fella called Miles Cato interviewed me at Savile Row police station about the hard drive. Ever heard of him?'

Amy shakes her head. She doesn't seem surprised that Jar was arrested, as if it was to be expected, which Jar finds disconcerting. 'Did he ask about Martin?'

'He suspects him of possessing indecent images – level four.'

Amy sits back. 'So why don't they charge him?'

Jar can't help wondering if she's not sure either. 'They think the incriminating evidence is on the hard drive. I guess they haven't been able to access it yet.'

Amy sits up, leans in towards him, for the first time looking animated, like Rosa used to. 'You do realise this has nothing to do with any obscene images, don't you, Jar? Martin's arrest, your arrest, Miles Cato. It's about Rosa, her death,' she continues. 'There must have been something in her diary.'

She's asking a leading question, desperate to know more, but Jar's not sure where to start. Before the entries began to arrive, there was still a chance that he was deluded, that the authorities' interest in the hard drive had nothing to do with Rosa. But the contents of her diary have changed everything.

He begins by telling Amy about Dr Lance's initial concern for Rosa, and then her meeting with Karen, the college counsellor, but he doesn't mention the likeness with Kirsten, his own American therapist. Not yet. Carl's words – *it's just a coincidence, Jar* – are still ringing in his ears and he has no wish to undermine his case. Amy is listening, leaning in.

He talks about Rosa's trip to the retreat in Herefordshire, signing the Official Secrets Act, being offered a second chance in life. And then he tells her about Max Eadie's story on the dark web, its striking similarities with Rosa's diary.

'I checked online,' Jar says. 'Sejal, her roommate in Herefordshire, "died" a few weeks after Rosa, body never found.'

'Be careful, Jar,' Amy says, resting a hand on his arm. Jar looks away, glancing around the café, and then turns to her, holding her gaze.

'Can I ask you something?' he says.

'What's wrong?'

'Did Rosa ever talk about us, as a couple?'

'Of course. Why?'

'This sounds pretty vain,' Jar begins, before checking himself. 'She doesn't write about us very much, that's all. In her diary. For sure, there's stuff in there about how we first met, but she never—'

'Jar, she loved you,' Amy says, taking both his hands in hers. 'With all her heart.'

'Nice of you to say so, but—'

'I remember her telling me once, before she began at Cambridge, that she hoped she would find someone there to share the rest of her life with. Just like Jim had found her mother when they were students together. It didn't happen for a while – she was still missing Jim too much – but then, one day, in the summer term, when she came up to Cromer on her own, she took me aside, breathless with excitement, and told me that she'd found that person. We hugged for a long while, cried a bit and laughed. I insisted that she brought this lucky man along the next time she visited. Which is how you and I met.'

32

Cromer, Summer Term, 2012

I'm feeling low tonight. I had hoped that getting out of Cambridge with Jar and staying with my aunt might help, but my downers are getting darker, and each time I wonder if I'll ever manage to resurface. It's like slipping over a cliff into an expanse of black material that has no limits and wraps you up as you fall, shutting out the light until you can see nothing but blackness and there's no longer enough air to breathe. My only solace is that it will all soon be over. I know I've made the right decision, even if it means leaving Jar behind and it won't bring Dad back.

Jar is asleep beside me – he drank too much whisky with Martin after dinner. They get on well, talk a lot about writing. Maybe I've missed something about Martin, placed too much on Dad's distrust of him. A part of me wants to share with Jar how low I am about Dad, but I feel so guilty about our relationship, knowing what lies ahead. In other circumstances, another life, he might have been a part of my future, but that's not possible now. I shouldn't have asked him to come up here with me this weekend.

Something weird happened when Martin picked us up

from the station in Norwich today. (He does all the driving because Amy's too much of a liability in the car, with all those meds she's on, though she's trying to wean herself off them now.) There was a pheasant lying in the road. I'm not sure if it was alive or whether the wind was just ruffling its feathers, but instead of avoiding it, Martin veered and drove straight over the bird, turning to me after the sickening thud beneath the car. None of us said anything. Jar thought I was making too much of it when we talked afterwards, said Martin was putting an injured bird out of its misery, nothing more, and I should give him a break. Perhaps he's right. Martin's just a natural loner, happiest in his own company, high up in the wheelhouse.

A few minutes ago, while I was lying here, I heard Martin and Amy arguing. Jar didn't stir. (He looks so at peace when he sleeps, it seems a crime to wake him.) Dad used to say he was amazed they ever got married, but then Dad was biased. He and Amy were very close. Dad was always the protective elder brother, particularly when she had a breakdown of some sort in her late teens – too much heavy partying, apparently.

It was never going to work between Dad and Martin. Dad had a thing about Big Pharma, said he'd seen so many horror stories in the developing world: unethical clinical trials, overpriced essential medicines. He said Amy had a natural aversion to it too, until her teenage neuroses blossomed into a full-blown anxiety disorder after uni. The stress of restoring famous paintings, I reckon – scratching away at a £10 million Brueghel with a scalpel and a microscope is enough to make anyone anxious. That's when Martin stepped in and 'saved' her.

She's a lot better than she has been, but she's still not back at work, which makes me sad.

Anyway, I tried to hear what Amy and Martin were arguing about tonight, but this is a big home ('the house that
Valium built', Dad used to joke) and our bedroom is on the
opposite side to the kitchen. So I crept along the landing,
past the bookshelves, also arranged alphabetically (Knausgaard next to Le Carré), and stood at the top of the stairs,
remembering not to step on one particular floorboard that
always creaks.

'You don't see her for years and now she's here almost
every weekend,' Martin was saying.

'I'm her only family now. We should have seen more of
her.'

'She sits in the back, like I'm her chauffeur, and says nothing the whole way. I don't know what Jar sees in her.' His
voice was heavy with resentment, unaware that Amy was
not being entirely truthful, that she and I used to meet up in
London for secret shopping sprees, encouraged by Dad, who
was acutely conscious of the need for a female influence on
my life. In my early teens, it was trips to Oxford Street to
buy bras together. Since Dad's death, it's been more drinking
than retail therapy, Amy showing me the Cambridge haunts
of her own youth.

'They did offer to take the train to Cromer,' Amy said.

'It would be all right if she contributed. Walked the dogs.
Cooked a meal. I can't understand why you bother.'

'It's what families are meant to do,' Amy said, seemingly
trying to salvage something from the conversation. 'Care for
one another.'

Then there was silence for a bit, maybe because they'd
moved to a different part of the kitchen, before they started
up again.

'I know this isn't an easy time for you,' Amy said. 'I get

that. I'm just saying it would be nice if you made more of an effort with her.'

A pause. 'If you promise to make more of an effort with me – us.'

Another pause, then Amy spoke. 'Martin, not now. We've got guests.'

Her voice sounded playful, but then a plate smashed. I listened, straining in vain to catch more of their conversation. Should I wake Jar, I wondered, go downstairs, check Amy's all right? Martin is tall and physically strong, but he's never lost his temper, at least not in front of me. I thought I could hear muffled sobbing, but perhaps I imagined it. I walked back down the landing to my room, no longer caring if the floorboards creaked.

Jar hooked a leg over mine when I slipped back into bed just now. I tried to tell him what I'd heard, but he was barely awake.

'All couples argue,' he managed to say, a smile waking his sleep-heavy lips. 'Except us, of course.'

33

'I owe you an apology. One too many.'

'We'd all had a few scoops.'

'It wasn't professional, I should never have come along.'

Kirsten is sitting behind her desk, Jar is on the sofa. She is back to how she was on their first meeting: buttoned up, businesslike.

'Can we move forward, as if the other night never happened?' she asks.

'We can try.'

'Great. I still have questions I'd like to ask about your post-bereavement hallucinations, for my research.'

Jar doesn't say anything. He knows that Kirsten didn't expect him to come to his morning appointment with her today, after they had got drunk together three days earlier, and he's had the upper hand ever since he rang her intercom on Harley Street. She played it well, he has to admit, hardly missing a beat as she let him in.

It feels strange being back in this high-ceilinged Georgian room, particularly as he knows he is about to confront Kirsten about Rosa, but he is quite calm. He's been thinking about today's meeting ever since he left Amy at the café yesterday. The only surprise is why Kirsten is persisting with the pretence for so long.

'Can we go back to the most recent sighting, when you saw her at Paddington.'

'Do we have to?'

'Excuse me?'

'Do we have to carry on like this? You acting like a sleeveen.'

'I'm not following you, Jar.'

Jar swallows. He is nervous now. 'I know about Karen.'

'Who's Karen?'

Jar's had enough. He gets up from the sofa and walks over to Kirsten's desk. He knows he's scaring her. He's scaring himself. He's not a violent man, never keen on confrontation, but something's just snapped: five years of frustration, other people's resolute disbelief.

'I lied. Last time I was here. Rosa did keep a diary. And she wrote all about you in it. How Dr Lance introduced you to Rosa, how you took her to the retreat in Herefordshire, got her to sign the Official Secrets Act.'

'Jar, I have no idea what you're—'

'Enough, now,' Jar says, slamming his palm on to the desk. They look at each other for a moment as the noise reverberates in the air around them, then Kirsten sets a mug upright that's been knocked over. Her hand is trembling. Does she have an alarm somewhere underneath the desk, he wonders, to ring when a patient goes postal? Are burly male nurses about to walk in and bundle him away in a straitjacket? Or maybe Miles Cato will appear from nowhere. After all, Jar knows she rang Cato last time he was here, arranged for him to be picked up in an unmarked police car on the street outside.

'I just need to find Rosa and I'm figuring you're looking for her, too, otherwise you wouldn't have tracked me down, changed your name, pretended it was chance that you met Carl and became my therapist and then tried to become my lover.'

Kirsten inhales deeply, as if she's calming herself. It's different from the telltale short intakes of breath she took before. She hasn't done that today, not yet. It's a while before she speaks and her eyes are closed as she begins.

'OK, you're right. I didn't find you by chance.'

Jar can't stop a sudden burst of satisfaction, punching out a sigh from deep inside him, more like a sharp cough. Her adamant denials had begun to sow little seeds of doubt. He walks over to the window and stands with his back to her, looking out through the blinds on to Harley Street, hands thrust deep in his pockets.

'So why all this pretence? The time-wasting? I need to know what happened to Rosa. Are you here because you think I might find her first? Is that it? That she might have grown disillusioned with her new life and be trying to get her old one back, to seek me out? Who do you work for, Kirsten? Karen? Whatever your name is? Who do you fucking work for?'

He turns around and then faces the window again, without pausing long enough to look at her. He guesses her eyes are still closed as she composes herself.

'OK, Jar, I'll tell you. I'm "working" for Amy, Rosa's aunt, if that's how you want to describe it.'

'Amy?' He turns around.

'We're friends. We were at Cambridge together, twenty years ago. She is very concerned about your welfare. You were dating her niece, after all. When she heard that I'm now practising in London, and still have an interest in post-bereavement hallucinations, she asked me to "seek you out", as you put it. I agreed. She once asked me to talk to Rosa.'

'Rosa? How long ago?'

J. S. MONROE

'When I was still in America.'

'And she was at Cambridge?'

'Yes.'

'But you never saw her.'

'No. Of course I now desperately wish I had. I guess it's why I said yes to Amy this time. She knows you're stubborn, not in the habit of accepting help when people offer it, so I approached Carl as a stranger, made up some story about music in therapists' waiting rooms, when in fact I'd been given his name by Amy. You'd mentioned Carl to her a few times, I think? And it was easy enough to contact him via your workplace. It was dishonest of me, but we both reasoned that the only way you'd agree to see a therapist was if you thought it was your choice, or at least on the recommendation of Carl, the one person you seem to trust in this world. And when I feared you wouldn't come to any more sessions, I joined you for a drink, which was totally unprofessional of me, but I was concerned for you. Just like Amy, who loves you dearly by the way.'

Jar turns back to the window. At least Carl isn't in on this, too, he thinks. He knows what's coming next and this time he fears she's not lying.

'I don't know anything about a woman called Karen, or a Dr Lance, or Herefordshire.' Her voice is quiet, calmer now, more confident. 'I have no idea what you are talking about. Truly.'

'But...' Jar knows how ridiculous the words sound even before he says them. 'Rosa wrote in detail about Karen, her therapist at college. She was American, had blonde hair...'

'There are a lot of us blonde Yanks about, you know.'

'And she...' He pauses again. 'She sometimes took a sharp intake of breath before she spoke, just like you do.'

His eyes are welling now, his voice more broken.

'That's not so unusual, is it?' she asks.

Jar gathers himself, wipes the back of his hand across his eyes. 'According to Rosa, Karen once used a particular phrase: "there should be no record, no contrails left in the Fenland sky". You said something very similar at our first meeting.'

'That's probably because I wrote a paper a few years back called "Post-bereavement hallucinations: contrails in the creative mind".'

Jar falls silent, trying to process what she's saying.

'When I was in America. My titles have become a lot more boring since then. More academic.' Kirsten comes around from her desk and joins him at the window, looking out on to the street. 'Do you want to talk some more about her diary? It seems to have stirred a few things up.'

Jar's old fears kick in again – why does she want to talk about the diary? – but this time he ignores them. He can already hear his father's voice: *yous been a feckin' eejit*. Misread coincidences as connections. It doesn't change anything, he tells himself. Rosa did have a therapist at college called Karen. It's just not the same person standing beside him now.

'I'm still off the clock,' she adds.

His phone is ringing in his jacket pocket, vibrating, on silent. He slips it out to see who it is.

'And if you don't mind me saying,' she continues, walking back to her desk, 'I've seen you looking better.'

But Jar isn't listening. To her, to the noise of people walking past on Harley Street, an accelerating car. All he can hear is the sound of his own deafening heart, growing louder with each beat. He looks at the name showing on his phone again, in case he's imagining it. But he's not.

It's Rosa.

34

Cromer, Summer Term, 2012 (continued)

I couldn't sleep after I heard Amy and Martin arguing, haunted by the sound of the smashed plate. I still don't know all the details of why Martin retired early, but Dad had his theories: excessive cruelty to laboratory animals ('Beagle-gate', he called it), sexual harassment, medical grounds. Take your pick. The last one was his favourite (Dad had a dark sense of humour): he reckoned Martin left because he was suffering from chronic depression, which would have been deeply ironic, given he was researching antidepressants just before he was 'let go'.

At about 2 a.m., I decided enough was enough. Sleep was not going to happen. So I slipped on jeans and a jacket, opened my bedroom door and crept down the stairs, careful not to wake Jar.

My life would be so much more straightforward if I hadn't met him. Jar's complicated things in the brief time we've known each other, muddied the waters. The way forward was once so clear to me, but he's introduced an element of doubt, made me question at times whether I've taken the right decision. When I'm with him, I feel happier than I ever thought possible, but I scare myself with my ability to disconnect the moment we're apart. It seems I can erase him from my thoughts like deleting a file. I know there's no turning back.

I unlocked the back door and walked across the flagstones at the rear of the house. It was a clear night and there was enough moonshine to make out the garden – a manicured lawn (Martin's big on stripes), then a long, narrow orchard, bordered on either side by high, drystone walls. Beyond the apple trees, more than five hundred yards from the house, I could see Martin's 'shed'. It's a proper garden office, about the size of a double garage, with windows looking out across the garden. My plan had been to go down Hall Road to the beach – about a twenty-minute walk – and watch the rising sun from the pier, but curiosity got the better of me. Instead of going through the side gate, I stepped out on to the lawn, keeping to the shadows of the wall, and looked back at the main house. All the lights were off.

I carried on walking, through the orchard, ducking under branches weighed down with ripening fruit, until I was standing to one side of Martin's shed. There was a padlock and chain on the door. His computers were stolen a few years ago and he's obviously taking no risks now. I glanced back at the house again and then moved up to the windows and peered in. There was an open area, with a few garden chairs stacked up inside, and beyond it a partition wall. A pale red light was seeping out from under a door to what must be a second room. I was about to walk away when I heard something: a whimper, perhaps, more animal than human. I strained my ears, listening for the sound again as the hairs pricked on the back of my neck, but there was nothing. I'm imagining things, I thought.

I walked back up the garden, taking less care to stay in the shadows as I lengthened my stride, slipped open the side gate and set off down the road towards the town, shaking off the fear that had descended on me like a fog. The two beagles stay in the house, sleeping in Amy and Martin's bedroom at night. 'Martin doesn't walk his dogs, he takes them for a drag,' Dad used to joke. Not funny, when you think of puppies being forced to inhale cigarettes. God, I miss Dad more than ever.

Down in the town, I headed straight for the beach and picked my way along the sand, close to the water's edge, stepping over the groynes that punctuate the shoreline at regular intervals as I looked for shells. It was almost 3 a.m. and the moon was so strong, it cast shadows.

There was no one around – I couldn't even see any boats on the horizon – so I decided to go up to the Hotel de Paris and walk down the pier, past the Pavilion Theatre and on to the end, by the lifeboat station, where I'd seen dads and their kids fishing earlier in the evening.

I'll apparently know when the time's right. This was not that moment, but I still felt a surge of adrenaline as I leant against the railings and looked out to sea, relishing the salty wind on my face. I gripped the rusting iron, but then I stepped up on to the first rail and stood there, with nothing to stop me falling into the sea far below. It was a calm night, but a strong current was swirling around the pillars of the pier far below. I started to feel dizzy. For a second, I wondered if perhaps the time had come, but there is still much to be done. I want to put everything in order, leave no loose ends, write to Jar, explain what I can, which is very little. Say my goodbyes.

I stepped down off the railing and headed back up Hall Road towards the house. My legs were shaking.

35

'Who is this?' Jar says, looking up and down Harley Street. He is standing on the pavement, outside Kirsten's consulting rooms, talking into his phone. 'Why are you ringing from this number?'

There is only silence on the other end of the line. His first thought is that someone has managed to get hold of Rosa's phone – it has never been found – but as he listens, his anger gives way to hope. The silence feels female.

'Rosa?' he asks, almost whispering, waiting for the call to disconnect at any moment. 'Is that you?' He listens, for the sound of breathing, anything, but there is no noise. He hangs up and leans back against the door, eyes closed.

When he opens his eyes, he sees Kirsten at the front window, looking across at him. He walks away, down towards Oxford Circus.

'Wait, Jar,' he hears her call after him, but he doesn't turn. He's still not sure Kirsten is being straight with him. A moment later, she is at his side.

'Who was on the phone?' she says, struggling to keep up with Jar.

'What's it to you?'

'I'm worried, Jar. It's my job.'

'Last time I visited your office, I was picked up by the police. I hope you'll understand why you being here now is making me a wee bit jumpy.' To confirm his point, he looks up and down Harley Street as he walks on.

'That had nothing to do with me. Was it Rosa on the phone?' she asks.

Jar stops on the pavement and turns to her.

'Was it her?' she repeats. 'Rosa?'

'Why would you think that?'

'Because of the way you reacted. I've seen it before. I can help you, Jar.'

'You think I imagined the call? Is that it?'

'Grief manifests itself in many ways, Jar. I don't doubt that someone called you.'

'But you don't think it was Rosa. What's that, then?'

He holds his phone out, Rosa's name clearly displayed on his list of received calls. Kirsten looks at it and then back at Jar.

'Her phone must have been found by someone and they rang me by mistake. A pocket call. It was her phone – her number is still in my contacts – but as everyone keeps telling me, she died five years ago.'

He is offering an explanation for his own benefit as much as for hers. His mind hasn't stopped racing from the moment he saw her name displayed. Of course it wasn't her, he tells himself, walking on.

Kirsten hasn't given up and is still jogging at his side. 'Come back tomorrow morning,' she says. 'I'll be in early. Please. I can help you.'

Jar walks away, sensing that she is watching him until he disappears into the crowds.

His phone rings again as he approaches Oxford Street. It's Carl.

'Are you coming into work?' Carl says. 'I can't keep making excuses for you.'

'Can you locate a phone for me?'

'I told you to turn on your "Find My iPhone"—'

'It's not mine, Carl. It's Rosa's.'

Carl pauses before he speaks. 'Where are you?'

'I need you to ask your friend at the phone company.'

'We've been through this before, Jar. Her phone's dead.'

It's true. In the early days, Jar asked Carl the same favour, after he was woken by a call on his phone in the middle of the night. The caller ID had been blocked, but Jar, half asleep (and possibly still drunk), had lain in his flat in the darkness, listening to Rosa talk to him about all the good times they had spent together. When he awoke in the morning, he thought it had been a dream, but he checked his phone and he had accepted a call from an unknown number at 2.05 a.m. that had lasted twenty-five minutes. He rang Carl, who had an old college friend who worked in the IT department of Jar's mobile-phone provider, but there was no trace of Rosa's handset on the networks.

'Someone's just rung me on it,' Jar says now. 'The caller ID said Rosa, just like it used to when we were at Cambridge together.'

There's a pause on the other end of the line.

'Did they say anything?' Carl asks. His voice is quiet, more supportive now.

'Nothing. I'm guessing it's been found by someone.'

'Five years is a long time.'

'Maybe they put the SIM card into a new phone. I don't know, Carl. You tell me.'

'Let's talk when we meet. You are coming in, aren't you? The boss is giving me hell, like I'm personally responsible for your continuing absence.'

'I'll talk to him. Now will you call your friend? Please?'

'Only if you promise to come into the office.'

'Sure. And Carl? You were right about Kirsten and Karen, Rosa's counsellor at college. It was just a coincidence.'

'There's a surprise.'

'But we were both set up, by Rosa's aunt. Kirsten didn't come into our lives by chance. Amy arranged it – thought I needed help.'

There's another long silence before Carl speaks. 'You mean she's not playing Congo Natty to her patients?'

'Not this morning.'

'And it was such a good story. You still seeing her, then? Professionally, I mean?'

'I've just been lying on her couch.'

'I'll call you. About the phone.' Jar detects a certain weariness in his friend's voice. 'But you are coming in?'

'Promise. And thanks. For everything.' Carl's gone the distance in recent days, trawled the dark web, put up with more conspiracy theories than usual, covered for him at work. Jar's about to hang up when he spots someone across the street. It's the man who sat in the café opposite the office, there's no doubting it's him this time. 'I'm coming in now.'

36

Please forgive me, Jar. I tried to call you earlier today, but I couldn't bring myself to talk. Not after all this time. It was good to hear your voice. So good. And I don't blame you if you've moved on with your life. But it's important we talk. It's best, I think, if we meet face to face and then I can attempt to explain everything from the beginning.

Meet me where I said I'd go if the world ever slipped off its axis. Do you remember the place? I can't risk writing its name here. I'll be waiting for you. At least give me the chance to explain. You're not safe and nor am I. Take care, babe. Always.

37

J ar stares at the screen and then checks behind him. The message in his email inbox – his own private gmail account, the one he's had for years – is so unreal, he wonders if an audience is watching him and he's not in the office but on stage in some tasteless reality TV show.

Meet me where I said I'd go if the world ever slipped off its axis. Do you remember the place? I can't risk writing its name here.

Jar glances across at Carl, who is typing, punching at his keyboard with podgy index fingers. When he looks back at his screen again, he expects the message to have gone, but it's still there. He reads it slowly, from the beginning, mouthing each word, and when he gets to the end he reads it again. And again. It's her language – she wrote something similar in her diary, after her father's funeral – and it's her old gmail account, but is it from her?

Think, think. He stands up at his desk, running a hand through his hair, looking around the office. Carl glances up at him and then returns to his own screen. Somewhere in the deep recesses of his troubled mind, Jar has a memory of a conversation with Rosa about a place of retreat in times of crisis. *If the world ever slipped off its axis.*

Still standing, he leans forward, scrolling through the diary, reading random, flickering snapshots from their conversations at Cambridge. Then he looks again at the email. It means only one thing: Rosa is alive. The phone call was from her too. She's trying to make contact, remind him of a crazy rendezvous plan she once told him about. If only he could recall where it was.

'Are you all right?' Carl asks.

'I'm good,' Jar says, but the blood is draining from his face. He sinks down into his chair, feeling nauseous.

'Don't worry about it. Just tell him the truth, that you've been unwell.'

He's not been off sick, but Jar lets it go. He is due to see his editor in ten minutes, explain why he has only written one story – best celebrity 'nudies', as opposed to 'selfies' – in the past week. He'll try to bluff his way through the meeting, but he fears the worst. At least if he's out of a job he'll have more time to find Rosa. His life has changed irrevocably, nothing else matters now.

And then he remembers. The night he met Rosa for a drink at The Eagle. She'd been with her actor friends, but they'd gone off in a group, leaving her behind. Rosa had rung him, feeling abandoned. She was worse for wear when he found her, talking about a report in the news about a meteorite that was going to pass close to earth.

'I know it's due to miss us by a few hundred thousand miles,' she said, nursing her pint of bitter, 'but if, say, something like that ever did happen, and the world got a fright, jumped a little and slipped off its axis, you and I need to have a plan.'

'What did you have in mind?'

'Somewhere we could go, away from all the chaos, far

from the cities. A place where we could shelter together, in a post-apocalyptic world.'

She took several runs at apocalyptic – 'acopalyptic', 'alopa-cyptic' – before giving up and burying her head in Jar's neck, giggling, her eyes closed.

'Galway's got a lot going for it,' Jar said, putting an arm around her. Her actor friends had behaved poorly, he thought, should never have left her behind.

'Galway's too far,' she said, perkier now, sitting up, one hand resting high on Jar's leg. 'And planes won't be flying – there'll be dust clouds in the atmosphere.'

'You've really thought this one through, haven't you?'

'There's a place in Cornwall where Dad visited after Mum died. And I went there after his funeral. Somewhere to hide – and heal. We should meet there.'

She turned to Jar, looked at him with her big eyes. She had never mentioned her mother's death before. He was about to ask her about it when she leant forward and kissed him, a long, slow, drunken kiss.

'It's named after a pig-ugly fish – the gurnard – but it's one of the most magical places in the world,' she said, sitting knee to knee with Jar now, holding both his hands in hers. She leant in to kiss him again. 'It's really important you remember this,' she chided and then hiccupped. Jar smiled, still not listening properly, thinking instead how beautiful she looked tonight, a touch of the capricious Carmen about her. 'Are you concentrating? You never know when we might need an emergency rendezvous in life.'

'I'll remember.'

She took a sip of her pint and continued. 'You get down to this place by a steep track – after you've had a drink at a pub at the top. Bright yellow-ochre walls, can't miss it. There's a sandy beach at low tide – some delicious hidden coves – but it's best to walk on around the bay, past the remains of an ancient chapel, and up to Gurnard's Head. You'll see some big rocks on the headland, and a place you can hunker down, out of the wind. Shall we meet there? We could watch the seals below, maybe even porpoises if we're lucky. The air is so pure.'

'Gurnard's Head,' Jar says.

'What's that?' Carl has stopped typing and is looking at him.

'I've got to go.'

'Jar, you're seeing the boss in five minutes.'

'He's only going to sack me. I've got a train to catch,' he says, breaking into a run.

But before he's reached the exit, one of the regulars from the post room stops him. 'Sign for this before you go, Jar?'

Jar takes the package – a book for review, he assumes – and runs out of the office.

38

Silent Retreat, Herefordshire, Spring Term, 2012

It's the last day of our briefing in Herefordshire. Tonight we return to our colleges, start to put our affairs in order – and wait.

Todd told us everything this morning. We were all called into the classroom again, where we first met him, and he treated us to a run-through of the whole programme. He was more relaxed than before, I think because our numbers have been thinned. Almost half of us have been 'allowed back' to our colleges early, leaving only the chosen few.

39

Jar checks the email folder on his mobile again, hoping there might be another message, but there's nothing. Just one item in the drafts folder: a brief diary entry that appears to have been cut short.

He looks up at the platform indicator on the concourse at Paddington. The next train to Penzance departs in an hour, leaving him just enough time to see Anton. It will take him twenty minutes to get from here to the skate park at Ladbroke Grove. He wants to thank him – and ask about the latest entry, why it's incomplete.

No one seems to be around when he reaches the skate park, so he makes his way over to the shipping container where he came with Carl six days ago. It's even messier than before. Is this where Anton decoded Rosa's diary? The computers have gone, though, just boxes of skate wheels, trucks, tools, scooter bars, broken decks, scattered everywhere.

'Can I help?'

Jar spins round. A man he recognises from the ticket gate is staring at him.

'Is Anton about?'

'Who's asking?'

'A friend – of a friend. He was helping me with a computer problem.'

'He ain't now.' The man picks up a skate deck from the ground.

'Is he OK?'

'Ask the Feds.'

'The Feds?' Jar repeats, dread rising in him.

The man smirks. 'He left in a hurry. Last night. Took all his computers with him.'

Jar's heard enough. Two minutes later, he's walking under the Westway, towards Ladbroke Grove Underground station, talking on the phone.

'Carl, it's Jar. Anton's disappeared.'

'He does that sometimes.'

'I think it's the diary, Carl.'

Jar hangs up and turns into the Underground. As the train draws into Paddington he remembers the package in his pocket. It's not a book. Inside is one sheet of official-looking A4 paper, covered in type. On the top of the sheet are the words: 'TOP SECRET STRAP 3, UK EYES ONLY'. The sheet has been wrapped loosely in cardboard packaging, which was why he thought it was a paperback. He checks the carriage, his heart quickening, and begins to read.

40

Programme: Eutychus (US)

DoB: 08.11.1992

University: St Matthew's College, Cambridge

DoD: 01.07.2012

CURRENT STATUS: Global SIS station heads informed. Border Agency also alerted. No immediate next of kin. Deceased father's sister in Cromer and a former boyfriend in London under 24/7 (A4/MI5).

41

Tucking the sheet of paper into his jacket pocket, Jar looks around the carriage. He doesn't want to be seen reading a confidential document if he is under surveillance. There's nothing unusual about the man standing at the far end, by the door's open window, he tells himself. Just a regular commuter, getting some air, who happens to be looking in his direction. And the woman on her phone, catching his eye and turning away?

Who in the name of the Holy Mother Mary couriered this to him? *Relax*. He should have checked with the post room. There's nothing on the envelope apart from his typed name. Could it have been sent by Rosa? *Breathe*. It's her date of birth and death and it name-checks Eutychus, the programme she mentioned in her diary, and refers indirectly to Jar. If she's been a part of a covert operation for the past five years, she must have had high-level access, got good at reading things she's not meant to see.

It looks genuine enough, but he's never been privy to raw intelligence, just a few documents that he's read online, courtesy of Edward Snowden. He gets off the Hammersmith and City Line train at Paddington. His stomach churns when the man and woman do the same. As he accelerates down the ramp to reach the main station concourse, he feels so sick he's almost giddy. Then his phone rings, cutting through his lightheadedness. It's Max Eadie. Jar wants to tell him everything, about the memo, Anton's sudden disappearance, but Max speaks first.

'Jar, we need to meet.'

'Everything OK?' Jar asks, trying to ignore the tension in Max's voice.

'I've finished going through the diary.'

After much deliberation, Jar gave Max the password to the email account Anton's been using. He figured that he couldn't expect Max to help unless he shared everything he knew with him, including his late girlfriend's private diary, sitting in his drafts folder.

'And?'

'We need to meet. Today. Now.'

Jar looks around him again. The woman has vanished, but the man still seems to be following him.

'I'm at Paddington. About to board a train.'

'Don't. I'm in the West End. I'll be there in fifteen minutes.'

Max's serious tone worries him. Jar was hoping the diary might provide enough evidence for Max to resurrect his article, iron out the inconsistencies, republish it. But he sounded far from vindicated on the phone just now.

Jar puts away his mobile and sets off in search of somewhere to photocopy the document in his jacket pocket, as a precaution. After finding an office shop on Praed Street, where he makes a copy, he returns to the station.

The main concourse is packed, even for a Friday afternoon. An incident of some sort has delayed trains leaving the station and commuters are milling around, waiting for information. If he misses this one, he'll have to catch the overnight sleeper service and find Rosa in the morning. (It's more expensive, but it was payday this week.) She won't sleep out at night on the headland. She'll stay at the pub, where she can keep an eye on people walking down to Gurnard's Head.

He glances at his watch, takes in the group of smokers standing just outside the station. He could do with a cigarette right now. His whole body feels taut. And then she is at his side.

'Don't even think about it,' Rosa says, smiling. Jar stands there, stunned, hoping that if he doesn't move, she might stay. But she's already gone. At least she seemed well, her eyes radiant, like she used to look at university, not how she was when he saw her rushing for the train the last time he was here at Paddington. He knows it was a hallucination, but it gives him hope. She's not far away now.

Five minutes later, Max Eadie is walking towards him in a creased linen suit. 'Shall we walk?' he asks, his voice still serious, urgent. 'I hate crowds.'

'Me too.' As they pass the diaspora of smokers, back up towards Praed Street, Jar turns to him. 'I think someone followed me here today.'

'Are you serious?'

'My friends say I'm paranoid.'

'How many?' Max continues to walk on, buttoning the middle of his bulging jacket as he quickens his step. 'On your tail?'

Before Jar can reply, Max has broken into an unlikely run and jumps on to the back of a passing red Routemaster bus. Jar follows, hopping on to the footplate just as the double-decker pulls away.

'That should buy us a few minutes,' Max says, trying to conceal his breathlessness. 'Upstairs.'

Jar wants to ask him what he's doing, but Max is already mounting the stairs, two steps at a time. They take the front seats – the only other passengers are two older women at the back of the bus – and look down on to the Edgware Road as the bus makes its way towards Marble Arch.

'If we're dry-cleaning properly,' Max continues, without explanation, still breathing heavily, 'we should get off at the next stop, cross the road, catch another bus in the other direction, walk quickly through it, hop off again at the front, hail a taxi, and head into heavy traffic. But I'm too old for that.'

'Have you done this kind of thing before?' Jar asks. He is already prepared for Max to reveal that he once worked as a spy, too.

'I've always thought that espionage and journalism make easy bedfellows: we're both in the business of getting people to reveal things they shouldn't. It doesn't surprise me you're being followed. We might not have long,' he adds, more serious now. 'There's something you need to know about Rosa's diary.'

'Did it help? With the article?'

'Not exactly. Do you remember Rosa ever talking about going on a retreat?'

'Once. It was before we met.'

'Anything else?'

'It was a passing remark, nothing more.'

'She didn't say where it was?'

'It might have been Herefordshire. I can't be sure.'

Max pauses. 'I'm not proud to say this, but there were – how to put this? – elements of my story for the website that were... elaborated... adorned... embellished.' He coughs theatrically. 'Made up.'

'Like what?' Jar asks. 'Much of it seemed to tally with Rosa's diary.'

'That's what's worrying me.'

'I'm not getting you here.'

'You've read the article. I believed – and continue to believe – that a number of student suicides at Oxford and Cambridge were suspicious. Bodies never found. And I wrote that these students had been recruited by the intelligence services through a network of welfare officers and college counsellors.'

'Which is what Rosa's diary implies.' And the document burning a hole in his jacket pocket, Jar thinks, but he says nothing about that. He doesn't know Max well enough yet to show it to him, doesn't quite trust him.

Max is holding up his hand like a traffic policeman as he glances around the bus, checking to see if anyone can overhear them. 'I also wrote that the students were sent off to a retreat outside Hereford—'

'That fits with what Rosa said, too,' Jar interrupts.

Max clears his throat again, as if he's about to confess a crime. 'And that some of them were subsequently transferred to a secure site on the military base currently occupied by the Special Air Squadron.' He pauses. 'That's the bit I made up. Informed guesswork – not my finest hour. A local told me the retreat's owner was American and had a Special Forces background, nothing more. It surprised me at the time, didn't fit in with a retreat. But I knew if I got the SAS into the story, preferably in the headline, it would sell. That was my hope, at least.'

'What do you mean, you "made it up"? Rosa—'

'I know. She implied in all but name that she was taken to the SAS headquarters. I'm not proud, Jar, but I had no proper evidence to support that part of the story. All I knew was that some unhappy Oxbridge students were once taken off to a spiritual retreat outside Hereford.'

'It doesn't mean some of them weren't actually transferred to the SAS base.'

'I'm sorry, Jar. I don't think you quite understand what I'm saying here. I have no idea who wrote the diary, but whoever it was had read my story and copied some of the details.'

'But that's not possible. Rosa wrote it.'

'My article was published on the dark web in July 2013 – a year after Rosa died.'

'I remember the things she describes in the diary, our times together. Breakfast after the May Ball, skinny-dipping in the Cam, the first time we met in the restaurant. No one else could have written those words.'

Max pauses before he answers as their bus sits in heavy traffic, so still that Jar wonders if its hybrid engine has cut out. But then it shudders into life and the bus pulls away. Below them, a group of men sit outside a café, smoking hookahs, watching passing commuters with a mix of indifference and disdain.

'I'm really not sure what to think, Jar. It was all a long time ago and my research was sketchy at best. I was under a lot of financial pressure in those days, desperate to get the story published somewhere. It was one of the reasons I switched to PR. What I do know is that there was no counsellor at Rosa's college. I did a lot of digging around, made quite a nuisance of myself with the porters. Her dean, Dr Lance, was a well-known recruiting officer for the intelligence services, but I couldn't find any evidence of a counsellor or welfare officer at St Matthew's. Which was odd. I chose to overlook that in my story, focused on the colleges that did have counsellors.'

'But Rosa writes a lot about Karen. She can't have made that up.' Jar tries to ignore the fact that Rosa never talked to him about any counsellor either; that he too had never been able to find evidence of a Karen at St Matthew's or prove that Kirsten was Karen, as he had first thought. 'That must help your story – it gives you something new, a reason to republish it.'

'All I know for certain is that the part I fabricated – about the SAS – has somehow found its way almost word for word into Rosa's diary.' Max falls quiet before speaking again. 'There's something else, too.'

'What?' Jar asks, but Max remains silent. 'Tell me.'

'The name of the American who owned the retreat. I didn't want to use his real one in my story so I made one up – I was on shaky ground, remember.'

'What name did you give him?'

Max pauses. 'Todd.'

'The instructor Rosa mentions?'

'I'm sorry, Jar. I think someone's playing you.'

42

I shouldn't be emailing you like this, Jar, but if we meet, we won't have long together. They'll find me. I know they will.

I don't know where to start, how to explain the choices I made. I owe you so much more than an apology, but let me at least begin with an explanation (I hope you got the document I sent to your office). You knew I was unhappy at college, but I never told you how low I felt, the dark days. When I was with you, the sun came out and the trees in the Fellows' Garden were shiny, like they were after heavy rain, but when we were apart, the storm clouds returned and I was ready to end it all.

Do you remember Dr Lance? The college dean and Goethe expert? A good friend of Dad's, too. He was the one who set this all in motion, spotted my unhappiness and offered me the chance to start again. He and Karen, our college counsellor, the American blonde all the boys fancied. And I took that opportunity, shut out what you and I had together and looked to the future, to my father. Because the first thing they told me was that Dad had been part of a programme to help unhappy students. I don't think I would have signed up if he hadn't been involved – it felt like a way of getting closer to him.

The work was dull at first. I can't say where we were, because just the mention of the name of the programme in this email would make the next few hours even more difficult than they will be (even though I'm using 'onion routing' to send this – you wouldn't believe what I've learnt, Jar). But once we'd finished our training it became interesting.

The only problem was that they were training us to discover things we weren't meant to find out and one day, a few years into our new lives, I learnt something about my father that changed everything. Dad had made a discovery that he shouldn't have. He found out that people like me, British students recruited from Oxbridge, were deemed ultimately expendable by the Americans who were running the programme. We were dead already, as far as the outside world was concerned, so what was the problem if we died again? We were disposable, ideally suited for the more dangerous missions. Dad was about to blow the whistle, but they stopped him, made it look like a car accident in Ladakh. From the moment I found out, I was looking for a way to escape, but you can't just leave. It's not like that.

One day, though, an opportunity arose – they made a mistake – and I took my chance. I thought I was free when I finally reached the UK, but I realise now they were just watching and waiting to see what I would do. The Americans took me in after a couple of days and I was kept in isolation on a US airbase – in the UK, I think; I wasn't flown anywhere – for months, maybe years. It's hard to tell. They tortured me, body and mind.

But then, last week, I managed to escape again. I was out, on the run. I still am.

I need to see you, babe, prove to you that I'm alive. If we manage to meet, however briefly, you must tell my story. They'll take me back and I'll disappear, most probably be killed. I'm dead already, so nobody will care. But at least you now know and it's up to you what you do with this knowledge. Find me, Jar, at the place we talked about, where we'd go if the world ever slipped off its axis.

43

The two people appear on either side of Jar as he reaches the ticket barriers for the night train to Penzance. Jar recognises them at once: the man and woman whom he had suspected of following him when he boarded the Underground train from Ladbroke Grove to Paddington.

'Someone wants another chat,' the man says, locking his arm in Jar's and steering him away towards the taxi rank beside Platform 1. The woman moves in on the other side just as a car pulls up, the two of them lifting Jar's feet off the ground as the rear door opens.

Miles Cato manages a thin smile from the far seat. 'Sorry about the cloak and daggers,' he says, as Jar is bundled into the car.

Jar stares straight ahead as they drive off into the London traffic, shocked, too angry to say anything or to be afraid, still thinking about the email he was reading on his phone a few moments earlier. There's just the driver, separated by a thick glass screen, and Miles in the car. The man and woman have stayed on the pavement, melting into the crowds.

'I don't think you quite realise what or who you are dealing with here,' Miles says, after a pause. He too is looking ahead. Jar wants to tell him that he has a good idea who he is dealing with, that he knows Cato is more than a policeman and that this is about Rosa, but he says nothing.

'It's an addiction, an illness. We've been following Martin for quite some time now. People like him operate in syndicates. They share indecent images on the dark web, hundreds of thousands of them. And they'll do anything to get more. This is not some online fantasy – real lives are at risk here.'

'I don't know what you're talking about,' Jar says, his voice shakier than he would like.

'Try to see this from where I'm sitting, Jar. We get a tip-off about Martin and his computers. When we investigate, it turns out he just happens to have given you one of his hard drives that might contain crucial evidence. You reluctantly hand it over to us, but not before it's been heavily encrypted. Odd, by anyone's standards, don't you think? Some would say wilfully obstructive. I'm trying to give you the benefit of the doubt here, Jar. Others might not.'

Jar tells himself to hold on to what he knows. The email he's just read from Rosa; the confidential document in his jacket pocket; the earlier anonymous phone call; Rosa's diary; Max's story...

'Can we stop this charade?' Jar says, raising his voice. 'Stop pretending that your interest in the hard drive has nothing to do with Rosa and her diary. I know what happened to her, where she went.'

There's a pause while Cato checks his phone for a text, letting Jar's words wilt in the stuffy air. He's good at this sort of thing, Jar thinks, his technique honed over many years in windowless interview rooms.

'I'm sorry about Rosa,' Cato eventually says. 'And your struggle to accept her death. It can't be easy. But that really is not what I'm here for. I just need access to the hard drive.

And I need to know why you asked your friend to encrypt it. As things stand, we've got grounds for charging both you and Anton with impeding a criminal investigation and possible complicity to commit a crime under the Sexual Offences Act.'

Jar turns away, trying to shut out the possibility that Cato is telling the truth and has no interest in Rosa. They seem to be taking in a wide loop of Paddington, up the Edgware Road and back down behind the station.

'Last night we paid Anton a visit,' Cato continues. 'We need him to show us how to remove the encryption from the hard drive, or better still, hand over the unencrypted copy he was using. Only he seems to have disappeared, gone to ground. Any idea where he might be?'

'Why don't you just go ahead and arrest Martin?' Jar asks, wondering if Cato is bluffing, if Anton is already being interrogated about the diaries.

'We don't have enough evidence yet to bring charges against him.' Cato pauses. 'Understand this very clearly, Jar: you need to get a message to Anton, tell him to make contact. For both your sakes. Apologies if you've missed your train.'

They are now back at Paddington. The rear car doors unlock automatically. Jar knows it's a mistake, but he can't stop himself, can't prevent his arm from bending at the elbow and his hand slipping inside his jacket pocket. He wonders for a moment if Miles thinks he's about to pull a gun on him, but he doesn't flinch, doesn't show any reaction at all, even when Jar pulls out the confidential memo he was sent. It's an irreversible escalation, a rash decision to show all his cards, but Jar can't let the pretence carry on any longer.

'You need to understand how much I know,' Jar says,

handing it over to Cato. He's glad he made a copy, which is in his other pocket. 'This isn't about Martin. It's about Rosa, who wants to come back. And if you and your people continue to follow me around, try to stop me finding her, there are others who are aware of the Eutychus programme, who know that Rosa is alive.'

Jar is bluffing now. Only Carl knows, and Max, and he's not even sure if he can be trusted.

'How did you get this?' Cato says, taking the memo. Jar looks across at him, desperate for a sign, something to tell him he's right. Cato is almost whispering – has the air been knocked out of his lungs? The colour has drained from his boyish cheeks, his normal equanimity replaced by hesitation. Or is Jar just willing it to be so?

'That would be telling. Herefordshire, Karen, Sejal – I am aware of everything that you persist in denying. That's Rosa's date of birth, by the way,' Jar adds, stabbing at the document, breathless now. 'And here's her date of death.'

'You know you are in breach of the Official Secrets Act by being in possession of this.'

At last Cato is taking him seriously, Jar thinks. 'So I'm giving it back to you, handing it in, being a good citizen now. It's lost property, like all those laptops MI5 keep leaving on trains.'

'This is Strap 3, the highest.'

'It was a very serious thing that Rosa did,' Jar says, trying to control his breathing, desperate for Cato to drop his act, come clean with him. But Cato says nothing, wrong-footed by the turn of events, Jar tells himself, the incontrovertible evidence now in his hands. What can he do? Arrest him under the Official Secrets Act? That would only prove Rosa was still alive.

'Just one thing,' Jar says, opening the car door. He needs to get far away from Cato, who is still looking down at the document. Why the hell hasn't he reacted more, made a call, told him he's been right for the past five years of his life? 'If you find Rosa before I do, be gentle with her.' He banishes the thought that Cato is only interested in Martin. 'She means quite a lot to me.' He is on the pavement now, leaning into the car. 'I'll never forgive you if you're not.'

44

Tread carefully with MC. I've learnt enough over the past five years to know that he will be the one who approaches you, if he hasn't already. He will probably be using police cover, plain clothes. And he loves a good Scottish accent. I have no idea what story he will spin, but don't believe a word of what he says. He's trying to find me, just like the others.

The Americans will be pressuring British intelligence to do all they can to locate me. Needless to say, the programme will be over if it ever becomes public, along with the careers of all who are involved in it. Rather puts Snowden's revelations in the shade, doesn't it? And it would probably spell the end of the Special Relationship, too.

It's important that we meet, however briefly. Come soon. I'm scared, Jar, scared that they will take me back to where I've been kept. Killing me will be a mercy.

45

J ar stands by the carriage door, breathing in the salty sea
air through the open window. The train is snaking around
Mount's Bay, drawing up to its final destination, the railhead
at Penzance. St Michael's Mount is to his left, its fairytale
castellations rising out of a blue pall of sea mist. Above him
mournful gulls are wheeling.

Rosa used to speak about arriving on the sleeper in Penzance with her dad when she was young. In those days, you
could put your car on the train, too. They would head off
along the coast road in their VW camper van, driving through
Newlyn to Mousehole, where they'd stay in the net loft her
mum had inherited.

Jar's plan is to take the bus, picking one up from the stop
opposite the station. He will have to go to St Ives first, and
then change on to another bus that will take him along the
north coast, past Zennor, to Gurnard's Head.

At Paddington, after he left Cato, he'd done what he could
to shake off any further tails, but he didn't have Max's inside
knowledge of 'dry-cleaning'. How did Max know all that
stuff anyway? Jar had boarded a late train bound for Swan-
sea on Platform 5, where the ticket barriers were open, and
sat there for as long as he dared. A minute before his night

train to Penzance was due to depart, he had leapt off, run round to Platform 1, ignoring the guard's shouts to stand away, and jumped on board.

Breathing hard, he had lowered a window and looked back down the platform, waiting for the train to move off. But there was a delay of some sort. It was as if the train was mocking him, his paranoia. Jar told himself this was a futile line of thought and moved away from the window. Embarrassing 'cloak-and-dagger' stuff, as Cato had called it. What was he thinking? This wasn't his world. No one was following him. And then he took another look out the window. A tall man was showing his ticket to the guard, gesticulating towards the train. An argument ensued. Jar glanced at his watch. The service was two minutes late already. It was nothing, he told himself, but then the man pushed past the guard and ran towards his carriage. Jar pulled back from the window, as if he'd seen another train coming, before daring himself to look out again. The train was finally moving.

It was the man he'd spotted so often in the café opposite work, no question, and he was now almost level with Jar, the open window. They looked at each other, Jar transfixed, still trying to calculate if there was any way this man who had been following him for so long could board his train as it slowly gained speed.

Jar pulled up the window. His pursuer was younger than Jar had imagined, early thirties, rash-red skin, small gimlet eyes, and his face was out of balance in some way, swollen, contorted perhaps with the effort of running, and devoid of all emotion. As he realised the futility of the situation and fell further back, his features collapsed, punctured by exhaustion and despair. It was odd, but Jar sensed the man had no personal animosity towards him as he watched the train move away, just a sense of professional failure. He had lost his target.

It was only as the train sped through Reading, twenty-five minutes later, that Jar had finally felt calm enough to move away from the window and take his seat. The first stop was Exeter, which he was already dreading, but the rest of the journey passed without incident. At each station, Jar looked out for the same man on the platform, in case he had somehow managed to catch up, but he was nowhere to be seen and no one else caught his eye. Maybe it wasn't the man from the café. Maybe it was just some regular fella trying to catch his train to Cornwall.

Now, as Jar walks out of the station in Penzance on a bright Saturday morning, he glances at the people clustered at the entrance, waiting for friends and family to arrive for the weekend. If Jar wasn't so tense, he would have stopped to take in the scene: the thick granite-walled station marking the railhead, the limits of Victorian endeavour. No station is further west than Penzance. He has a sudden yearning to be back home in Galway. Perhaps it's the smell of the sea, the big skies.

Outside in the sunshine, a taxi driver, standing by the door of his car, raises his eyebrows in hope, but Jar keeps going to the bus stands beyond. The next bus to St Ives is in twenty minutes, so he heads across to a café, where he orders a bacon sandwich. Again, no one seems to be following him.

Nursing a mug of dark tea, he looks around the café, thinking about the man who had tried to board his train. He must be working for Cato, whose role in all this is to find Rosa and shut down the case afterwards – silence anyone like him who might know too much. His police inquiry into Martin is just a cover, as the latest email from Rosa confirmed.

He recalls his conversation with Max, the suggestion that

he's being played by someone. It doesn't seem possible, particularly since the emails have arrived. Rosa is on the run from her captors, hiding out at Gurnard's Head, where she is waiting for him. *If the world ever slipped off its axis...* He swallows at the thought of seeing her after all these years, pushes Max's scepticism away.

An hour later, Jar spots the bright yellow-ochre walls of the pub at Gurnard's Head, standing out like a beacon of hope. Or maybe it's a warning sign, he thinks. He has been on edge ever since he changed buses at St Ives and is now the only passenger. He rises to his feet.

'The pub?' the driver says. He sounds northern, Jar thinks.

'Thanks.'

'Cracking cream tea further on. Rosemergy, about a mile or so,' the driver continues. It's the first time they've talked and Jar wonders why it's taken so long. 'Best in Cornwall – cream on top, of course.'

'I might well try it now.'

Jar stands on the roadside, watching the bus disappear into the barren moorland landscape. He should have talked to the driver more, enjoyed the company of a fellow human being, but he doesn't trust anyone any more. There is no one around and the pub looks shut up. Then, behind him in the distance, he hears a car approaching from Zennor. He steps into the shadows of the building, to one side, by a track, and watches as the car, a racing-green Mini, slows as it passes the pub. Jar can't see the driver, whose head is turned away. He waits until the car has disappeared over the horizon before he steps out again.

The pub turns out to be open and at the bar he strikes up a conversation with a young barmaid. At first it's about cream teas, rumours of top scones nearby. It's good to be talking. He's spent too much time inside his own head in recent hours. She too recommends the place down the road, letting her jade eyes linger on his a moment longer than necessary for an exchange of information about tea.

Jar smiles, notices how good-looking she is: tanned, sunbleached hair tied at the back. 'I'm also trying to find a friend,' he says, turning a beer mat in his hands. 'A woman in her early twenties, black hair, big eyes.'

The woman looks up, her smile more muted now, professional rather than personal.

'I was wondering if she was staying here,' Jar continues.

'Only couples at the moment,' she says, checking the book in front of her. 'And a family, two kids.'

Jar nods. Of course she wouldn't be staying in a pub. What was he thinking?

'Thanks now.'

As he turns the handle on the front door, she calls out to him. 'We did have someone in last night.'

Jar stops, his hand resting on the side of the door.

'A woman on her own, been walking the coast path. I think she's camping.'

'How old?'

'Early twenties? Big eyes.'

Jar manages a smile, which is returned. Rosa loved to camp, used to go on camping holidays in the Lakes with her father.

The trek down to the sea is about a mile and Jar takes most of it at a steady run, feeling the sea air on his face. He tries to recall her description of this place, her crazy drunken contingency plan in case of a meteorite strike. Jaysus, how much he loves her, misses her mad mind.

There's a sandy beach at low tide – some delicious hidden coves – but it's best to walk on around the bay, past the remains of an ancient chapel, and up to Gurnard's Head. There are some big rocks on the headland, and a place you can hunker down, out of the wind. Shall we meet there? We could watch the seals below, maybe even porpoises if we're lucky. The air is so pure.

It might be pure, but the Cornish air is still busting Jar's lungs. He has allowed himself to get unfit in recent months – ever since Rosa died, if he's honest. His whole life has slipped: no interest in his job, too much alcohol, a lack of discipline. Rosa used to talk of huge hikes, he remembers, sometimes in the Lakes, once in Ladakh.

He stops at the bottom of the track, next to the ruins of a stone building overlooking the sea. This must be the old engine house for the copper mine that he'd googled on the train. To his right is a small, steep cove and ahead is a cluster of rocks. To his left is a big bay that sweeps around to a dramatic rocky headland: Gurnard's Head.

After glancing back up the hillside, he walks out on to the top of the cliffs, noticing some old iron girders embedded in the rocks. They look like bits of a winch or crane that must have lowered copper into boats below.

He turns and heads back to the ruined engine house, picking up a path that will take him around the cove and to the headland. Halfway there, he stumbles across the low remains of a wall: Chapel Jane, he guesses, its outline barely visible in the long grass. He pauses for a moment, wondering if Rosa has stood at this exact spot in recent days. She liked all that: Cornwall's ancient past, the wells and chapels, water springs and Iron Age fogous.

The coastal path is deserted in both directions as he walks on towards Gurnard's Head. Dark, ominous clouds are gathering in the north, over towards Zennor, but the headland stands vivid against what's left of the blue sky. Atlantic rollers are bursting against the rocks below him, throwing up spray that glints in the sunshine.

At least they will have some warning, Jar thinks, if someone has followed him down here. There is nowhere else to go, nowhere further to run, but they will have a precious few minutes to be together after five years apart.

Jar is nearing the tip of the headland now, walking down a precarious path that runs along the rocky ridge leading out to Gurnard's Head. It reminds him of Cleggan on the Connemara coast, that day he thought Rosa was walking by his side, when she called him a clumsy bogger. He smiles at the memory.

To his left, sheer cliffs and a two-hundred-foot drop to the sea below. To his right, a gentler slope leads to cliffs on the other side. There is an easier path there, through the grass, but he prefers the rocky route. He can see all around from up here.

It's only as he reaches the final outcrop of rocks, Gurnard's Head itself, that he acknowledges how nervous he feels. And how foolish. Why would she be here, of all places? He tries to run through the reasons again: she loved Cornwall, the land of her childhood; she feared meteorite strikes and once told him to meet her here if the world ever slipped off its axis. It's not enough and he knows it.

There's something else that has driven him to Cornwall, something he's been trying to put out of his mind ever since it happened. The woman standing on the escalator at Paddington, with the rucksack and shaved head, the woman boarding the Penzance train: it was Rosa, for sure. No post-bereavement hallucination, or projection of his own grief, or *spéirbhean*, as his da would have him believe. It was the woman he loved at university, who supposedly took her own life one night in Cromer and whose body has never been found.

He sees the tent first, low and floral patterned, pitched on a small patch of long grass in the lee of some rocks, overlooking the Atlantic. It could be anyone, he tells himself, moving forward, but he has seen that pattern before, swinging from a rucksack on the concourse at Paddington.

His first instinct is to look back to where he's come from, his gaze sweeping around the coastal path to the ruins of the old engine house at the foot of the track. The coast is still clear. Then he turns to the tent again, expecting it to have gone: another hallucination, brought on by five years of grief for a woman who never said goodbye. But it's still there, rippling in the sea wind.

Jar approaches the tent, cutting down through the rocks and tufts of grass, and is soon level with it. Is Rosa in there? He peers inside the open entrance. There is a roll mat, a sleeping bag and a rucksack.

He tries to control his breathing and turns to look around him. The headland is deserted. He walks over to the edge of the cliffs, where there is a path out to the furthest point, an exposed group of boulders below the big ugly rock that gives this place its piscine name.

There, sitting on a boulder, clutching her knees to her chest as she looks out to sea, is a woman, shaved head, baggy trousers, rocking gently. Her back is to Jar. He hesitates, feeling the pulse in his tired eyelids, and holds on to a rock to steady himself. His first thought is to call out her name, but he checks himself, in case it frightens her, in case she is not real. Instead he stares at her, perched on the edge of the sheer cliffs. Sometimes, when he has a hallucination, he shuts his eyes and opens them again, only for her to have disappeared. He closes his eyes and starts to count to five, willing her to stay. This time he knows she is real, that he has finally found her. At four, he opens his eyes, fighting back the tears.

'Rosa?' His voice is a whisper and the wind is against him. 'Rosa,' he manages again, louder this time.

She turns and looks at him, giving a distant smile, squinting in the sunlight. He has thought about this moment so many times. He wants to rush over, fold her in his arms, in case she disappears, fades *through the brightening air*.

'Beautiful, isn't it?' she says, turning back to look out to sea. A shudder of relief runs through him. It's Rosa. He's not hallucinating. 'I've seen so many seals today,' she continues, 'too many to count. We used to come here all the time. Dad had a way of talking to them, cupping his hands and blowing into his thumbs, making sounds more like an owl than a seal.'

'Rosa,' Jar repeats. He can already feel his euphoria slipping, giving way to a creeping dread. 'Rosa, please come away from the edge.'

Rosa stands up, almost stumbling as she does so, and steps back from the cliff face. Jar can't move as she picks her way down through the rocks and walks past him to the tent. Her eyes are cast down, as if he doesn't exist.

'I always forget to close it,' she says, squatting down to zip up the front. Jar stares at the back of her, trying to work out what's happening, take in her physical presence, the roll of her shoulders, the sound of her voice.

'Where have you been, Rosa?' he asks, watching her struggle to close the tent. 'Where did they take you?'

Rosa doesn't respond as she continues to wrestle with the jammed zip. 'Festival tent,' she says. 'Dad always said don't waste money on a cheap one. I think the zip's gone.'

Jar bends down to help. 'Here, let me try.' His hand brushes against the back of Rosa's, the contact making her real. A moment later, she is sobbing into his shoulder, her arms wrapped around him. Jar folds his arms around her, too, absorbing the shudders from her frail body, not daring to believe she is flesh and blood. Then he starts to sob. He knows he must stay strong, but five years of not knowing is way too long.

They stay like that for a while – ten minutes, half an hour, Jar cannot be sure, doesn't care – hugging each other in silence as they sit beneath the rocks, the wind whipping the tops off the waves far below them. Eventually, he pulls away and looks into Rosa's eyes, holding her face, smudging away the tears with his big thumbs. And then he kisses her lips. She turns away.

'I know everything, Rosa. And I don't blame you, for taking the chance to start again. I want you to know that.'

'It's true, then.'

'What's true?'

She looks at the ground. 'My life.'

'How do you mean?'

'Tell me, everything you know about me. Please.'

Jar searches her eyes, looking for an explanation and then turns away, realising there will be no quick or easy answers. She has the same distant look he saw in Amy: disengaged, lost.

He starts at the beginning, her unhappiness at college, Dr Lance, Karen the college counsellor, her trips to Cromer, the retreat in Herefordshire, the offer of starting over. Then he talks of how they met at the restaurant. Her reaction is the same: a blank indifference, deadness in the eyes. They are sitting close to each other, facing out to sea, but there is no intimacy.

Jar looks across at her again. If only he had trusted himself when he saw her at Paddington, for he is certain now that it was Rosa rushing for the train. He should have followed her to Penzance, trusted his instincts. So much of the last two weeks could have been avoided.

'Am I right?' he asks. 'About the Herefordshire retreat? Karen?'

She nods. Jar lets out an involuntary sigh of relief: no one's playing him. The diary was written by Rosa.

'I never knew how unhappy you were at college,' he says.

She looks away, out to sea.

'Of course I knew you missed your dad, I just didn't realise...'

'It's OK.'

Jar stares at her again as they sit there, the wind rippling her baggy trousers, a realisation mounting like nausea. She hasn't said his name yet.

'Rosa?'

She turns to him with the same look that she gave from the train: stranger to stranger. 'Yes?'

'Do you know who I am? My name?'

Tears start to well in her eyes again and she turns away. Jar puts an arm around her and, after a few seconds, she rests her head against his shoulder.

'It's Jar. My name's Jar. Jarlath Costello. We were at Cambridge together.'

'I know who you are, babe. Sometimes I know everything. Then it all clouds over.'

'What did they do to you, Rosa?'

It's a while before she answers. 'I was on my own.'

'Where?'

'I don't know, Jar. I don't remember ever being flown anywhere, but an airbase was mentioned. Lakenheath? I think someone once said Lakenheath.'

The US airbase in Suffolk, Jar thinks.

'There was a pale light. They shaved my head and I was forced to wear an orange jumpsuit. Day and night, food lowered down to me like they were feeding a dog.'

'How long were you there?'

'Six months, six years? I don't know, Jar. I'm sorry.'

'It's OK,' Jar says, cradling her. But he knows it's not.

'They are going to come for me again, aren't they?'

Jar glances across the bay. 'Did you tell anyone you were coming here?' he asks.

'No.'

'Have you got a phone?'

'No.'

'You're "off grid"?'

Rosa looks at him again, her eyes seeming to flicker with recognition at the expression. 'The pub has Wi-Fi, though,' she says.

She must have used it to send the emails, he thinks, borrowed someone's phone or iPad. 'They can't track you if you don't have a phone,' he continues.

'No. They can't.'

Jar stands up, looks out at the old engine house across the bay. A tall figure has appeared at the foot of the track. He tells himself to stop being so paranoid.

'Are you warm enough?' she asks. 'It's getting cold.'

'I'm fine,' Jar says. He sits down on the ground next to her, like two school friends on a park bench. He never meant their reunion to be like this, never thought it would be so mundane.

'So this is the place where we agreed to meet if "the world ever slipped off its axis",' he says, looking out to sea. 'I got your emails.'

She pauses, smiling at a distant memory. 'I've seen some shooting stars. No meteorites, not yet.'

'You wrote about it in your diary once but never said where it was.'

'I never told them,' she says. 'Our secret.'

And now I've revealed it, Jar thinks, as he looks across to the figure again, its familiar gait. His heart sinks. It's the man who tried to board his train at Paddington. He is walking at pace along the coast path towards the headland where they're sitting. Jar looks around him, searching for an escape route, but there is no place for them to hide, nowhere to run. The headland is surrounded by sheer cliffs and the sea. Jar's led Rosa's captors to her.

'You need to tell me everything you can about where you've been, what happened,' he says, his voice more urgent.

'It's all in my diary. My whole life's written down there.'

'Have you got it with you?' Jar doesn't know whether to tell her that he's already read most of it.

'I know it all anyway. They made me memorise a different entry every day.' She pauses. '"There was only one thing unnerving about Karen: she did this short intake of breath just before she spoke. It was as if she'd suddenly remembered to breathe. The more she talked... the more I couldn't help noticing it, until in my mind it became a deafening gasp. Dad would have found it funny."'

Karen, the counsellor who saw her at college, Jar thinks. The one she never mentioned to him. The one Max could never find any record of. 'Do you remember Herefordshire?' he asks. 'Going to the retreat?'

'Eating dark chocolate with Sejal.'

'And being briefed by the Americans?'

She pauses. 'I think so.'

This is what he needs her to talk about: the last, incomplete diary entry, the one that was cut short, in which she was going to reveal all.

'Can you tell me anything else about the programme? Eutychus?'

'Our nickname was "the invisibles". We were dead to the outside world, no one knew we existed. Dad never meant it to be like that. We were supposed to be given new lives, and we were, for a while, but the Americans...' Her voice tails off. 'They had other ideas, saw us as dispensable.'

'What was your new life like?'

It's a while before she answers. Jar tries not to be impatient. The man is almost with them now. Jar should have taken a train back to Paddington instead of coming out here from Penzance, led his tail down a few rabbit holes, taken him far away from Rosa and Cornwall. Instead he's brought him here, and they are trapped.

'There was a lot of training.'

'Encryption?'

'I don't remember.'

'Is that how you found out about your dad?'

'Then I escaped. I wanted to tell the world. But they caught up with me, put me in...' Rosa's voice breaks off again, her eyes welling.

'It's OK.' He cradles her in his arms, telling himself that she is real. Will they ever be together like this again? Just the two of them? He glances once more at the approaching man.

'Awful things happened,' she whispers. 'Like you never imagined.'

'To you?'

'He said he owned my soul.'

'Who did?'

Rosa pauses. '"When we save a human life, we own their soul..."'

'Was he part of the programme?'

Rosa appears not to have heard him. 'Then I was taken away.'

'To the airbase?'

She pauses again, this time for longer, and starts to sob. 'They tried to drown me.' Her voice is barely a whisper now.

'Jaysus, Rosa. I'm so sorry.' Curiosity is giving way to anger.

'You think you're going to die. The cloth in your mouth, pouring water. You can't breathe, so you panic, which makes it worse.'

Waterboarding, Jar thinks. An American speciality at Guantánamo. He wasn't aware it's also on the menu at Lakenheath.

'And then they...' Rosa whispers. 'Again, and again, and again.'

Jar closes his eyes, remembers Cato's words of warning. *I don't think you quite realise what or who you are dealing with here.*

'We have to tell the world, Rosa. Tell everyone what happened. To you, to your father. We need to prove that you are alive.'

'Am I?' She manages a weak laugh, a trace of a smile. Jar holds her tighter, in case she disappears.

'I hoped you'd come here,' she whispers. 'To our secret meeting place. I knew you would. It's one of the few things I did know about my life. My old one. We really had something, didn't we? You and I.'

'We need to take a photo,' Jar says. The tears are coming again. Her diary entries had begun to raise doubts as to whether their relationship was as strong as he remembered.

He pulls out his phone and holds it at arm's length in front of them. His hand is shaking. They lean in to each other.

'A selfie,' Rosa says, smiling.

'Quick. Look at the camera.'

He takes a photo and checks the phone.

'No signal. There was a signal.'

'Wait for the wind to blow,' Rosa says.

'We don't have time.' Jar stands up, holding the phone high above him like he's asking a question in class. 'One bar's enough.'

He has already typed in Carl's number. The photo is attached to the text, which just says 'Rosa and Jar today' with the date in brackets. He presses send.

'Jaysus, send, will you?' he shouts, watching the data wheel spin on the phone.

A moment later, the man has appeared on the rocks above them, silhouetted against the Blue Curaçao sky. He is wearing a black balaclava now and holding a handgun. Jar stares at him, trying to imagine the features underneath, the gimlet eyes, rash-red skin. Then he hurls the phone high into the air, over the cliff, and watches it twist and spin in the sunshine as it arcs out to sea and drops out of sight. A second later, the man has jumped down next to him. Jar steps forward to protect Rosa, but the man is too quick, whipping the butt of the gun across Jar's face. He falls to the ground, his cheek against the soft, mossy grass. He tries to get to his feet, to stop this man from taking Rosa away, but he can't move. His legs are heavy, his head spinning.

'Rosa!' he cries out. 'Rosa!'

He watches, helpless, as Rosa is led away across the rocks, her wrists tied behind her back and a cloth held to her mouth. He has failed her, he thinks. Then his world darkens.

PART TWO

46

'Did you get the photo?' Jar asks.

The young woman behind the bar at the pub, the one with the green eyes, is pretending not to watch him. Jar has offered to pay for the phone call, but she won't hear of it. She is more concerned by the gash on his forehead – received, he told her, when he stumbled on the rocky cliff path – and how long he was unconscious for.

'What photo?' Carl says.

'I texted you a photo of me with Rosa. Carl, she's alive. I've just been with her.'

'Are you prangin' out, bro? You don't sound so good. Where are you?'

Jar's aware of what Carl is thinking. His friend has had another episode, like the one at Paddington (he won't try telling Carl he knows that was Rosa too). Jar hoped the photo would clinch it, end all doubt, but Carl hasn't received it. Jar's sure the photo went through before he threw his phone over the cliff.

'Will you look at your messages again? Please? Are you sure it hasn't arrived? They can often take a while to go through. You can check the date and location on the photo when you get it.'

There's a long pause. 'Jar, listen, bro, there's no photo. To be honest, I've no idea what you're talking about. We've really got to deal with this, you seeing Rosa everywhere. Get yourself back to London, talk to the Feds and I'll make sure Kirsten sees you again – in a professional capacity.'

'You don't understand. This is different, Carl. You've got to publish the photo. Put it up on our website. Send it to a newspaper. Anything. Just get it out there as soon as it arrives.'

Jar glances up at the barmaid and forces himself to smile. He knows he's talking too fast, not getting enough oxygen into his lungs. His life never used to run at this pace.

'It might not look like Rosa, but it was her. She's shaved her head, lost a lot of weight. This wasn't a hallucination, Carl. Not this time. I've just been with her. Before they took her away.'

'Are you with anyone now?'

'Carl, listen to me. I'm fine. Rosa's alive. She's not well, but she's alive.'

Jar hangs up, holding the receiver firmly down on the base for ten seconds, maybe longer, extinguishing all life from it, as if he's drowning a kitten. When he takes his hand away, the barmaid is staring at him.

47

Cromer, 2012

I picked up Rosa from Norwich this morning. A insisted on it, despite the perfectly good, if slow, train service that operates between Norwich and Cromer. Rosa was more moody than ever – takes after her father. A says she's been through a lot in recent months, tells me that I'm being unsympathetic. I know I need to care more, but it's hard when someone won't accept help. I've talked to her about the benefits of benzodiazepines, but she's not interested.

My latest creative-writing task is to keep this daily journal, gradually mixing in some fiction with the facts of my unexpectedly early retirement. It's my literary Petri dish, before I start on the big novel. I'm to write it as if I'm addressing someone in particular, a person in a room. Like a letter only more direct: right up close, in your face. The danger is lapsing into an overly chatty style – 'first person on steroids', as my online tutor put it, in what I assume was a touching attempt to bridge the gap between my previous life in the lab and the writer's one that beckons. ('First person on nootropics' would have been more appropriate.)

I'd prefer to sit down with a published author for a few

hours rather than do all these tedious exercises. Last week's was the worst: compose a CV for each of your main characters. I thought I'd left the corporate world behind.

The good news is that Rosa's got herself a new man. He's evidently not doing a great job of cheering her up, but he has written a collection of short stories. They've also been published – and not by himself. I tried to extract some information from Rosa in the car, but she was even less interested in conversation than usual, so I looked up the book on Amazon when we got back.

I'm not sure it's quite my bag, but it's had a lot of five-star reviews. (Where would we be without friends and family?) I've already ordered my copy. If it's halfway decent, I'll invite Jar out one weekend with Rosa and shoot the literary breeze. My problem's not so much writing CVs for my characters, it's coming up with an original story. Maybe I just need to revisit existing material. Tell it in a new way.

My tutor also says that I should keep a notebook to write down character observations, snatches of dialogue and so forth, and feed them back into my journal. It's something I used to do before I went up to Cambridge, when I thought I would become an author and was trying in vain to write a beatnik novel, scribbling down things I'd overheard before passing them through the prism of peyote and other psychedelic alkaloids. So I bought a notebook in Norwich today, when I was waiting for Rosa to turn up (she was late, of course). It's a Moleskine. While I was there, I bought a new sketchpad too, in anticipation of next week's life-drawing class. A says it'll be good for me, all part of managing the midlife crisis she insists I'm having. I tried to get out of it, but she was adamant: I need to keep my mind busy. If only she knew.

Things are tense between us at the moment, not least because she's decided to see our 'changed domestic circumstances' as an opportunity to reduce the benzos and other medication that I've been giving her for the past twenty years. 'New beginnings,' she keeps saying, although she hasn't actually told me that she's trying to come off her pills and I'm pretending not to have noticed.

No one should be on anxiolytics for that long, of course, but it's managed her anxiety disorders over the years. And, as I've told her many times, coming off them is no simple matter: it has to be done slowly and carefully to avoid crippling withdrawal symptoms, which tend to mirror the benzo's primary benefits: sleeplessness rather than hypnotic effects, anxiety rather than calm, tension rather than relaxed muscles.

I'm also around the house a lot more, even if I'm mostly down here in my shed. I've explained that I've signed up for a writing course in a bid to rekindle the passion that once made me consider reading English at Cambridge. It's the first step on the long road to becoming a published author, I told her, but we both know it's not enough to justify the amount of time I'm spending here. She's too decent to challenge me about it, accepting that I need space to sort out my head after I was 'let go'. (I prefer 'fired': there's a sense of propulsion, going places.) If I could eat, drink and sleep alone in this shed, I would.

I thought that having time to focus, finally, on what I've always wanted to do in life – write a novel – would be a tonic, but I've forgotten that putting words in the right order on a page is a slow, painful process, after years of dealing with data. I've always kept up my reading, devouring several books a week, but it's no substitute for the process of writing.

If I'm honest, I spend more time surfing the web than working on my book, keeping up with former colleagues (today I've been reading the latest on serotonin 2c receptors in *Molecular Psychiatry*) and, OK, comparing my cycling times with others on Strava. That's the one good thing about the writer's life: the scope for endless displacement activities. There are more hours in the day for getting out on the bike, for example. But not as much as I thought there'd be: the internet's a distracting place.

48

I started to file my nails today. It wasn't intentional, not at first. One of them snapped off when I was hammering my fists against the wall.

I looked down at my other nails, some broken, one removed, several extending by almost half an inch, beginning to curl up like peel, and remembered showing my hands to Dad before Sunday lunch (roast beef, homemade horseradish sauce, just the two of us). He used to take my fingers in his and turn them as if they were the most precious objects in the world. What would he think of them now?

So I rubbed them all against the walls until they were smooth. Jar had beautiful hands, nails like polished marble.

49

J ar keeps having to check himself as he walks back down the track to Gurnard's Head. The barmaid – she's told him her name is Morvah – is struggling to keep up with his long, purposeful strides, breaking into an occasional jog at his side.

He bounced around the pub for half an hour until Morvah's shift finished at 4 p.m. After she'd fetched a bandage for the bruise on his head and fastened it with an oversized safety pin, her gentle hands lingering afterwards, he'd sat at the bar, drinking Guinness, trying to calm himself down, telling her about Rosa when she wasn't serving customers. She had listened patiently, throwing him suggestive glances that might, in different circumstances, have stirred something in him. Jar was happy to be distracted when the conversation turned to literature. She read a lot, when she wasn't surfing, she said: Proust, Joyce, Sebald.

He'd enjoyed talking to her until he'd seen Rosa, sitting in a corner. She was gone again in a blink, but not before Jar had caught her frowning. He knew it was a hallucination, but it stopped him in his tracks. He was drunk, pretending to admire authors he had never read. And still speaking way too fast. Carl was right: he sounded like he was on amphetamines. His mind was all over the place after he'd spoken to his friend on the phone. Carl's refusal to believe him about the photo had forced him to doubt what had happened on Gurnard's Head, whether Rosa had been there at all. He was impatient to revisit the spot with someone, a third party, to reassure himself, validate the moment, and Morvah had offered to come with him. He was aware she'd taken to him, but no one could accuse him of leading her on. He'd made his feelings for Rosa more than clear.

Now, as they reach the old engine house, they pass an elderly man walking two dogs. When he nods at them both, glancing at Jar's bandaged head, Jar stops to talk, trying in vain to sound normal, friendly.

'Rare sunny day, did you see anyone here earlier?'

Slow down, he thinks. The man, wisps of his grey hair flying in the sea wind, looks at Jar and then at Morvah, who comes up to join them. He seems to recognise her.

'Hello, Morvah,' he says.

'It's OK, he's with me, Mr Thorne,' she says, sensing his unease. Jar thinks she must be a good barmaid, goes the distance, looks out for people in the community, when she's not surfing. She was meant to be meeting up with friends at Sennen Cove but had bailed and accompanied Jar instead.

'I was just asking if you might have seen anything strange earlier,' Jar continues. 'Maybe an hour ago.'

'Depends what you mean by strange,' Mr Thorne says, growing in confidence, winking at Morvah before nodding towards Jar.

'Mr Thorne lives in the house up the track here,' Morvah says.

The man looks at them both and continues. 'A car drove up the track an hour back,' he says. 'I didn't see it arrive.'

'What sort of car was it?' Jar asks.

'Green Mini. Rental from Penzance. It had a sticker in the rear window.'

The same vehicle that had passed him earlier, when he stepped off the bus.

'Did you see who was in it?' Jar asks. 'How many people?' Mr Thorne looks like the sort of man who would have: Neighbourhood Watch material.

'One in the front. Big-looking bloke.'

Jar manages a smile, trying to seem less deranged. He needs to encourage this man to reveal more.

'My friend here is looking for someone,' Morvah says. Jar clocks the word 'friend', makes a note to thank her later. 'He thinks she might have been in the car.'

Mr Thorne seems to sense that no one is being entirely straight with him. He's right, Jar thinks. All he can think of right now is Rosa curled up in the boot, hands and feet tied with rope, a gag in her mouth.

'Is there something wrong?' he asks, looking from Jar to Morvah.

'Did you catch the name of the hire-car company?' Jar asks.

'It's the one down by the harbour.'

Morvah nods knowingly. Jar has asked enough. Any more questions and Mr Thorne might ring the police, the last thing Jar needs. He'll ask Morvah about the car hire.

Jar thanks Mr Thorne and they hurry on to Gurnard's Head, Morvah jogging at his side. He pictures her running into the waves, board under one arm. Why do surfers always run down to the sea like that?

'Where exactly are we going?' she asks.

'I want to show you where she was, where her tent was pitched.'

'I do believe you.'

'I know. I appreciate that. Really. And thanks back there, for reassuring Mr Thorne about me. Do you know the car-hire firm he mentioned? We need to go there after this.'

Ten minutes later, they are standing on the top of Gurnard's Head. Jar's head wound is starting to throb again. Either the painkiller that Morvah gave him at the pub is wearing off, or it's being back at the scene where he was hit on the head.

'She was here, sitting just here,' Jar says, indicating the patch of grass by the cliff where he had first set eyes on Rosa a few hours earlier. 'And this is where her tent was,' he adds.

'You would expect the ground to be flattened in some way,' Morvah says, pushing her sunglasses up on to her hair as she looks more closely.

She's right, Jar thinks. Why hasn't the tent left a mark on the grass? It's thick here, strong tuffs to withstand the sea gales, but there's no depression. Perhaps she had only just pitched the tent. He turns to the sea and looks out across the bay, where Atlantic waves are rolling in. The afternoon sun is still high, but its rays are beginning to weaken. If the whole thing was a post-bereavement hallucination, then it's the most convincing one yet.

He breathes in the fresh air, wishing the photo had got through to Carl.

'We took a selfie, standing right here, a few seconds before she was taken away.'

His words linger between them.

'I think we should head back, get that cut looked at properly.'

'I'm not concussed, if that's what you're thinking.'

'I know you're not.'

'She was right here,' Jar says again, but Morvah is already out of earshot, walking back up the narrow path.

50

Cromer, 2012

A held her life-drawing class tonight. She's drawing again, thinks it can replace the pills. I tried again to get out of it, but she insisted. There's only so much resistance a man can offer.

'I don't feel so good,' I protested, but she saw through it. Truth is, I felt better than ever, my senses sharpened by the cognitive enhancer I took twenty minutes earlier, and I was keen to see how it would affect my drawing skills. It's been helping with the writing.

'Come on, babe, you can't sit in your shed all the time.'

She knows I like it when she calls me babe: it makes me feel younger, less like an ageing scientist. And it's what Rosa calls Jar, too.

I composed myself, adjusted the cuffs on my shirt and walked out of the kitchen. The sitting room was full. It was a nice crowd – A used to love a good party, in the early days – but I needed to be away from there, from the young female student sitting naked on the table in front of me.

'Last week it was a man,' the only other male, a partner of one of A's friends, whispered to me as we got out our sketch-pads and pencils. 'Perched on the dining room table like an inappropriate bowl of fruit.'

Sasha, our model, wore an expression that suggested she would rather be anywhere but naked in a house in Cromer, surrounded by strangers sucking on their HB pencils. I couldn't blame her. I assumed she was an actress. Most of them are, apparently.

In some ways, she reminded me of Rosa. Same big hair, full mouth, surly attitude. A good figure, too: more apple than pear. Swimmer's shoulders, slim hips.

After forty-five minutes, I took a break to serve some South African Shiraz. A came out to the kitchen, where I was filling the glasses she'd set out on a tray.

'How's it going?' she said, resting her hand on my arm, leaning in to me.

She still thinks I haven't noticed that she's reduced her dose – and is drinking more to compensate.

'Some people are put on this earth to draw. I'm not one of them.'

'Oh I don't know,' she said, leafing through my sketchpad, which I'd left on the sideboard.

'Don't,' I said, closing it firmly.

She assumed I was being playful and snatched the sketchpad away, shielding it with both arms as she held it tight against her chest, her whole body swaying. 'Don't be shy,' she said, smiling.

I couldn't protest any longer. Reluctantly, I resumed pouring the wine, trying to picture what I'd drawn.

A leant against the sideboard as she opened the page, then turned it on its side. 'It's good. Not bad at all.' Then she looked at the picture a bit more closely. My chest tightened. 'I don't remember her wearing a choker necklace.'

'Artistic licence,' I said, and took the Shiraz through to the sitting room.

51

Shahrayar's palace is finally complete in my mind, each piece of marble, every block of granite laid with care and precision in its rightful place. I wasn't aware of how much I knew about architecture until now. Alhambra arches, no problem: none of those corbelled jobs for me (amazing what I can remember from Dad's talks on holiday).

The last room I built was Scheherazade's bedroom, where she retreated each night to think up the next story to keep her alive. Tomorrow I will start to tell Scheherazade's stories, followed by some of my own.

I'm looking forward to the weekend. Dad and I are going on holiday, the best one we ever had. I'm packing tonight and I'm already excited. We will leave for the airport early – warm bacon ciabatta sandwiches wrapped in foil for the car journey – and then, ten hours later – 36,000 seconds – we'll be in Delhi. It will be a dull plane journey, a lot of sitting around, but I think I can cope with that. At least I'll be able to choose the movie.

Now, though, I must keep writing this diary – not the one that I am asked to memorise every day, but this one, which no one knows about. I found some scrap paper and a blue biro down here. I try not to think about what will happen when the ink runs out or if they discover where I hide the paper, behind the sink. Writing a diary is the only thing that's keeping me sane – that and the mind games.

My past has become a sickening blur, but when I concentrate, I can still pick out a few snapshots from my memory that I know to be true, like the night Jar and I walked for miles through the streets of Cambridge, ending up at a Turkish restaurant on Mill Road at 1 a.m. They asked us to leave at 3 a.m., but not before I'd realised I'd found the man I wanted to spend the rest of my life with.

We were drunk and the only people left in the restaurant.

'How long have we known each other?' I asked, resting my hand on his.

'All of a month,' he said.

'It already feels like a lifetime.'

'In a good way? Or in a world-weary-married-couple sort of way?'

I lifted his hand to my lips and kissed it.

'My reality fractured when Dad died – broke clean in two. In one, that split second when I first wake up, he is still alive. In the other, I know he's dead. Since we met, I am finding the strength to accept my life as it now is – one without Dad. Thank you.'

'I wish I could have met him,' Jar said, turning my fingers in his big hands.

'Me too.'

'Will you come over to Ireland this summer? Meet my da and ma?'

'Sounds like a plan.'

'I can show you the Connemara coast, Cleggan Head.'

I paused, losing myself in his eyes. 'I'm not sure what I'd have done if I hadn't met you. It frightens me to think about it.'

'Then don't,' he said, leaning in to kiss me. 'Didn't you say you'd once been on a mindfulness retreat? In Herefordshire or somewhere? They must have taught you how to cut out negative thoughts. And meat. And whiskey...'

I don't know what I said next. I wish I did, but I can no longer remember what memories are mine, what really happened on that dreaded retreat.

52

Jar and Morvah sit in silence in her VW Beetle, looking out across the car park in Penzance at the green Mini. A surfboard is wedged in the back of the Beetle, its nose protruding between them, pressing against the car roof. After this, Morvah is off in search of waves.

He studies the Mini, certain it's the same one that Mr Thorne, the man on the coast path, saw yesterday. And the one he saw passing him at the pub. When they arrived at the car park five minutes ago, the sight of it had stunned him.

'Are you going in?' Morvah says, glancing across at him.

Jar puts a hand up to the plaster that she gave him for his head.

Yesterday evening is a blur. He took up her offer of an empty staff room out the back of the pub and went to bed early, his head aching with the wound and too much Guinness. 'Irish anaesthetic,' someone at the bar quipped, and Morvah had smiled nervously. Alcohol seemed the only way to slow himself down and cope with everything that had happened: finding Rosa after five years, only to watch her being taken away from him minutes later.

He's now certain that the tall figure on Gurnard's Head was the same person who tried to board his night train. And he'd led him to Rosa. Acting on Cato's orders, Jar assumes, the man must have come to Cornwall by car, having missed the train, then followed his bus out from Penzance to Rosa's hiding place on the cliffs. The night train was an eight-hour journey – the drive from London could be done in six. He'd had plenty of time to wait for Jar.

'He must have hired the Mini when he arrived in Penzance,' Jar says. 'Switched vehicles, just to be careful.'

'Why don't you ask them?' Morvah nods at the small Portakabin office beyond the Mini.

Jar gets out of Morvah's car, walks across the car park and pushes open the office door. There's only one person on duty: mid-thirties, weather-beaten skin hardened by sun and surf. Feisty.

'Is the Mini for hire?' Jar asks, gesturing out the window.

'It will be,' the woman says, in a strong Cornish accent. 'When I've cleaned it.'

'Mind if I take a look?' Jar says. No need to apologise, he thinks. Not cleaned yet? The woman turns and takes a set of keys from a board behind her, next to a map of west Penwith.

'Shall I take the hoover out with me?' Jar says. He'll be asking her if she wants a pint of the black stuff next. Her face, high cheekbones, hard round the edges, melts into a smile. Jar makes a point of returning it with interest, and then notices her glancing at his forehead.

'Nothing serious,' he says. 'Low ceiling in the pub last night.'

As he walks across to the Mini, he's aware of Morvah stepping out of her car.

'It's not been cleaned yet,' he whispers, opening the driver's door as Morvah joins him.

'What exactly are you looking for?' she says.

He leans in and glances around the passenger seat and at the seats behind, trying not to act suspiciously. Slow down, he tells himself. He's a regular punter just off the train and in need of a car for a holiday, but he feels his every gesture must look suspicious to the woman in the office, who is watching them through the Portakabin window.

'And?' Morvah asks.

'If it hasn't been cleaned since it was last used, we're looking at a crime scene.'

'You're scaring me now, Jar. You really should just call the police.'

Jar doesn't reply as he walks around to the back of the car and opens the boot. He's scaring himself. The boot is empty apart from an emergency triangle folded up into a red plastic sheaf. He leans in, all his senses trying to detect a trace of Rosa. Was she sedated, unaware of her cramped surroundings, or alert, terrified, desperately trying to claw her way out of here? He looks again, inhales the stuffy air, runs his hands slowly over the floor. And then he sees it, at the back, where the passenger seats meet the floor of the boot: a bent tent peg that has fallen down a gap, almost completely hidden, glinting at him. Attached to it is a tiny shred of floral tent material.

Jar reaches in and removes it, his heart thumping so hard he thinks his chest is about to collapse.

'He put her in here,' he says, one hand clasped tight around the tent peg as he snaps the boot door shut with the other.

Without waiting for Morvah to react, he walks back to the passenger door and opens it, slipping the tent peg into his pocket. He looks around the interior of the car again, but this time it's to disguise another glance across at the office.

The woman is no longer watching them. Without hesitating, he slides off his watch, the one that his da gave him on his eighteenth birthday. A few seconds later he is standing in the office again.

'I found this, down the back of the driver's seat,' he says, putting his watch on the counter.

The woman pushes at it, can't quite bring herself to pick it up. This is a complication in her working day that she could do without, Jar hopes.

'Do you have the contact details of the person who hired the car?' he asks. Easy, he tells himself.

The woman looks at Jar for a second and then turns to her computer, typing idly at the keys. Her heart's not in this job, Jar thinks, which could work to his advantage.

'I booked it out myself, yesterday morning,' she says, sighing.

Jar leans across the counter and looks at the computer screen, smiling. She glances up at him and then angles the screen away before continuing to type. But it's a half-hearted gesture, almost coquettish.

'I once worked in a car-rental company,' Jar says, his arms folded on the counter now, as if he's chatting at the bar. 'Avis, in Dublin.'

'Shabby, isn't it?' she says, still looking at the screen.

'Is this a franchise?'

'You are joking.'

'Not exactly jumping, is it?'

'I've got an address, it's in Leeds.'

'Seriously now?'

'Got a problem with Leeds?'

'It's where I'm heading. End of the week. I could drop the watch off.'

She eyes him for a moment, making a calculation, Jar assumes. The hassle of having to go to the post office when the customer calls, package up the watch, send it off – it will fall to her to do it, he guesses, the only member of staff apart from a lazy boss, who never works Sundays, like she is today. Or she could give the watch to him and be done with it.

'I did just hand it in,' Jar says, sensing her hesitation. 'If I was going to steal it, I wouldn't have brought it in here, would I now? I would have—'

He checks himself as she reads out a name, 'John Bingham', and an address in Leeds, both of which Jar assumes are fake. Whoever wanted to cover their tracks by renting a car would have used a false driving licence. 'Shall I write it down for you?' she asks.

'You're very kind,' Jar says. And not bad-looking either, but he checks himself. Job done, no need to keep playing the libidinous eejit. 'How will I know I've got the right man?' He pauses. 'Do you remember what he looked like?'

'Tall.' She glances around the empty office in an unnecessary gesture of confidentiality. 'And a little bit creepy?' she adds, her voice rising at the end of the sentence.

'I hope you're not suggesting a link there,' Jar says, smiling again, leaning back, rising to his full height.

The woman finishes copying down the details on a sheet of paper, unimpressed by Jar's attempt at flirting.

'His eyes were also way too small,' she adds, pushing the paper over to him. They both pause for a moment, looking at the watch that lies between them like seized contraband.

'Let me give you my number,' Jar says, taking the watch, keen to end the awkward silence. 'In case there's a problem.'

'I'm sure there won't be,' she says. She just wants to be shot of this whole thing, Jar thinks, and the weird tall fella with a plaster on his head who keeps smiling at her. 'And if you don't manage to find him, you can always keep it yourself,' she adds. 'Looks like you could do with a watch.'

She glances at his left wrist, where there is a neat band of lighter skin, and then up at his face. Does she know?

'We won't be taking the Mini,' Jar says, as he walks out to Morvah's car.

53

Cromer, 2012

A's worried about Rosa, says she reminds her of her own darkest days. Rosa's unhappy, mourning her father, but she's not suicidal. Not yet. I wish I could muster more sympathy, but I can't. A's been filling her head with the joys of cognitive behavioural therapy and the girl is less keen than ever on the idea of medication.

Rosa's presence in the house has stirred up something in A. She hasn't said anything, but I can see what's happening, how maternal she's being towards her: the child we never had.

I'm beginning to sound like Kirsten, A's old college friend who she's suddenly got in touch with after all these years. Last night, when I was loitering downstairs, waiting for A to fall asleep, she was FaceTiming Kirsten in the States. She was still talking to her when I came to bed, chatting on her new iPad.

Kirsten's a counsellor specialising in 'bereavement therapy'. Enough said. A and Kirsten were at Cambridge together, but we never met. I know she's been talking to A about coming off her medication – as if therapy can replace benzos.

I tried to focus on *Tinker Tailor*, which I've been rereading, but Kirsten kept catching my eye. A was telling her all about

Rosa, how she lost her father, how low she seems, asking whether Kirsten might be coming over to the UK any time soon and if she might meet up with Rosa for a few counselling sessions, how it's easier to accept advice from someone who's not family.

Since I've started the writing course, I've found myself constantly running the rule over anyone I see or meet, sizing them up to use as the basis for a character. My tutor tells me to look out for defining traits, tics, mannerisms – a line here or there that will capture the person, like the single flick of a caricaturist's pen. It's addictive once you get into the right mindset and I'm filling my notebook with observations. I haven't felt this alive since I tried – and failed – to write a novel when I was younger. The observations were sharp enough, my problem was that I could never come up with a decent story with a beginning, a middle and an end. I'm hoping this online course will help with that.

Kirsten's blonde and good-looking: too clichéd, even for a male writer like me. There's an intensity, an immediacy about her that I like. Not every time, but occasionally, she takes a short sharp intake of breath, just before she speaks, as if she's forgotten to breathe.

I put Le Carré down and reached across for my Moleskine.

54

Let the mind games begin.

We check in early, to avoid the queues, but there's a big delay up at Passport Control. I stand in a long line for thirty minutes – 1,800 seconds – and when I finally reach the security scanner, beside the fetid sink, the woman doesn't even smile as she frisks me (it must be my orange jumpsuit).

It's not easy going on holiday with your dead father when you're imprisoned in a cell, but I have to try. It's all I've got, the only way to pass the time, to try and hang on to a trace of sanity.

I hold my arms out as wide as I can, but the chains stop me from extending them fully. She scowls and then waves me on into the main room, where I wait for Dad beside my bed. We've got plenty of time, which was always the plan. Dad loves airports as much as I do. He's not one for Duty Free. Instead, we head for the bookshop in the corner of the room and browse for forty-five minutes (2,700 seconds), comparing books, working out our shared 3-for-2 offer.

The flight attendant at the door to the aeroplane is friendlier, particularly when I show her our tickets. 'This way,' she says, pointing to the left. Left! We always dreamed of turning left.

Dad lets me sit by the window, and we settle down with our books before the movies start. Once we're airborne, we watch one of Dad's all-time favourite films. And I shout out his favourite lines, forgetting for a moment that I'm in first class.

'It's 106 miles to Chicago, we've got a full tank of gas, half a pack of cigarettes, it's dark and we're wearing sunglasses.'

'Hit it!'

Silence. Then a distant scream that I've heard too many times before.

55

Jar spots the two men as soon as they board his train at Exeter. They walk into his carriage together, not talking to each other, but there is an unusual synchronicity to their movements: one takes a seat by the exit nearest to Jar, the other walks down to the far end and sits near the door, past a lot of empty seats, the two of them effectively bookending the carriage. Neither looks familiar, but they both blend in well with the mix of holidaymakers and locals: one's wearing a fleece and jeans, the other a leather jacket and chinos. Anonymous, faceless.

Jar sinks down into his seat. Cato will have told these two men to keep an eye on him in case he makes trouble, maybe bring him in for a final chat, some closure. Did they help the other man on the cliffs with Rosa? Transfer her, hog-tied, from the hired Mini to another car? Cato will continue to deny that he has any interest in Rosa, or that he oversaw her recapture in Cornwall. No doubt he'll urge Jar to get help for his hallucinations, too – until he shows him the selfie of him and Rosa together. Carl must have received the text by now.

Why is his best friend always so sceptical? Even Morvah, who barely knew him, had showed more faith, believed that he had been with Rosa on the cliffs. He said goodbye to her at the train station, after he'd finished at the car-hire company in Penzance and had bought a cheap phone on Market Jew Street. They swapped numbers and he found it strange – disloyal, even – to own a phone with only her number in it, as if she was some sort of fleeting holiday romance that had blossomed out of a shared love of literature. She had been kind to him in the past twenty-four hours, which made him feel guilty that he didn't want to linger in her presence.

'I'm not going to see you again, am I?' she asked on the concourse.

There seemed little point in lying. 'Thank you. For believing.'

'I'll read your book,' she offered, and walked away.

Now, as his train pushes through the countryside to London, he glances over to the man at the far end of the carriage, who is staring out the window, and then at the man nearer to him, talking into one end of his mobile. More pipe smoker than pizza eater, Jar thinks, the handset to one side and angled up at forty-five degrees. Not normal. Carl would find it funny.

Jar begins to relax, increasingly reassured by the two men's presence. Yesterday's meeting on Gurnard's Head has left him feeling stronger, vindicated. Even Rosa's distant manner (she didn't know his name, he's trying not to linger on that) and her disappearance again, so soon after they were reunited, somehow seems tolerable. The woman everyone thinks died five years ago in Cromer was walking the Cornish coast yesterday in the sunshine. For a moment he wants to go over and confront both men, ask them now to try denying that she is alive. He curls his fingers around the bent tent peg in his pocket, rehearsing in his head what he'll say to Cato.

It's as his train pulls into Paddington that he begins to think he's mistaken about the two men. Both are queuing at the front end of the carriage, waiting to disembark, neither acknowledging the other, or Jar. He waits his turn to join the queue in the aisle and then walks down the carriage. As he steps off the train, he notices that it has arrived at Platform 1, where there is no barrier – and where he first saw Rosa. If Cato doesn't want to meet him, what then? He hasn't considered that no one might be interested in him any more. Rosa has been recaptured, the diary has been shut down before anything too compromising was revealed. Who is going to believe him, someone with a track record of bereavement hallucinations and paranoid behaviour?

The two men are moving off into the distance now. They couldn't be less interested in him if they tried. Jar focuses on the back of one of them, tracing the lattice of ageing creases in his leather jacket. He hopes to God that Carl has received the image.

'Could we check your ticket please, sir?'

Jar hasn't noticed the two ticket inspectors, standing in the flow of passengers like boulders in a stream.

'Sure now,' he says, distracted, still looking after the two men. Where are they going? Why haven't they made themselves known to him?

He shows the inspectors his return ticket and tries to keep an eye on the men. Turn around, he thinks. Jaysus, you've played it cool enough. You can drop your cover now.

But the two men keep on walking until they've vanished, lost in the crush of evening travellers.

56

Cromer, 2012

J ar came up to Cromer yesterday. I'm always interested to meet a published author, but, sadly, he's not
my kind of writer. Not my kind of person, to be honest.
(No wonder Rosa's feeling suicidal.) There's a smug blarney tone to all that he says, a smoothness of speech that
gives him a confidence that borders on arrogance. He's not
loud, or overtly cocky, just a bit too laid back and pleased
with his southern Irish self, a soft 't' knocking 'Thursday'
into 'Tursday', 'three' into 'tree', and he quotes W. B. Yeats
as if he knew the man. He's well dressed, though, which
is unusual for a student: polished brogues, dapper cordu-
roy jacket. Looks like a writer ought to look. I will try to
see beyond his faults, do my best to befriend him. He could
be useful.

I pulled him into the sitting room for a Scotch before the
Sunday roast, which has never been the same since A decided
to become vegetarian. Jar prefers Irish whiskey, but we all
have our crosses to bear. I asked him a few encouraging
questions about his book, pretending I'd read it (I failed to
get past the first two stories).

'Character first, or plot, then?' I began, pouring him a large Talisker. He seemed a little nervous.

'You probably noticed my stories don't have a lot of plot now,' he said. Understatement of the year, but I kept quiet. 'I'm more interested in getting someone's voice right and see- ing where it goes from there. If a story emerges, so be it, but I don't rely on a strong narrative drive.'

'What about research?' It was central to my previous career and I want it to play a key part of my new one.

'The procrastinator's friend.'

'So authors should just write about what they know?'

'Not at all. That's usually boring, unless you've lived an exceptional life.'

'I'm a scientist.' In my experience, that's on a par with telling someone you're an accountant: their eyes glaze over, they're not sure what to say, particularly if you add that you're employed by a Big Pharma contract research organisation, working to ensure that new drugs are as safe as possible for mankind, animals and the environment. Only I don't work for them any more.

'There you go, now,' Jar said. 'Imagination is the key.'

I wasn't going to rise to his bait, defend the life scientific. Besides, his words were oddly comforting. I've never had a problem imagining things, fantasising. 'Do you have a note- book?' I asked, moving on. 'To write things down?'

'I scribble things on scraps of paper, then put them on a computer, if I remember. I have a special file. What kind of book are you writing?' Jar was beginning to relax. He stopped glancing over towards the kitchen, where Rosa was talking to A.

'To get my hand in, I'm writing a journal, semi- fictionalised – I'm intrigued by Karl Ove Knausgaard.'

I was showing off, of course. I've only just begun to read the Norwegian writer, but Jar seemed impressed.

'Now there's a fella who *only* writes about what he knows,' he said. 'Much to his ex-wife's dismay.'

'Then I thought I'd have a go at genre fiction, see where it leads me. I'm a big fan of Le Carré,' I added. 'Spy fiction in general.'

'Le Carré's interesting. The story's central, but we all remember Smiley the character.'

'Of course, when I was your age, I was more into the Beat Generation, the influence of psychoactive drugs on creativity, that kind of thing. I'm sure you know that Kesey wrote the first three pages of *One Flew Over the Cuckoo's Nest* after choking down eight peyote.'

'Wasn't he working on a psychiatric ward at the time?'

'As a night watchman. He claimed the little cactus plant had inspired his narrator. Ten to twenty grammes of dried peyote buttons yields enough mescaline to induce a state of profound reflection that can last for up to twelve hours.' I paused. 'So I'm told.'

Just as we were beginning to get into our stride, Rosa came into the room and linked her arm through Jar's. 'How's it going?' she said, looking at Jar with the uncomplicated affection of youth, and then at me, surprised, perhaps, by how well we were getting on.

'We were just assessing the medicinal benefits of writing,' Jar said, raising his whisky glass in my direction.

57

Dad wants to head for Old Delhi first, which is fine by me. Anything to take my mind off what's really been happening to me here. We start at the top of Chandni Chowk and weave our way down the road, turning off into Wedding Street, an old favourite when I was younger.

'Can we go to the jalebi wallah?' I ask. 'Please?'

The pain has been unbearable, despite the medication.

'Of course we can,' Dad says.

'Please stop,' I sobbed, but he never listened.

I try to taste the jalebi in my mouth, the sweetness of the crystallised sugar, but the memory of the wet cloth being pushed so far down my throat means that I can't taste anything.

'It's sweet, isn't it?' Dad says, oil dripping down his stubbly chin. I love it when he forgets to shave – a sign we are truly on holiday. 'The sweetest thing I ever tasted.'

Dad loves it even more than me. And he always chats to the man who sells it, perched on his plastic chair behind a deep bowl of bubbling oil, happy to serve tourists as well as locals.

I reach out for Dad's hand.

'Look at your nails,' he says, turning my fingers over. 'Aren't they pretty?'

They nearly drowned me.

We're no longer in Old Delhi. We're rafting down the mighty Zanskar, our rubber dinghy spinning in the rapids. Dad, laughing, tells me to hold on as we rise up over the surging water and crash down again. And then we're both in the river, swimming beside the dingy, holding the rope that runs down its side. The water is calm now, but so cold, even with our wetsuits on. Our instructor is urging us to let go of the rope. There's no danger, he says, nodding at his Nepali friend, who is in a kayak, downstream, watching over us. And we do, floating down the river on our backs, one of the happiest moments of my life.

But not even Dad could save me from him.

'Stop,' I tried to cry, the icy water flooding my lungs. 'Please stop.'

58

Jar pushes open the door of the lock-up, checking the street in both directions. He knows something's not right: Nic, the photographer on the floor below, had tipped him off when they met at the bottom of the towerblock a few minutes earlier. At dawn this morning, he said, while Jar was still in Cornwall, police had been seen taking away a computer from one of the lock-ups, along with several boxes. Nic is the only person who knows that Jar rents one of them.

The padlock has been broken but made to look as if it's working. Jar braces himself, but he is still taken aback by the sight that greets him inside. Everything has been removed from the walls – all the maps, photographs, newspaper cuttings. The computer has gone, too, and the drawers of the desk are open, their contents taken. Whoever was here – Cato's people, he assumes – was interested in anything that might be linked to Rosa and her disappearance. There's no vandalism, no sign of violence, apart from the broken padlock. Why doesn't Cato want to talk to him in person any more? Why didn't his men on the train pick him up when they reached Paddington?

Jar's first thought is that he no longer has any photos of Rosa, nothing to stop her fading away from him. He has deliberately kept all traces of her out of his flat, away from the life he presents to the world. Every material connection with her – letters, photos, newspaper cuttings about her death – has now been taken from him.

A week ago he would have been distraught, but it doesn't bother him now. The empty lock-up, the efficiency of the sweep, is confirmation that someone is trying to stop Rosa from returning – and him from finding her.

Back at his flat, he is almost disappointed to find no evidence of a break-in. The books are all on their shelves, not in any order but present and correct. His guitar, too, is still underneath his bed. He's about to slide it out when he remembers the photo that fell from a book the night his flat was raided. He goes to the shelf and retrieves it from a copy of *Finnegans Wake*. She has aged, he realises; when he saw her yesterday, she looked like another person.

Jar pours himself a large Yellow Spot, one of his da's favourites. He won't call him about his Cornish encounter, not yet; he knows it will only upset him, suggest that he is far from over his grief. And he won't call Amy. She is too unstable already and Jar wants to know more before he tells her.

He knocks back the whiskey and pulls the tent peg from his jacket pocket, placing it on the kitchen surface. The piece of floral fabric has frayed and the peg is buckled a bit in the middle. He wonders if Rosa swore as it hit some granite in the Cornish earth. She could swear with the best of them, Jar remembers, smiling to himself, thinking back to the time when he averted his eyes as she stepped out of the Cam, frozen to the core.

His phone rings.

'How was Cornwall?'

Jar recognises Miles Cato's measured Scottish tones at once. How the hell did he get his new number? Someone must have talked to Morvah, after he boarded his train.

'I am trying very hard to eliminate you from our investigation into Martin, Jar,' he continues, 'but you aren't making it easy for us. Have you heard from Anton?'

Jar runs his fingers along the shelves as he listens, bringing errant books into line, standing the idle to attention.

'How did you get this number?' he asks.

'I'm a policeman, Jar.'

He's good, Jar thinks. Sticking to his script like a leech. He recalls Rosa's warning in her email: *Tread carefully with MC. I've learnt enough over the past five years to know that he will be the one who approaches you, if he hasn't already. He will probably be using police cover, plain clothes. And he loves a good Scottish accent. I have no idea what story he will spin, but don't believe a word of what he says. He's trying to find me, just like the others.*

'We now think Martin may be into torture videos,' Cato continues.

Their cover story is getting more ludicrous by the day, Jar thinks. Why not accuse Martin of something more plausible, like an unhealthy interest in beatniks? Or being addicted to Strava?

'I know who I saw yesterday in Cornwall,' he says.

'Another one of your hallucinations?'

'Are we done here?' Jar is annoyed now. Cato's pretence has gone on long enough.

'Don't run away again – and call me on this number as soon as you've made contact with Anton. I'm sorry about your computer. Routine procedure. You'll get it back.'

Jar walks out on to the balcony and looks across towards Canary Wharf, blinking in the night. Nic, the photographer in the flat below, is playing his sax. If only the selfie of the two of them together, taken yesterday on Gurnard's Head, had got through to Carl. Then he thinks about the emails again and pulls out his phone.

'It's Jar, Jarlath Costello. Still working?' Jar hopes that he has found Max Eadie at his office. A lot of the lights in the tower are still burning.

'Always working, twenty-four hours a day. You've read the website. Where have you been? I've been trying to call you for two days.'

'Can we meet? A lot's happened.'

'Your lift's out of order,' Max says. 'Had to take the stairs, which stink of camel's piss, by the way.'

'Do you want a drink?' Jar asks, closing the door and taking in the strange shambolic sight of Max in his flat. For a moment, he fears for the man's health.

'Some of that, no water,' he says, gesturing at the whiskey bottle on the table. 'Is your head OK?'

'Max, I saw Rosa,' Jar says, keen to cut to the chase as he pours himself another whiskey. 'Yesterday, in Cornwall.'

Max pauses before answering, his face more serious now, respectful, the bluster gone. 'Properly?'

'It wasn't another bereavement hallucination, if that's what you mean.'

'Whereabouts in Cornwall?'

'At a place where we once agreed to meet in a crisis.'

Jar goes on to tell him everything: the emails, the meeting with Cato, the man who tried to board his train, their secret rendezvous agreement in Cornwall, how he inadvertently led Rosa's captors to her. 'She didn't even know my name,' he says, his eyes welling.

Max listens intently. He doesn't seem surprised by the

encounter, nor that Rosa struggled to remember everything about her past.

'I found this, too, in the rental car that took her away.' Jar picks up the bent tent peg from the kitchen table, looks at it and then tosses it back down again. 'She'd been camping on the cliffs.'

'And you think Miles Cato's behind all this?'

'That's what I want to talk to you about. I'm worried about the emails Rosa sent, asking me to meet her,' Jar says, handing Max his phone. 'Something's not right about them. She would have mentioned the meeting place by name. Read this one.'

He watches as Max lifts his glasses up on to his eyebrows and peers at the phone. 'It's not from Rosa,' Jar says. 'It's from someone pretending to be Rosa, who didn't know where she was hiding, where she'd go if she was on the run – "if the world ever slipped off its axis".' Jar hesitates, can sense his voice is about to crack. 'They knew I knew where this place was and waited for me to show them, to lead them to her. Which I went and did – like a stupid eejit.'

Max glances up at Jar as he walks over to the window and looks out.

'You think Cato sent them?' Max asks.

'Read the second email,' Jar says, trying to regain his composure, his back still to Max. '"Tread carefully with MC" – that's Miles Cato. "He will probably be using police cover, plain clothes." Why would he want to raise suspicions about himself? Whoever sent them was trying to frame Cato – to divert attention away from themselves.'

Jar knows what Max is thinking, that he was right when he suggested someone was playing him. 'I still believe the diary was written by Rosa,' he says in anticipation, but Max stays silent, turning the whiskey in his glass.

'While you were away, I went back over all my old research files. For that article I wrote.'

'Did you discover anything?'

'Only that I was a lazy sod. No wonder I never made it as an investigative journalist. Christ Almighty. I did discover one thing, though. The retreat's just been put on the market. I was planning to call the owner tomorrow, pay them a visit. Want to come?'

59

After A finished FaceTiming Kirsten again, she put her iPad on her bedside table and went to the bathroom. I switched off my light and turned away to sleep, but there was something about A tonight – the way her cotton nightie moved against her buttocks. We haven't made love since I lost my job, since she started to reduce her daily medication. And we now often sleep in separate bedrooms. Tonight, though, she asked if we could be together – new beginnings, she said.

Benzodiazepines affect people in many different ways. Long-term use generally depresses sexual activity, but there are exceptions. In an interesting case study by Fava and Borofsky from 1991, a woman with a history of drug and alcohol abuse and sexual promiscuity as a teenager (not dissimilar to A's own experience) led an abstemious, almost monastic life as an adult until she started to have panic attacks. She was prescribed clonazepam, a potent anti-anxiety benzo, and became sexually disinhibited, with a particular fondness for striptease.

Benzos have helped to control A's general anxiety disorders, eased her insomnia and, it's fair to say, made things simpler in the bedroom. In the early years, I switched her between diazepam and alprazolam, chlordiazepoxide and clobazam, swapping in fast-acting compounds such as flunitrazepam (aka Rohypnol) when I needed to be sure she'd forget what had happened between the sheets.

When I changed jobs from Huntingdon to Norwich, we began to test a variety of new benzos with very long half-lives, one of which fell at the last phase of regulatory trials because its side effects included sexual disinhibition *and* memory loss – a potent combination perceived as making it too dangerous to be licensed. It was a shame, as it was a decent product (similar to clonazepam, with one chemical arm of the molecule substituted), but I had access to our warehouse and made sure we had almost a lifetime's supply of the drug at home. (There have been many advantages, not least that it doesn't show up in blood tests whenever A visits her GP.) It wasn't easy, but I managed to take away other benzos, too, powerful new ones that were awaiting first-in-human trials.

Did A forget to take her dose tonight? I usually substitute it for one of her innocent sleeping pills, which she takes like clockwork an hour before bedtime.

She slid into bed next to me and nibbled my ear. I lay there for a few seconds, eyes open. For as long as she's been on benzos, it's always been me who has initiated, her response compliant rather than enthusiastic. A tear ran down my cheek as her fingers circled my stomach before they descended. I should have slept in a separate bedroom, or gone down to the shed.

I turned towards her, feeling her face in the dark with my fingers, slipping my thumbs between her lips. Her mouth was warm, her excitement arousing something in me that had no right to be remembered in any conscious mind.

'Gently,' she whispered.

I knew I should stop, make my excuses, but I told myself I could control what was about to happen, as I have done so many times before. And for half a minute, maybe longer, we were like any normal couple, evenly matched.

It was only when I turned her over on to her front and pinned her arms above her head, my fingers circling her thin wrists, my knees pushing her thighs apart, that she cried out.

'Martin, what are you doing? You're hurting me.'

She tried to wriggle free from beneath me, but for a second I held her there, martyred on the bed, legs and arms splayed like St Andrew. Then I let her go and rolled away.

'I'm sorry,' I said. 'Are you OK?'

'No, I'm not OK. What the hell were you doing? You nearly broke my wrists.'

'I said I was sorry.' I was sitting on the edge of the bed now. But she was already walking to the bathroom, where she slammed the door behind her.

60

What makes me human has flown this bruised body of mine and is perched at a safe distance, looking on, wings folded, waiting one day to return.

'It's just resting,' Dad says. 'The underwing markings help to keep it unnoticed.'

My guard visits in the afternoons, bringing me a daily dose of pain, and a clean orange jumpsuit once a week. He refuses to give me any underwear, but at least he's now accepted the need for sanitary towels (my periods have almost stopped anyway).

Today's visit began like all the others: a test on what I had memorised the day before, followed by new entries that I must commit to memory.

'Silent Retreat, Herefordshire, Spring Term, 2012: It's the last day of our briefing in Herefordshire. Tonight we return to our colleges to put our affairs in order.'

*'**Start** to put our affairs in order – and **wait**,' he shouted, emphasising 'start' and 'wait'.*

'Tonight we return to our colleges, start to put our affairs in order – and wait.'

He punishes me when I make mistakes, beats and abuses me, but is any human company, even his brutal presence, better than the isolation that follows when he is gone?

61

It's as they are driving over the Severn suspension bridge that Jar decides that he can trust Max. For the first few hours, he slept – Max had picked him up from outside his block of flats at dawn in his navy blue Land Rover Defender – but he stirred somewhere between Swindon and Bristol on the M4 and they have been talking ever since.

Perhaps it was Max's opening remark that convinced him: 'You should write a novel – I enjoyed your short stories.' When Max went on to say he'd ordered copies of his book for several friends, Jar knew Max was wasted in corporate PR. It also became apparent that Max has unfinished business as an investigative journalist and that his article about Oxbridge students means more to him than he at first let on. He's keen to help Jar, but he also wants to nail the story, prove to himself once and for all that he has what it takes to write a front-page scoop.

Jar confided in him that he was working on a novel when Rosa disappeared – she was the only one that he'd told – and hasn't written a word of it since. They went on to discuss their favourite collections of short stories – everything from Joyce's *Dubliners* to Saunders' *Tenth of December* – before Jar returned to his meeting with Rosa on the cliffs in Cornwall forty-eight hours earlier.

Once again, Max said nothing to suggest he didn't believe him. He just listened. As he is now, to Jar's account of Rosa's uncle and aunt in Cromer, the weekends away they spent there together, Cato's ongoing investigation into Martin.

Jar adjusts his feet, realising that he's been resting them on a squashed banana. The floor on his side is littered with sweet papers, crushed juice cartons and an empty Paddington Bear lunchbox.

'I was convinced that Cato was after her diary,' Jar says. 'But he really is just a policeman trying to clean up the darker recesses of the web. I accept that now.'

'Who do you think took Rosa from Cornwall then?' Max asks, drawing up at the row of toll booths at the far end of the bridge.

Jar waits before he speaks, watching Max pay the toll and accelerate away from the booths. 'There's something I need to show you.' He pulls out a sheet of paper from his coat pocket, the copy he'd made of the confidential memo he'd handed over to Cato in the car. He holds it up for Max to see.

'Christ, what's that?' Max says, as if Jar has just produced a ticking bomb.

'Top Secret Strap 3, UK Eyes Only, that's what it is.'

'Where the hell did you get it?'

'The original was sent to me at work.'

'Who by? Edward bloody Snowden? What does it say?'

'It's about a programme called Eutychus and gives Rosa's date of birth and date of death in Cromer.'

'When did you get this?'

'Three days ago, on Friday, the day before I saw Rosa.'

'Why didn't you say anything, show it to me last night?'

Jar hesitates. 'I wasn't sure whose side you were on.'

'Fair enough.' Max glances again at the document. 'It might be a fake, of course.'

'Or the proof you were looking for when you wrote your article.'

'I assume you know who Eutychus was? The man so bored of listening to one of St Paul's sermons that he dozed off and fell to his death from a third-floor window. St Paul was horrified – embarrassed too. Not great if you're trying to get on the after-dinner-speakers circuit. So he rushed over to the body and managed to resuscitate him. Brought him back to life, Jar. Like Lazarus.'

'I get it.'

'And just like all the bright students who supposedly committed suicide and were given new lives,' Max says. 'It's dynamite if it's genuine – a front-page splash. "Highly shareable content".'

Jar smiles at Max's derisive tone and then turns away, looking out across the passing countryside.

'Sorry. Insensitive.'

'Not at all,' Jar says. 'You've got to tell the world. Properly this time. It's the only way I'll get Rosa back.'

62

Cromer, 2012

'We should talk about last night,' A said, nursing a mug of rooibos tea at the kitchen table.

We have never talked about last night.

'I said I was sorry,' I replied, standing at the sideboard, my back to her. I was making another pot of coffee to take down to the shed. Strava was calling. I went out on a long cycle ride first thing this morning to clear my head, avoid the retributions.

'I know things aren't easy at the moment,' she said.

'I'm fine, honestly,' I said.

'I wasn't talking about you.'

I waited for the kettle to boil.

'I'm trying to get clean, Martin, wean myself off all my medication. Get my life back. Our life.'

'I had noticed. You could kill yourself if you come off too quickly, you do know that?'

There's no danger of that, of course, as I'm still administering her main benzo through her daily 'sleeping pill'. (It turns out she did forget to take it last night, and took one later, after she eventually emerged from the bathroom.) But she doesn't need to know. If she thinks she is regaining control of

her life by reducing some of the other fast-acting compounds
I give her, so be it.

'I can cope until something like this happens.'

A wasn't listening to me. 'And Kirsten's therapy won't be
enough on its own. Not with your condition.'

'It reminded me of when we were first together in Cambridge,' she continued.

'In a bad way?'

I have only happy memories of that innocent period of our
lives. She had just graduated in history of art and started her
first job, restoring pictures at the Hamilton Kerr Institute in
Whittlesford, a few miles south of Cambridge. I was a PhD
student, dividing my time between the university and working up the road at the contract research lab in Huntingdon.

'You once asked me something: whether you could tie my
wrists to the bed. We were drunk at the time and I laughed
it off, forgot all about it. You never asked again. Last night,
I remembered.'

'It was nothing, Amy. I was being clumsy, that's all. And
I don't recall ever asking to tie your wrists.' I was lying, of
course. I remember it well.

'Are you watching porn? Is that what you're doing in the
shed?'

'I'm trying to write a book.'

'We should talk about it if you are. I'm not completely
naïve, you know... We could watch it together, as long as it's
ethical porn. I was reading about it the other day, would like
to see what all the fuss is about.'

'I'm trying to write my novel, Amy. Finally. That's all.'

She turned to the newspaper on the table and idly flicked
through the pages. 'With weird sex in it?' She was smiling now.

'It's going to be a spy story. Maybe.'

63

My debut haiku
It took me half the summer
A joke? If only

64

The retreat is more comfortable than Jar was expecting. During the three-hour drive down from London he had imagined a sparse mountain barn where students sat cross-legged on cold stone floors. Instead, he and Max find themselves standing outside a Victorian former farmhouse surrounded by an orchard, a walled garden and clean, converted outbuildings with lots of glass and exposed oak beams.

'The property sits on high ground at the head of the Olchon Valley, in the shadow of the magnificent Hatterall Ridge,' the estate agent says. She points first down the valley and then up at the ridge, like a flight attendant gesturing towards a plane's exit doors. Jar senses that it's not the first time she's given this spiel.

'The famous Offa's Dyke footpath follows the Hatterall Ridge, marking the border between England and Wales. If you place your right hand palm down, then we say around here that you are holding the Black Mountains: your thumb is the Cat's Back, over there, your first finger is Hatterall, your second finger is Ffawyddog...'

The estate agent had met them at the house. They'd hatched a plan in the car: the two of them are representing an overseas client – no details offered, Russian if asked – who is keen to buy a weekend country retreat. Now, as they stand outside the front door, waiting for the agent to find the right key, Jar feels quite emotional. He wants confirmation that Rosa came here, that the diary hasn't been doctored, as Max suggested.

'This is the main reception area,' the estate agent says, once they are inside the house. 'It was used for the larger meditation classes but could easily be converted back into a traditional drawing room.'

Jar looks at the white walls, the pale blue carpet. There are no pictures or bookcases, just one mirror above a bricked-up fireplace. At the far end, in front of a pair of imposing floor-to-ceiling windows, two meditation stools are the only evidence of the room's former purpose. Jar tries to picture Rosa sitting there, eyes closed perhaps, listening intently to Karen in the morning light as she attempts to make sense of her life, the death of her father, the disappointment of Cambridge.

Upstairs, the estate agent shows them a number of bedrooms, most of them with two beds, some of the bigger ones with four. Again, she talks about how easily they could be converted for private use.

'Our client's main concern is security,' Max says, winking at Jar before turning to look out of a bedroom window on to the Olchon Valley below. Jar glances out too, spots a buzzard soaring in the wind, flying in the currents rising around Hatterall Ridge. *Turning and turning in the widening gyre, the falcon cannot hear the falconer...*

'The nearest neighbour is almost a mile away,' the estate agent says. 'And there's only one road into the valley, so you would know well in advance if you had visitors.'

'Do you mind if I take a look around?' Jar asks.

'Of course,' the woman says. 'The place is yours.' She throws a hopeful glance at Max.

Jar leaves Max to discuss security for their fictitious Russian client and walks out on to the landing, wondering which of the rooms Rosa might have shared with Sejal. Hesitating at the doorway to the smallest room, occupied by twin beds, he decides to take a closer look before going back downstairs. Perhaps she wrote her name on the wall, or carved her initials into the bed?

It's not a prison, he tells himself. It's a peaceful retreat – a place of silence. He glances at the two beds, both made up, the duvets tucked in with Indian patterned bedspreads. Rosa would have liked that touch. He turns and is about to go down the varnished wooden staircase, when a voice calls out to him.

'You know we're not meant to have visitors.'

Rosa. Jar pauses, checking himself, and then looks around. Rosa is sitting on the bed, smiling coyly at him. She puts her fingers to her lips, to indicate that he should be quiet, and pats the bed beside her, encouraging him to sit down.

'Rosa?' he says, the whole weight of his body free-falling through his legs.

'Sejal will be here in a moment. We haven't got long. They can be quite strict here.'

Jar closes his eyes. When he opens them again, Rosa has gone. He walks over to the bed and sits down, relieved to be taking the weight off his legs.

'You OK?'

Jar looks up to see Max standing in the doorway. He pauses before answering. 'This was the room where she stayed, here in this bed.' He taps the bedspread.

'How do you know?' Max glances back along the corridor.

'It tallies with what she said in her diary.'

'Are you coming?' The tone of Max's voice suggests an order rather than a question.

Down in the hall, Max continues to discuss other aspects of the property with the agent – power supply, water, planning restrictions – while Jar asks if there is a lavatory.

'At the far end of the corridor,' the estate agent says, glancing at Max as if to ask if Jar's OK. Jar guesses he looks spooked after his hallucination.

'Thanks,' Jar says, and walks away from them as quickly as he can without arousing suspicion.

A room had caught his eye when they first entered the property: a small office, off the main corridor. Through a half-open door he'd glimpsed a computer and books on a shelf.

Checking that the agent isn't nearby, he pushes the office door further open and steps inside. There is a desk littered with paperwork, a phone and an old computer. A wipe board on the wall has a few phone numbers written at a sharp diagonal. Jar pulls out his phone and takes a picture of them.

He can still hear Max and the estate agent chatting in the hall: oil deliveries, security lights. The man's a born bullshitter, Jar thinks. He turns to look behind the door, where there is an old grey filing cabinet. The drawers are all open, the dark green envelope folders lying empty. Even the index labels have been removed. But it's what's on the wall above the filing cabinet that interests Jar: a forgotten patchwork of photographs, at least fifty of them, faded snapshots of young people smiling, posing.

Jar walks over to take a closer look, his eyes moving rapidly from one to the next. It's a while before he spots Rosa, but there she is, standing next to an Asian girl. Sejal, he guesses. There is snow on the ground and they have one scarf wrapped around both their necks and are leaning in to the camera, smiling.

Jar prises the photo off the wall, extricating it carefully

from the surrounding photos. He takes one from the edge of the patchwork and puts it in the gap left by the one he's taken. There's a date on the back: March 2012. It chimes with what Rosa told him about having gone on a retreat in Herefordshire before they met.

The emails might not have been written by Rosa, Jar thinks, but Max has got it wrong about the diary. Rosa was here, just as she said she was.

65

Cromer, 2012

It seems that I'm not the only person who's caught the writing bug. I came down this morning to find Rosa sitting at the kitchen table, tapping away at her laptop.

'Revision?' I asked, not expecting an answer. She came up from Cambridge yesterday. Usual friendly routine – barely a word in the car from Norwich, spoke to A over dinner as if I didn't exist. She's making it very difficult to like her.

It was a while before Rosa answered. 'I'm keeping a diary,' she said, not looking up. 'Amy said it might help.'

'With what?' I asked, thinking it was time we flushed out the subject of her father, if only to agree to disagree.

'Dad was a special man,' she said, almost to herself.

'Time's a great healer,' I offered, then immediately wished I'd said nothing.

'You weren't close to yours, were you?'

Her question took me by surprise. 'It depends on what you mean by "close". Things were different in my day.'

She looked up. 'In what way?'

'Parents didn't try to be their children's best friends.'

'So you weren't close, then.'

No, we weren't, I thought, but I'm not going to give you the satisfaction of being right in your cod diagnosis. The man I thought was my father was a stranger to me in childhood.

'I can't pretend your father and I saw eye to eye,' I said, deflecting her observation. 'But that doesn't mean I don't understand how difficult it must be for you.'

Rosa remained silent.

'You know,' I continued, 'there are a lot of proven medical strategies that can help with bereavement, depression.'

She typed on in silence.

'They've helped Amy to turn her life around,' I added, but I knew it was a lost cause. A's been confiding in Rosa, boasting about having reduced her medication. It will only end in tears. 'I've been writing a diary, too,' I continued, changing the subject. 'More of a journal.'

'Was Jar helpful?' she said, less hostile.

'We chewed the literary cud together.'

'He's a good teacher. Patient.'

'I'll bear that in mind.'

'Is your Wi-Fi working?' she asked. 'I can't seem to connect.'

'Let me take a look.'

'I just need to send some emails.'

I searched for the card, but it wasn't in the normal place on the mantelpiece. A uses a different router in the house – narrow bandwidth, but enough for her needs. I have my own fibre-optic broadband in the shed. Then I saw the card, over by the phone. I picked it up, glanced at the access code scrawled in A's illegible hand as I gave it to Rosa, and left the kitchen. Two minutes later, Rosa was at the back door, calling out to me as I recycled our wine bottles. A might be cutting down on the benzos, but she's drinking more. We both are.

'There still seems to be a problem with the Wi-Fi,' Rosa said.

I came back into the kitchen, sat down at the table and looked at her MacBook Air. Rosa had moved to one side and was standing behind me. As I opened up the Wi-Fi preferences, her mobile phone rang.

'Hi, babe,' she said, walking away to stand by the open back door. *Babe.* I glanced across at her. She was looking at me but turned away, as if I was intruding on her conversation. Sometimes I'm taken aback by how much Rosa reminds me of A when she was younger. I wish we could get on better.

Rosa's gmail inbox window had been minimised, but I wasn't interested in reading her college emails. It was her diary I was after. I couldn't resist the opportunity. For purely professional purposes, of course – I wanted to see how a real one measured up against my own attempts at writing a journal – but I told myself there was another reason, too: I need to understand Rosa better if I am to learn to like her, understand her world, get closer. She's A's niece, after all. Family. I must make more of an effort.

Turning Wi-Fi off and on in preferences, I selected A's router. Rosa had entered the code incorrectly. A few moments later, her computer was connected.

I glanced again at the door. Rosa was deep in conversation. Without hesitating, I maximised her gmail window, created an email, attached the diary document, which I found easily enough on her desktop, and sent it to my own address. I then opened her sent emails, deleted the email, selected the deleted box and deleted it from there, too, before I returned the screen to the inbox, as it had been, and minimised. Literary theft. Does it count as a proper crime?

'All sorted,' I said, looking up at Rosa, who was walking

back over to the kitchen table. I was struggling to control my breathing.

'Thanks. What was the problem?' she asked, sitting down at the table.

'Amy's handwriting. You'd entered the access key incorrectly.'

'Jar sends his regards, hopes the novel's progressing.'

'I've just made an important breakthrough,' I said, unable to conceal a smile.

66

My guard brought me some 'civilian' clothes today – Ali Baba trousers and a fleece. He gave them to me after the session, said it was to reward my good behaviour. I am no longer a non-compliant detainee, apparently.

I won't wear the clothes. I will keep them for the outside.

He will never let me go, not after this long. My only chance of freedom is if I escape. I try not to be excited at the thought, even though I can feel the adrenaline rising through my body as I write these words. I must remain neutral, on a level, grey. No colour, no joy or sadness. Nothing.

My guard is a man of habit, of order and routine, but he will make a mistake. We all do, sooner or later.

67

'I found it in the office,' Jar says, turning the photograph over in his hands. They are back in the Land Rover, driving through Herefordshire. 'It's a photo of Rosa with Sejal, the woman she writes about in the diary.'

Max glances at the photo. 'It still doesn't prove a connection, though, does it? With this place?' Max nods as they pass the entrance to an army barracks on their left. Jar looks in at the gate, the guard on duty. The military life has always been a mystery to him, its uniformity.

'It proves that Rosa stayed at the retreat, which happens to be just up the road from the SAS headquarters. And it proves that she wrote the diary herself.'

'Does it?'

'She wrote about staying at a retreat in Herefordshire. Exhibit one: a photo of her staying at said retreat.' He looks at the photo in his hand. 'You can even see the front of the house in the background.'

Jar had been happy until he got in the car, pleased that Rosa had actually visited the retreat she'd written about. But Max's mood is troubling.

'I saw Rosa again,' Jar says. 'Just now, at the house.'

Max turns to him and then looks ahead. 'In the bedroom?'

'It was a post-bereavement hallucination. I experienced a memory trace – a contrail in the sky. At least, that's what my therapist calls them.'

'I lost my mother when I was fourteen,' Max says, after a pause. 'I was boarding at the time and back at school within the week. The waters closed over as if nothing had happened.'

'Did you see her at all? After she died?'

'Couldn't even remember her face for the first few weeks. My own dear beloved mother! I was terrified, thought I'd never be able to picture her again.'

'But you did?'

'I had the most extraordinary dreams. Just the good times, night after night, after I'd cried myself to sleep in my pillow in the dormitory. Us on holiday, her always smiling, laughing, hugging me. It was a gift from her, lasted for a month. After that, I felt I could get on with my life, move forward without her. Was Rosa happy when you saw her today?'

'She was.'

They drive on in silence, out of Herefordshire.

'We haven't got enough to publish something, have we?' Jar asks. He pulls out the tent peg, smiling at the bent evidence. He doesn't know whether to laugh or cry. Jaysus, it's not much, Jar knows that. Not much at all. Max doesn't even glance at it.

'We need that photo – the selfie you took together on the cliff edge.'

'I'm seeing Carl when we get back,' Jar says. 'He hadn't received it when I rang him.'

Max's mobile rings in a holder, below the radio. It's connected to a Bluetooth microphone somewhere above him.

'Speak to me, Sally,' he says.

'The MD wants to talk to you. Urgently.'

'I can't right now. Tell him I'll ring back later.'

'It sounded urgent.'

'I'm sure it is. He shouldn't have blown his bonus on crack cocaine and £1,000-an-hour hookers.' He hangs up.

'Was that wise?'

'He can wait. This can't. I've not felt this alive for years.'

The phone rings again.

'Yes, Sally.'

'He's cancelled the contract. Going elsewhere. Said you were meant to be available twenty-four hours a day.'

'Thanks, Sally,' he says, smiling at Jar as he ends the call. 'I never landed a big story when I was a journalist. This one was the closest I ever came. I was devastated when it wasn't published in a newspaper and I jacked it all in. It was Orwell who said, "Journalism is printing what someone else doesn't want printed. Everything else is public relations." This is journalism, Jar, what we're doing right here. It matters.'

Jar sits in silence for a while, grinning to himself as he listens to Max's wheezy breaths, then he glances at a Vauxhall Astra in the wing mirror.

'That car's been following us ever since we left Herefordshire,' he says.

Max looks in the rearview mirror. 'Are you sure?'

'For sure, for sure.'

A moment later, Max turns hard left, the Land Rover's tyres screeching as they veer off the main road and down a small track, only just making the turn.

'Hold on,' he says, as Jar clings to the door. 'This might get bumpy.'

68

Cromer, 2012

A thinks all the cameras are for security. They are – or, at least, they were. I knew I would be a target for animal rights activists from the moment I joined the lab in Hunting-don, and it was the same when I moved to a different firm in Norwich. The police have advised me that the risks will remain for some time after my departure.

It's now two months since I left that world. By chance, one of the antis who was interested in me has just been locked up, but two of them were let off with suspended sentences. I made an issue of this to A, who is easily frightened and thinks we're being watched, when the technician came to instal new cameras last week. He replaced all the external units, as well as the internal units. A hated the ones inside the house, said they ruined the decor, so I promised her more discreet cameras, without going into detail. She was out at the time.

I'm sitting in my shed now, in front of a bank of small TV screens, waiting for Rosa to go to bed. I left her talking to A in the kitchen. She seems more depressed than ever. A has told her to run a deep bath and has given her some sort of oil or essence to put in it, to help her relax. Five milligrammes of lorazepam would have been more helpful.

Rosa's diary has turned out to be fresh, raw. I've read most of it and I'm on the right lines with this, my own semi-fictionalised effort. There's too much sentimental stuff about Jar, and it's overly chatty – 'first person on steroids' seems more apt than ever – but there's a story in there somewhere, something I can steal for the novel. I'm just not sure what it is yet.

I'm particularly intrigued by her college dean, Dr Lance, who moonlights for the intelligence services. I've heard a lot about how Oxbridge colleges tip off MI5 and MI6 about suitable candidates. It will be interesting to see if Rosa ever gets a tap on the shoulder. (Sadly, no one ever bothered to approach me.) Would she write about it in her diary? Having a father who worked for the Foreign Office must increase her chances of being recruited, even if he wasn't involved with intelligence matters – officially.

This is the first time I've checked on the cameras in the guest room, and I keep telling myself that I am doing this purely for security reasons. They are only activated by movement and I didn't want to ask A to test them, in case it alarmed her unduly.

I've emailed my tutor about adopting a diary format for the novel, something I've been practising here in my journal, and he says it will only work if my use of the present tense is as 'vivid' as possible. Which is where I'm hoping the cognitive enhancers will come in handy. I'm going to practise commentating on the camera test, using dictation software that turns my voice into typed words. Throw in 500 mg of the nootropic I was working on before I left the lab, add two hits of LSD, and we're in business.

I've decided that I'm not going to share this journal with anyone, not even my tutor. It's just for practice after all, the amuse-bouche. Since I started writing, it's become more confessional than I planned – far too honest – which presents a few problems, however much I dress it up as fiction. To be on the safe side, I'm going to have to encrypt it at some stage, as we had to do with a lot of our more sensitive documents in the lab.

Rosa's just entered the room.

She walks into the bedroom and drops on to her bed. She is looking tired, defeated. She checks her phone for messages and then reaches across for her laptop, which is on the bedside table. She opens it up and starts to write. I can't see what, but I want to think it's her diary. I like the symmetry, the connectedness: I'm 'writing' my journal at the same time as she's writing hers. I'd like it even more if she took some clothes off.

Five minutes have passed and I'm typing this again, keeping one eye on the screen in front of me. If I were a more loyal husband, I'd be checking on the new camera in our bedroom. Would A understand if she saw me now?

Rosa's stirring.

She walks through to the en suite, where one of the new cameras is rolling. She starts to run a bath. Now she's heading back to the bedroom, removing her T-shirt as she goes, shaking down her hair. Not exactly 'event' underwear: practical, white. The jeans are coming off too, her (no-frills) knickers slightly pulled down at the back. Here we go: bra and knickers tossed to the floor like so much flotsam and jetsam.

Back into the bathroom, leaning in to stir the water, adding the oil. Now she's in the bedroom again, walking around on her phone, which must have been ringing (no audio on these cameras – yet).

I should stop now, turn off the monitors, stop violating Rosa's privacy, but I can't bring myself to reach for the switch.

Call me an old hippy for using LSD, but I've always admired its dopaminergic properties, something not often found in serotonergic psychedelics. And its ability to treat depression and anxiety is astonishing. It will never become accepted as a medical treatment, though. Ever since the sixties, Big Pharma has been wary of developing 'countercultural' psychedelic therapies. LSD would prove hard to patent, too. The trouble with peyote, the effects of which are similar to LSD, is the variation in potency. You need to extract the mescaline from the dried cactus buttons first, which is easy enough but takes time, along with some sodium hydroxide, benzene and a pressure cooker (just don't use aluminium). Give me a tab of acid any day. And when acid is mixed with a nootropic, the trip is significantly enhanced in a way that works well for me: a more intense peak (and a more sudden comedown, regrettably). The visual experience is more mathematical, too: clear-headed, ordered and connected. None of the swirling, surreal dreaminess you get with LSD on its own.

I've been using the nootropic when I work on the novel – we were close to going to market with it before I left and I know it will change the face of nootropics when it's finally released. The clarity and enhanced cognitive abilities are one thing (it worked particularly well on Alzheimer's patients in trials), but it's the positive interaction with a whole host of recreational drugs that will make it a market leader.

Rosa steps into the bath, stirring the water as she sits down. She lies back, staring at the ceiling, directly up at me, one leg idly cocked. Has she seen the camera? I look away, unable to maintain eye contact. No. We're safe. Her eyes are now closed. It's going to be a good evening.

69

Sometimes, when a butterfly's wings are folded, it's hard to tell if it is resting or dead.

14 x 9 = 126

zyxwvutsrqponmlkjihgfedcba

'Age cannot wither her, nor custom stale her infinite variety.'

My nails are long again. He has not made a mistake.

70

C arl is waiting for Jar at the rear of the office, near the post room and loading bay. There's a large generator, painted battleship-grey and, beyond it, a dilapidated smoking shelter. Two buckled bikes are wedged into an old cycle rack beside a wheelie bin. Jar likes it around here: no corporate façade. He's pleased to be with Carl, too, even though his pal is mad at him.

The boss finally snapped when the police raided the office and removed Jar's computer. After that, he told everyone that Jar no longer worked for the company and should not be allowed back in the building under any circumstances.

'I've got no mates left at all now,' Carl says. 'What am I going to do?'

'There's always the IT department.'

'You are kidding?'

'You're a geek at heart, Carl. Admit it.'

Jar had wanted to meet further away from the office, but Carl had insisted. Things were busier than usual, he said, and his workload had doubled with Jar gone. No one to share Google Doodle duties, or X Factor stories, a particular bane of both their lives. Carl's text had woken Jar – he and Max had got back late from Herefordshire the night before. Carl said it was urgent and he wouldn't speak on the phone.

'How's it going anyway?' Jar asks, looking around him at the security guard in his leaking Portakabin. This is where Jar used to enter the building when he was running later than usual. If you took the ramp beside the loading bay, you could arrive unnoticed, beyond the main reception, in the canteen, via a door behind the toaster machine.

'Since you ask, we're 40 per cent down on page views this month,' Carl says.

'Nothing a Jennifer Lawrence picture gallery can't sort,' Jar says. He misses the office camaraderie but not the work.

Carl lights a cigarette and offers one to Jar, who declines.

Ever since Jar told him that he'd seen Rosa on the cliffs in Cornwall, Carl has been short with him, no doubt frustrated that he's still hallucinating and is not getting proper help. But his manner is different today, more sympathetic, like old times.

'It arrived overnight. Woke up this morning and there it was, on my phone. I wanted to tell you in person.'

'The photo?' Jar asks.

'No, a text from Santa saying he's for real. Of course it was the bloody photo – of you and Rosa in Cornwall.' Carl gets out his phone, pulls up the image and hands it to Jar. 'I'm so sorry, bro. You know... That I didn't believe you.'

Jar's hand is shaking as he takes the phone from his friend, suddenly aware of the crackle of a nearby bike courier's radio. He has to shield the phone, but then he sees the image clearly: him and Rosa, squinting up at the camera, fear in his eyes, emptiness in hers, moments before the man arrived and she was taken away from him.

He lets out a long, slow breath. No one can doubt him

now. 'And you can tell when it was taken?' he asks, his voice quiet but firm.

'Time, date, location. You had it all switched on in your preferences.'

'Thank Mary for that.'

'What does this mean, Jar?'

'Mean? It means that Rosa's alive. That she didn't take her own life five years ago.'

Carl shakes his head, taking a drag of his cigarette. 'I can't believe it, bro. Of course, I do believe it, I believe you, now I've seen the photo, it's just that—'

'I know.' Jar glances at his friend, who is beginning to well up. 'Why did the photo take so long to arrive?' he asks, steering the conversation towards less emotional territory. Carl knows where he is with technology.

'Ask your provider. Multimedia messages can take a few hours, sometimes days. In this case, three days. She doesn't look so well, bro.'

'She wasn't. She isn't.'

'And they got her just after this was taken?'

'A second later I was lying on the grass, hit on the head, and she was gone.'

'What do we do now? With the photo?'

'Can you send it to me? I'll get it to Max. He's writing the whole thing up.'

'Max?'

'The corporate PR fella who wrote the article about Rosa.'

Jar realises the awkwardness too late. He should be asking his old friend to help.

'You mean the fantasist,' Carl says.

'He's not so shabby now.'

'He's a PR for bankers, Jar. It doesn't get dodgier than that. Unless he's an estate agent on the side.'

'Or a traffic warden.'

Carl takes another drag of his cigarette and looks around him. 'Or a barber.'

'Barber?' Jar glances at Carl's long, dreadlocked hair.

'Spawn of the devil.'

Jar will send the photo to Miles Cato too, but he decides against telling that to Carl, who distrusts policemen even more than hairdressers. A second later, a text with the photo attached lands on Jar's phone.

Jar opens it up and looks at it for a moment before putting his phone away.

'Thanks,' he says, fighting the urge to ask Carl for a cigarette. 'There's one more thing. I need you to show me how to get on to the dark web.'

71

Cromer, 2012

R ound and around she swims, looking for a way out. Rosa's been in the water for more than four hours now, and her head is beginning to sink below the surface, her legs are tiring. I could watch her all night if she had the strength, but she is exhausted. Even the panic in her eyes is turning to resignation as the water rises over her head.

For twenty years, the Porsolt forced swim test was an integral part of my working life at the lab. Also known as the behavioural despair test, it's one of the standard ways to measure the efficacy of antidepressants. Roger Porsolt, a psychopharmacologist from Auckland, came up with the simple idea in the late 1970s. Place a mouse in a one-litre beaker of water (filled up to the 800-millilitre mark) and observe how it deals with unavoidable and inescapable stress: the threat of drowning (mice hate water). To begin with, the mouse swims around, even tries to climb the sides of the beaker, but after a while it becomes immobile, doing just enough – an occasional twitch of a paw – to keep its head above water.

Porsolt discovered that if mice are given antidepressants, they put up more resistance, swim for longer, try harder.

He also hypothesised that mice's immobility in the water correlates with depressive disorders, despair and a state of hopelessness in humans. Which is why the test is so ideal – low cost, fast, reliable – for the primary screening of antidepressants (along with the muricidal test, in which rats that are given antidepressants seem to suppress their natural urge to kill mice placed in their cages).

The cylindrical beaker is on my desk now, as I write into the early hours. After Rosa finally went to sleep in the guest room, I slipped her namesake into the water and have been watching her swim around ever since.

We used transgenic mice in the lab, because of their ability to mimic human illness, but it's not so easy to get hold of them when you are on the outside, so I have to settle for what I can find on the dark web. Amazing what you can buy with bitcoins.

Rosa, the one beside me now, has been in the water for four hours twenty minutes. Five minutes is the normal permitted time for a forced swim, but I prefer to let things develop into a 'terminal exhaustion test' – when you keep them in the water until they die. It tends to yield more interesting data. Given the right medication, a mouse can stay alive in the water – and remain more mobile – for three times longer than a control. My PB is 840 minutes – fourteen hours.

Sadly, I don't think Rosa's going to survive for much longer. Her legs have stopped moving now. She is sinking beneath the water, her sodden body giving one final twitch before falling still for the last time.

72

My guard comes at two o'clock every afternoon. I know this because I count the seconds, from the moment I'm woken up by a plane passing over, high in the sky. The flight might not be regular, of course, what with wind speed and air-traffic-control delays, but it marks the beginning of my day: 6 a.m. Rosa Time. And then I count every second: 28,800 until he arrives.

Sometimes he comes with another guard, but he was on his own today and late, which is unusual. Or maybe the plane this morning was ahead of schedule.

It's quiet here now, but I know the cries will start soon. I've been counting them in too, from the moment he leaves. The first minute is hard, because I am in such pain after the session, but I've managed it all week now. During the day it's silent out there. Perhaps the other prisoners get moved out.

If I am right, the cries will begin any minute now, 240 seconds after he left. (I have learnt to count in the background, while I write this. Multitasking – that's me.) A low moan followed by banging against bars. Six bangs, every time. Then, two minutes and thirty-five seconds later, a scream followed by sobbing and more bar banging, communal this time: a show of support, cut short by abuse from a guard – American, I think.

237

238

239

240

I pause from the counting, listen to the silence. A few seconds either side will not matter.
And then it begins: a long, slow moan followed by banging. It's too routine, even for a prison.

73

'Ithought I was close to finishing the article, sending it over to a paper, but we're missing something.'

Jar listens to Max as they both look out of his office window down on to the concourse. This low-key reception from Max isn't what he expected, given that he texted Max the photo earlier. Miles Cato hasn't responded either, though Jar sent the photo to his mobile, too. Christ, what more proof does everyone need that Rosa is alive, that he was with her on the cliffs in Cornwall three days ago?

Far below them, commuters are swarming towards Canary Wharf Underground station, past the bank of clocks that stand sentinel, measuring out their daily lives in seconds: the ones, like Jar, who arrive late for work, and the bath-dodgers, as Max calls them, who leave work just late enough to miss their young children's evening ablutions. 'Never missed bath time in six years,' Max boasted to him.

Five minutes earlier, Jar had walked by the clocks on a far more urgent schedule. Rosa managed to escape once, but whoever is holding her won't let it happen again. They will have punished her, if she's not dead already.

'We've got the photo, stamped with time and place,' he says. 'What else are we missing?'

'There's definitely no college counsellor. No American called Karen has ever worked at St Matthew's. I've been back to Dr Lance, finally got through to him on the phone.'

'He would say that. If he's recruiting for the intelligence services.'

'I'm not sure if that's true either.'

'Ask anyone.' Jar is annoyed now. 'Everyone knows Dr Lance is on their books.'

'I've also looked into Sejal. They found her body.'

'What? Sejal was part of the programme. She—'

'Six months later.'

'They must have made a mistake, found someone else's body.'

'Not so easy with DNA testing.'

Something's got to Max, Jar thinks. His enthusiasm has gone. 'Is it still OK to use your computer?' he asks, keen to steer the conversation on to more neutral ground. He doesn't like Max's mood. 'I can find an internet café if it's easier.'

'Of course. Plenty of space, as you can see. Make yourself at home.' At least he's making an effort to sound positive, Jar thinks, but he's not his usual ebullient, shambolic self.

Earlier, Jar had rung him and asked if he could do some research online in his office, explaining that he no longer even had a work computer to use – or a job. He didn't go into details, omitted to tell Max that he planned to use his computer to dive the dark web in search of Rosa's captors, but Max couldn't have been more welcoming. He'd had to let two colleagues go yesterday, after losing more banking clients, and Jar sensed he wanted the company.

'Maybe you're right. Maybe we are missing something,' Jar says, hoping to sound conciliatory. He settles down at an empty desk and pulls out his phone, opens the photo of

Rosa and props it next to the computer like a family snap. He can't get over the emptiness in Rosa's eyes.

'A part of me thinks that this might all have nothing to do with the intelligence services, or the police,' Max says.

Jar looks up at him. 'What about the confidential memo? Eutychus?'

'I don't know what to think any more, Jar. If someone faked the emails, maybe the memo is fake too, and the diary—'

'Rosa writes about events that only I know happened, Max,' Jar says, raising his voice. 'Swimming in the Cam, staying over in my room.'

'And she writes about things that didn't happen, too. There was never any counsellor at St Matthew's called Karen. What if there wasn't a programme called Eutychus?'

Jar looks out the window, watches a plane take off from City Airport and arc across the London sky. He doesn't want to argue. Max is right. The similarities between Rosa's diary and the article, the elements of it that Max made up, are too striking to ignore. He needs to revisit the spy site where the article was published, dig around the dark web. He picks up his phone, glancing at the photo of him and Rosa together, and calls Carl. If Jar found Rosa once, he can find her again.

74

Cromer, 2012

Kirsten and I were on our own in the sitting room and, it's fair to say, we'd both had a lot to drink. I had planned to serve a regulation claret this evening but, when Kirsten walked in through the front door, from America, I decided on impulse to break open the champagne. Tonight's other guests – a pair of retired History of Art lecturers – hung around for a bit after supper and then left, leaving A to take a long call in the kitchen and me on my own with Kirsten.

The last time I saw Kirsten was when A was FaceTiming her in bed a few weeks back. Computer cameras are never flattering, but Kirsten, with her blonde bob and high cheek-bones, caught my eye. I even wrote a brief character sketch in my Moleskine, hoping to use her in the book. Now that she's here, in the flesh, I'm keen to observe her more closely.

Tonight, she looked radiant, stunning even. What's more, she likes to flirt – a raised eyebrow here, a napkin-suppressed giggle there. As we talked on the sofa in the sitting room, our knees closer together than strictly necessary, my mind was already fast-forwarding to later.

Her manner – a touch on the arm, lingering glances – is so

intoxicating that I found myself wondering if I'd taken any-thing earlier, but I was clean. I was even prepared to overlook her choice of profession and enter into the sort of toe-curling conversation that she no doubt holds with her clients. She plans to move over to London in a couple of years, open up a practice on Harley Street. It's enough to make me sign up for some sessions.

I'm joking. As I was explaining to A yesterday, if counsel-ling really was as good as she claimed, we wouldn't be living in this big house and an entire antidepressant industry would be out of business.

'How would you characterise your relationship with women, Martin?' Kirsten asked, preceding her brazen inter-rogation with that same odd intake of breath that I'd noted when she was FaceTiming A.

'That's a very personal question.'

'Habit, I'm sorry. Let's talk about the weather. That's what you guys do in England, right? Way more interesting.'

'My parents left me when I was three,' I offered, drinking deeply from my glass. I had no idea why I'd told her that, why I was even having the conversation. Maybe it was some weird defence of our national character, proving that we can talk about something other than rain. The only other per-son I've spoken to about my parents is A, and that was when we first met, when I was trying to impress her with my emo-tional openness. (Ha!)

'I'm sorry to hear that. Were you taken into care?'

I laughed, with more derision than I intended. 'They divorced and I was sent to stay with my grandparents.'

'You've talked to Amy about all this?'

'And she's asked if you can get me to talk a bit more about it.'

'Not if you don't want to.'

'She says I'm too closed, but I'm not sure that this is the time or place to "open up". A bit unprofessional, isn't it?'

A voice in my head was telling me to get up, walk away and do the dishes, but I stayed where I was. Deep down, I've always known I need to talk to someone. And why not to the foxy Kirsten, a choice seemingly endorsed by my wife? If only my motives were so pure.

'I hoped I might be able to talk to you informally, as a family friend, but you're right. It's unprofessional. Let's leave it.'

'I thought Amy would be a substitute mother – is that the kind of thing you want me to say?'

'I don't *want* you to say anything, Martin.'

'Perhaps she was looking for a father figure. I am seven years older than her.'

Sheesh, are you really? You don't look it. Must be all that hill work on the bike, she replied, but only in my head.

'Did your parents ever get back in touch?'

'I tracked down my mother when I was at Cambridge. She told me never to contact her again. My father drank himself to death a few years after the divorce.'

'And were you close to your grandparents?'

'My grandfather was a POW in Japan. He married my grandmother just before the war. When he didn't come back, she presumed he was dead, so she had an affair with an American here in the UK. My grandfather then returned and never forgave her. Spent the rest of his life punishing her and the daughter she was pregnant with – my mother.'

'Was the American the father?'

'My grandfather never let anyone forget it. Consumed with anger until the day he died.'

'Was he angry with you?'

'He used to lock me under the stairs.' I was now in

uncharted waters. I haven't even told A about the cupboard that smelt of Traffic Wax and was so small that I had to sit with my knees pulled up to my chest (I was a tall child). How I feared the stairs would collapse above me as my grandfather stormed up to his bedroom. Dust used to fall from the cupboard ceiling and I had to suppress my sneezes. Any noise and he would drag me out to beat me with a wooden brush. One time he kept me in there for sixteen hours.

'That's criminally abusive behaviour, Martin.'

'It's fair to say my presence in the house was resented. I hate to think what the Japanese must have done to him in the war. My grandmother was too frightened to intervene.'

'How did you survive?'

'I had hope.' I know I shouldn't have told her, but I couldn't help myself. 'And hope's an extraordinary thing.' I paused again, thinking through the implications of what I was about to say. 'There was once this scientist called Curt Richter, you might have heard of him. He did a lot of groundbreaking research in the 1950s, not least about the biological clock.'

'Mine's ticking so damn loud it keeps me awake at night.' She laughed.

I held her gaze for a moment.

'But Richter's most important findings concerned hope – what came to be known as his "hope experiments". He once put some wild rats in a high-sided container filled with circulating water – there was a current on the surface to stop them floating – and recorded how long they swam for before they died.'

'That's horrible.'

'They were all dead within fifteen minutes, drowning after an initial period of struggle. But then he did the test again with a second group of rats, and when these rats were just at the point of exhaustion he scooped them out of the water

– he saved them – and dried off their fur. Then, after a few minutes' rest, he put them back in the circulating water. This time, the rats kept swimming – for sixty hours. *Sixty.* That's 240 times longer than the first group. These rats had hope – hope that they might be rescued again. Doesn't that tell us something? They could visualise an end to their suffering and that thought kept them going.'

'And you had hope under the stairs?'

'One time my grandfather let me out after I'd been in there for barely an hour. Full of remorse, contrite, he cradled me in his arms as he sobbed his heart out. After that, I always thought he would do the same again and let me out early.'

'But he never did?'

I shook my head and took another large sip of champagne, wondering where our conversation was going, why I'd confided in her. I've studiously avoided talking about animal testing with A, at least the details.

'Do you regret not having had children?' Kirsten asked.

Her direct question finally pulled the plug on our charade. My drink tasted sour, her bright eyes faded.

'I didn't realise we were here to talk about family planning.'

'People respond in different ways to childhood traumas. Some don't want to see their own experiences repeated; others continue the cycle, abuse their offspring.'

'Amy always wanted a child. I'm sure we both know that.'

'She's been enjoying having her niece here to stay.'

'Sometimes I think she's using Rosa to punish me.'

'Does her presence in the house make you uncomfortable?'

'Let's talk about the weather,' I said.

And that's how we left it. She went back to find A in the kitchen, I retreated down here to my shed. And now Kirsten's bedroom door has finally opened. She's coming to bed.

75

The moon is bright tonight. The stars must be out, too. Ursa Major, Orion's Belt, the North Star...

I can't remember all their names any more. Jar once taught me how to use the Plough's pointer stars to locate Solaris. We were lying on our backs on the grass in Christ's Pieces in Cambridge, after necking too much Belgian beer. The small pub where we'd been drinking was candlelit in the evenings – we were there when the barman lit them and when he blew them out at closing time, snuggled into a corner playing Scrabble. It was one of the happiest nights of my life.

I can't remember Jar's face, either. Or Amy's.

The other prisoners are crying out tonight again. Same time, same routine. It gives me hope.

76

It's late and Jar is sitting at the window desk in Max's office. Max has gone out in search of food and Carl is at Jar's shoulder, helping him navigate the dark web. Jar had hoped to be able to do this on his own, after Carl had talked him through the basics over the phone, but he lost his nerve early on, when he found himself looking at a directory page that read like a summation of every twisted depravity known to man.

'Tor directories are always pointing you towards Torch, claiming it's a great way to search onions, but it never works, not in my experience anyway,' Carl says, leaning over to type on Jar's keyboard. 'You can reach Torch's homepage easily enough, but have you tried doing an individual search? They time out. Always.'

Jar has no idea what his friend is talking about, but he watches as he scrolls down and opens what he recognises as Max's old article on the spy junkie website: a long series of numbers followed by the .onion suffix.

Carl had been reluctant at first to come over to Canary Wharf, still moaning about Max and his corporate PR work, but when the two of them actually met, they got on fine, particularly when Max revealed an encyclopaedic knowledge of London's nineties reggae scene and an unlikely fondness for UK Dub.

'I'll be all right from here,' Jar says, looking at the spy site.

Carl hesitates for a moment, unconvinced, and then retreats to the third desk in the office, across from Jar's, where he's conducting his own searches.

Diving the dark web scares the hell out of Jar. It's the thought of making a wrong turn, a wrong click, and finding himself in a paedophile chatroom, or unintentionally buying heroin with bitcoins in an FBI sting, even though he knows the Tor software he's using is meant to ensure anonymity. He tells himself he's doing this for Rosa.

'We never accessed the comments on Max's story,' Jar says, twenty minutes later. It's good to be back in an office with Carl, even if the plush Canary Wharf surrounds are a far cry from the website offices. 'It's attracted quite a lot of interest over the years. See here?'

Carl comes over to Jar's screen again. 'The bandwidth in this building is exceptional, I'll give you that,' he says. 'Must be for all those bankers live-streaming their HD porn.'

'This guy,' Jar continues, ignoring him, 'ChristiansInAction—'

'That's the CIA, a common nickname,' Carl says.

How does Carl know that? 'He comments on other stories on the site, too,' Jar continues. 'Look what he says here: "Nothing about my old firm surprises me. When I was working clandestine in Europe, I heard rumours about a programme called Eutychus. Never got to the bottom of it – way past my pay grade. All I know is that it was some sort of recruitment project, targeting bright British kids at Oxford and Cambridge universities. Clean skins given new IDs, faked deaths, that kind of thing. Sounds like donkey dust, but you never know with this shit."'

'How did we miss this?' Carl asks.

'The comments were hidden,' Jar says. 'It took a while to find them.' Carl raises his eyebrows, impressed. 'And see here.' Jar points again at the screen. 'The comment below: "This reads like a Le Carré spy thriller. Or maybe Len Deighton. I wouldn't put it past the Americans to do this kind of thing, with or without the cooperation of Britain's intelligence services." It's posted by someone calling themselves Laika 57.'

'How are you spelling that?' Carl asks, going back to his desk.

Jar spells it out – there's something about the name that sounds familiar – and continues to scroll through other comments on the story.

'Laika 57 shows up in one or two other places, nothing on the surface web,' Carl says, five minutes later. 'He's posted a few times in some batshit Guantánamo torture forum.'

'About what?'

'Rectal feeding,' Carl says, sounding distracted. Jar's beginning to wish he hadn't asked. 'And something called "learned helplessness".'

'Which is...?'

There's a pause as Carl reads. 'They did it to dogs in the 1960s – subjected them to so much pain that they no longer tried to avoid it.'

'And they did that to prisoners in Guantánamo?'

'That's what it says here. Seems like the prisoners were more compliant if they felt they had no control over their environment. The idea is to "breed passivity in the face of traumatic events". Not sure why, but it somehow feels a whole lot worse doing that kind of thing to animals.'

Jar looks up at his friend for an explanation.

'I mean, in Guantánamo, they were enemy combatants, right?' Carl says. 'The bad dudes.'

'Some of them.'

'But with the dogs, one minute they're minding their own business, being dogs, sniffing each other's patooties, the next they're banged up in a lab and being tortured. What did they do to deserve that?'

'Anything sounds better than rectal feeding,' Jar says.

'Vindaloo anyone?'

They both look up as Max enters with two brown paper bags of takeaway curry.

77

Cromer, 2012

Kirsten stumbles a bit as she walks over to the bathroom. She's drunk a lot tonight, we all have. A and her must have been chatting in the kitchen for a good two hours, no doubt complaining that men don't know how to open up, talk about their feelings.

I already know the guest-room cameras are working, but I can't help myself. The earlier champagne has erased what remains of my guilt. It's 1 a.m. and I think my patience is about to be rewarded. Kirsten's cleaning her teeth vigorously at the basin, her arse cheeks wobbling with the effort. I told her earlier that there's plenty of hot water to run a bath. Sadly, it seems like she has other ideas. She turns and looks around the small bathroom, glancing at the walls, the ceiling, now looking straight up at the central light fitting. Has she seen the camera? Her eyes are staring directly into mine. I'm holding her beautiful gaze, but there's no love there, only anger and suspicion.

She's turned back to the sink now and is looking hard at the mirror, running her hands along its sides, trying to see behind it. What's she up to? Now we're back in the main room and she's doing the same: moving around the walls, checking behind a picture (lifting it off the hook, returning it), removing books carefully from a small bookcase above the dresser.

My mouth is drying. She's in the middle of the room, looking around her. Again, she glances straight up above, staring at the light, at me. Christ, something's caught her eye.

She goes over to the bottom of the bed, picks up a wooden chair and moves it to below the light. Then she stands on it – her drunken imbalance has gone – and examines the fitting, where the wire joins the ceiling. Her cheek is so close to the camera I could reach out and stroke it, smell her sweet breath (citrus?).

What am I going to say? Explain about the need for security? Make something up about CCTV film being deleted after twenty-four hours? How the hell did she know to look? Does A know? Did she warn her? Has she been down here, to the shed?

The cameras are tiny, concealed as small screws and Kirsten would have to know what she's looking for. Unless she has a screwdriver, I'm safe.

She's climbing down off the chair now, places it back at the foot of the bed. Is sitting on the covers. Come on, Kirsten, quit all this mucking about: it's time to get your clothes off.

But she doesn't. She knows. How the fuck does she know? She's pulling back the sheet and climbing in, fully clothed. Side light off.

Kirsten is swimming beside me now, round and around in

the water, keeping to the edge, peering up at me. I've turned down the lighting in the shed – it's glowing blood red here, like in a submarine.

Her legs are tiring, her body sinking beneath the surface. Four minutes and thirty seconds. The longer she is in the water, the more disorientated she will become, until it's too late. Panic is tiring.

But then, just now, without warning, she summoned every last ounce of strength, scratched at the sides of the beaker and caught the rim with a claw. The next moment, she was out, perched on the table, staring at me, triumphant. Too much water in the beaker. I grabbed Kirsten and tossed her into darkness.

78

I'm late for my date, but Jar's pleased to see me. We've agreed to meet in the park, on a concrete bench, far away from anyone. On our own. I have washed my face in some water I kept from earlier (my guard turns off the mains when he's not here, which means the basin stinks – so does the loo), and I am wearing the clothes I was brought a few months back: the Ali Baba trousers and fleece. I can't brush my hair because it's been shaved off.

Tonight I just want to talk, without alcohol or distractions, which won't be difficult. I want to tell Jar a few things, sort out in my mind what really happened.

'I didn't write that letter,' I begin, on safe ground. For I am certain that it wasn't me who wrote the email. My guard has shown it to me on countless occasions over the years, explained how I left it in the drafts folder on Amy's computer. Jar takes my hands in his, which are so much bigger than mine. Better manicured, too – not saying much. I turn the silver ring on his thumb.

'I still should have realised how upset you were,' I hear him say. 'You never said anything.'

'It was difficult, after Dad died.' I've got used to hearing myself talk, but I'm surprised by the emotion in my voice. I thought I'd stripped out all feeling from my life.

'You went for a walk,' Jar says. 'At two in the morning. Why?'

'I needed to clear my head. I'm sure I left a note in my room saying I was going out for a bit. Handwritten.'

'But not a suicide note?'

'I want to live now. That's all I know.'

I look around the cell, tears welling. I have no way of telling if Jar cares about me, even believes that I'm alive. And then I remember his wry, pinched smile, the unrushed Irish brogue, intelligent eyes.

'I think that you walked to the pier and stood on the railings, looked down at the dark water, gave it some serious thought,' he says.

'But I didn't jump.'

'What stopped you?'

I think about my diary again, what it says happened next. I have read that diary over and over, so many times. It's all typed – I used a laptop then, not like now. I remember the retreat outside Hereford, Sejal, Dr Lance. But I am less sure about Karen. Was there a counsellor at St Matthew's with that name? There could have been. My memory has been shredded by medication – so many different pills.

'How long will you keep looking for me?' I ask. I'm sure we had so much more than what's written about us in the diary. It's as if great chunks of our life together, however brief it was, have been removed from my past.

'Till I am old with wandering.'

Jar loves Yeats, used to read it out to me late at night, when I stayed over in his college rooms. 'One day we will meet at the place we agreed that night,' I say. 'When we got drunk at The Eagle, remember? Our secret.'

79

J ar is on his own in the office now. Carl left first, just after
midnight, followed by Max, who told him to sleep on
the sofa in reception if it got too late. The air is stale with the
smell of curry and Jar wants to get home before dawn.

He glances at the clock behind Max's desk. It's almost
1 a.m. He wonders if he's the only person left in the tower,
apart from the Spanish-speaking cleaning staff he saw entering the building earlier. Jar's glad they're around. He doesn't
like the idea of being on his own up here in the tower. Max
said a security guard was supposed to do a circuit of their
floor a few times a night, but Jar's yet to see him.

For the past hour, Jar has been searching for other posts
by people who posted a comment on Max's original story.
He is now convinced that the article is central in some way
to finding Rosa, given the similarities between it and Rosa's
diary. *I'm sorry, Jar. I think someone's playing you.*

He has found no further mention of Eutychus, but he
keeps coming back to Laika57, who has posted more widely
elsewhere than Carl initially thought. If only he could find
his real name. ('Onionland's anonymous. That's kind of the
whole point,' Carl had said earlier, when Jar had asked him.)

He goes back to the disturbing Guantánamo torture site

that Carl found. There are several other posts from Laika57, one pointing out that what the CIA were doing to detainees owed much to experiments conducted in the 1960s, another about vivisection. ('With the dark web, it's a question of knowing where to look rather than searching randomly.' That's another thing Carl said before he left.) And then Jar finds a video posted by Laika57.

Most of the footage Jar's watched tonight was posted by prison guards. At first glance, this video looks like it was filmed at Guantánamo, but there's something different about it.

Jar swallows. The quality is poor, but it's possible, as the camera pulls back, to make out the body of someone suspended horizontally from the ceiling in what looks like a straitjacket or a hammock, coloured bright orange. The person's legs and arms are hanging down through holes in the harness and an electric cable is connected to one foot. Another cable runs up between the legs.

He can't see the face as it's covered by a black mask of some sort, a stitched grille covering the mouth. Only the eyes are visible.

Jar puts his hand to his mouth as the person's body suddenly convulses, head thrashing like a pinball between what looks like two panels that have been placed either side of the face. Some sort of yoke, connected to the two panels, has been secured around the neck.

'Jaysus,' Jar says, as if the electrical current has just passed through his own body.

He pauses the video and searches for the comments, which are not immediately visible. After locating them, he finds a post from Laika57, who describes how the CIA paid $81 million to two psychologists to oversee the interrogation of high-value detainees in Guantánamo.

Jar goes back to watching the video, flinches at a second shock. There's no sound, but he can hear the screams. He pauses the video again, glances around the empty office – why, he's not sure – and leans in to the screen to look more closely. The person's head has been caught in freeze frame, turned to one side. Jar is transfixed by the image in front of him.

He studies the eyes, and then traces down the trunk of the body to the legs and then the calf muscles. The victim is female, no question.

He presses play. A third shock rips through her body. Jar pauses it again, the woman's thrashing head clearly visible. It couldn't be her. But his gaze lingers on the woman's eyes. It doesn't look like Rosa and anyway, why would they take Rosa to Guantánamo?

He scrolls back through the footage and freezes the image of the woman's face. After scrutinising it, he gets up from his desk and makes a circuit of the office, trying to hold on to the thought that it's not her. He comes back to the screen. The face is contorted, blurred, the eyes behind the mask all wrong: too lifeless. But as he turns his head to one side, Jar can't help but see the woman on the cliffs in Cornwall.

He sits down, closes his eyes and opens them again. He's seeing things. From another angle, the woman doesn't look like Rosa. He begins to work methodically through all the comments – there are more than he originally thought. Torture trolls have crawled out from their caves en masse. And then he sees it, a few words near the beginning of the thread:

Nice work, Laika57 – best video yet.

Jar repeats the words in a whisper, noticing another, anonymous thread below the comment.

Psychochem: You still writing novel? When's it out?

Laika57: Fiction not so easy. I've written a journal – not sure will ever be published.

Psychochem: Could publish here?

Laika57: Too honest about my Seligman experiments – ha ha. Makes Knausgaard look reserved.

Jar's mouth dries. Fingers trembling, he googles 'Laika' on the surface web. A stray dog on the streets of Moscow, she was the first animal to orbit the earth, launched into space in *Sputnik* 2 in 1957. 'Muttnik', as the American press dubbed her, died after four circuits of the earth, from overheating. Rosa told Jar once that Martin's two beagles were named after Russian dogs that had been sent into space.

Martin. Is Laika 57 Rosa's uncle?

Jar switches back to Max's article, trying to control his breathing, and finds Laika 57's comment again that compares the story of Rosa's disappearance to a spy novel. What about all those times over the years when Jar emailed Amy and Martin with his theories about Rosa's disappearance? Martin was always so scornful of them, dismissing Jar as paranoid, unhealthily obsessed with conspiracies. What's he doing posting on an article on the dark web that suggests Rosa was recruited by the intelligence services?

What's he doing posting videos of a woman being abused in Guantánamo?

We now think Martin may be into torture videos. Jar should stop, ring Miles Cato, tell him what he's found. If Cato's investigation into Martin and his dodgy computer habits is genuine, this video is the proof that he's been looking for. But what exactly has Jar found? What if it is Rosa in the video...

He tells himself again that it's not her. Martin's interest in the site is purely professional: a self-confessed spy-fiction fan who worked in Big Pharma, he just wants to point out similarities between CIA torture techniques and animal experiments in the 1960s. Jar exits Max's story and looks for other Laika 57 posts, for something that will prove Martin's innocence in all this. On the site's main index page, he spots a thread on the origins of George Smiley, an innocuous enough subject. Martin would never pass up a chance to show off his knowledge.

Sure enough, Laika 57 is in full flow:

> Bingham or Green? On balance, Smiley owes more to John
> Bingham, 7th Baron Clanmorris, Le Carré's MI5 colleague and a
> fellow novelist.

Jar blinks. John Bingham was the fake name used to hire the car in Cornwall.

80

Cromer, 2012

The tail-suspension test has a lot going for it, not least its cost-effective simplicity. Using medical adhesive tape, mice are hung from their tails, away from any objects that they might try to hold on to or use to escape. Rosa is currently dangling in front of me as I write, secured to the underside of the shelf above my desk. But this shed is not ideal for these sorts of experiments.

In the past few months I've realised that I can't just stop what I was doing in the lab before I was fired, can't just turn off my interest like a tap. It's been my life for thirty years and I was close to a breakthrough: developing a next-generation antidepressant that works within days rather than weeks, in a wide variety of people and with limited side effects. If I'm not allowed officially to continue my research, I must find a way of carrying it on unofficially and complete the work that I was doing when I was sacked.

We used to have an off-site lab in the late 1990s. I went out to have a look at it this afternoon, took me an hour on the bike to get there. It's in a converted Nissen hut on a disused Second World War airfield on the far side of Holt.

There are lots around here: in the war the flat expanses
of north Norfolk were one giant airfield for Flying Fort-
resses and Wellington bombers. This one finally closed in the
1960s and part of it was then used for intensive poultry
farming, but that business shut down too, leaving rows of
low, empty buildings. For a brief period in the 1990s, some
of them were used by local businesses, including us, but they
are all derelict now.

I'd forgotten about the facility in the intervening years and
was pleased to see that the place hasn't changed much. The
original hut, which is in a clump of pine trees on the side of
the airfield, has been converted to include a series of dormer
windows along the front that allow in more light. I looked
in through a broken window – one of the original ones in
the brick walls at either end of the building. There wasn't
much to see: just some empty office space, peeling wall paint,
a couple of broken chairs. Nothing to suggest that it was a
laboratory, which is probably why the antis never found out
about the place. The real lab was in the basement, away from
prying eyes, in a converted former air-raid bunker.

I was one of only a handful of people who knew about the
facility, what we did there. The ground floor was used for
company admin – a good front for anyone passing by (part
of the airfield was occasionally used by light-aircraft crop
sprayers) – but there was a fully equipped, if rather small,
lab in the basement, entry to which was via a panel in the
floor, covered by a filing cabinet, that led to a short set of
steep iron steps.

It's a measure of the paranoia in those days that we had to
resort to such lengths in order to carry out tests on animals
(mainly canines), but that's how things were.

I managed to get into the building this afternoon through

the broken window, but there was still a heavy padlock on the floor panel preventing me from gaining access to the basement. I'm planning to go back there tomorrow, on my daily cycle ride (these days A expects me to be gone for at least three hours), with a pair of bolt cutters in my rucksack. I'm hoping there's still some equipment in the basement – we left there in a hurry, I remember.

Rosa's been hanging from the shelf for six minutes now, the normal duration for the tail-suspension test. It's not dignified: she should be in a proper lab. At first, her body wriggled and writhed, but now she is still, shrewdly conserving energy, or limp with despair, depending on your point of view.

What we do know is that antidepressants decrease the duration of immobility, making the test another useful method of primary screening. But there's only so much you can do with animals. Everyone agrees there are limits to the sort of psychiatric problems that can be modelled in a mouse: complex human bipolar disorders and schizophrenia are far removed from the 'state of despair' that a rodent feels in a beaker of water.

It was Protagoras who said that 'man is the measure of all things'. He had a point. Unfortunately, clinical trials of antidepressants in humans have long been plagued by controversy. Their efficacy is best demonstrated in the severely depressed, but such people are rarely recruited for trials. Instead, tests are carried out on patients with only mild to moderate conditions. The placebo response in depressed patients is also quite high, partially negating the treatment's effectiveness. The result? Big Pharma has put on hold much of its research into antidepressants.

I quoted Protagoras in my resignation letter, but senior management didn't want to know, even if a rethink of first-in-human trials is the only thing that's going to save the antidepressant industry.

I still stand by the basic premise that chronic high stress is a key component of most depression. And if, like me, you want to validate a next-generation antidepressant that you've been working on for almost all of your career, one that you know will transform the lives of millions of depressed people, then human patients, rather than rodents, need to be put into high-stress situations before being administered trial drugs. Big Pharma missed a trick in Guantánamo. I won't.

Rosa's eyes have closed.

81

It happened so quickly: the mistake.

He had only been in my cell a few minutes, long enough to remove my chains and administer the medication he always gives me before the session begins, when his mobile phone rang. I couldn't hear what the other person was saying, but it made him angry. So angry.

He left almost immediately, the door snapping shut behind him, but there was no sound of a padlock, no scraping noise. He always locks the cell door and something is dragged across it. But not today. And he forgot to chain me back up, too.

I waited five minutes before I moved, 300 seconds. He's done this before: tested me. On the last occasion I was left unchained, he kept the door open and disappeared. After two hours, I still hadn't moved from the floor. I had no desire to escape. None. When he returned, he congratulated me, gave me some fresh food – rice, chicken – and told me I was an example to other prisoners, a credit to science: 'a paradigm of learned helplessness'.

Today, though, something is different. I know it. He didn't mean to leave me like this. I've changed into the clothes he brought me a few months earlier, the ones I've been keeping for this moment: the Ali Baba trousers and fleece.

He's made a mistake. There's no other explanation. Now I must run.

82

'Amy, it's me, Jar. Did I wake you?'
'I got your text. I was up anyway.'

It's 3 a.m. and Jar had hoped that would be the case. She'd once told him about her insomnia, when the pills wear off or after she has secretly failed to take them. Jar is still in Max's office in Canary Wharf. He'd texted her a few minutes earlier, asked if she was awake, if he could call her. She had texted back straight away, told him to ring in ten minutes.

'Is Martin with you?'

'He's upstairs. Asleep.'

She sounds disconnected, unconcerned by being rung at this hour of the night. It's six days since Jar saw her in Greenwich Park, when she hadn't been looking well. He takes a deep breath, wonders where to begin, how much to tell her. He needs to get hold of Martin's journal, the one he mentioned in the comment he posted about the torture video, in which he's 'too honest about his Seligman experiments'.

'I need you to do something for me,' Jar says.

'Are you OK? Where have you been? You sound—'

'I'm fine. I was away.' Now's not the time to tell her about seeing Rosa in Cornwall. He doesn't know how she will react. 'Have you ever been into Martin's shed?'

'His shed? No, why?'

'I need you to go there now.'

'He doesn't allow anyone inside.'

'Is it locked?'

'Of course.'

'Do you know where the key is?'

'He hides it in a tankard on the kitchen dresser, but I—'

'I need you to go down there.'

Amy pauses. Jar can hear her breathing.

'Amy?'

'What is it, Jar?'

He wonders if she has had the same thoughts as him, buried, never acknowledged.

'I just need you to look for something.'

'I can't do this. He'll go crazy if he finds out.'

'He's asleep.'

'Is this about Rosa?' Amy is beginning to sound more engaged, Jar thinks. No need to tell her about his worst fears, not yet.

Two minutes later, Amy says that she is standing outside the front door of the shed, at the bottom of the garden.

'What's this about, Jar?'

'Please, just unlock the door.'

'You're frightening me.'

Jar's frightening himself. Canary Wharf is a lonely place at night. He hears her fiddle with the padlock, imagines her hands trembling, struggling to see what she's doing in the darkness, looking back up at the house in case Martin stirs.

'I've never been in here before, tell me that's weird.'

'A man's shed is his castle,' Jar says. And maybe his prison cell, he thinks. 'But yes, it's weird.'

'What am I looking for?'

Jar tries to picture the scene. He knows he should focus on the computer, get Amy to search for Martin's journal, but he can't stem the flow of thoughts. There might be a basement in the shed, or a hidden room, concreted over. A place where Martin makes his films, where...

'Tell me what you see,' he says.

'Some garden chairs, his croquet set.'

'Is there just one room?'

'There's another, at the back.'

'How many keys are on the ring?'

'Two.'

'Open the second door.'

Jar waits, listens to the sound of a padlock being sprung open.

'Are you in?'

'There's a strange red light in here.'

'What else?'

'A desk, a computer, some TV monitors. That's for the security CCTV. The cameras will have picked me up coming down here, Jar. There's one on the outside of the shed, and one on the back of the house, the back door.'

'He'll only look at the tapes if he suspects a security breach.' Jar's bluffing, but he can't think of anything else to say. CCTV tapes are usually wiped after a few days, aren't they? Unless there's been an incident.

'I want to go back to the house, Jar. I shouldn't be in here.'

'Tell me what else you see. Is there a door, a trap door?' He knows she should be searching the computer, but he can't help himself.

'There's a wine cellar somewhere, he mentioned it once.

When I was drinking all his best claret. I can see a panel on the floor.'

Jar's heart is racing as he pictures the scene: Rosa, confined in a dark space, terrified, out of her mind.

'Can you lift it up?'

'There's a box of files half covering it.'

'Try, please.'

He hears Amy put the phone down, move the box, but then there's silence.

'Amy?' Has she found her?

'Martin's up.' Amy is whispering.

'Can he see you from the house? Is there a window?'

'No. Not in this room. I can see him on the screen. There's a camera on the landing.'

'What's he doing?'

'He's coming down the stairs. He'll kill me, Jar, if he finds me out here. You don't know Martin.'

'You need to lift up the panel,' Jar says. 'The wine cellar door. Tell me what you see.'

Another pause.

'I'm lifting it up.'

Jar closes his eyes. 'What can you see?'

'It's just some wooden boxes of wine. Lots of boxes. What am I looking for, Jar?'

Martin's her uncle, Jar tells himself. John Bingham's a common enough name.

'Are you sure there's nothing else?'

He wouldn't keep her there, not so close to the house.

'Nothing. I'm sure. I want to get out of here, Jar. He's downstairs now, in the kitchen.'

'Lock up and then go for a walk, away from the shed. You've just gone for a night-time stroll, unable to sleep.'

'OK.' Jar's never heard Amy sound so scared. 'He's going upstairs again – to his bedroom. We're sleeping separately.'

Jar sighs with relief and then remembers the computer. 'There's one other thing. Is the computer on?'

A pause. 'Sleep mode, I think.'

'Can you activate it?'

'Jar, I want to go back to the house.'

'Please?'

Silence. He thinks he can hear Amy suppress a sob.

'You're doing brilliantly. Is it a Mac?' Jar asks.

'Yes.'

'There might be a password.'

'I'm looking at the desktop now. I think he left in a hurry. His desk is a mess.'

'Can you search for the word "journal"?'

'OK.'

'Anything?'

'I'm no good with computers.'

'You're better than you think. Is there a file called "Journal"?' Jar tells himself not to be so impatient. Amy's taking a big risk for him. For Rosa.

'Nothing's coming up.'

'Try "diary".'

'No.'

Jar knew it wouldn't be easy. He thinks of key words or phrases that Martin might have used in his journal. If he was recording everything, did Martin write about Jar's visits to Cromer?

'Try searching for "peyote".' He can hear Amy typing.

'Lots of files are coming up – what's a peyote?'

'Dried cactus. Try "Jar + peyote",' Jar says, remembering

the conversation he'd had with Martin about writing, drugs and the Beat Generation.

'It's found one file with those words in it,' Amy says. 'A Word doc called "My Struggle".'

'That's it,' Jar says, remembering Martin's interest in Knausgaard's autobiographical novels of the same name. Nothing if not ambitious.

'Should I open it?'

'Not so easy.' Jar assumes that Martin has encrypted the journal. Carl, or maybe Anton, if he ever resurfaces, should be able to decode it for him.

'Jar, I think it's already open, on the screen.'

'Are you sure?' Jar's palms begin to moisten. If the document is open, it won't need decoding.

'It's off the bottom of the screen, but I can drag it up.'

'Be careful.' Martin must have been writing his journal this evening, left it open. Jar doesn't want Amy to alter the document in any way, leave any trace of her visit – or look at it.

'He's written about Strelka, my beautiful dog,' Amy says. 'The day she died.'

'Don't read it, Amy, please,' Jar urges, trying to stay calm. 'I want you to listen to me, very carefully.'

He proceeds to talk Amy through how to open Firefox and log into her email account (Martin is signed into his own email in Chrome). He then gets her to copy and paste the entire contents of Martin's journal into a message to him, before asking her to copy some blank text to cover her tracks and delete the journal from the copy-and-paste memory.

'Now log out. That's important,' Jar says, after her email has dropped into his inbox.

'OK.'

'And quit Firefox, drag the Word window back to where it was, put the computer back to sleep.'

'Done.'

'Thank you, Amy.'

'What's this about, Jar?'

Jar takes a deep breath. He knows he owes Amy an explanation. 'I saw Rosa. I found her four days ago in Cornwall.'

83

North Norfolk, 2012

I've been coming out here every day for a week now and the lab is finally ready. The bolt cutters made short work of the old padlock on the floor-panel door, and I've installed a new one that should be harder to break. I've also sealed off the smashed window, screwed down the catches so they can't be opened, and put a new lock on the main entrance.

The lab is in relatively good condition, given it hasn't been used for more than ten years. The white paint might be peeling, but there's still a central experiment area, surrounded by worktops, and an operating table in the middle. Off to the side is a post-mortem room and at the back there's a small incinerator, a washbasin and lavatory.

There's no mains electricity – it must have been disconnected years ago – but there's a sunpipe that casts an eerie, pale light. We used it to keep certain animals synched with daylight. There's also more ventilation than there would have been when it was an air-raid shelter – vents were put in around the ceiling, again to make sure the animals stayed alive.

I've set up a video camera in the main area as there's a lot of interest in learned helplessness from colleagues on

the dark web, following suggestions that it was used to justify interrogation techniques at Guantánamo. Yesterday I
announced that shortly I hope to be re-creating a version of
the original experiments on dogs carried out by Martin Seligman at the University of Pennsylvania in 1967. I'll be low-res
live-streaming to a select few. Although there's no Wi-Fi here,
there's a 3G mobile signal. The dark web caters for niche
preferences even more than the surface web: sixties animal
testing meets CIA enhanced interrogation techniques, with a
twist of BDSM. Talk about a long tail.

This is what I posted today in one of the secure Tor forums
that I've come to trust:

*Learned helplessness is a condition in which an animal
– or human – becomes passive in the face of painful
or unpleasant stimuli. Concluding that they have no
control over their environment, they lose all desire and
incentive to escape. For various misguided 'ethical'
reasons, the experiments, pioneered in the 1960s by
Martin Seligman, have not been continued in recent
years, despite their efficacy in antidepressant drug
testing.*

An old colleague soon replied – a lab technician I haven't
heard from in a while. He was 'let go' too, for similar fabricated reasons. And he's taken up cycling – we're going to
meet up, ride out together. The two of us used to conduct our
own learned helplessness experiments at HQ, adapting Seligman's canine tests for rodents and other animals, but when
the antis started to make life tricky for us, we moved the
more sensitive work from Norwich to the facility out here.

It's strange being back, but I also feel very at home. Old

habits die hard. The daily precautions I take in order not to be seen entering the airfield – I leave my bike locked up in the woods and walk the rest via an overgrown footpath that runs along the southern perimeter – are not so different from the measures we all used to adopt at the lab (different routes to work each day, back doors, false commutes). And if A's suspicious of my prolonged absences from the house, she's not showing it.

All I need now is an animal on which to conduct my experiments.

84

J ar gets up from Max's desk, his legs heavy with adrenaline, and walks over to the window, looking out at the neighbouring Docklands towers. It will soon be dawn, but not yet: the night feels darker than ever.

He's been reading Martin's journal for the past half an hour: his early scribblings about 'first person on steroids' writing styles, his own visit when they discussed George Smiley, peyote and beatniks, the drunken conversation with Kirsten, and now the lab out in the Norfolk countryside, his trips there disguised as long-distance bike rides.

Is Amy reading it at the same time? Did she go into her sent folder and open the email? Jar can't get out of his head Martin's throwaway line about the benzos he's been prescribing her for the past twenty years: *it's made things simpler in the bedroom.* What's he been doing to Amy? And is it safe for her to be on her own with him? Jar knows that he should call the police, or at least social services, but he has an overriding compulsion to find out everything first.

He's about to read another entry when he hears a noise in the corridor outside, like a door closing. He assumes it's the cleaners, but there's something about the sound, the suggestion of force, that makes him stand up and go to the door. He's just over-tired, he thinks.

He walks out into the empty corridor. After listening for a few seconds, he turns to go back into Max's office, but then the double doors at the far end of the corridor swing open and two cleaners walk through, pushing a trolley loaded with mops and buckets. They are both Hispanic, a man and a woman, in their forties.

Jar smiles as they approach, relieved, but they seem tense and avoid eye contact. Perhaps they are surprised to see him, or have been told not to interact with the people who work here. It's what Carl calls 'corporate apartheid'. (He and Carl used to leave notes for the night cleaning staff at work, telling them to help themselves to the various freebies that had been sent to the office that day.)

Jar doesn't know whether to say goodnight or good morning, so he settles on an 'OK now?' There's no acknowledgement from either of them, not even a smile. They speed up as they pass, one of them glancing back towards the swing doors and then at Jar.

Jar hesitates for a moment, looking up and down the corridor, then returns to Max's office, locking the door behind him.

85

Cromer, 2012

A fell very quiet when I told her, asked me to repeat exactly how it happened, explain why I returned with only one dog. I didn't tell her why, but the how was an easier story to tell.

A and I used to go out for a morning walk together, in the days after I lost my job, both of us hoping for better things, 'new beginnings', as if all that was wrong with our marriage would disappear because I was suddenly at home all day. But it wasn't to be.

So after breakfast today I went out on my own with Belka and Strelka. I wasn't given the dogs as a leaving present from colleagues, as Rosa used to joke (like father, like daughter), although it's true we did use beagles a lot in our experiments. A and I got the pair of bitches from a rescue home in Norwich a few weeks before I knew I was leaving. Another false dawn. I named them after two Russian dogs who were put into space in 1960 on *Sputnik 5*, along with forty-two mice, two rats and a rabbit. Belka was mine, Strelka was A's. That's how we came to see them anyway.

My walk's always the same: down the road to the water

meadow, along the river, across the rail track, and back around to the house. A good twenty minutes at a brisk pace. This morning, Strelka was pulling at the leash from the off. A has always spoiled her, hasn't disciplined her as she should. I only ever let them off the leash once we've crossed the river on a small footbridge, then I allow them to run in the water meadow beside the railway, where there's good fencing.

Except today. The gate where the footpath crosses the railway line had been left open. I should say that on the far side there's a smaller strip of meadow, where rabbits often play. Strelka saw the rabbits before I did and ran along the fencing, desperate to get through. Belka was less interested, looping in small circles around me as I walked.

I saw the open gate before I heard the train, but I knew there was time to reach for the dog whistle I keep in the pocket of my waxed jacket. My hand found the whistle but I held it tight in my fist and watched.

Strelka was getting closer to the gate, barely five yards away from it, desperate to reach the rabbits. If I blew the whistle then, it would overrule her visceral urges and she would return to my side.

The whistle remained in my pocket as Strelka ran through the gate. She saw the approaching train but still headed up the low bank and on to the railway line, where certain death awaited her. It wasn't suicide, of course, just a healthy appetite for rabbits, but a life could have been saved. I didn't look away. Instead, I stood transfixed by the consequences of my inaction as Strelka's body was knocked backwards into the air by the front of the train and then landed on the track, before disappearing under the wheels.

The driver glanced across at me, accusation in his eyes, as the train continued on its way. Belka fell quiet at my side.

Perhaps her sister emitted a sound that I hadn't heard: fear in a higher register than the human ear can detect. I didn't hear anything at the moment of impact, just a dull thud.

There was no point in bringing Strelka back to the house. Nor did I tell A that what was left of her was scattered down the track in bloody clumps.

86

Jar is still reading. He can't stop. Amy loved Strelka. Like a child, he remembers Rosa telling him. When she finds out what really happened, she will leave him. Perhaps she has tried before. He wonders if he should call her now, make sure she reads the journal, discuss with her whether the police should be informed. Keeping someone on benzos like that must count as domestic abuse.

His train of thought is interrupted by the sound of movement again in the corridor, swing doors closing. Have the cleaners returned? Jar glances at his watch. It's 3.30 a.m. Max told him the place would start to get busy at dawn: early risers, trading stocks in Hong Kong and the Far East.

He turns back to the screen, thinking of Amy, Rosa, Strelka, but then he hears a second sound, like a muffled scream, and swallows hard. He tries to ignore what he's just heard, but he can't. It was too human.

Out in the corridor, Jar looks both ways. The journal has confused him, heightened his paranoia. The sound was nothing, he tells himself, but he is unable to shake off the image of the cleaners as they rushed to leave the floor half an hour earlier, unsmiling, eyes averted.

He walks down to the swing doors and pushes them open.

Nothing. The lifts stand silent, in repose, waiting for the morning rush. And then he sees a peaked cap on the floor, by the fire exit, beside an empty chair. He goes over to pick it up. The inside is still warm, the lining torn at the back. Jar looks around again and then pushes open the heavy fire door.

'Hello?' he calls out, his voice echoing up and down the stairwell. Silence. He lets the door close and places the hat on the chair, trying to ignore its clammy warmth. The guard will return shortly to collect it, Jar reasons, as he walks back down to Max's office, locking the door again behind him. His heart is racing.

87

North Norfolk, 2013

The bitch is suspended from the ceiling of the lab, con-strained in a rubberised cloth hammock, just as Seligman prescribed in 1967, her limbs hanging down below her through four holes in the harness. I haven't been able to replicate all the original details, but enough to make the experiment valid. The shock source is a twelve-volt car battery and a parallel voltage divider, conducted through brass-plate electrodes (first covered with commercial electrode paste), one of which has been taped to the bottom of the bitch's foot. The shock intensity is 20 mA, based on skin resistance of 1,000 ohms.

Her head, protected by a riveted black leather muzzle, is held in position, again exactly as Seligman prescribed, by a panel on either side of it, connected by a yoke across her neck. She can press either panel with her head, in the hope that this will make the current stop, but there is no causal connection between pressing the panels and termination of the electricity.

The only difference from Seligman's equipment is that I have made the harness out of material similar in colour to the jump-suits worn by high-value detainees: Guantánamo orange.

I've just checked to see that the video is working and am picturing the colleagues around the world who are watching: disenfranchised scientists, CIA psychologists, the odd terrorist, perhaps.

Seligman's theory is that dogs who are administered a series of inescapable electric shocks while in a harness, and have no control over the shocks, do not try to escape from further pain when they are subsequently put into a different situation – a 'shuttlebox' with two joining cubicles – where they can easily avoid it. In his original experiment, a second control group of dogs was placed in the constrained harnesses and, when they pressed the panels with their heads, the shock stopped. This second group went on to escape pain when they were put into the shuttlebox, unlike the first, who felt that they had no control over their environment.

The test I'm currently conducting is, therefore, only part one. Later, she will be placed, unharnessed, into a shuttlebox where she will receive further shocks (administered through a metal grid on the floor) and can move freely to a connecting cubicle to avoid them. If Seligman is right, she will choose *not* to escape to the pain-free environment but will instead cower and whimper in a state of learned helplessness.

Her body convulsed with impressive vigour when the first electric shock ran through it.

At the second electric shock, enough to initiate sustained muscular contractions, I worried for the harness as her whole body twisted like a beached fish, so I've just checked where it's fastened to the ceiling. She banged her head against the panels and emitted a high-pitched screeching sound.

The automatic relay circuitry proceeded to administer a series of decreasing shocks, totalling 226 seconds.

We must now wait twenty-four hours before placing her

in the shuttlebox's adjoining cubicles to see how she reacts to further pain. Will she try to escape? Or has her failure to terminate the shocks while in the harness – her inability to control her environment – induced a state of true learned helplessness?

88

Jar wipes the sick away with the back of his hand and leans over again, bent double, gripping the sides of the bin in Max's office. He should ring Max, tell him what he's just read. Give it a few minutes, he thinks. First he needs to go for a walk, get some fresh air, clear his head.

The bitch is suspended from the ceiling of the lab.

He heads out into the corridor, walking towards the bank of lifts. As he reaches the swing doors, the fire alarm goes off. It's just an early-morning drill, he tells himself, trying to stay calm. The sound makes him flinch, much more than it should. His nerves are shot. A recorded voice, far from reassuring, is telling people to evacuate the tower using the stairs.

He considers going back inside Max's office, locking the door and ignoring the alarm (no one knows he's here), but he needs to get away from the place, put some distance between himself and Martin's journal.

The lifts have been disabled. Jar turns to the fire exit, glancing at the peaked cap, still on the chair. He tries not to think about its owner, where the guard has gone.

At the second electric shock, enough to initiate sustained muscular contractions...

Martin was torturing a dog, Jar tries in vain to reason, as he pushes open the door. Maybe it was just a made-up story and Strelka didn't die on the tracks? This time the stairwell is no longer silent. Loud extraction fans are churning somewhere far below, keeping the stairs ventilated. He listens for footsteps. No one else is evacuating the building. He looks up. There, slumped in the corner of the stairwell above, is the security guard.

Jar approaches the body, struggling to suppress a rising nausea. The guard's eyes are closed, a bruise beginning to blossom on his forehead. Jar feels for a pulse and is relieved to find one, even more relieved when the guard manages a faint moan. He knows he should ring the police, but the desire to get out of the building, away from the alarm, the fans, the video, is overwhelming.

'You'll be OK now,' Jar says, as much to reassure himself as the guard, and begins the long descent to the ground, twenty floors below. Despite himself, he accelerates, taking the stairs two at a time. After three floors, he stops, catching his breath. He can hear footsteps above the din of the fans. Someone is on the stairs higher up.

Jar starts to descend again, forcing himself to maintain a steady pace. If he goes any faster, he'll fall down the unnaturally steep steps. He looks up and sees a familiar tall figure, two floors above him. Is it the same man who tried to board his train in Paddington, who took Rosa away on the cliffs in Cornwall?

Jaysus. Jar runs down the stairs, taking them three at a time now, too fast to keep his balance. He falls and lands heavily, his momentum carrying him down the next flight of steps.

When he comes to rest, he lies stunned, trying to assess where the most pain is coming from. Blood is gathering around his cheek on the cool concrete floor. He thinks of the guard, his warm hat. Someone is walking down the stairs, standing above him. Jar closes his eyes and offers up a prayer for the first time in years, waiting for his life to flash before him. All he can see is Rosa on a clifftop.

At the sound of a gun being cocked – mundane, existential – Jar grabs at the man's legs, wrapping his arms around them. The man topples and falls, pulling Jar down with him. They tumble down several stairs together before Jar manages to extricate himself. He watches as the man's body folds and turns beneath him, before it comes to a halt at an awkward angle. On a step between them is the gun, the same one that had been pointed at him in Cornwall.

Jar knows nothing about guns, but he picks it up, finds the safety catch and slips the weapon inside the pocket of his suede jacket. For a moment he imagines shooting the slumped figure below him. It's what he should have done on the cliffs, seized the gun from him and stopped Rosa being taken away. Instead, he turns and runs.

'Christ, are you still there, at the office?' Max asks, sounding half asleep.

'Someone just tried to kill me,' Jar says, his voice cracking with emotion.

'What? I can hardly hear you.'

'I thought I was going to die, Max. In the tower. The man who took Rosa, he chased me down the stairwell, tried to kill me.'

'Where are you now?'

'I'm at the bottom of the tower, by the DLR.'

'And you're safe?'

'I'm not sure.' Jar wipes some blood from his mouth as he looks around him. Dawn is breaking. He is cut and bruised from the fall, nothing more.

'You need to tell me exactly what happened,' Max says quietly.

Max is familiar with panicked, confused calls in the dead of the night, Jar thinks. It's his job to deal with them, calm the caller, assess the collateral damage.

'It was when he started to talk about "the bitch",' Jar continues. 'That's when I knew.'

'Knew what?'

'He hired a car in the name of John Bingham. For his pal who just tried to kill me. The tall fella.'

'Who, Jar? You're not making any sense.'

'Rosa wasn't taken away by the police, or the spooks, or kept in Guantánamo. She's being held by Martin.'

'Martin?' There's a long pause. 'Her *uncle* Martin?'

'Her uncle Martin.'

89

North Norfolk, 2013

Seligman was very specific about the equipment he used for the second half of his 1967 experiment, 'escape/ avoidance training', and I have tried to follow it to the letter, despite the limited resources out here.

In Seligman's experiment, those dogs that had been in control of their environment in part one – when they'd pressed the panels with their heads, the shocks had stopped – quickly learnt in part two how to hop over the barrier between one cubicle of the shuttlebox and the other. But those dogs that had no control of their environment in part one – pressing the panels had failed to stop the shocks – made little or no effort to escape the shocks in the shuttlebox. (Seventy-five per cent of them stayed in the cubicle for a full fifty seconds, painful electricity coursing through their bodies.)

This was the tenth and last time – Seligman specified conducting the test ten times – and the results were exactly the same.

The lights went out and I counted down the seconds until the shock began. When the current started, her whole body began to shake and she emitted a low growling sound that built in intensity. She made no effort to rise to her feet and climb over the partition into the sanctuary of the other cubicle. Instead, she just sat there on her haunches, staring back at me, a textbook picture of learned helplessness.

She is still looking at me now, slumped in the corner of the left cubicle.

90

'Can we hold back on the details?' Max says. 'You know, until we've dropped the kids off?'

'Of course, sorry,' Jar says, glancing in the Land Rover's rearview mirror at Max's two young children, rolling around on the back seat, school bags and lunchboxes beside them.

'The next generation needs to know what was done at Guantánamo in the name of Western democracy, but maybe wait until they're a little older. When they're ten, say.'

Jar manages a half smile, watching as Max pulls up outside the primary school in Dulwich. Earlier, Max had insisted on driving over to pick him up from Canary Wharf, even though it was 4.30 a.m. Jar had slept for a couple of hours on the sofa, much to the excitement of Max's children, who had peered wide eyed around the sitting-room door when he stirred.

'What's your name?' the girl had asked.

'Jar,' he replied, guessing they were about six years old, twins but not identical.

'Jar,' the girl said, 'what's the matter with your head?'

'That's a funny name,' the boy interrupted, before Jar had time to explain why, for the second time in two weeks, he was sporting a bandage, this time courtesy of Max's wife.

'My friends call me Jam,' he said.

'Daddy, the funny man's called Jam Jar,' they chimed, running off to the kitchen.

Jar had struggled to stop himself from crying, wishing he could wind back the clock, to when life had been simple.

Now, as the children climb out of the Land Rover and walk over to the school gates, a wave of fear washes over Jar. He was wrong to come with Max on the school run, put his kids in danger. The man in the stairwell was unconscious but breathing.

'I'm sorry, I shouldn't have called you or come over to your place,' he says, glancing up and down the street.

'Why on earth not?'

'He could have followed me here.'

'I thought you left him for dead,' Max says, starting up the Land Rover.

'I did.'

'I'm more worried about the police. There's CCTV all over the tower.'

'I couldn't see any in the stairwell.'

'Maybe not.' Max pauses, checking either way for traffic. 'It wouldn't be the first time someone's injured themselves during a fire practice. A girl in the next-door office broke her ankle the last time the building was evacuated. People can get a bit freaked out using those stairs – the crowds, the noise of the fans.'

Twenty minutes later, they have picked Carl up from his house in Greenwich and are on their way towards Cromer, driving down the A2 to the M25, round London and then north. Jar had rung Carl after he'd called Max and asked if he would phone in sick from work – a funny excuse didn't seem appropriate this time.

The atmosphere is tense, the reality of what they are doing, where they are going, sinking in. Jar still can't quite believe the implications of what he saw and read last night, or that a man had chased him down the stairwell. He's convinced now that it was the same person who came to Gurnard's Head to retrieve Rosa – maybe the former lab colleague that Martin mentioned in his journal, his tall cycling companion.

Jar wonders if Carl is asleep in the back as he talks through what has led to them all driving to Cromer on a rainy Wednesday morning.

'It's kind of a journal,' he begins. 'Martin wrote it as part of a creative-writing course he signed up for, practice before beginning a novel.'

'So it could all be bollocks,' Carl says, stirring.

'Could be. His house has heavy security, because of his old job. Cameras everywhere. He writes about watching his guests undress in the spare room.'

'A peeping Tom,' Max says. 'Old-school perv but not a psychopath.'

'He watched Rosa take a bath,' Jar says.

'I'm sorry.'

'And he carried on testing animals, mice, in his writing shed. Drowning them in beakers of water, hanging them upside down by their tails with medical tape. He gave them women's names, too: several of them were called Rosa.'

The car has fallen silent, except for the mesmerising noise of the windscreen wipers. Jar glances in the wing mirror.

'But it was the last test that made me realise what's been going on. Martin described how he re-created a famous 1960s experiment in which a dog is repeatedly electrocuted in a hammock. Only the "bitch" he describes wasn't a dog. Their dog.' He pauses. 'It was Rosa.'

'How can you be so sure?' Max asks.

'It was the same experiment as in another video I found earlier, after you left.' He turns to Carl. 'Of a woman I thought was in Guantánamo.'

'So what are you saying, bro?' Carl asks. 'That Martin worked for the Yanks? Tortured Rosa in Gitmo?'

Sometimes Carl doesn't realise how he sounds, Jar thinks.

'Two weeks ago, Amy gave me a diary written by Rosa. At least, I thought it was written by her. Parts of it were, for sure. The passages where she describes our time together in Cambridge. But Martin managed to get hold of it when she stayed with them once, accessed her computer, emailed himself a copy when she was having problems with the Wi-Fi. He writes about it in his journal.'

'Which might be a work of fiction,' Carl says.

Jar ignores him. 'So Martin reads Rosa's diary, about her time with me, how we met, how she struggled to get over the death of her father. Her college tutor—'

'Dr Lance?' Max asks.

Jar nods. 'Dr Lance picked up on her unhappiness. He suggested she go off to a retreat in Herefordshire. Maybe he even said she could drop out of college for a year, return when she felt stronger. But there was no college counsellor.'

'What about Karen?' Max asks. 'She writes a lot about her.'

'So does Martin, in his own journal. He writes all about her strange short intake of breath before she speaks. Except he's not writing about Karen, he's writing about one of Amy's old friends from university, an American psychologist called Kirsten, who came to stay.'

'Hot Kirsten you saw on Harley Street,' Carl says.

'Amy was worried about my bereavement hallucinations,

asked her friend Kirsten to help me. Kirsten approached you as a way to reach me, knowing that I needed persuading.'

'She said she wanted to play jungle to her patients,' Carl says. 'I was duped.'

'Amy acted with the best intentions. When I met Kirsten, I thought, wrongly, that she was really Karen, Rosa's old college counsellor, and was trying to find Rosa too. But Karen never existed. Martin created her. Ever the aspiring novelist, he made her up, based her on Kirsten when she came to stay. He sketches out her character in his journal as a writing exercise – the short intake of breath, her blonde hair, high cheekbones – nothing to trouble the Booker Prize.'

'But why does "Kirsten" become "Karen" in Rosa's diary?' Max asks.

'Martin had always wanted to write a novel, ever since he nearly read English at Cambridge. He'd tried and failed once – I know the feeling. Then he gets hold of Rosa's diary and has an idea. He starts to embellish it – adds bits here and there, drops in characters of his own, makes things up. It explains why you were never able to find a counsellor at St Matthew's, let alone an American one called Karen.'

'So Martin borrows Rosa's diary for the basis of his big novel,' Max says. 'That doesn't quite explain why he's posting videos of her being tortured by the Americans.'

'He's not.' Jar pauses, glancing again in the wing mirror. A white Transit van has been behind them for a while now. He feels for the gun in his jacket pocket, not sure if he's reassured by its cold presence. He hasn't told Max or Carl about it.

'Rosa was more depressed than I realised in her last weeks, I understand that now. And she wrote about it in her diary. I don't know how much Martin changed things, but whichever way you look at it, I underestimated her sadness.'

Not by much, Jar hopes. Martin might have added things to her diary, but Jar is sure that he took things away too, redacted their relationship, diluting the genuine love they had for one another.

'Martin suspected this,' Jar continues, 'knew that suicide was at least a possibility, so he followed her when she walked out of the house that night and went down to the pier.'

'I still don't get why,' Max says.

'He saw an opportunity in Rosa – for his novel and his experiments, the writer and the scientist. His journal's full of the need to test antidepressants on humans – stressed humans – and his frustration that regulations prevented him from doing so. Guantánamo was the perfect place for unauthorised clinical trials. Now he had a chance to conduct them in similar conditions, test all those potent antidepressants that he'd been working on. Which is why he'd been preparing his special place, a disused animal-testing laboratory that belonged to his old firm in Norwich. It's where they went for the really bad experiments, away from the prying eyes of the protestors.'

'Jesus, Jar. And he writes about all this in his journal?'

'In a manner of words.'

Jar pauses, gestures for the bottle of water beside Carl and takes a sip. His mouth is dry.

'Once he's talked her down from the pier's railings, he walks Rosa back to his car without being seen by the broken CCTV cameras on the pier, or the one below the hotel. He sedates her – not difficult, given his old job – and then makes an anonymous call to the emergency services, before driving her away to his lab out at the disused airfield, where she spends the next five years.'

'Christ,' Carl whispers.

'And it's there that he starts to experiment on her. Doing all those things he was never allowed to do on humans in his work. That's why he took her. It also provides fuel for his novel, the one he has always wanted to write. He begins to embellish her diary with character sketches he's been writing in his journal. A year later, he comes across your story on the dark web, which gives him his storyline. We know he read your article – he left a comment as Laika 57. Rosa hasn't committed suicide, she's been taken by the Americans, been given a new life as part of a covert programme called Eutychus – a name he got from one of the comments on your article. Perfect for someone who loves spy thrillers. He includes other details from your story in the diary, too.'

'Like the SAS,' Max says. 'And Todd. The bits I made up.'

'As the years roll on, he feeds all these details back to Rosa, gets her to read the altered diary every day until finally she believes it. She told me as much when we met on the cliffs in Cornwall. It was another one of Martin's mind experiments – and also provided feedback for an author worried about credibility, the ring of truth. The scientist and the writer again. So she really thinks that she was recruited to Eutychus in Herefordshire, escaped the programme and is now being held prisoner in a US airbase by the CIA. But she's not, she's being abused on an old Second World War airfield in Norfolk by her uncle.'

Jar pauses. Everyone is silent, waiting for him to continue. The van is still behind them, seemingly drawing closer.

'One day, she does actually manage to escape – the day Amy called up a computer man, asking for help with her laptop. Martin is furious with her, worried by what the man might find, all those torture videos. Most are on his hard drives in the shed, but did he download some on to Amy's

laptop, before he gave it to her? Had he erased them properly, or left a trace? He panics, makes mistakes. Rosa sees
her chance, breaks out of the lab, flees across the Norfolk
countryside.'

'Which is when you see her at Paddington,' Carl says.

'Only I don't believe it's Rosa. I put it down to another
bereavement hallucination. But then I do finally meet her,
at Gurnard's Head in Cornwall. She's damaged. Of course
she is.'

'Five years of being experimented on by Martin,' Max says,
'believing she's being punished by the Americans for trying
to leave a fictitious covert programme called Eutychus.'

'And she's taken back again,' Jar continues. 'Not by the
intelligence services, but by Martin – he books out a hire
car in the name of John Bingham. He can't help himself: the
name of the man Le Carré based George Smiley on. He has
help, too, a big fella who shares his perversions – an old lab
colleague he cycles with. I know I should have stopped him
from taking her away, challenged him at Gurnard's Head,
but he had a gun and we had nowhere to escape to.'

'The same person you saw in Starbucks, across from the
office?' Carl asks.

Jar nods. 'And who hit me with a gun in Cornwall, and
tried to kill me in a stairwell at Canary Wharf. I'm sure
of it.' Jar hesitates, swallowing hard. 'I helped Martin find
Rosa again, led him to Gurnard's Head.' His voice is cracking now and it takes a while before he can continue. 'When
she escaped, Martin knew exactly what to do: he had a contingency plan in case she ever broke free. He calculated that
she would head for a special place – she'd written in her
diary about fleeing there "if the world ever slipped off its
axis". Except she had always refused to tell Martin where it

was. But I knew. And Martin knew I knew. So he sends me her diary, the one he's embellished, gives it to Amy to hand over to me. He encourages me – me, the paranoid conspiracy theorist – to think that Rosa is on the run from a covert intelligence programme. I am easy prey, ready to believe she's alive, unable to accept her death, even after all these years. He sends me emails pretending to be from her. Even fabricates a confidential document, "Strap 3, UK Eyes Only", based on what he's gleaned from hidden spy sites on the dark web. He knows that Rosa will head for our secret meeting place and that I will lead him there. Which I do.'

Jar can't talk for the tears now.

'So she's been with Martin all this time,' Carl says quietly.

Max struggles to clear his throat. 'They do say the attacker is often known to their victim.'

'And now he's taken her back, to his lab,' Jar says, trying to sound strong. 'And we've got to find her.'

A second later, all three of them are thrown forwards.

'Jesus Christ,' Max says, struggling to keep the Land Rover on the road. 'Friends of yours?' he asks, looking in the rearview mirror.

Carl and Jar both turn to look behind them. The white van that Jar saw earlier is tailgating them, so close that they can see the driver. Jar recognises the man he left for dead in the stairwell. He is staring ahead, his face without emotion as the van rams into the back of the Land Rover again.

'Nobody fucks with a Defender,' Max says, short of breath.

'Is it him?' Carl asks.

'It's him,' Jar confirms, turning to Max, fearing what he's about to do. An hour earlier, and the kids would have been in the car.

'Hold on,' Max says, as he stamps on the brake.

A screech, accompanied by the smell of burning rubber, then everything slows down, or that's how it seems to Jar, before a loud crack as the van runs into the back of the Land Rover. Jar's head is throbbing, but he turns to see that the windscreen of the van has shattered in front of the driver, the top of his head pushing out through the lattice of fractured glass. Before anyone can say anything, Max has accelerated away, the van limping to a standstill amid a cacophony of horns.

91

The last dose of medication he gave me must have been stronger than usual because I'm struggling to remember the past few days. I was found, in Cornwall, and I'm now back here again. That much I do know. And I'm being punished, like the early years. Treated like an animal. But this time I know that I'm on my own. When I got out of here, there were no other prisoners. Instead, I found an abandoned office, and a tape recorder near the trap door that leads down to my 'cell'. I pressed play and the cries began. A low moan followed by banging against bars. Six bangs.

I remember the bright sunlight, an airfield, walking across flat farmland, a campsite where I stole a floral tent, a rucksack and some money, running off like a feral child. I don't remember getting to London, but I got a train from there to Cornwall and a bus out to Gurnard's Head, where Jar and I agreed to meet if the world ever slipped off its axis.

And he was there. My beautiful Jar.

At least I think it was him.

92

Cromer, 2013

S uicide is such a waste. People should offer their bodies up
to science instead. There's so much we can do with them.

I'm signing off from this journal now. It's served its purpose.
I have found a voice and at last I have my main character, a
living, breathing one with a past I can plunder and a future
that I can shape. Before I finish, though, I should recount the
night Rosa disappeared, an event that presents a writer with
so many different narrative opportunities.

We had argued that night, Rosa and I. At first it was about
depression, the merits of counselling versus SSRIs, but then
it broadened out into a generational dispute, what I called
reality-TV-show openness versus dignified reserve, blubbing
versus stiff upper lip.

A asked me to apologise to Rosa, so I went up to her room
and found a handwritten note next to her laptop. She had gone
out for a walk, down into town – to clear her head. A few minutes later, I came back downstairs, told A. She begged me to
go after her, follow her out into the night. I took the car, certain she would be heading for the pier. She'd written about it
in her diary once, how she had contemplated jumping from it.

When I found her, by the lifeboat house at the far end of the pier, she was standing on the railings in the wind. An easterly wind was roughing up the sea below. I knew she would have been picked up by CCTV as she walked along the front towards the pier. But the camera on the pier itself was out of action.

For a while, I just stood and observed her, the way the wind played with her hair.

I'm not sure how committed she was to jumping, but three things could have happened next. She could have overcome her doubts and leapt into the darkness, her body carried away by the vicious riptides that circle the pier's pillars far below like sea snakes. She could have been removed from the pier in the still of the night as part of a covert intelligence programme called Eutychus, given a new life after her death was faked. Or she could have turned to see a man in the shadows watching her, waiting to intervene.

If she took the latter course, the man would have begun with a simple, Faustian question: 'When a man saves someone from certain death, does he own their soul?' She wouldn't have understood what he meant. Nor would she have protested as he unpeeled her cold fingers from the metal railings, tears streaming down her confused, frightened young face. She'd just be grateful to be alive.

Slowly, they would have walked back down the pier together to the car, carefully avoiding the CCTV below the Hotel de Paris that had recorded her arrival. They would have talked some more as her shaking subsided, and then driven away, she sleepy now, warmed by a thermos of tea that tasted slightly strange, he stopping only to make a call from a payphone. To A, she presumed.

So what did she do? Which of these three narratives did she follow?

It's time, at last, to turn to my novel. I know now that I will stay with the diary format. I even have an idea of an opening: something about contrails in the Fenland sky.

93

When did I know it was him? Year two, maybe year three. When he finally started to speak to me. At the beginning he wore a black balaclava, poked me with an electric cattle prod, said nothing. The gap in the balaclava around his mouth made his lips look feminine, despite the stubble. My medication was so heavy I wouldn't have cared if I had recognised him. Dad knew. From the moment he met him. It was only Jar who had a blind spot. I feel so sorry for Amy. Has she suffered like me?

He won't let me call him Martin. He's my 'guard'. But I address him as Martin if I'm feeling strong, which makes him mad with anger. He takes away my food, turns up the dials, forces pills down my throat that turn my fingers into writhing maggots and make the walls crush me until I cannot breathe. But I'm not going to play his games.

94

It's a while since he was last at Amy and Martin's house, but Jar remembers enough to be able to direct Max up Hall Road, away from Cromer's seafront. After a mile, he asks Max to slow down as they pass under a railway viaduct. About five hundred yards further on, the road bends to the left and Jar tells Max to slow down even more. The house, he thinks, is somewhere up on the right. And then he spots it, set back from the road, at the end of a long drive, partially hidden by trees.

'Drive on,' Jar says. 'If we park somewhere along here, I can walk back up.'

The plan is for Jar to call Max and Carl once he's established that it's just Amy at home. Martin should be out on his bike, according to his journal, as he is every day at this time. Jar will ring the front doorbell, and in the unlikely event that Martin does answer, he will explain that he's come to say goodbye, make up some story about going abroad, moving on with his life, finally putting Rosa behind him now that he's read her diary and come to terms with her death.

'It's a long walk to the pier,' Max says as he pulls over, a few hundred yards beyond the house. He sounds tired, Jar thinks, after the three-hour drive up from London.

'Twenty minutes, maybe half an hour.' Jar tries not to think of Rosa setting off down the road on her own in the dark that night, Martin following at a distance in his car. There's a path for most of the way but not the first quarter of a mile. 'I'll call you,' he says, getting out of the Land Rover.

'Martin could be hostile,' Max says. 'His friend was.'

'He won't be here – he'll be out cycling.'

'I think I should come with you, bro,' Carl says. 'Just in case.'

'I'll ring.'

Five minutes later, Jar knocks on the front door.

'Who is it?' a voice calls out, after Jar hears a chain being put on the door. It's Amy.

'It's me, Jar.'

The door opens a few inches, still on the chain, and Jar smiles at Amy. She's looking terrible, worse than he's ever seen her: dark eyes, heavy make-up, a vacant half smile.

'Is Martin in?' he asks.

She shakes her head. 'On his bike.' Her voice is vague, dreamy.

'Can I come in?'

Amy takes the door off the chain and lets Jar into the hall. Jar notices her fingertips are black as she closes the door behind them.

'I read it, after I sent it to you.'

Jar nods, not sure how much to say, trying to establish what she now knows about the man she's shared a house – her life – with for the past twenty years: the cameras in the guest bedroom, the lab out at the airfield, the learned help-lessness experiments. At least she hasn't seen the video, might not have suspected that the trussed-up 'bitch' was Rosa.

'Tell me it's fiction,' she says, walking into the kitchen. Jar follows her. It's not even teatime, but there's a half-empty glass on the sideboard, an open vodka bottle nearby. There are some charcoal sketches on the table – cross-hatched, violent images – and balls of screwed-up paper on the floor.

'Did you read it all?' Jar asks, glancing again at the drawings.

'Of course I did.' She pauses. 'He let her jump that night, didn't he? Down at the pier.'

She's fallen for the journal's crude obfuscation, Jar thinks, chosen to buy in to the wrong narrative. He wonders how much medication she's taken. Her voice is weak, her sentences trailing off. 'He let my Strelka die, too.'

'We can talk about the journal later,' he says.

'Kirsten knew,' Amy says. 'She suspected him of having cameras in the guest room.'

'Martin writes about an old lab, out at a disused airfield,' Jar interrupts, worried by Amy's state of mind. 'We need to find it. I think it's where he goes on his bike ride every day. Do you know where it is?'

Amy pauses, her eyes focusing on Jar's, more alert now. 'I think I might.'

'Where?'

'I'm a Strava widow, Jar. He's out on his bike for three hours every day. When he gets back, he goes down to his shed, downloads the route, his times. The airfield will be on his computer.'

Jar is already calling Carl. 'Thank you, Amy.'

Max is keeping watch outside the shed with Jar, holding a pair of bolt cutters they found in a nearby outhouse. They have severed both padlocks and the main door is open. Carl is inside the back room, working fast on the computer, helped by Amy, who has come alive, energised by the hunt.

'Have you found it yet?' Jar calls.

'Give us another minute,' Carl says. 'He's got a lot of security on here.'

Jar looked in briefly on the back room, but the sight of the TV monitors, the desk, Martin's computer, the roll of medical tape next to a paperweight unnerved him, brought Martin's journal to life. He needs to keep it together for what he fears lies ahead. It was also very dark in there, even with the door open, the room lit by a red lightbulb.

'We're in,' Carl says. 'Now we just need to see where he's been pedalling. People compare times on Strava for particular routes, stretches of road.'

Jar glances at Max and goes back into the shed, leaving Max outside. His worry is that Martin might return at any moment.

'Looks like he's been taking the same identical route every day for years,' Carl says, going through the data.

'Where's the airfield?'

'Other side of Holt, right here.' Amy points at a map on the screen. 'I know where that is.'

'Fifty-five minutes and forty seconds away, cycling at an average speed of sixteen miles per hour,' Carl adds. 'He leaves here at the same time every day: 1 p.m. – like clockwork.'

'And returns at 4 p.m.,' Amy says.

Jar glances at his watch. 'He's still there.'

'I'll show you the quickest way,' Amy says.

95

I've got so used to the pale, diffuse light down here that when the ceiling lightbulb exploded into life today, I thought it was lightning. But the light has stayed, yellow and artificial and as bright as fire, and it's burned a plan into my mind. I know now what I must do.

The light reminded me of when we lived in Pakistan. 'Dim-dum' – that's what our cook called it when the power was weak and flickering. Then one day we were connected to a private-generator powerhouse, the current surged and all the lightbulbs popped like firecrackers.

I walked over to the cell door, my chains just allowing me to reach the light switch. I flicked it off and then on again, looking at the light. Power.

Someone has connected the mains power.

'Do you remember that time you touched the bare wire in the garden?' I turn to see Dad behind me, examining the plug socket on the wall. He was always good at DIY. 'If we'd been connected to the powerhouse, you would have died,' he continues. 'Volts, current, resistance, remember?'

All I can recall, apart from Dad trying to explain the physics to me (I was only five at the time), is being given a glass of lemon water afterwards by the gardener. Dim-dum had saved my life.

I turned the cell light off again, my plan already formed.

'Sounds like you were lucky to live,' Jar says, emerging from the shadows and standing next to Dad.

I always wanted them to meet.

They seem relaxed in each other's company, leaning against the cell wall together, arms folded. The two men I love more than anyone in the world.

'Thank you, babe,' I whisper, 'for coming to Cornwall, for being here now.'

'Your dad's a good man,' Jar says.

'He's a charmer, this one,' Dad replies, nodding at Jar. 'Your mother would have liked him.'

I closed my eyes, happy at last, and opened them again. They were gone, but the light is still burning.

96

J ar, Max, Amy and Carl sit in silence, looking across the wide expanse of the disused airfield, surrounded by pine trees and the vivid yellow of rapeseed fields. Amy showed them a back route and, as they drove, Jar broke it to her as gently as he could that Martin might be holding Rosa at the airfield. He didn't want to say too much – she's too fragile – but she wasn't completely surprised. Although it never referred explicitly to Rosa's capture and torture, Martin's journal had prepared the ground. Jar also mentions Kirsten, says he knows that she had his best interests at heart, and promises to be more open-minded about therapy in the future.

Max has parked the Land Rover next to a long row of abandoned poultry sheds, down a track and away from what was once the main runway. They ignored a sign that said 'Private Property: No Unauthorised Persons Beyond This Point' and drove around an old barrier where cars had once had to stop to have their wheels cleaned with antiseptic spray. Jar wonders what had come first: the intensive poultry units or the secret animal-testing laboratory.

'They look like something out of Belsen,' Max says, nodding at the poultry sheds. Jar had had the same thought:

low grey huts with grain silos at each end, rising up like sinister chimneys.

'According to Strava, the lab should be over there,' Carl says, pointing to a clump of pine trees on the far side of the airfield, more than half a mile away.

'In his journal he writes about leaving his bike by the southern perimeter,' Amy says. Her voice is quiet but strong. 'If we can find the bike...'

Jar stops, struck by the reality of what lies ahead of them all. What will they do when they find the bike? Confront Martin? He feels for the gun in his jacket pocket. He's never fired one before. It would be so much easier to call Cato, but this is his time now. He has waited five years for such a moment and he's not going to let anyone else get in the way. He knows, too, that some dark corner of his soul wants to confront Martin with no authorities about.

'Shouldn't we be calling your police friend?' Max asks, reading Jar's thoughts. 'Leave this to them?'

'After,' Jar says. 'We'll call him after.'

⋆

'You look so helpless today.' He smiles.

I glance down at my naked body, the chains around my sore ankles and wrists, trying to focus on the plan.

'A picture of helplessness,' he says, holding my chin in his fingers as he turns my head from one side to the other. Sometimes I have spat in his face, but not today. Today I will do whatever he says.

He's talked to me a lot about 'learned helplessness', claiming it's the key to unlocking the neurobiology of clinical depression. 'Debility, dependency, dread' – that's another thing he goes on about.

If I believe I have no control over what he does to me in the harness, I will begin to think I cannot influence any traumatic aspect of my life or environment. But I do have control, ever since I saw the light, ever since Jar and Dad met each other down here. They have given me strength, shown me a way out.

★

Max brakes when Amy spots her husband's bike, partially hidden in the trees, on the far, southern side of the airfield. The location couldn't be more remote, Jar thinks, out of sight of the main road. The nearest house, in a hamlet beyond the airfield, must be more than a mile away.

'There should be a Nissen hut nearby. Let's leave the car here,' he says, turning to Amy. 'I think you shouldn't come any further.'

'Call the police,' Amy says. 'Please.'

'We will, I promise,' Jar says, hugging her. 'As soon as we've found him.'

The three of them climb out of the Land Rover, closing the doors as quietly as possible and leaving Amy on her own. She has a phone with her and will call Jar in an emergency. Max is carrying the bolt cutters he used on Martin's shed door. If Jar is right, they will need them again. There are no buildings in sight, but there is a strip of old concrete on the far side of the trees where the bike has been hidden. Jar gestures for the others to stand still and listen. The only noise is the sound of the wind in the pine trees: plangent, restless.

Jar walks over to the bike and looks around, trying to see if any undergrowth has been trampled. An abandoned white facemask catches his eye, lying beneath some brambles.

'I think there's a building over there,' Max says, pointing further along the perimeter. 'Green roof.'

Jar looks and can't see anything at first, but then he spots the distinctive curve of a Nissen hut, partially hidden by trees, about five hundred yards away.

They walk towards it, hugging the edge of the trees, Jar first, followed by Max, breathing heavily now, and Carl, who has fallen very quiet. A second later, they all jump, a pheasant rising up from beside them, cackling loudly.

'Jesus,' Carl says. 'I hate the countryside.'

The bird frightened Jar too, but he tries not to show it. Max is right, he thinks. They should have rung Cato. He tells himself to concentrate on what lies ahead. Rosa is fewer than a hundred yards away from them now, alive, he hopes to God, but there's a chance they might be too late.

*

It's the moment we've both been waiting for: when he releases the shackles from my legs and arms. He beams with pride as he stands before me, key in hand.

'For those of us interested in learned helplessness,' he says, bending down to unlock my ankles, 'the absence of any desire to escape is a sign of success, proof that Seligman was right.'

He rises to his feet, close to my naked body, and frees my wrists, letting the chain drop to the floor like discarded clothing. 'Can you imagine how exhilarating it must have been, that first time, when the dogs just stood there, electricity coursing through their limbs? They were able to leap free of the pain, but they chose not to. They had given up hope, felt unable to control their environment. The dogs were depressed!'

He laughs as he says these last words and then slaps me hard across the face, watching for a reaction in my eyes. I stare ahead, trying to block out the stinging in my cheek.

'Good girl,' he whispers.

'Keep your wings folded,' Dad says, appearing behind him. Jar is there, too. I can see the butterfly, resting on a sail bag in the sunshine.

We have been here before, many times. In the early days, when Martin took me upstairs, showed me the open door, the countryside, he was right: I didn't want to escape. Today is different. It's the first time he has unchained me since I ran away to Cornwall, and he wants to prove that he is in control again, that we are back on track with his experiments. The pain he has inflicted on me in the past week, my punishment for escaping, has been the worst I can remember, but he can't break me, not with Jar and Dad here.

'You know what to do,' he says, nodding towards the table where he has placed the car battery and electrodes.

To celebrate my submission, my return to a state of learned helplessness, he wants me to prepare the instruments for my own torture. I have been expecting this – he's asked me before. I go over to the table as he checks the harness, tugging on the ceiling chain. I don't have long. Moving quickly, I disconnect the wires from the car battery, slip them into the left and right holes of the mains plug socket on the wall and press the switch to on as quietly as I can. He won't notice what I've done unless he's looking. With the sunpipe blocked off and only candles *for illumination, which is the way he likes it on these occasions, the light is poor.*

I come back to the harness, holding the other end of the wires, and place them on a small table that he always puts below the harness. I take care not to touch the electrodes together, or allow them to touch my skin. In a moment, he will ask me to climb into the harness and clamp the electrodes on to my body – different places, depending on his mood. I fear the worst today. First, though, I must apply conductive paste. We both know the routine. He opens the tin of paste, twisting the lid as he looks me up and down. Does he know something's wrong? That this time the electricity in the electrodes is enough to kill me?

'Volts, current, resistance, remember?' Dad says.

'I never did get physics,' Jar adds, under his breath.

I look up but they have both gone. I am on my own now and know what I must do.

*

They walk around the back of the Nissen hut first, peering in through a window at what looks like a derelict office. There are no obvious cameras, no sign that the building has been anything but abandoned for years. As they stand in silence again – listening for what? Rosa's screams? – Jar notices something in the undergrowth, a few yards away from the building. It's an old car battery. Then he spots another, and another. There must be at least a dozen of them. Heavy to carry on a bike, Martin has clearly only bothered to bring them this far – no point ferrying them back afterwards, once they've served their purpose. Jar's angry now. He feels Carl's hand on his shoulder.

'Let's do it,' Carl says.

*

I tell myself I'm doing this for all the animals that he has ever tortured, but I know I'm doing it for me, for Dad, for Amy, for Jar.

'Put on the mask,' he says. 'You forgot the mask.'

He passes me the black leather face protector with stitching across the mouth, one that I have worn on so many occasions, trying to bite into its leather to ease the pain.

I swing around in the hammock, arms and legs hanging down freely below me, as I secure the mask with ties at the back of my head.

'Can I help?' he asks, as if I'm struggling to put on a coat.

I shake my head. The mask is on. All that's left now is for me to reach down for the electrodes below me. Normally, once I have picked them up, he kicks away the table like a hangman's stool and I attach them, ready for him to turn on the car battery.

'Ready?' he asks.

I nod again, struggling to breathe in the mask. My heart is racing. The moment has come. I hear myself praying.

'It's a new battery, fully charged,' he says. 'Should be quite a tingle.'

*

The main door of the Nissen hut is locked, as Jar had suspected, but there is a pile of wood stacked up at the front, along with some old agricultural equipment, and Max and

Carl are already walking over with a large log. Jar takes one end from Max and with Carl they swing it back between them and launch it at the door, close to the lock. The noise reverberates across the airfield. There is no turning back now. They wield the log again, and again, until the door finally splinters and Max kicks it in.

'It's hidden by a filing cabinet,' Jar says as they look around for the entrance to the basement. There are more than five cabinets dotted around the room, some with doors hanging open, others closed.

'Over here,' Carl says. The three of them walk across to a cabinet in the far corner. All its drawers are closed and behind it there is a panel on the grey linoleum floor with an inset catch. There are scratch marks to the side where the cabinet has been pulled backwards and forwards.

Jar doesn't hesitate now as he bends down and lifts the catch on the panel. He starts to pull, lifting it upwards, with Carl's help.

The smell hits them first: a rancid mix of excrement, airlessness and something else that reminds Jar of hospitals. Or is it what he smelt at the morgue, when he went with Da to say goodbye to Mamó? Max pulls out a spotted handkerchief and holds it up to his mouth. Carl turns away, walks to the door and retches. Jar puts his hand over his mouth and nose and pulls the panel back fully. Despite the darkness below, he can see the top rung of a metal ladder.

'I'm going down,' he says.

'Use this,' Max says, passing him his handkerchief.

Jar takes it, turns and feels with his feet for the ladder.

'Tell Carl to keep a watch out for Martin,' he says. No human would be down in the basement of their own volition, he thinks, not with that smell. Perhaps Martin has popped out. To get some fresh air? A pint of milk? Jar is no longer thinking straight, his heart beating fast, his hands clammy on the metal ladder. Did Rosa climb down these stairs that first night? Or had she been so drugged that Martin had had to carry her down, or maybe drop her like a sack of coal?

★

I close my eyes and open them again, holding the electrodes apart in my hands below me. I can't go through with this. I can't.

Dad has slipped back into the room, cutting it fine again for a school performance. He gives me a look of reassurance, the you-can-do-it smile he gave me when I was wobbling on the beam, arms held high, about to cartwheel. Then Jar appears, too, with that same look he had given me when my credit card defaulted in the restaurant. 'There's enough money in the tip box, from other diners, for me to cover it,' he said. I loved you for that, Jar.

'I'm ready,' I say, as he steps forward to remove the table so my body can hang freely when it begins to twist and contort.

'One on your foot, the other on your tongue,' he whispers. There is sweet alcohol on his breath and his skin is beading with sweat.

I check with Dad, who nods and turns away. Jar nods, too.

And then I plunge both electrodes into the sides of his head, one against each sweaty temple, pushing as hard as I can as his body convulses beneath me.

★

Standing at the foot of the ladder, Jar peers around the dark room, using his mobile phone as a torch. He holds the hand-kerchief against his nose, wanting to be sick, but he forces himself to swallow. Where's Rosa? Is she here? Or is this just used for animals? *Taped to the bottom of the bitch's foot... She just sat there on her haunches, staring back at me...*

The first thing Jar sees is an orange hammock suspended from the ceiling. It's empty, hanging limply, two electric cables trailing away from one end into the darkness. This is where the video was made, Jar realises. He turns to retch into the handkerchief.

'You all right down there?' Max calls out, but Jar barely hears him. He flicks the mobile phone light around, hoping it answers his question.

'Rosa?' he says, wiping his mouth. His voice is weak. 'Rosa, it's me, Jar. Where are you now?' He walks over to the har-ness, making sure it's empty.

'Rosa?' he calls, gaining confidence.

He walks past the hammock into a side room, where there is a lavatory and a basin, and shines the light around the tiny space, flicking from one object to another: a glass beaker, a car battery, electrodes, two large wooden crates, like cubicles, that have been joined together, and a stack of what look like lampshades. The sort you put around a dog's neck to stop it scratching, he thinks. He shines the light on the shelf above. A row of tins: dog food. Below it, on a work surface, one open tin with a spoon in it.

And then he hears a sound, the faintest shuffle. He shines the light down at the floor. There, crouched beneath the basin, naked, arms clutching her knees, trembling, alive, is Rosa.

'Where is he?' she whispers, as Jar reaches down to cradle her in his arms.

'It's OK,' Jar says, starting to sob, shocked by the coldness of her skin. 'Take my jacket.'

'He's here, Jar.'

'It's over,' Jar says, not hearing her words as he lifts her to her feet and wraps his suede jacket around her, just like he did on the banks of the River Cam. It's hard to believe she is the same woman. Her hair is shaved, the side of her face bruised and swollen, her body skin and bones. 'We need to get you out of here.'

He will never let her be taken away again, he thinks, holding her close to him, closer than he's ever held anyone. But his own skin is beginning to cool too, chilled by her silence. *He's here.*

'I tried,' Rosa whispers.

Jar feels the chain around his neck before he hears Martin. His hands shoot up to the heavy links, desperate to release the pressure as he is pulled into the middle of the room, away from Rosa, his legs kicking out in a hideous cancan. He can hear himself choking, as if it's someone else.

'I hate stories with happy endings, don't you?' Martin says, his mouth close to Jar's ear.

'My jacket,' Jar manages to say to Rosa, who has sunk back down to the ground, curled up in fear – or is it helplessness? She looks up at him. Jar motions with his bulging eyes at his jacket pocket, unable to speak. He doesn't want her to watch him die, but she fails to understand. There's no energy left in his body now. The chain is hard against his windpipe and he is losing consciousness.

'I saved her soul,' Martin says. Jar is aware of a different smell, singed flesh. He closes his eyes. It doesn't matter any more. Life is leaving him. Where's Max? Carl? Haven't they heard them? 'So the bitch is mine.'

With a final effort, Jar drops one hand from the chain and pendulums his elbow behind him. Martin doubles up, releasing his grip enough for Jar to free himself. He staggers over to Rosa, trying to ignore the pain around his neck, grabs his jacket and takes the gun from the pocket.

'You wouldn't dare,' Martin says as he looks up at the gun Jar is now pointing at him. 'Wouldn't know how.'

'Shoot him!' Rosa shouts, rising to her feet.

Jar glances at her and releases the safety catch. He needs no persuading. There's a wildness in Martin's eyes, a lethal unpredictability about him. His trousers are bloodied and the sides of his face are covered in raw burn marks and blood. He's a simple enough target.

'Five years you kept her down here.' Jar grips the gun to stop it shaking. His neck is on fire. 'Five fucking years,' he repeats, louder now.

'How time flies,' Martin says, smirking.

'She thought she could trust you, her own uncle.' Why's Jar saying all this? The three of them know the charges against him, but it's as if he needs to spell them out, rest his case before he can pull the trigger. Or is Martin right and he's not up to it? 'She thought you'd come to save her on the pier. Instead—'

'Are you OK down there?' It's Max. Jar looks across at the ladder. Max would have shot him by now.

'Jar!' Rosa screams.

Jar turns to see Martin rushing towards him. He pulls the trigger, but there's just an empty click. Instinctively, he adjusts his grip and swings the butt of the gun into Martin's face, as hard as he can, thinking back to how he'd been felled – with the same gun – on the cliffs in Cornwall. It's enough to stop Martin. Jar grabs the back of his neck and pulls Martin's head up and then down on to his raised knee with a brutality that Jar never knew he possessed. Martin collapses.

'Call the cops, Carl!' Max shouts up the hatch as he rushes over to Martin's motionless body and stands guard over it.

Jar, breathing hard, glances from Martin to Rosa, who is slumped against the wall, clutching his jacket around her. He reaches down and helps her to stand. Her whole body is shaking. He holds her tight, trying to calm her, calm himself, resting his forehead against hers.

'This time it is over,' he whispers. 'I promise.'

97

'You should have rung me,' Miles Cato says, standing outside the Nissen hut.

'I thought I just did,' Jar replies.

'Before you came out here. As soon as you read Martin's journal. This is a major crime scene – with your fingerprints all over it.'

'It was personal,' Jar says, looking at all the people now in attendance: four police cars, two ambulances, a fire engine with cutting and lifting equipment, and the police helicopter that Cato had hitched a ride in from London, not to mention the patrol cars down on the road that has now been sealed off. There is blue-striped police-incident tape everywhere, strung between trees, rippling in the breeze.

'She's going to be all right, you do know that,' Cato says.

'Her body, maybe.'

Jar has just stepped out of the ambulance where Rosa is being looked after. The paramedics have cleaned her up, given her a smock to wear, and will soon be taking her to the Norfolk and Norwich University Hospital, but not without Jar. He has insisted on going everywhere with her, and this is the first time he has left her side since he found her more than an hour ago.

Carl and Max are still with him, giving statements to the police, offering reassurance. Martin was arrested and whisked away to Norwich police station, for his own safety as much as others'. No one has yet established the whole story, what happened before Jar arrived, but he assumes Rosa seized her moment and somehow managed to administer a near-fatal shock to Martin, enough for her to escape the harness. As for the gun, Cato has confirmed that it was a fake, which isn't much consolation. Another reason why Jar should have challenged Martin's colleague on the cliffs in Cornwall.

'I'm going back in to see her,' Jar says, motioning towards the ambulance. 'They want to drive her over to the hospital now.'

'We'll need to talk to her, when she's feeling stronger,' Cato says. 'There are a lot of questions. I'm sure you understand.'

'As you like.' Jar holds Cato's gaze, thinking back to the first time they met. He still doesn't trust him.

98

Cornwall, 2017

This won't be long. I find everything tiring at the moment and spend much of my day sleeping. It was Jar's idea to start writing a diary again – my own words written in freedom – and it feels good, the first steps to reclaiming my life, my past.

It was Jar's suggestion to come down here, too, to the place where Dad used to bring me: a sanctuary, even though the last time I was here was for his funeral. I walk up to Paul every day with Jar, to visit Mum and Dad's grave. It takes a long while (2,700 seconds), but I tell myself it's good for body and soul.

It's been a month since Jar found me. For the first few days I was in hospital, before he brought me here. A counsellor comes from Truro every day and we talk for two, sometimes three hours, depending on how strong I'm feeling. She shows me pictures of my 'cell', photos of Martin, with and without his balaclava, and I read her extracts from my 'prison diary', the bits that I wrote on scraps of paper. She's suggested that I write up the final hours of my incarceration as well, when I electrocuted Martin. It will help me to get some closure, she says, if I can recall the events in real time.

I feel so sorry for Amy. One day soon, I hope, she will feel able to visit me. I've written a letter, telling her not to blame herself.

Bright sunlight remains a problem. I wear big sunglasses wherever I go, which also helps to conceal my identity. Sometimes I put a wig on, too – one of the advantages of having short hair. There's still a lot of interest in what happened to me, how I survived.

I want to go back to college, that much I do know. Complete my studies. Dr Lance has written to me, says my place will be kept open indefinitely. I've just got to persuade Jar to come back with me, do a PhD or something. He's agreed to have some more counselling with Kirsten and his writer's block has finally lifted. He says he was always too fearful of borrowing from other writers, but now he's not so bothered and is going to steal an idea that was stolen from someone else before they could use it. What goes around comes around.

I never want him to leave my side.

99

J ar holds Rosa tightly. It's the first time they've kissed properly since he found her in Norfolk two months ago. They are lying on the bed upstairs in her parents' old net loft in Mousehole, the sound of the sea rolling up through a large double window. Noisy gulls have gathered on a neighbour's rooftop.

'It's OK,' Jar says, stroking her hair, which is growing back. A tear rolls across her cheek. 'Shall we go down to the harbour wall?' She smiles back at him, shielding her eyes from the light. Jar leans over to the bedside table and passes her sunglasses.

They dress and take two Union Jack mugs of tea with them: Earl Grey for her, Barry's Gold for him. It's too early for the shops on the front to be open. They have spent a lot of time sitting on this particular bench on the harbour wall, talking quietly, trying to piece together her life, one second, one hour, one day at a time. If the daily walk to Paul hasn't taken it out of her, they climb Raginnis Hill, behind the village, and venture along the coast path. They haven't got beyond the coastguard lookout yet, but they hope to make it to Lamorna in the coming months. Jar is pleased with the progress she's making. The counselling sessions are helping, and she's started to keep a diary again, but there's still a long way to go.

This morning, though, they venture no further than the bench on the harbour wall, cradling their mugs of tea in cold hands, watching as a mackerel fisherman steers his boat out of the narrow harbour entrance. He raises a salty hand in acknowledgement.

Jar senses that a lot of people come to this far-flung part of the country to heal. The village has left Rosa to herself, despite a five-page article in a Sunday broadsheet, which triggered worldwide media interest. Rosa gave only one interview, to Max, who told her story from the beginning. The rest of the world's press has accepted that she won't speak again.

It wasn't quite the spy scoop that Max had been expecting to write, but the sub-editors still managed to get the SAS into the headline, much to Jar's and Max's amusement.

Max has been down to visit a couple of times, first to interview Rosa for the article – sensitively, slowly, over three days, writing notes longhand with a fountain pen – and then with his family for a short holiday, during which he and his wife came over regularly to check on Rosa. Jar played French cricket with their twins on the small beach below the car park. And Max is back being a journalist, having decided to wind up his PR business in Canary Wharf. 'Bankers will have to tell their own lies now.'

Carl has been down too, sleeping on the sofa in the net loft. He came with good news from the office. Jar can have his old job back, with two provisos: he mustn't be late, and when he is, he must lay off the lame excuses. Anton has also resurfaced. Turns out he'd had some girlfriend problems, nothing to do with Rosa's diary, which he has now finished decoding and sent to Jar. Carl's even had a skateboard lesson with him, claims he's now mastered the pop shove-it.

Cato's visit was more businesslike. After conducting further formal interviews with them both, he'd stayed the night in Mousehole, at the Old Coastguard, and called Jar over in the evening for a pint of Betty Stogs and an off-the-record update. For half an hour, Jar almost began to like him.

According to Cato's ongoing inquiries, Martin was fired by the company in Huntingdon because of excessive cruelty to animals. He went on to lose his second job, in Norwich, for similar reasons, although there his cruelty had manifested itself in an unauthorised first-in-human trial on a new antidepressant that he was testing for the company. A lab assistant was fired at the same time – the same person who had taken Rosa away in Cornwall and had chased Jar in Canary Wharf. He was Martin's cycling companion but also his partner in crime, helping to keep Rosa captive and assisting with Martin's experiments on her. The police had found him unconscious, his head through the windscreen of a white Transit van, on the same day as Martin's arrest.

Cato confirmed, too, that Martin's old company had reconnected the electricity to the facility out at the airfield, in advance of plans to use it again. In other words, he explained, Rosa would have been found soon enough. It wasn't much comfort. Nor was Cato's reluctance to reveal more about the ongoing police investigation into the circumstances of Rosa's abduction five years ago.

Only Amy has failed to visit them. A heaviness descends on Jar as he thinks back to the letter from her that arrived earlier in the week, darkening their sunny corner of Cornwall. Very soon, in a matter of minutes perhaps, he will know whether he and Rosa can move on with their lives.

'Some days I want to know what happened,' Rosa says, getting up from the bench to walk along the harbour wall. 'On other days, like today, I don't care. I just want to hitch my past to another person's life, put a different name on my diary.'

'Martin changed much of what you wrote,' Jar says, repeating what he's told her many times.

'I know that.'

Together, they have been through a printout of each diary entry, highlighting with a green marker pen those memories that are hers, focusing on what they both know to be true, and redacting with a black pen Martin's numerous additions: from the entire Karen character to signing the Official Secrets Act in Herefordshire, and much in between. Jar was intrigued when Rosa confirmed that her dad was awarded a KCMG – she's got the medal somewhere. She even remembered the private ceremony at St Paul's – at least she thought she did. Was he a spy? *No, he was much more important than that.*

'I also like to think that he toned things down – between us,' Jar says, with an optimistic smile. He's already suggested to her that Martin altered their relationship in the diary to imply that there was less love between them.

'You know I'd never end it with you like that,' she says, linking an arm in his. He hopes she's right: it's a belief that has kept him going for the past five years.

They are at the end of the harbour wall now, watching as a second small boat, laden with mackerel, passes through the narrow gap beneath them.

Jar has had to accept that Martin wrote the suicide note to him, leaving it in her drafts email folder on the laptop in her room. He was duped into believing they were Rosa's words, the ones that he had learnt by heart. *I just wish I didn't have to leave you behind, babe, the first true love of my life and my last.* It was the use of 'babe' that had tricked Jar. He feels such a fool. Martin, the aspiring writer, had learnt to mimic other people's voices.

He had also made the silent phone call on Rosa's old phone (which the police found in his shed) and used it to send Jar the emails, pretending they were from Rosa, when Jar was searching for her in Cornwall. He had hacked into Jar's work email account, too. Martin had become adept at spoofing IP addresses in the last months of his job, when he was pushing the boundaries of human trials in his quest to develop a next-generation antidepressant and posting the results anonymously online.

But he had left the surveillance of Jar (around London and down to Cornwall) to others. According to Cato, Martin's lab-technician friend had once worked for a bailiff and knew a few tricks.

Jar glances at his watch. The time has come.

100

Dear Jar,

I hope you are both coping with all the media attention and that Rosa is making the best recovery she can in the circumstances.

I am sorry I haven't been down to Cornwall yet to visit you both, or replied to Rosa's sweet letter. It's taking longer than I thought to come to terms with what's happened. I don't want anyone to feel sorry for me – Rosa is the only real victim here – but my guilt is almost unbearable. All I can say, as I tried to explain to the police, is that I wasn't alive to the world. The doctor said I was lucky not to have died on the prescriptions Martin was giving me. I didn't realise that the 'sleeping pills' were in reality a strong – and illegal – benzodiazepine. I was cutting down on the minor benzos, wondering why I didn't feel much different. My senses had been blunted, to put it mildly – I was 'emotionally anaesthetised', as my GP put it (he was appalled when he discovered that he'd failed to notice the illegal benzo Martin had been administering). But I should have known, asked more questions, challenged Martin.

One day soon I hope to be strong enough to come down and join you both in Cornwall, walk the coast path with Rosa, go on the same walks I used to take with Jim, when Rosa was *a little girl. In the meantime, I've been clearing out the house. I can't carry on living here. It's not just the traces of Martin, it's the police, too, who have been through everything, from top to bottom, even my knicker drawer.*

They missed one thing, though, and I'm sending it to you now, as you'll know what to do with it better than me. It's a letter that I found when I was clearing out Martin's books in the sitting room. It was tucked into a copy of The Spy Who Came in from the Cold, *one of his favourites. I don't know who it's from, whether it's even genuine. Martin seems to have lived in a fantasy world for much of the last five years. But I think it's important.*

The address is Langley, Virginia, where even I know the CIA has its headquarters, and it's typed. It's not addressed to Martin, or signed by anyone, but it's a personal thank you letter, that much is clear, for sharing his professional expertise in the war on terror.

I remember he did travel to America, on a number of occasions, and it would have been in the years immediately after the awful events of 2001, but my memory has never been good. I could try to find out, if it helps, dig out his old passport, look at the visa stamps. I'm not sure where he kept it, though.

I hope this hasn't complicated things further. My mind is in such a mess already, I can't begin to work out its importance, if it has any.

It was painful, but I read your friend's article, of course, and watched every bulletin on the news. I didn't recognise the kind man I married as a student more than twenty years ago, who promised to help with my anxieties, and I still cannot fathom how he could have been so wickedly cruel to my own niece. Sadly, the media won't leave me alone, but security here in the house is good, of course. A small irony.

Destroy the letter to Martin if you want – do whatever makes your life easier. You and I always felt our darling Rosa was alive, but there's no satisfaction in being proved right. The shame and disbelief that a man I once loved could have done this will live with me for the rest of my life.

All my love to you both,
Amy

101

It's 9.05 a.m. when Jar notices the black car. They are back on the harbour wall with two more mugs of tea and an extra cardigan for Rosa – she feels the cold a lot more since her incarceration. The car enters the village slowly, nosing around the sharp right-hand bend and on to the narrow road in front of the deli. After disappearing for a minute, it reappears as it enters the car park below them.

'Definitely not a local,' Rosa says idly. They've played a game in recent weeks, trying to guess whether people are born-and-bred, blow-ins, tourists or journalists. It's not hard, but they have sometimes been wrong. Not today, though.

The car comes to a halt. The driver sits there for a while – Jar knows he's had a long journey through the night – and then steps out of the car. He looks up at the two of them, sitting on their favourite bench on the harbour wall. He doesn't raise a hand like the fisherman, but he nods an acknowledgement of sorts in their direction.

'Do you know him?' Rosa asks.

'Not yet.'

'Has he come to talk to me?' Rosa links her arm through his for reassurance. 'You know I don't want to talk to anyone.'

'Why don't you go back to the house,' Jar says, squeezing

her arm against his. The man rests one hand on the roof as he makes a call on his mobile, looking around him like a tracker finding his bearings from the sun.

'Is everything OK?' Rosa asks.

'Everything's fine now. He's just come for a chat. With me.'

'Thank you for sending Cato the letter,' the man says, sitting down on the bench next to Jar. The man, Asian, early thirties, is wearing a cotton shirt and chinos. 'He forwarded it to us.'

'It's a fake, right?' Jar asks, more in hope than anything. 'Just like the other document.'

Jar knows now that nothing is ever black and white. This man wouldn't have driven all this way, from London to Cornwall, if it was just a fake.

'The honest answer is that we don't know yet.'

'For sure it is.'

Ever since the typed letter from Langley arrived with Amy's own handwritten letter, Jar has been telling himself that it's not real, that it's just Martin being delusional. But when the man who's now sitting next to him rang him late last night, giving no name, saying only that he would be with Jar by 8 a.m., the old fears came tumbling back, keeping Jar awake until dawn.

'You know I can't comment,' the man says.

'Why have you come here then?'

Jar tries to remember the wording in the letter, the oblique suggestion that Martin had some sort of connection with the CIA.

'We need to talk to Rosa.'

'She's not ready.'

'She seemed happy enough to talk to your journalist friend. And to Cato.'

It's true, Jar thinks. Rosa had opened up to both men, but he doesn't want Rosa being interviewed by the intelligence services. It's not relevant or necessary. Max had mentioned MI6 in his article – along with Herefordshire and the SAS headquarters – but only in terms of Martin's perverted spy fantasies, to explain how an animal-research scientist had kept Rosa incarcerated for five years, tricking her into thinking that she'd been recruited by the CIA at Cambridge and then punished – tortured, Guantánamo-style – for trying to escape from a covert programme. (Max had specifically not mentioned Eutychus by name – he wanted, he said, to keep his powder dry just in case more evidence ever came to light on the dark web.)

'We have no evidence – beyond this letter – that Martin ever worked for the CIA or had any connection with it.'

'So what if he did?'

'There would be implications for Rosa's disappearance five years ago and her subsequent incarceration.'

'What sort of implications?'

'Her disappearance would become a matter for the intelligence services rather than the police.'

'Because Martin might or might not have once worked for the CIA, which might or might not have once run a covert programme that doesn't exist?'

Jar is pleased with how unlikely the scenario is beginning to sound. It hadn't been like that at four o'clock that morning.

'Is Rosa remembering any more about her imprisonment?' the man asks.

'The altered diary has confused things. That and the industrial quantities of medication Martin tested on her.'

'We're particularly interested in the early years, when she first disappeared in Cromer.'

Jar shakes his head in disbelief. 'Martin was a scientist. A sick pharmacologist who fantasised about working at Guantánamo. Nothing more.'

'That's what we want to clarify.'

'Sure to God he wished he did work for the CIA. All that torturing in Guantánamo. Home from home. But he didn't. He worked for a contract research organisation in Norwich – until they fired him, for cruelty to humans.'

'Post 9/11, the West turned to the most unlikely people to help with the war on terror. A Big Pharma research scientist with an interest in learned helplessness might just have appealed.'

Jar studies the old stones in the harbour wall beneath his feet, trying to draw comfort from their longevity, their resilience through centuries of storms and gales.

'Will you do one thing for me?' the man continues.

Jar looks across the harbour towards the village. Rosa is at the window of the net loft now, standing in the big double windows, looking down at them on the wall. The man follows his gaze. They both stare up at her in silence.

'Her father was a good man – we all miss him.' He pauses. 'When she starts to remember what really happened, call me.'

He hands Jar a plain white card with a single mobile number.

'Rosa was kept for five years against her will in a basement on a disused airfield in Norfolk,' Jar says quietly. 'She was imprisoned there by an uncle who despised her, despised women in general, even more than he despised animals.'

'I hope you're right, Jar. For everyone's sake.'

Jar watches the man walk over to his car, key the ignition and drive away, this time up Raginnis Hill. When he's out of sight, Jar looks back at the net loft window. Rosa is still standing there, looking out to sea. Jar closes his eyes, breathes in the fresh salty air, and opens them again.

What's in that beautiful, damaged head of yours, he thinks. What dark secrets do you unknowingly keep?

She raises a hand and gives him a distant wave.

Acknowledgements

The character of Martin, a psychopharmacologist, is, of course, entirely fictitious. Thankfully, I know of no one who shares his view that "Big Pharma missed a trick at Guantánamo". In 2014, however, the US Senate Select Committee on Intelligence published a report on torture and the war on terror that revealed the disturbing role played by psychology in CIA detention and interrogation programmes post 9/11. According to the report, two former US Air Force psychologists used "learned helplessness", a theory first developed by Dr Martin Seligman in the 1960s, to justify a controversial CIA technique known as "enhanced interrogation".

Dr Seligman, now a leading self-help author and advocate of positive psychology, told The New Yorker in 2015 that he was shocked and mystified to discover how his research had been used by the CIA. He was "grieved that good science, which has helped many people overcome depression, may have been used for such a bad purpose as torture".

In the course of researching this book, I read a number of original papers concerning early experiments on rodents and dogs, including Dr Seligman's 1967 canine tests, as well as more recent papers on stress, depression, learned helplessness and human trials:

On the Phenomenon of Sudden Death in Animals and Man, by Dr Curt P Richter (*Psychosomatic Medicine*, 1957)

Failure to Escape Traumatic Shock, by Martin E Seligman and Steven F Maier (*Journal of Experimental Psychology*, May 1967)

Depression: a New Animal Model Sensitive to Antidepressant Treatments, by RD Porsolt, M Le Pichon and M Jalfre (*Nature*, 1977)

The Tail Suspension Test: A New Method for Screening Antidepressants in Mice, by Lucien Steru, Raymond Chermat, Bernard Thierry, and Pierre Simon (*Psychopharmacology*, 1985)

Adult Hippocampal Neurogenesis Buffers Stress Responses and Depressive Behaviour, by Jason S. Snyder, Amélie Soumier, Michelle Brewer, James Pickel and Heather A. Cameron (*Nature*, 2011)

Redesigning Antidepressant Drug Discovery, by Professor Florian Holsboer (*Dialogues in Clinical Neuroscience*, 2014)

The dark web, by its very nature, poses a number of terrifying challenges for the ingenu, and I couldn't possibly have written this book without *The Dark Net: Inside the Digital Underworld*, by Jamie Bartlett (Windmill Books, 2015). His BBC Radio 4 programme, *Psychedelic Science* (2016) was equally invaluable.

I'd also like to thank: Will Francis, Rebecca Folland, Kirsty Gordon, Jessie Botterill and Kirby Kim at my literary agents, Janklow & Nesbit; Laura Palmer, Madeleine O'Shea, Nicolas Cheetham, Lucy Ridout and the Head of Zeus team in London; Liz Stein, Emer Flounders, Jena Karmali and the MIRA team in New York; Wiebke Rossa at Verlagsgruppe Random House in Germany; Jon Cassir at C.A.A.; J.P. Sheerin;

Giles Whittell; Nic Farah and Nadine Kettaneh; Louisa Goldsmith; Lisa Beale and Helen Gygax; The Gurnard's Head near Zennor; Mark Hatwood at the Harbour Gallery in Portscatho; Len Heath; Discover Ireland (*@gotoIrelandGB*); Adrian Gallop; Nick K.; Stewart and Dinah Mclennan; Polly Miller at the Gallery Norfolk, Cromer; Dr Raj Persaud; Rufus Lawrence; Andrea Stock; The Lullaby Trust; Mike and Sarah Jackson for use of "top hut"; and most of all Felix, Maya and Jago, who kept me going with their encouragement and joie de vivre; and Hilary, the love of my life, to whom this book is dedicated. Without her wisdom, humour, patience and love, it would never have happened.